I0645580

THE
GEMDARK
DYNASTY

CONSPIRATOR

ELLA PYNE

Copyright © 2023 by Ella Pyne

All rights reserved.

No part of this book may be reproduced in any form or by any electronic or mechanical means, including information storage and retrieval systems, without written permission from the author, except for the use of brief quotations in a book review.

Cover by MiblArt.

CONSPIRATOR

THE GEMDARK DYNASTY
BOOK TWO

ELLA PYNE

CHAPTER 1

*L*eda Locarno never thought she'd enjoy being lonely.

She'd been intimately connected with the feeling, of course, for most of her life. She'd spent her youth surrounded by her sister and foster parents, and then the rest of her insane and dysfunctional family at the palace in Gemdark. Bringing up the rear had been a whole court of noble sycophants and servants.

She'd stood in her father's throne room, year after year, drowning in a crowd of people. And she'd felt utterly alone.

And the questions, all those infernal unending questions, had swirled continuously around her mind. What if she'd been *better*? Prettier, funnier, more charismatic? What if she'd eclipsed their expectations of her, become special enough to matter, to be worthy of notice?

Would they have looked at her then? Would they have been interested in the things she had to say?

She didn't know.

She'd drawn the conclusion back then that she'd never know, because she wasn't and couldn't be special. She'd been raised only to die; why should anyone bother investing in the middle part?

Now, having escaped the palace that had been her prison, the roar that had once been those questions was a murmur in her mind. She was no longer fated to die at the hands of her sister Azaria. She wasn't a Counterpart, at least not in a way that meant anything. The gods wouldn't be getting her blood in exchange for her father's prosperity.

The old King was dead, her siblings scattered, the man she'd idiotically fallen in love with gone, seduced by the power of the throne.

She was far away now, where she'd dreamed of being ever since she'd read about the glittering sea that surrounded a land as close to paradise as it was possible to get. A book she'd read in Pyrrhus's library had once described the water around Saint-Trevale as being a blue comparable to the aquamarines on the King's crown.

She was happy to report that the book had been correct.

The thought of Pyrrhus, though, made her chest tighten, even a year after she'd last seen him.

She'd been true to her word and left him and the remnants of her father's awful court. She'd declined his entreaties to stay, to help him build a better future for the Five Kingdoms. Instead she'd followed through with the plan she'd developed when she was just ten years old, escaping the palace and starting life anew where nobody knew who she was.

A life of independence.

She'd climbed out of her chimney, camped out on the palace roof, and driven herself crazy wondering whether she'd made the right decision. She'd watched them send out guards to see where she was. Flocks of them, moving into the woods behind the palace.

Just as she'd counted on her father doing, Pyrrhus had

sent the full extent of his resources out after her. Whether it was an attempt to keep her safe by identifying her new location or to bring her back, she hadn't known. She suspected the former, but fear of the latter had fluttered within her.

Her treatment at her father's hands had instilled a wariness in her, an expectation of betrayal, that it was hard to break even now.

Leda had seen Pyrrhus one night as she sat just beyond the precipice of the golden roof, going over her plan for the millionth time. She'd been resting her chin on her knees, watching the light of the full moon shimmer on the river that swept behind the palace.

A dark, solitary figure had moved from the edge of the rose garden and down the steps to the lawn, and her heart had contracted painfully in her chest.

He was too distant to see in detail, but she knew him the moment her eyes fell on him. There was something so distinctive in the way he moved. He held himself rigidly upright, every gesture made with economy and purpose. This was a man who prided himself on always being in control.

He was alone, no guards trailing him. The longer she watched the more she saw small differences in him. Something almost defeated in the line of his posture, shoulders, that she'd only ever seen strong and square, slightly stooped.

He'd sat by the river, seemingly uncaring of the mud under his pristine coat.

Leda had fought the ridiculous urge to call out to him, but she couldn't. He'd made his choice. He could have come with her, and he'd decided not to.

Pyrrhus had desired power and influence even though they suited him so ill. He'd felt morally obligated to hold the broken pieces of the Five Kingdoms together despite how violently they were trying to tear themselves apart.

He'd felt this obligation more than he'd wanted her. And so he wouldn't have her.

Leda had buried her face in her hands, unable to keep looking at him.

She waited for three days on that rooftop, watching the guards in the gardens being drawn more frequently into the palace to compensate for the numbers missing. One night she rappelled down using the rope she'd stolen from the armoury and tied around her chimney, setting fire to it once she hit the ground to remove the evidence.

She'd practised the trick in the winters in Leatherfell, descending the walls of Fayne and Dalev's home in the dead of night until she could do it without wanting to vomit. With a leg that showed its weakness at the worst times, it had been difficult.

Her journey to Saint-Trevale had been a perilous and exhausting one that took weeks and drained most of her funds. She'd been chased by a pack of curious wolves in the woods and got lost for two days when her map-reading skills proved terrible.

When she reached civilisation she stayed in coaching inns with rotting floorboards and spent two nights curled up under the stars in grassy fields. She'd even slept in a temple under the eye of a priestess who clearly didn't believe a word of her lies about her identity.

The journey had been uncomfortable and unpredictable and dangerous and Leda had never felt more alive. For the first time, *she* dictated her destiny. If she was in a perilous situation it was because she'd got herself into it and it was bloody well her job to get herself back out again.

She arrived at the cabin that her foster mother, Fayne, had told her about so caked in dirt and grime she no longer had to worry about being recognised. The relief that had rushed through her as she touched the key hidden in a nearby tree stump had hit her with such force she'd cried.

Fayne's old home probably shouldn't have been described as anything so nice as a cabin judging by the condition Leda found it in. The wooden exterior, though painted a charming blue, was faded and rotted. When she shoved open the door with an ominous crunch, a cloud of dust made her cough and she heard the scurrying of nearby rats.

She found a rusted kitchenette, a bed that had seen better days, and a bathing room in surprisingly good condition.

All was quiet, the thick layer of dust having a muffling effect.

She'd therefore nearly lost her mind in panic upon hearing a tiny cough behind her. Guards and carriages and the gold-infested palace flashed before her eyes as she whirled around.

An old woman stood in the doorway, her skin dark and smooth, eyes a vibrant green, with steel-grey hair flowing to her shoulders. It looked like her body was inclined to start stooping with age but she had not permitted it to do so. She regarded Leda with raised eyebrows.

"Who sent you here?"

What an interestingly specific question that had been.

Caught off guard, Leda looked into those wise eyes and felt a cautious, tenuous kind of trust. This woman stood in the doorway like she owned the place, and her gaze was fixed squarely on Leda. It did not drift about the room as it might if the house was unfamiliar to her.

Leda straightened up and opened her hands in front of her, showing that she had no weapons. "Fayne sent me."

The woman's posture relaxed ever so slightly. "So you're

the friend, then. Fayne wrote that I should expect you within the last five years. You took your time."

Relief flooded her, and Leda gave a choked laugh. "You could say that. Do you mind if I ask who you are?"

The woman finally released her from that piercing gaze, looking around the room. "The name's Iris. I'm the person who's going to make sure you don't die of disease in this wreck of a shack."

Leda couldn't help the scepticism that clung to her wherever she went. "Why would you do that?"

"Don't be suspicious, girl. We take care of each other around here. If Fayne says you're one of ours, you're one of ours. No questions asked."

Leda had really hoped she meant that last part.

Leda sighed as she curled her toes in the sand of the nearly deserted beach upon which she sat. It was pure white and finer than anything she'd ever seen before, soft and shifting beneath her. She'd visited this beach every day, rain or shine, for a year now and had yet to lose her fascination with it.

She waved to Iris, who was trudging over to join her. The sun had begun to set, casting the sky in radiant orange.

Iris paid it no attention, inadvertently kicking sand all over Leda as she came to a stop beside her. She waved the basket she carried with a grin.

"Thought I'd find you here. Two new orders just came in; it's time to get sewing."

Iris lived in the cabin opposite Leda's and had crowed with delight upon discovering that she had the makings of a seamstress, recruiting her immediately into her tailoring business. She had three children herself, but they were all grown and had gone to seek their fortunes on the outer islands of Saint-Trevale, so she was pleased to have Leda to boss around instead.

Leda had been happy about it, too. Something to occupy herself, some purpose. And, of course, a source of income. It wasn't much, but it was enough for her.

"Did you finish the dress for that priestess?"

Leda's shock had been hard to conceal when Melia, Exalted Priestess of the Grand Temple in Slofray, had walked up to their market stall a month ago. She'd been blasé in her attitude while Leda had frozen in place.

When Iris had turned away to note down the details of her order, Melia had murmured to Leda that she was on holiday and simply wanted a dress made. She had no intention of reporting back to the palace on Leda's whereabouts when she returned there. Then, she'd winked.

When no knocks came on her door for weeks afterwards, Leda had been cautiously optimistic that Melia would keep her word.

"The dress is nearly finished, just some embroidery on the skirt left."

Iris nodded approvingly.

"You need some more sun on your face, girl. You've a deathly pallor." Iris gestured to where Leda had chosen to sit in the shadow of the Monument to the Gods. It towered over them from the back of the beach, a fifty-foot monstrosity of ugly iron with a small viewing podium peeking out on top.

Twisted depictions of the faceless gods climbed its side. It was supposedly built to draw good luck for the fisherman who sailed out every morning, to protect them from the brutality of the sea. Leda wasn't sure about that, but she did know that the shadow it cast would allow her to spend time outside without getting horribly sunburned.

She'd learned that she was susceptible to the sun very quickly after she'd arrived in Saint-Trevale. She'd turned an unrecognisable shade of beetroot and had shed so much skin she'd briefly wondered whether she was part snake.

The beauty of their location more than made up for it, however. Leda had been struck as soon as she'd arrived by the array of colours she'd never seen before in her life. The beaches were all pearlescent sand, fringed with huge green palm trees. Colourful shells filled with tiny hermit crabs skittered to and fro. Hundreds of small atolls and islands spread out from the coastline, rings of aquamarine water encased in the deeper blue of the sea. The air was warm and humid, not so much as a breeze stirring it.

Well, usually. Today the wind was stronger than was comfortable, and waves crashed in a white froth upon the beach.

Leda's attention shifted to Iris's basket. "Are those the satins?"

"Yes. Got a right good price for them too," Iris said, all satisfaction.

Leda couldn't suppress her answering grin. "They can't resist your charms."

"Exactly. That's why I do the customer work and you sew silently in the back," Iris said with a wink.

Leda rolled her eyes good-naturedly. Iris had found her aversion to people strange at first, but had shrugged it off as one of Leda's quirks.

The wind was picking up, lifting Leda's hair from her shoulders and smacking it back into her face. She pushed it away impatiently.

"Do you—oh!" The ground trembled beneath them and Leda looked down in bemusement, watching the sand shift under her fingers. It only lasted for a second, but it was enough to send Iris stumbling down to her knees.

Leda hurried to help her up.

"I just laundered this dress yesterday," Iris said crossly, whacking her skirts with her basket in an ineffectual attempt to get the sand off. "Oh, for the sake of the gods!"

The grey sky had finally opened up above them, letting loose a deluge of warm rain.

It hung so thick in the air it felt like it should be impossible to breathe. It was nothing like the cold, refreshing rain that Leda remembered cutting across her skin in a Viridiana rainstorm.

That was one thing to add to the, thankfully short, list of things she missed about her home.

Iris watched Leda tip her head up towards the sky and let the rain hit her face. She tutted.

"Silly child. You'll catch your death." She adjusted the cover on her basket to ensure the fabric within was protected from the downpour. "Let's go back now; I've a pot of stew on the fire. You can have some if you like."

Leda's stomach was telling her that a little food was just what she needed, though Iris's recipes were hit-and-miss at best. The woman was a fine seamstress and saleswoman, a pillar of the community and an abominable cook.

"Squirrel again?"

"You loved it until you found out what it was. Spoiled, you Rivernesse people, the whole lot of you."

Leda was careful not to let her smile get too tight as she was presented with the lie she'd told the first day she'd met Iris. No one, even the person she trusted most in this wonderful new place, could be allowed to know where she'd come from. She couldn't risk any enemies of the Crown finding out that she was here.

The fact that she'd chosen Pyrrhus's home as her fake country of origin wasn't significant. It was merely a coincidence.

Iris dropped her basket. It hit the sand with a wet *thunk*.

"Iris?" Leda went to pick it up for her and paused, following her gaze. The older woman was staring at the sea, basket and Leda completely forgotten, watching the surf bubble as it met with the beach.

Leda could have sworn that the tide had been much further in only seconds ago.

"What's going on?"

"It can't be …"

"It can't be what?"

"The Ounam," Iris murmured, eyes going from narrow to wide and panicked in a heartbeat. She drew shaking arms together and cupped a hand on each of her opposite shoulders, a Saint-Trevalian sign of supplication to the gods. "Tsunami."

That word, Leda knew.

"*What?*"

Leda looked out at the water churning a good distance from the beach. The horizon was oddly blurred, and she realised with a jolt that the birdsong that usually surrounded them was absent.

The palm trees lining the cobbled road behind them were devoid of life, but they had started to sway violently from side to side in the wind that continued to whip Leda's hair and skirts around.

"We need to get to high ground. Now," Iris croaked.

There was fear in her voice, real and raw. Leda had never heard Iris anything but confident, and that scared her more than the rapid churning of the water did.

"Alright, no problem," Leda muttered to herself, spinning around to see what was behind them.

A road, and behind that a vast, flat expanse of rocky sand upon which were perched hundreds of squat little houses with thatched roofs. No hills lay behind them. No tall buildings they could climb. "Oh, gods."

Iris appeared similarly panicked by their lack of options. She looked up at the sky, dropped to her knees, and began to pray.

Leda had no time for that, though she was looking at the roiling grey sky as well. The gods had no interest in her, would probably laugh if she attempted to pray to them.

Something caught her eye as she desperately scanned the clouds: a tall, thin metal construct.

If the gods were minded to not see them die a horrible death, they might as well allow it using the sculpture that had been built to honour them. There was an observation deck at the top for tourists, which Leda hadn't visited, but its existence told her there must be stairs hidden within the ugly rusted legs of the structure.

A deafening roar sounded behind her, and Leda spun to take in a sight so horrific her mind couldn't process that it was real. A wall of water was building on the horizon. It surged towards them in a huge, continuous wave that moved at almost supernatural speed.

Leda yanked Iris's basket off the sand and hooked it over her elbow. "Get to the monument!" she yelled, all but dragging Iris behind her.

They wasted precious seconds as Iris looked back to the sea and let out a spine-chilling screech of fear. Leda redoubled her efforts to pull the older woman across the sand, sure she was about to dislocate one of her arms.

Adrenaline gave her strength she was extremely grateful for as they hurtled towards the door at the base of the monument. Leda hit it with such speed her body slammed against it, before stepping back to haul it open. She pushed Iris in ahead of her as the whoosh of approaching water reached them.

She kept her hands on Iris's back and shoved her up the stairs.

Despite her advanced age, Iris was spritely, and Leda had a leg that chose the most inconvenient times to give up on her. Within seconds a gap had opened up between them, but Leda still pulled herself upwards as quickly as she could. They climbed the stairs in tight circles, hearing only the sound of rushing water and the creak of metal as they ascended. The air tasted like salt and kelp and decay.

A discordant, rattling *bang* sounded as the water hit the structure. The metal screamed under the onslaught and Leda forced her eyes to stay open as they ascended the shuddering stairs.

Iris exploded through the door at the top and out on to the observation deck. Leda was right behind her, panting. She dropped the basket of fabric to grab the railing and bent double to catch her breath. It felt like she was choking on her own lungs.

Iris let out a moan of despair as she surveyed the world beneath them. They'd been in that stairwell for a minute at most, but what they could see of the place they'd just left was almost unrecognisable.

Leda blinked, hardly believing her own eyes.

The beach was gone.

A carpet of muddy brown water churned beneath them, as high as the top of the signs warning swimmers to be wary of dangerous tides. The boats in the harbour to the east had been overturned, and what remained of the houses Leda had been looking at in desperation earlier had been smashed to pieces. Some had been lifted from their foundations and swept away entirely.

The monument on which they stood swayed alarmingly, a few inches left and right, and every important moment of

Leda's life flashed before her eyes as her stomach swooped sickeningly.

She awaited the screech of splintering metal that would herald the structure plunging them into the treacherous depths below. Pyrrhus's face appeared in her mind, quick as a whip, an image that stubbornly refused to disappear while the others faded.

And then, to Leda's shock, the monument stopped moving and seemed to hold steady. She let out a shuddering breath and opened her eyes, which she'd screwed shut at the first ominous lurch.

She was face to face with one of the black metal carvings of a god's face, smooth and indistinct as it peered around the side of the structure, out towards the ocean. She had the insane urge to kick it, to scream and to beat her fists against it.

It was not an exaggeration to say that Leda hated the gods.

Well, if she were being specific about it, she hated *her* god. She wasn't even sure if a god had ever been designated to her. They'd certainly never made any attempt to smooth her path through life. They'd never spoken to her, never given the slightest hint of their existence. She was supposed to be able to conjure their face in her mind, as everyone did from a young age, but their image had remained as blank as the statues on this monument.

She and Iris stood there for what had to be at least an hour in stunned silence, watching the water slowly begin to recede. When Leda went to approach the stairs, Iris seized her sleeve and shook her head.

"There could be multiple surges; we need to stay at least a few more hours."

"Oh, of course," Leda said weakly, absurdly grateful that she had someone with her who knew what they were doing.

And so they waited, and she tried not to think about the calamity below, the senseless death and destruction. It wasn't the first impossible-to-explain weather event that had happened recently, and a feeling of dark foreboding in her chest told her it wouldn't be the last.

"Are you alright?" Leda asked.

Iris shook her head, lips pressed tightly together, but she allowed Leda to place a comforting hand on her shoulder.

They were both shivering and shaking out tense limbs by the time Iris finally allowed them to descend the monument. The water was halfway up to their knees when they emerged, opaque with mud. But it was finally calm, allowing them to make their way slowly towards home.

The devastation they passed was humbling. They'd been prepared to help survivors, to hear their cries and try to pull them from the debris, but the only sounds were of swirling water. Everything else was terrifyingly silent.

The road they lived on was far enough from the beach that the buildings hadn't been ripped away, but the destruction had Leda and Iris exchanging a desolate look.

Without another word to one another, they split off to inspect the damage to their homes.

What Leda found when she managed to get the door to her cabin open had her freezing in shock.

Two figures stood before her, water swirling around their ankles. They didn't seem to care, given how they turned to stare at her as she entered.

Leda took in a sharp breath as recognition rocketed through her.

"What in the gods' names are you doing here?"

CHAPTER 2

Former princess of the Five Kingdoms, Elina Locarno was as radiant and pristinely put together as always, or as well as she could be given the circumstances. She'd clearly given up on trying to keep the emerald fabric of her gown dry, the bottom of it dyed a dark brown by the water.

Her eyes were beautifully large and dark. They were also so judgemental that Leda had trouble meeting them.

The crickets screeched outside of the window, their cries melding with the shouts of people as they inspected the damage to their homes. The unsettling silence throughout the town had finally broken.

Leda moved to snap the door shut in a whirl of sodden skirts and disturbed water. That done, she drew her hands into fists to stop them from shaking.

Her Counterpart brother Eber had taken up his customary lounging position on Leda's bed and didn't seem to care that he was getting it wet. He'd grown over the past year, lost some of the softness of youth in his face. His posture had a new confidence to it that was pleasant to see.

But guilt kept Leda from looking at him for more than a second at a time.

"What are you two doing here?" Leda looked around with dismay at the ruined inside of her cabin.

She'd left it that morning in perfect condition, all her fabrics sorted into neat piles in wicker baskets along one wall. They were gone now, sad streamers of taffeta and silk rippling around their legs. The beautiful maroon rug she'd bartered for at the market was nowhere to be seen, probably ruined beyond recognition.

She'd spent so much time fitting out her cabin exactly the way she liked it, making it a home, and now her furniture floated past her in pieces. "How did you even find me?"

"We've always known where you were," Elina said, arms crossed to keep her from inadvertently touching anything. "You were seen leaving the Prestglass Woods by a stag hunting party. Atticus picked up your trail and followed you here. Pyrrhus told anyone who knew to leave you alone."

So Pyrrhus had known where she was, all year long. And he'd made sure she stayed free. That was something, at least.

Leda was gratified that he'd followed her wishes. Still, the stab of pain that came with the knowledge that he'd chosen her father's poisonous crown over her hurt as much now as when she'd left the palace.

"Alright," Leda said carefully. "That's the *how*; now I need the *why*."

Eber was uncharacteristically silent and Elina seemed to lose her train of thought as she inspected Leda with a critical eye.

"What are you wearing?" she burst out. Leda looked down at her white cotton dress, practical and comfortable and one of the best things about moving away from the stuffy, image-obsessed royal court. It was, however, as soaked as Elina's dress and much thinner. It clung to her in a way that would mortify any courtier, particularly her most pious sister.

"My wool dresses didn't fit the climate."

"So your next best option was underwear?"

Leda abruptly remembered that Elina was from Saint-Trevale herself, had grown up here with her Counterpart, Sofie, and their foster parents. She should have known better than anyone what the heat was like here.

Realisation hit her.

"I'm so sorry this happened to your home; you must be upset," Leda said with as much diplomacy as she could muster.

Elina's expression grew impossibly more angry. "Why did you even come to Saint-Trevale? This is my place!" She snapped her mouth shut, looking momentarily mortified by her outburst.

Leda rolled her eyes. Even in the face of all this, Elina couldn't control her emotions, couldn't stop them spilling over and attacking anyone in proximity. She was as self-involved and petty as ever.

"You both need to make this quick; we're going out to help survivors before it gets dark."

"Who's 'we'?" Elina snapped.

"No one." Leda was reluctant to expose Iris to the madness of her family; she needed to keep her two lives as separate as possible.

Elina looked about ready to splash dirty water in Leda's face.

Eber's voice, when he spoke, was deeper than she'd remembered it. "We've come to take you home, Leda." The usual affection when he spoke to her was missing. She'd hurt him by running away, she knew it, but hadn't been confronted with the truth of it until now.

"*This* is my home," she said weakly, bending to retrieve the detached leg of one of her wicker chairs as it floated past. "Destroyed as it may be at the moment."

Elina had no time for Leda's words; she waved them away like nuisance insects. "No, it isn't. You belong at the palace and we need you there. Now, preferably."

"Why?"

"Because this tsunami is only the latest in a line of horrific events. The people who lay dead here are only a few of tens of thousands who've been killed. Storms and heat-waves and earthquakes all across the Five Kingdoms. Tornados have been ripping Slofray apart for weeks. It's possible that crop failures across the lands will lead to starvation on a scale we've never seen."

Leda's mouth was dry. "And what does that have to do with me? How could I possibly help?"

"Your family needs you."

"Pyrrhus needs you," Eber interjected.

Leda's traitorous heart thundered against her ribs.

"The king has advisors; he has no need of me."

"Is that so?" Elina said.

Eber sighed. "There's also the fact that Caspari is dead."

It was like being punched with an icy fist. Leda spluttered. "What? Dead? How?"

"He was found drowned in a lake near where we grew up, two days ago," Eber said with such little emotion he reminded her jarringly of Azaria. "There were signs that he struggled, that someone held him under."

Elina turned away, her shoulders stooped with grief.

"Oh, gods. I'm so sorry." Insofar as Leda could be sorry at the death of one of her more violent and malicious brothers, albeit one she'd never known very well.

Eber, as Prince Caspari's Counterpart, had borne that burden. He didn't seem particularly sorry that Caspari was gone. And yet, something about his death had brought Eber here to Leda when he clearly couldn't stand to be in the same room as her.

"Are you alright, Eber?"

"You're to come home." That was a command that might as well have come directly from Pyrrhus's mouth, it sounded so much like him.

"I ... I'm ... no," she said stubbornly.

"They're calling him the King of Calamity now."

Leda's heart sank at the words. "Yes, I read that in the newspapers."

"You cared about him."

"Of course I do, but—"

Elina made a noise of frustration. "And yet here you sit in this squalid little hut, sewing dresses, not getting yourself into a bother about anything. You care nothing for any of us, do you?"

That wasn't fair. "That's rich coming from you, Elina. Shall we ask Sofie how much you care about *your* family?"

The reminder of their sister's death at the final Counterpart ceremony struck them all like a physical blow, but none so effectively as Elina. All the colour drained from her face.

"How dare you speak her name to me?"

"I'm not the one who killed her, Elina. If there's anyone here who shouldn't say Sofie's name it's you."

It appeared she'd landed right on top of her little sister's trigger and struck it with all of her might.

Elina let out a screech of rage and bolted across the room, sending water flying in all directions. When she reached Leda, she slapped her clear across the face.

Leda reared backwards with a cry of shock, her hand coming up to the stinging skin. There was the sound of Eber sloshing his way towards them. He took Elina by her upper arms and yanked her away, just barely preventing her from striking Leda again.

"You want to bring her up to *me*?" Elina shrieked, battling to get out of Eber's grip so hard she nearly toppled them both over. "You HYPOCRITE! I saved you when Thorodin was about to gut you; do you remember that? Or does that not count?" Elina let out another unhinged scream of rage, ragged with pain at the edges. "I shouldn't have bothered to save your pathetic life; all I did was unleash another bland, snivelling *nobody* on the world!"

Leda had been feeling penitent, that she'd gone too far, but that last statement had her seeing red. Eber, in his haste to immobilise Elina, had inadvertently made her an excellent target.

Leda had never slapped anyone in her life, but she found her arm winding back to strike her bitter sister right across her smug face.

Thankfully, Eber was faster than any of them. He shoved Elina behind him and stepped up to Leda. His hands against her shoulders pushed her back so firmly she had to brace herself against the wall to avoid falling over. There was an almighty splash in the kerfuffle that drenched them all up to their shoulders.

"You're as selfish now as you were when you sneaked away through the Prestglass Woods. You're a coward," Eber said flatly.

He might as well have struck her like Elina had.

"I just want to live out my life in peace. I won't go back there; I can't. Please," her voice cracked.

"Leda—"

"I *can't*. I'm so sorry. Nothing will change my mind."

Eber stared at her for a long moment, his eyes glassy and tinged with red.

"We'll see," he said, his face uncharacteristically grim as

he released her. Shaking his head, he gestured to Elina that they should leave, which she seemed only too happy to do. "We have other cards up our sleeve."

Leda flinched as the door shut with a bang behind them.

~

Between the sullen spirit of the community following the aftermath of the tsunami, the damage to her cabin and the fallout of her visit from her brother and sister, Leda spent the following week in a dour mood. She busied herself with helping her neighbours to clean up their homes and working into the nights with Iris to make new clothes for those who'd lost their own.

She was exhausted and sleep-deprived, but the work had done what she'd needed it to, driving all thought of her family and Viridiana out of her mind.

She wasn't selfish; she was helping the people of her community. So Eber could bloody well shut up about that.

The royal family weren't the only ones who mattered, despite what they thought.

When the worst of the damage had been swept away and the marketplace reopened two weeks following the disaster, Leda was one of the first to claim her table and haul in her wares.

The atmosphere was more genial than it had been in some time as townspeople began to creep back into what had once been a hive of activity. One by one, each stall filled up with items, from floral displays to stacks of steaming bread loaves to an array of multicoloured fish.

Two flautists joined them at midday to entertain the crowds as they milled about.

Leda wiped the sweat from her brow as the afternoon

sun beat down on her, looking forward to telling Iris about the amount of trade she'd done.

Something, she didn't know what, made her look up from her table.

A flash of black hair, pale skin, arctic blue eyes and a heavy feeling in her stomach; there, between two people conversing at the edge of the market.

Could it be?

No, there was no way Azaria would be here.

Nevertheless, Leda strained to find the figure through the crowd.

She must be seeing things. She was used to being with Azaria every day and even after a year spent away from her, some small part of Leda expected to see her in every room she entered.

She shook herself and handed over a fistful of change to a customer with a tepid smile.

And yet, she wasn't able to stop scanning the crowd for another glimpse of ebony hair.

She needed to put the Locarnos and anyone else who lived in that godsforsaken palace out of her mind, for good.

"I'll take this, please."

Leda glanced at the silk cravat held aloft by a black-clad arm, her hands already buried in her change purse as she nodded.

"Yes absolutely, that'll be seven sov—" She was struck dumb as the image her eyes had just captured flared and twisted in her mind: that cravat dangling from a characteristically ink-stained hand that she knew in her very bones.

Her mouth was desert dry as she looked up. "Pyrrhus."

CHAPTER 3

Pyrrhus Selhurst, ruler of the Five Kingdoms, looked out of place in the bright sunlight, with blue water sparkling in the distance behind him. This was a man who belonged indoors in a library, lit by candlelight with a mug of hot chocolate he pretended wasn't his vice in hand.

Standing in the heat in his black tailcoat must have been a particular form of torture for him. Sweat glistened on his forehead as he shielded his eyes from the light with one hand.

He was magnetic. He was mesmerising. He was ... not supposed to be here.

"Leda." That frustratingly handsome mouth curled into a small smile. He looked even better than she remembered. How was that fair?

He stood upright and relaxed, not as stiff as he'd been when she'd first known him. The difference in his bearing made her brows pull down into a frown.

She snatched her cravat from him and tucked it back into the display on her table. "What do you want?"

"I really did want to buy that," he said mildly.

"Tough luck," Leda said, putting her hands on her hips. He threw her into shadow; had he always been this tall? How could she possibly have forgotten? "What are you doing here?"

The question was redundant; she knew she stood before the card that Eber had claimed was up his sleeve. A dirty trick, if ever there was one.

She'd detached herself from most people in her life, and here was the one she could never quite let go of, despite the abhorrent position he held. It didn't matter that she hadn't seen him in a year, he haunted her dreams constantly.

Well played, Eber.

A prospective customer sidled up to her stall and Pyrrhus waved her away with a subtle gesture. To Leda's irritation, the woman ducked her head and moved to the next table with no fuss. These people hadn't realised who stood among them, yet they couldn't help but treat him with deference.

Leda grabbed a linen shift from her table to keep her hands busy. She glared up at him as she unfolded and refolded it.

"I can't come and visit you?" Pyrrhus said with all of the confidence of a man who'd had an entire court hanging on his every word for a year.

Visit her? He was supposed to be *with* her. That was what they'd agreed, all that time ago. They were supposed to be living their lives here together.

He'd chosen otherwise.

"Kings don't normally have time in their schedules to make visits to nobody seamstresses in Saint-Trevale. Unless you've abdicated?"

The smile slid from his mouth and his dark eyes, which

had fallen to the sunburn on her neck, snapped up to meet hers.

"Not yet, but soon."

A promise she'd heard before, too long ago for it to mean anything now.

He wasn't wearing his crown, but he didn't need to. She could imagine the shape of it on his head, the weight of it, the jewels that displayed the reach of his empire. The power he wielded, it was too much, unnatural.

Her father and his ancestors had amassed that power through blood and violence and death over centuries. He'd commanded that his people cleave to a religion they didn't understand, that his children die in service of it, and no one had dared stand up to him. He'd plucked Leda's mother from a crowd, killed her betrothed, and forced her to be his mistress, just because he could. And no one had said a word.

His whim had been law, the rest of the world obeying out of fear and reverence.

And she found it disgusting.

A harsh sound reached her ears and Leda realised she'd torn the linen in her hands. She forced herself to let it go, one finger at a time.

"Of course," she said, her voice more bitter than she was comfortable with.

With a sigh, she began to gather the wares on the table into her basket. A ring of poorly disguised guards had gathered behind the king, surveying the market with blatant suspicion and putting off any other customers she might tempt over.

Pyrrhus followed as she yanked her basket off the table and shouldered her way through the crowd and out of the market square.

He fell into step easily beside her. "You're looking well."

She was abruptly reminded that the last time they'd spoken he'd pulled her on to his throne and kissed her in a way that had stolen all the air from her lungs, plaguing her thoughts for far longer than it should have.

She'd run away from the palace less than twenty-four hours later.

He'd reneged on their deal and she'd abandoned him. The fact that he was speaking to her so civilly was baffling; surely he should be as resentful as she was about all that had gone wrong between them?

When they came to the beachside promenade that would start Leda's journey towards home, Pyrrhus made the mistake of trying to relieve her of the weight of her basket. She pulled it away from him with a glare.

"I'll ask again. What are you doing here, Your Majesty?"

Pyrrhus was silent as their feet crunched on the gravel of the pathway, his guards falling into a neat line behind them. They'd evidently decided that their unconvincing undercover act was no longer required.

The quiet was frustrating and Leda couldn't resist needling him. He deserved to feel at least a tenth as uncomfortable as she did in that moment. "And why aren't you wearing your crown? Afraid that people will recognise the 'King of Calamity'? That's what they're calling you, isn't it?"

She'd asked around after Eber and Elina's visit. The tsunami in Saint-Trevale had been nothing compared to the droughts and storms and earthquakes wreaking havoc across the lands. The newspapers hadn't been able to keep up with half of it.

The people of Saint-Trevale were resilient and had recovered quickly, but that wasn't possible for everyone.

Each time one of these tragedies ceased, another began, more lethal than the last. The people, superstitious and fearful of their gods as her father had made them, were minded to place blame on whatever had changed most recently. They found their answer easily. Their King had been deposed, and a pretender placed upon his throne. Pyrrhus was of noble lineage through Rivernesse, yes, but he had no royal blood. He was beneath even Leda in the estimations of many.

The man in question roundly ignored her insult. He'd become quite the statesman, it seemed.

"That's the reason I'm here. You need to come home."

Leda was heartily tired of hearing that.

The thought of going back to that palace, her prison of so many years, made all the blood leave her face. "I need do no such thing," she hissed, quickening her pace. "And that is *not* my home."

How could it be, when it housed the axe that was fated to kill her? When she'd been tortured there, the faint scars across her back a reminder she carried everywhere she went? When she'd seen the bodies of more siblings than she could bear sprawled throughout the palace and grounds, drenched in shockingly scarlet blood?

Her deepest nightmares knew to locate her there, that the sight of those golden walls would have her waking up panting and shaking so hard her headboard rattled.

Pyrrhus was a little ahead of her, his legs so much longer than hers, so when he stopped abruptly she nearly ploughed into him. His hands came to rest on her shoulders as he turned to her and she froze. She'd forgotten what it was like to be touched by him. "Your siblings need you. Your brother is dead. Your family—"

She exploded outwards and his hands dropped from her. In one step she stood inches from him, her hand balled into a fist on his chest. "I owe nothing to anybody—*particularly my family.*"

"You can't be that callous; these people are your flesh

and blood."

Leda's laugh was high, hysterical and utterly unrelated to humour. "*Oh*, but that's the real difference between us, isn't it, Pyrrhus? You would kill a king and sit on his throne to avenge your family, and I'd happily see most of mine dead of their ambition and cruelty."

His jaw visibly tightened at that, but he held his tongue, considering his response.

He allowed her to stand within inches of him, threat implicit in every line of her posture, while his guards hovered anxiously a few feet away. "You'd want that for Eber? For Ami?"

She hissed out a breath.

Even after a year, the effect this man had on her was as potent and ridiculous as it had ever been. It was infuriating. His presence severed the connection between her brain and her mouth.

She stepped back from him. "Of course not."

She was the worst. An unfeeling creature. What had happened to her?

Pyrrhus waved a hand and Leda heard the scrape of the nearest guard re-holstering his sword. She cast an incredulous look at the guard and he met her gaze with an unimpressed frown on his ruddy face. He clearly considered her more of a threat than his master did.

She supposed that could be a good thing. Though Leda was alarmingly heartless she was no shrinking wallflower any more. She wasn't a girl who things *happened* to. She could be dangerous if she wanted to.

"I'm not going back to the palace with you," she told Pyrrhus, pleased at how steady her voice sounded.

"You've changed over the past year, Leda."

"Likewise." Her tone implied that she did not consider his changes to be for the better.

"It appears we've reached an impasse." Pyrrhus looked down at her with a frustrated expression, seemingly having trouble deciding what to do with her next. He'd clearly thought his emotional entreaties about her family would have her falling over herself to accept his invitation, despite Eber and Elina's failure.

A guard shifted in the corner of Leda's eye and her back stiffened.

"If you take me back there by force I will *never* forgive you."

Pyrrhus appeared so revolted by the suggestion that he took several steps back from her. She'd offended him. Good.

The distance cleared her mind.

"I'm aware," he said stiffly. "But I'd thought better of you, Leda. I thought you were a person with a sense of responsibility, someone who cared for other people. I didn't realise you shared so many qualities with Azaria, but I see it now."

The rest of their conversation had bruised her, but that hit its mark.

He was genuinely disappointed in her. The thought made her skin feel tight. She wasn't the only one who looked at the changes the other person had undergone and found them wanting.

"Don't compare me to Azaria," she murmured, trying to repress the ridiculous urge to explain herself. "I had to be selfish to survive, to save myself."

Something in Pyrrhus's expression softened infinitesimally. "I know. But that was then, and this is now, and everything has changed. You no longer have to be selfish, and they need you. Your family needs you."

Eber, with his once-huge grin and irreverent humour. Ami, with her surly moods and delight in learning to read and write. Elina, with her remote demeanour and caustic wit. Even Azaria, unpredictable and violent and the other half of Leda, who had somehow burrowed her way in and created a gap that she could feel in her soul when they were apart. It was a strange ache that Leda hadn't managed to shift over the past year no matter how hard she'd tried.

"How would me being there even help?" she asked.

Pyrrhus shook his head. "After all this time you still don't understand the impact you have, do you?" he said. "You bring them together. You steady them. Not to mention you're the only one who knows how to handle Azaria. And until we find out who killed Caspari you're all in danger; we don't know if someone is exacting revenge against the Locarnos. You're threatened by these natural disasters, too, and you can't be protected while you're out here. They're worried for your life." He looked at the remnants of devastation around them with a tight, furious expression. "They *want* you to return and be safe with them at the palace. At least until the new king or queen is crowned. They don't want your name to be the next the papers bring them, after Caspari."

Oh, but he'd always been able to craft a good speech.

Leda looked across the seafront at the wreckage that had yet to be cleared, only a short walk from her home. So much death and pain, so many families torn apart.

Pyrrhus had said nothing about himself, whether he wanted her back at the palace for his own benefit. Leda highly doubted it, after the way she'd left him.

It was so difficult to deny him, and the thought of seeing him again, having him back in her life every day, relaxed a knot in her stomach that she hadn't been aware was there.

But it could change nothing.

She would not touch the Crown and he still *was* the Crown. She couldn't be brought into its toxic and evil influence; it would break something in her to do it. She had few principles for her life, but that was one of them and she would stick to it staunchly.

"Please." It looked like it cost him dearly to say the word. "Eber is floundering, without direction. Elina hides in her rooms all day. Ami is screaming for attention, and Azaria has all but moved into the armoury."

"I'm not their mother."

"No, but you are the eldest of them now, and they trust you. They need you to support them, to show them how to go out into the world and live independent lives."

It was the final nail in the coffin of her resolve. Leda wilted, her gaze falling to the ground as the guilt suffused her. Did she love being alone and free more than she cared for the safety and wellbeing of her siblings? She wondered if she would like the person she'd be if she answered that question in the affirmative.

Leda took a deep, steadying breath. She couldn't believe she was about to do this, that he'd managed to convince her. "Until my siblings are settled and safe. Then I'm coming straight back here. I won't be sucked in by false promises this time, Pyrrhus."

If Pyrrhus was surprised by her changed mind he hid it well. "As you wish."

It hurt to look at him. Averting her eyes, Leda waved him forward, resuming their walk. "I'll need to collect some things from my cabin, and then we can go."

He stayed silent by her side, as though convinced that further words might change her mind back.

When at last they reached her cabin she was thankful that Pyrrhus ordered his guards to remain outside. She stepped through the door that screeched on its hinges.

He followed, apparently unable to stifle his curiosity. He took in the rumpled, unmade sheets on her bed and the water damage to the floor as she whirled around the room, shoving what remained of her possessions into a large leather satchel.

When she was done and the bag was looped over her shoulder she found him focused on the nearly finished dress draped over her new sewing table. It was a profusion of thick sapphire silk, the delicate golden embroidery around the corset only just complete.

"You should take this back to the palace with you."

Leda snorted. "That's not for me. I've been making it for Madam Megara, the mayor's wife. If she knew you'd told me to steal her dress, the blights upon the land would be the least of your problems, trust me."

Something that resembled a smile crossed his features.

Leda stopped to scribble a hasty note to ask Iris to take the dress to Megara, requesting that she hold the final payment for when she returned, and placed it on the table. Iris would find it when she stopped by to see where Leda had got to.

With that, she was ready, and she followed Pyrrhus out to the shiny black carriage pulled by six horses that had appeared outside. Such a sight did not belong on her sand-paved street, and was drawing the attention of several neighbours. Each horse was pure white, sporting a ridiculous tufted gold feather in its bridle that trembled in the light breeze.

Leda slid an unimpressed look over to Pyrrhus as he offered a hand to help her into the carriage. With a toss of her head she wasn't entirely proud of, Leda hoisted herself up alone, her right leg shaking imperceptibly with the effort. A bolt of pain shot through it, mercifully quick that time.

The carriage was lushly appointed, the bench comfortable as she sank down on to it. By the time Pyrrhus entered and shut the door behind him she had her hands on the curtains over the window, the luxurious red velvet under her fingertips. Inspiration sparked for the next dress she would make.

She dropped the curtains at the sight of Pyrrhus's raised eyebrow as he lowered himself on to the seat opposite her. They both jerked as the carriage moved, the wheels shuddering over the rough road.

Leda had hoped that he'd entertain himself during the long journey, perhaps with a book. Instead his gaze was steady on her face, as though cataloguing the changes from the past year. Though he said nothing, she thought there might be something approving in his demeanour as he took in the evidence of sun in the freckles scattered across her cheeks and the erasure of the lines of stress between her eyes.

Still, Leda squirmed under his appraisal. "Stop looking at me."

His mouth quirked. "You're awfully angry at someone you haven't seen or spoken to in a year."

Infuriating man. "Power has made you obnoxious."

"An argument can be made that I always was," Pyrrhus said, momentarily distracted by the sparkling of the sea through the window as the sunset cast it in an orange and pink hue.

Leda snorted, then was annoyed with herself for finding him funny, and with him for daring to develop a sense of humour while she was away.

They lapsed into silence after that.

For all that he'd changed, Pyrrhus had not become a fidget, sitting as still as a statue in the corner of her eye. Leda had no way of knowing he was breathing if not for the fact that he hadn't keeled over.

The temperature dropped drastically as night fell and soon enough Leda had crossed her arms tightly around her torso to disguise her shivering. With a sigh that she could see condensing in the air before her, she took her hair out of its plait and spread it around her neck in a vain attempt to trap some heat.

She barely saw Pyrrhus move, but a second later he'd produced a blanket from the compartment beneath his seat and it was spread over her lap. It was made of a fine cream wool, and she murmured her thanks as she ran her fingertips over it. It eased her suffering, but Leda needed more warmth if she wanted to spend the rest of the journey in any kind of comfort.

She looked over at Pyrrhus, who was showing no sign of being the least bit chilly.

He looked warm, and comfortable. Damn him. In another life she'd have been able to lie against his chest, pull his arms around her, draw out all his heat and be asleep in seconds.

But that wasn't what they were to each other. She'd made that decision for them both a year ago.

They wanted different things, and they hadn't chosen each other over those desires. Leda was built to be alone. She needed to get over the part of her that was all giddy joy at seeing him again and return to rationality, even if her body screamed otherwise.

In the end, Pyrrhus made her decision for her.

"You're still shivering," he said, his voice gravelly and serious as he stood up with admirable balance in the rocking carriage, transferring himself over to her bench.

Leda imagined she had all the pliancy of a wooden floorboard as he circled her shoulders with an arm and drew her towards him.

She didn't like that he was close enough to be able to hear her swallow. "You don't have to, but thank you," she said stiffly.

"You're welcome."

A pause, then, "This doesn't mean anything."

"Doesn't it?" Pyrrhus asked in a tone of detached academic enquiry, his face unacceptably close to hers.

She looked staunchly away.

"I begged you to come with me and you said no, remember? You chose power."

Now he was the one who stiffened. "I chose to serve our kingdom, all of these countries. I'm providing stability."

Gods, he was so warm. "That's as may be. It doesn't change the fact that we have different goals in life. When I told you I wouldn't be anywhere near the throne I meant it, Pyrrhus. There's no future for ... for whatever this was." They'd never properly defined what they'd meant to each other, just careened towards one another and away like marbles on strings. A child's game.

"Is that so?"

"You've spent an hour of today talking about my selfishness and lack of family values. Surely you know we're incompatible?" It hurt something deep inside her to say that, but it didn't make it false.

Pyrrhus remained very still against her. "It seems you've come to your conclusions on the subject," he said, frustratingly remote. "I won't go against your wishes."

She bit her lip at that. "You would go with my wishes, if I felt differently?" She couldn't believe that were possible.

He'd stopped breathing, judging by the total lack of movement in his chest. There was her answer. He'd moved on. As he should have. She wondered if his twittering band of empty-headed advisors had forced him to select a wife to reign beside him yet, and decided not to ask.

A couple of months before, Leda had read a speculative piece in the newspaper about who might be chosen as his queen. She'd got about three paragraphs in before she'd thrown the newspaper into the sea. Then, cursing loudly, she'd splashed her way in to retrieve it. She was not about to be a polluter in her pettiness.

"Go to sleep, Leda."

A silence that made her want to claw at the walls.

"We can be friends again," she said staunchly. Anything more and she'd be unacceptably close to the corruption and pain that clung to the throne like a malevolent curse.

She could see Pyrrhus's jaw flex from the corner of her eye. "Friends. Yes."

"I think ... I think I'd like that," she said softly, all the fight leaving her as she finally began to feel warm. "I never really had friends, not proper ones, before you."

He grunted, clearly finished with that line of conversation. "How is your leg?"

"Fine."

There was that fascinating tick in his cheek as he repressed his annoyance at her reticence to share with him. He nodded tightly.

Leda's leg actually was relatively fine, though it still flared up from time to time. She'd continued in the treatment that the royal physician Ambrose had prescribed, and it helped immensely. The desire for a high dose of hibcus, the oblivion that it would bring, lingered at the edge of her consciousness as it always had, but she could put it aside now.

She felt his sigh against her.

"Sleep, Leda."

She was contrary, she knew she was, but it just so happened she was considering sleeping anyway, so there was no point in arguing with him. She allowed her eyelids to flutter shut and the gentle rocking of the carriage to lull her to sleep under his arm.

Her friend. She wondered how long she'd be able to keep that up without her resolve shattering.

It hadn't worked out so well for her the last time.

CHAPTER 4

$\mathcal{A}$ shriek of wind.

Leda started awake so violently she smacked her head against the carriage window. She looked up to see Pyrrhus opposite her, trying and failing to conceal his smirk.

He then did a very bad job of pretending to be absorbed in the book he held.

"Good morning," he said.

"Is it?" Leda asked croakily, bracing her hands against the seat either side of her as the screeching wind jostled the carriage back and forth. Thankfully she hadn't eaten recently, or the rocking would have her casting food up all over the upholstery.

The view from the window was miserable, as grey as if all of the colour had been sucked out of the world. The normally bustling and prosperous streets of Gemdark, capital of Viridiana, lay quiet and empty.

Surely they would normally be busy at this hour? Leda supposed the rain pounding at the carriage like handfuls of hurled stones must have discouraged people from leaving their homes.

Her eyes widened at the number of boarded-up shopfronts, all bearing the characteristic signs of water damage they'd just travelled away from.

"What happened?" Her breath fogged up the glass of the window in the frigid air.

"Drought," Pyrrhus said crisply, back to being engrossed in his book. "For months. The soil hardened, then the rains came. The earth was not equipped to soak it up and so ..." His expression was grim. "Floods."

"Why is this happening?"

"They say the gods are angry."

"Do you believe that?"

"I didn't at first," he said. "But the gods are refusing to address this with any of the priestesses. I've had scholars from the universities gathered at the palace for months and they all swear that none of this could be a natural occurrence. It's as if the weather has gone mad."

He was a man of logic, of course, and so explored every alternative before turning to the wrath of the gods as an explanation. Not that it would have helped him much; the gods were largely unknowable except to the secretive priestesses.

"Elina believes that the gods have placed a curse on us, that I've gone against their will by forcibly taking your father's throne without their dispensation," Pyrrhus said.

"Elina spends too much time crouched in the temple thinking the ringing in her ears is the whispering of the deities. I'd take her words with a pinch of salt if I were you." Leda's tone was confident, much more than she actually felt.

She shot an angry glance at the sky, in case the gods were observing them at that very moment.

They both fell silent, and she found herself glued to the window as they started their ascent towards the palace.

The glittering monstrosity loomed above them, casting their carriage into shadow, and Leda grimaced at the sight of it. It was as beautiful and imposing as ever, a sumptuously crafted prison, gold and gaudy against the muted grey backdrop.

Pyrrhus was looking at her strangely, and she found herself fidgeting under his attention once again.

"What?"

"You give your opinion far more confidently than you used to."

She shot him a challenging look. "Is that a problem?"

He turned a page in his book, utterly indifferent. "No."

"Good."

He kept turning pages despite the fact that his gaze was fixed on her face once more.

"How did you do it?"

Leda winced at the question, just audible over the whistling wind that rocked the carriage.

"How did you leave? No guards saw you go." Pyrrhus finally put the book aside. He crossed his arms and looked away as though the answer weren't particularly important to him. The tense quiet that followed indicated otherwise.

"I had ... a route out of the palace."

"I gathered that. If it's a breach of security you need to tell me so that the safety of the people in the building isn't in jeopardy."

Leda shook her head. "It's not a risk."

"I'll be the judge of that."

Leda puffed up in annoyance, about to give him a piece of her mind, when he held up a hand.

"Just tell me. Please," he added grudgingly. This was a man who couldn't stand a mystery.

She sighed. "A chimney in the armoury. Milos, the armourer, couldn't stand to be hot. He defied my father's orders to keep all the fires burning. I discovered it when I was very young. I snuck into that chimney most nights over the years I spent the summer at the palace, carving hand and footholds within so I could one day climb out to the roof."

"The roof," Pyrrhus said sardonically, like she'd lost the plot or was pulling his leg. He looked up at the myriad of sloping golden roofs atop the palace, the chimneys scattered through them, and the lack of other access points. A deep frown carved his face.

"Yes. It was always the plan, mad as it may sound. I'd take my supplies and stay there for a few days, invisible to anyone down here, until the King stopped searching the immediate grounds for me. His dogs were trained to scent me and my siblings, so I'd wait until the search expanded and they were sent with them. Then I'd rappel down into a guard blind spot and sneak into the woods. Of course, when I actually did it the experience wasn't so smooth. I sprained my ankle and nearly kicked through two windows. But I managed it in the end."

He shifted restlessly in his seat. "And that's it?"

"It is."

"Of all the melodramatic—you could have walked out the *front door*, Leda."

"I wasn't sure that I wouldn't be prevented from leaving or followed by your people."

That only appeared to incense him further. Pyrrhus's presence seemed to take up much more of the carriage than it had before.

"You know nothing about me if you think I would have ever prevented you from leaving. Instead, you risked breaking your neck to perch up on the roof, laughing down at us."

"I was *not* laughing."

There was an unfamiliar distance to him as he held her gaze. She wanted to explain more, to justify herself for what was, in hindsight, an insane decision borne of mistrust and desperation. But it seemed he didn't want the conversation to continue.

With a short nod Pyrrhus opened the door to the carriage, climbed out, and offered her his hand. She took it after a little hesitation, clambering out into the rain and the wind.

The heat of his skin was more of a potent shock to her system than the weather, and her breath hitched at the feeling of her fingertips sliding against his palm as he pulled away.

Three tall figures stood on the topmost steps leading to the palace, watching Leda and Pyrrhus with interest. They seemed undisturbed by the rain's concerted attempts to batter them into the ground.

She recognised them instantly. The Ariti brothers, royal representatives of Pyrrhus's homeland of Rivernesse.

Leda was surprised that any of the Five Families would be interested in her return; they'd barely paid attention to her before she'd left the palace.

The gossip in the markets of Saint-Trevale was that the trials to determine the new monarch should have begun over nine months ago, but fierce arguments between the families on the nature of the tests had caused delays. Leda remembered thinking that Pyrrhus must have been tearing his hair out when they didn't stick to his carefully formulated schedule.

She was distracted by the man in question stepping up to greet them.

"Gentlemen. You remember Leda." Pyrrhus gestured to her and was momentarily distracted by the groom as he came to detach the horses from their carriage. He missed Pan, Arsen and Castor looking at her with the identical blank expressions of three people who'd never met her in their lives.

Only they had. Twice.

Leda's fists clenched at her sides. She hadn't missed being reminded of how unmemorable she was to nobility.

Castor, youngest of the three, recovered fastest. A smile bloomed on his face and he executed a sharp bow. He was the most handsome and personable of the brothers, closer to Leda and Pyrrhus in age than to Pan or Arsen. His teeth were very straight and white and he took care to display each one of them in his eager smile.

The Aritis were famous, even outside of their home country. A family of wise and even-tempered academics who had ruled Rivernesse until Prince Fynn had conquered and slaughtered their parents. Pan, Arsen and Castor had relinquished their claims to the throne and scattered into the population to avoid drawing the ire of Leda's father, though they'd made impacts on society in their own ways.

Now forty years old, Pan was the heir eligible for the throne. He'd published many influential books and papers on horticulture and the cultivation of crops to avoid mass starvation using cross-breeding. Arsen, approaching his mid-thirties, taught military strategy at a university in Doviet and had even advised the former King on his invasion strategies once or twice.

Castor, well, he was more of a mystery. He bounced between universities, holding senior academic positions, but never seemed to have developed a speciality.

His reputation with the ladies, though, that was legendary. At least according to some servants Leda had once overheard giggling about him.

Leda bent her knees in the traditional courtly curtsey. How little she'd missed that; it felt odd to contort herself in such a way now.

"Miss Locarno," Castor said, his voice deep and pleasant as he raised himself smoothly from his bow. He gave a dismissive nod to Pyrrhus, who had come to stand next to her. "How lively we'll be with your company; things have been much too dull around here." He was still looking at Pyrrhus as he said that.

Pyrrhus remained stone-faced.

"Thank you," Leda said, wondering what was going on there. "It's nice to be back," she lied.

Someone new joined them on the steps, another face that Leda instantly recognised, this time because she'd seen her so recently.

Melia was the most powerful and influential priestess in the kingdom, the Exalted Priestess, and her family had been the rulers of Slofray before Leda's father had taken it for himself.

She was beautiful as ever, with fiery red hair that cascaded down to her waist. She wore a thick satin gown in light blue and a coat of white damask on top, complete with a fur-trimmed scarf.

Something about her was different from the last time Leda had seen her. She looked tired, her eyes circled in dark purple.

"Ledazaria," she said with a smile. The name chafed but Leda said nothing to correct her. "How lovely to see you again. I hope you're here to deliver my dress."

Pyrrhus turned to Leda. "Her dress?"

"Yes, she came to me in Saint-Trevale to commission one."

Pyrrhus was expressionless as he looked back at Melia. "Is that so?"

"I had heard of her talents, but only after she'd left the palace. I happened to be on holiday there," Melia said. "I needed a new dress and I wanted the best, so I sought her out to commission it." She swivelled to face Castor. "Have you been to the beaches of Saint-Trevale? Simply breathtaking, well worth a trip."

Castor seemed momentarily bewitched by her beauty and made no reply. Leda couldn't blame him; she'd been much the same when Melia had approached her for the first time.

"Unfortunately your dress was destroyed in the tsunami, but I'll begin work on a new one immediately."

Leda would need to track down a lot of expensive and luxurious fabric to do so, but the palace wasn't a bad place to source it.

Melia liked her gowns to weigh as much as another human. How she wasn't profusely sweating all day, Leda couldn't fathom.

"As we're all thoroughly drenched, why don't we step inside?" Pyrrhus suggested. He looked as though he might put his hand on Leda's lower back to guide her up the steps, but his arm fell down to his side so quickly she must have imagined it.

Instinct, quickly suppressed.

"I look forward to seeing you at the trials, Leda. It's military strategy first," Castor said jovially. "You'll be coming along to watch? We need more people to cheer on poor Pan; he can't tell the right end of a spear from a mathematical theorem so he'll need all the support he can get." He laughed as a scowl crossed his brother's face.

Leda actually was keen to see the trials, having heard so much about them the previous year. But it wasn't the public ones that most intrigued her; no, it was the secret trials that Pyrrhus had designed to test the heirs without them knowing. They had agreed in principle to them, if grudgingly, as they ensured that all of the trials hadn't been influenced by the candidates and thus there would be some objectivity.

A guard was quickly summoned to accompany Leda to her old rooms. His dark hair reached his shoulders, and he had russet brown skin and round, expressive eyes. He seemed young, a year or two older than Eber perhaps, but there were lines between his brows, like he spent a great deal of time frowning.

Speaking of Eber, her unsmiling brother appeared at the guard's shoulder almost immediately. His face was flushed, most likely a display of how angry he already was with her. What a treat.

Pyrrhus, the three brothers and Melia left them to it, and Leda looked after them anxiously. She'd rather have them as a buffer between her and Eber, but she supposed this moment had to come at some point.

The guard gave Eber an odd look, which piqued Leda's interest. As they made their way up the stairs, she turned to him.

"What's your name?"

He looked surprised to be asked, but his voice was steady. "Kadir, madam."

"How long have you been at the palace?"

"A couple of years. I'm from Rivernesse originally but my uncle is a clerk here; he suggested I join the guard forces when I finished my training."

The fact that he was still here must have meant he'd sided with the rebellion last year. Smart man.

That must be why he looked so familiar. He'd probably been one of the many faces she'd seen on the sidelines of more balls and dinners than she could count. "Well, it's nice to meet you properly."

Eber strode on the other side of Kadir, his feet clomping loudly on the floor.

When they reached her old rooms Leda turned to Kadir.

"Is the king still next door?"

"No, madam, he had his rooms moved last year."

She didn't need to ask when.

Eber didn't seem to be of the same opinion. "That was when you ran away and abandoned everybody, if you recall."

"Yes I do, thanks," Leda said shortly. She nodded to Kadir, who stepped back into the shadows but made no attempt to pretend he wasn't watching them. She sighed. Another thing she hadn't missed.

Eber stumbled slightly and his shoulder knocked Leda's. She reached out to steady him with a frown. "What's going on with you?"

He scoffed, and was it a trick of the light or were his eyes bloodshot? "As if you'd care."

Leda stood in his path as he made to leave. "Tell me what's happening, Eber."

"No."

Right, that was it. She fixed him with the most no-nonsense expression she could muster.

"Listen to me; I'm really sorry that I left you so abruptly. It was selfish of me. I know it and everyone else here knows it. But something is clearly going on with you and I want to help, so tell me what it is."

"Don't overexert yourself, *sister*." He said the final word like it meant nothing and everything all at once. "I'd hate for you to suffer a moment of inconvenience on my account."

His mouth remained slightly open, as though more words were stuck on the edge of his tongue. The young guard shifted in the shadows behind him, and he snapped it shut.

Without another word, he walked away from her.

As Leda stared after him she caught a glimpse of Elina turning into the corridor. She took one look at Leda, scrunched up her face, and pivoted around to disappear in the opposite direction.

Well, that was just great.

CHAPTER 5

$\mathcal{L}$eda stared after Eber and Elina for a long time, trying to clamp down on the odd gripping pain in her chest, and then opened the door to her rooms.

She traced her fingers over a stack of jewel-coloured silks that had been folded neatly on her dressing table. Alongside them was a basket containing an assortment of sewing instruments and her old knitting needles.

Only one person knew Leda well enough to have arranged all this for her, and the lump in her throat only got worse as she crossed to her bedside table and read the titles of the books stacked there. They were a mix of her favourites: a novel about the adventures of a Slofray knight, a brief history of Viridiana, and a book on the language of Saint-Trevale that she'd nearly worn through the spine of last year.

Pyrrhus had readied the room for her return. There was perhaps something arrogant in the way he'd done so, as though he hadn't entertained the possibility that she wouldn't come back with him. But she couldn't find it within herself to be annoyed.

She lifted a book from the table, frowning as she spotted

a piece of paper tucked under the cover. It had deep indentations, as though it had been unfolded and refolded a hundred times, but was otherwise in pristine condition.

It had been well cared for.

Her list.

Leda's pre-death list

1. *Learn to ride a horse*
2. *Swim in the river in springtime*
3. *Wear a proper ballgown*
4. *Shoot a bow and arrow*
5. *Find out what gold leaf tastes like*
6. *Learn to dance a waltz*
7. *Steal a 100-year-old bottle from the wine cellar*
8. *Sleep outside under the stars*
9. *Finish the Knight Errant book series*
10. *Kiss someone*

Stunned, Leda turned the book clutched in her other hand to see the cover. It was indeed from her favourite series about the knight, as she'd first thought, but it was one she hadn't read. The final instalment. It hadn't been in Pyrrhus's library when she was last at the palace.

She was horrified to realise how close she was to tearing up here, alone inside her room. She didn't know how to classify what she was feeling as she stared down at that list she'd made so long ago, when everything was different.

It shouldn't mean anything to her, not anymore. She was here for a purpose: to ensure that her siblings were stable and safe, to reassure them that she was just fine living alone in Saint-Trevale and then return there as soon as she feasibly could.

She tucked the list back into the book and placed it in the drawer in her bedside table, her hand shaking as she closed it.

As Leda perused the rest of her room her stomach rumbled, and she was grateful for the distraction from her increasingly tangled thoughts.

The banquet hall was empty of food, and therefore people, and so she made her way down to the kitchens to see what she could scrounge up by throwing herself at the mercy of the servants.

There were many things she hated about the palace, but the food wasn't one of them. Anticipation coursed through her as she made her way down the stone steps into the basement. Perhaps she'd be lucky and they'd have some bread rolls ready, warm from the oven.

The kitchens were bustling with life as servants began preparations for lunch. The air was hot and moist and the people flitting around paid Leda little notice as she made a beeline for a tray of steaming dinner rolls, their crusts mouth-wateringly golden. Taking the nod of a nearby chef as permission, Leda grabbed a plate and began to pile on rolls, trying not to burn her fingertips in her enthusiasm.

"Save some for the rest of us." A voice came through the steam and she nearly dropped the plate. "They have to feed four hundred people in a couple of hours."

Castor lounged at one of the wooden tables by the wall, an enormous red lobster on the plate before him in a puddle of sizzling butter. He held a sharp forked implement in each hand and gave her a dazzling smile as he tore into the tail.

Leda put two more rolls on to her plate, just because she could.

"You're one to talk," she said, sitting across from him. "That lobster could feed two tables."

"I'm a growing boy; I need sustenance."

Though he seemed to like to be thought of that way, in his mid-twenties there was nothing about Castor that was boyish anymore. There was a hardness to his eyes that even that smile couldn't hide.

"Yes, you do strike me as rather small."

She only dared make the joke because it was so obviously untrue. He towered over most people, even sitting down.

Castor snorted with laughter. "I remember you now. You've returned a changed woman, I see," he said, his smile transforming into something more appraising. He leaned so far back in his chair she was surprised he didn't topple it over.

Pyrrhus had made the same observation about her when he'd convinced her to return to the palace, only his face had held surprise and discomfort as opposed to Castor's amusement.

"Have I?"

"Look at you, making eye contact." Like a shot he was leaning forward again, his face so close to hers she clenched her muscles to keep from flinching back in surprise. "Such lovely eyes. And what a pretty voice. I'd heard no more than ten words from you before. How I missed out."

They were the sweet words of courtly flattery, ones she'd heard bored and indolent courtiers exchanging countless times. They had bathed in the decadence of her father's court; the music and rich food and dancing and, of course, the romance. They'd had nothing better to occupy themselves with.

Having these lovely words directed at her was disconcerting, and Leda had no idea how to respond. She'd never been taught how to do this.

Still, she needed to say something. Anything.

"Oh, well, thank you, that's very kind." Not impressive, but not terrible. She hesitantly returned his smile.

"Perhaps you'd like to take a walk with me in the grounds this afternoon?"

Good gods, no thank you. She was barely keeping up with this conversation as it was.

"I'm afraid I have to... go to the infirmary and pick up some medicine." It wasn't untrue, she did need to visit Ambrose and stock up on hibcus since the crop she'd been growing by her cabin had been ruined by the tsunami. She'd planned to settle in and go in the evening, but why wait?

"Of course," Castor said, undeterred. "Why don't I come with you and then we can walk after? A new hedge maze is being cultivated that I'm sure you'll find..." he trailed off, eyes fixed over her shoulder.

Leda didn't need to turn to see who had stolen the words from his head. Azaria Locarno was terrifying to those who didn't know her, and moreso to those who did.

Steeling herself, Leda turned to take in those bright blue eyes set in a perfect face. Said face was arranged in an expression that unsettled even those who would normally be predisposed toward her beauty. Her posture was perfect, as ever, but her hands were planted on her hips as though she were already in a bad mood and was ready to take it out on someone. Her gown was a rich green satin studded with jewels that set off the inky darkness of her braided hair.

"You finally left the dungeon, I see," Leda said.

"I did." Azaria cocked her head towards Castor. "Leave us."

He looked like he was about to protest, but Leda shot him a warning look. It was best to stay beneath Azaria's notice where possible. With admirable grace, Castor got to his feet and swept them both a low bow.

"Ladies, I look forward to speaking again."

Azaria waited until he'd left the kitchens and his shadow had disappeared along the corridor before she deigned to speak.

"You've been in the sun, I see. It suits you. You look less like a walking corpse."

Azaria was never one to give a compliment without a sting in the tail.

"Thank you," Leda said dryly. "Weren't you supposed to be exiled off to somewhere? They were talking about Slofray when I left—I assumed they'd make you a priestess like your mother. Or that you'd just build a lair in the volcano there."

"The priestesses wouldn't accept me, not that I would ever debase myself by joining their ranks," Azaria sniffed. "Quite frankly it was offensive for them to reject me given I did *not* seek admission. I decided to stay here." She didn't elaborate on her reasoning for that and Leda didn't want to know the details.

"I see."

Azaria crossed her arms, making her an even more threatening picture. "I missed your presence over the past year."

That was a perplexing admission. "You did? Why?"

"The seamstresses here aren't effective; my gowns are falling apart." Azaria gestured to her dress as though it hung off her body in rags.

She was delusional. It was perfect; Leda couldn't see a single fault in the stitching.

"If you say so," Leda said dubiously.

"I'm going hunting shortly. Join me? You can carry my kills."

Leda couldn't think of anything she wanted to do less.

She was moments away from calling Castor back and telling him she'd go on that walk with him after all.

"Perhaps next time," she said. "I need to see Ambrose for my medicine."

Azaria tilted her head to one side. "How inconvenient it must be, to be ill all the time."

Leda gave her a dark look. "We all have our burdens to bear." Hers was the horrific knife wound spanning her right thigh, inflicted by Azaria herself when they were children.

Her mood souring, Leda made her excuses and went to the infirmary to find Ambrose.

The royal physician was nothing if not predictable. He sat at his desk, absentmindedly consuming a sandwich as he read a book filled with diagrams that should have put him off eating for at least the next decade. He looked up as Leda approached and a scowl descended on to his face.

Missed you too, Ambrose.

"Well, well, look who's back."

He put his sandwich down as though the sight of her had made him lose his appetite, and not the gruesome drawings of bodily secretions in his book.

"You're here for your medicine, I suppose?"

"That, and the joy of seeing you," Leda said sweetly. Nothing annoyed him more than when she was nice to him. He had to struggle harder to justify his dislike of her then, and that was effort he didn't generally care to expend.

He made an indistinct noise and got up from his desk to rifle through the cabinet behind him, pulling various pots from shelves and muttering something she was sure she didn't want to hear.

He looked like an overworked physician who didn't have the best grasp of his sleeping schedule. The fact that he was one of the few remaining heirs to the Bixel family that had once ruled Saint-Trevale was baffling. The idea of him entering himself into the trials to have a chance at becoming king was laughable, though he was technically eligible. And yet, having brought down the throne with Pyrrhus and the other rebels, Ambrose had stayed as far away from ruling as possible.

He was a curious man.

"Are you going to compete for the Crown?" Leda asked as Ambrose handed her the medicine. At her words his hand clenched so hard around the pot that she struggled to prise it out of his grasp.

There was a loud snort from the corner, and Leda turned to see Elina sitting on the floor nearby, surrounded by jars on to which she was carefully applying labels.

"Why are you *everywhere* now?" Leda asked. Elina's iridescent white dress was spread over the flagstones, doubtless picking up all kinds of dirt, but she seemed not to care. Her back was stooped as she bent over the jars.

Ambrose had turned away and was busying himself arranging the paperwork on his desk into stacks. He had none of Pyrrhus's meticulous approach to organisation, his desk painful to look at, covered as it was in books and vials and one ominous yellow stain.

"I have no desire to lead," Ambrose said. "I doubt I'd be suited to it."

Leda agreed; he was hardly the most amiable. His face, though very handsome, held a perpetually unamused expression. And though he was a healer he seemed to hate nothing more than interacting with people. Particularly Leda, though she believed his dislike for her was special.

"Zephyr is even less suited to power," Elina said idly.

Ambrose's twin brother was almost identical in looks but diametrically opposed in personality. Zephyr had the same face and golden hair as Ambrose, but where Ambrose's eyes were a piercing blue Zephyr's were entirely black. It gave him an unsettling look, and so in the development of his personality Zephyr overcompensated to put people at ease. He didn't like to be the centre of attention, not at all, and he flitted around in the shadows. He flattered people and listened to their stories with such fascination they'd think they were the centre of the world.

Leda liked him even less than Ambrose.

Ambrose wore an expression that could only be described as pained. "Zephyr shouldn't be participating in these trials, and I can't think why he is. He'd hate to sit on that throne even more than I would. He wouldn't stand up to the scrutiny; I've never seen anybody take criticism worse than he does. It's why he dropped out of university in his first year, tried three other degree specialisations and then gave up completely."

Leda thought that judgement on how his brother responded to criticism was a little rich coming from Ambrose, but held her tongue.

Elina knocked over one of her jars with a loud clink and cursed under her breath.

"What are you doing?" Leda asked.

"Inventory. This *handwriting*," Elina grumbled, lifting a jar of what looked like dark green moss and tearing off the label with relish. "Do you have a child working here by any chance?"

"I wrote those," Ambrose said in a long-suffering tone.

"So you chose your penmanship at five years old and never deviated?"

Ambrose pinched the bridge of his nose, eyes closed. "I cannot deal with both of you here at the same time; I swear to the gods my head will explode."

Leda stifled her laugh, pitying him enough to bring the conversation back on track. "Zephyr is unlikely to win the trials, though, surely?"

It was true that Zephyr's competition far outclassed him. Pan Ariti was said to have a mind that worked faster than any except perhaps Pyrrhus's. He spoke four languages and held three advanced degrees.

Melia had a devoted following of hundreds of thousands and was one of the only people in the kingdoms who could commune directly with all of the gods. Elina literally worshipped the ground she walked on.

Then there was Thalia of the tribes of North Doviet, who was said to be pragmatic and a great strategist. She'd brought with her a silent husband who refused to speak to those not living in Doviet as part of a long-standing tradition. They also had a fifteen-year-old daughter, Selene, who did speak, though she was almost as sparing with her words as her father. She was a pretty girl with platinum hair sporting a streak of pure black, green eyes and a consistently mulish expression. She stayed concealed in her father's shadow most of the time.

Finally, there was Linus Bolsh of South Doviet, who had brought his wife and child to court. He was an enormous man, standing nearly seven feet tall. He had the eyes of a hunter, an aggressive aura that surrounded him at all times, and long brown hair braided down his back. He was said to have once killed a thousand men in a single fight with no weapon of his own. He was so terrifying he'd become a legend in his own right, and Leda tended to find an excuse to leave a room when he entered it.

"Who knows with these trials; any of them could take it."

That was what worried her.

As Leda stood there, fingers clenched around her pot of medicine, her mind whirred. She had to get back to Saint-Trevale, to the life she'd built there. But she'd need to stay here for a while first to see that her siblings were safe. That would give her time to inspect the candidates going through these trials more closely, to see who might become their new monarch.

Something to keep an eye on, then.

"Melia should win," Elina piped up from the corner. "She has the closest connection to the gods. She's divinely blessed."

Leda rolled her eyes. "Because that's all that matters."

"It is, as it happens." Elina pointed one of the empty jars at her. "You'd do well to be a little more deferential to the gods who gave us life and steer us in all things, Leda."

"I'll try," Leda said, voice saccharine sweet as she turned to leave.

Pious little twit.

CHAPTER 6

*L*eda had returned to the palace just in time, it seemed, as the first trial was scheduled to take place the very next day. Barely able to contain her curiosity, she went early to the banquet hall and made her way outside in a flurry of servants bearing chairs and rugs and baskets filled with food.

The sun was dazzling, beaming so brightly that she had to shield her eyes as she stepped into the cool air.

The candidates from the five families were to be tested on military strategy, a critical skill in a kingdom that consisted of so many resentfully conquered countries.

Six huge tables had been assembled on the lawn, with well over a hundred people crowded around them. What was particularly distinctive about this group was that nearly all of them wore armour, and the sun glinted so brightly off them that Leda had to squint as she approached on the damp grass.

She peered at the nearest table in awe. It was a minia-ture recreation of the palace atop its hill overshadowing Gemdark, surrounded by woods. The grass looked so realistic she touched her fingers to it and was shocked to find it was painted.

She crossed to the other tables to see that they were also impressively rendered and set up to resemble different regions of the kingdoms. There were the red mountains of Slofray, the islands of Saint-Trevale ensconced in jewel-bright water, the mossy green forests of Rivernesse, the arid dunes of northern Doviet and the ice fields of the south. All these places she'd never had a chance to go to, though she'd been lucky to experience Saint-Trevale.

All the exploration she had left to do made her ache.

Speaking of aching, she felt that familiar tightness in her chest when her gaze locked on Pyrrhus. She'd been aware of him, watching him from the corner of her eye in a way that felt excessive, from the moment he'd stepped on to the lawn.

She forced herself to look away.

So he'd given her back her list, so what? It should be a reminder of all of the terrible, dark things that had happened before she'd left. She should be furious at the sight of it.

And yet.

While the artistry of the scenery and the intricate little figures were interesting, the machinations of the war games were lost on Leda as the representatives of the five families gathered to respond to the scenarios. Each table was staffed by an army general, and at the end of each mock battle where the figures moved where the representative bid them, they would rotate tables. Leda watched as the military observers around the table cheered at a crafty play made by Linus with his ships at the Saint-Trevale table, and the groan at Melia's proposed defence of the icier territories of South Doviet.

A gap opened up in the spectators on the North Doviet table, and Leda slipped in to get a better look.

Thalia stood at the head of it, arms crossed as she frowned down at the pieces. Her face was lined in a way that indicated this was a common expression for her, but there was nothing aggressive or intimidating about her stance. Her daughter Selene stood beside her, her elbows on the table as she contemplated the scene with similar intensity.

Leda was close enough to hear them murmur to one another.

"You could place a squadron in the centre of the town and funnel the attackers in, then surround them from all sides," Selene suggested, her head bowed over the pieces.

Thalia hummed in approval. "Well done for spotting that." She picked up a fistful of the pieces and set them out to depict Selene's suggestion. "That was something I'd considered too, but see how that gives any survivors access to the heart of the city. This was a surprise attack, remember, and so citizens would still be there, vulnerable." She pointed to the buildings surrounding the square. "We protect the weak first, those who didn't ask to be in the conflict."

"No collateral damage?" Selene asked with a grin, as though it were a phrase that had passed between them more than once.

Thalia smiled. "Never, when we can avoid it." She tugged affectionately on the end of Selene's plait with one hand as she shifted the pieces with the other.

Leda looked away, feeling as if she was intruding on a moment not meant for her; a tiny, affectionate interaction between a mother and daughter that was unlike anything she'd ever experienced.

She couldn't imagine having someone she was that close with, who could guide and build up her morals with her. Not even Fayne had been able to provide her with that.

All of a sudden, the ache in Leda's chest had nothing to do with her desire to travel.

She was glad when the games were complete and they were called to lunch.

They picnicked on wide tartan blankets as the judges deliberated over their decision. Leda could see from her spot on the grass that Pyrrhus hadn't touched anything on his plate and appeared to be in a heated debate with two of the generals.

She tilted her head back and absorbed herself in the feel of the sun on her face, the sound of the birds singing from the trees.

The results were announced to great fanfare. Quite literally, as Pyrrhus stood to reveal the metrics by which he and the generals had made their decision and his words were heralded by trumpets. He commiserated with Melia, who was in last place but didn't seem concerned about it, followed by Thalia in fourth, Zephyr in third and Pan in second.

Linus let out a roar of triumph as he was announced the winner, thumping a hand against his chest. His delegation from Doviet let out a chorus of cheers.

Leda wasn't surprised that he'd won, as he possessed a worrying mix of brutality and strategic intellect. Still, she wondered if he'd fare so well in areas he wasn't naturally skilled in. Perhaps the trial of economic understanding would trip him up.

Linus didn't notice her watching him; why would he? But watch him she did, as he dropped on to a picnic blanket and snatched a leg of roast chicken out of his daughter's hand. The girl's face was wan, pale, and Leda didn't miss the way she flinched when her father reached out to her.

Anyone else might not have noticed the minute flash of expression, quickly stifled, but Leda had grown up in the most brutal court there had ever been. The violence she'd been exposed to had been constant, and she'd seen so many of her brothers and sisters recoil just like that.

Linus reminded her entirely too much of her father; he was more of the same. If Pyrrhus conceded the throne to him, then what would it all have been for?

It was then that Leda realised that her original plan to watch the trials as an interested observer wouldn't suffice. She *shouldn't* interfere, of course; it was against the rules and spirit of the competition, but what if her interference prevented atrocities from happening further down the line? Wasn't it justified?

She needed to investigate these candidates, that was all, to learn more about them. After everything that had come before, surely as a Locarno it was her duty to ensure that those who weren't worthy of power didn't get the chance to take it, to eclipse her father in new, more frightful ways?

She could watch from the shadows unnoticed, as she always had, and draw her own conclusions.

CHAPTER 7

*L*eda spent the following week settling back into life at the palace. It was depressingly similar to the day-to-day structure of the past, her life within these decadent walls more stifling now that she knew what freedom was like.

Still, her position was one of privilege compared to the citizens who were suffering across the kingdom. She had a warm place to sleep and all the food and medicine she desired, and so no one would hear a word of complaint from her.

And she had a purpose: ensure her siblings were as well adjusted as possible and to leave when appropriate.

Unfortunately, judging by the state of her family, 'appropriate' was an increasingly distant goal. They were anxious and temperamental and couldn't be together for more than a few minutes without fighting.

Pyrrhus seemed to be avoiding her once more, too, though that was unsurprising. He'd looked like she'd ripped up all his favourite books in front of him throughout their last conversation, so it made sense he had no desire to repeat it.

He'd set a trend, actually, in that most people Leda knew were avoiding her presence, despite having ordered her back there. Eber still answered her attempts at conversation with one-word sentences, Elina had a sarcastic response to anything that came out of her mouth, and Azaria stood at the opposite end of whatever room Leda was in and no closer.

Her ten-year-old sister Ami had mellowed in the year since their father died. She wasn't particularly interested in Leda, but didn't actively dislike her, so that was a success.

Besides, Leda was an independent and self-driven woman now. She could choose what to do on a daily basis; she didn't need her family to coddle her. She took her meals in the banquet hall with her siblings, trying to coax them into conversations that didn't end in cutlery being thrown. She spent her mornings walking out on the grounds to strengthen her leg, afternoons in the royal library working through her stack of books, and evenings crafting a new dress for Melia.

Sometimes Castor sought her out, diverting her with witty conversation. He was hard to ignore given he commanded attention wherever he went, and she conceded that he had some interesting stories about growing up in Rivernesse.

One particularly lazy afternoon Castor found Leda lying on her favourite settee in the library. She was close to dozing, lulled by the steady ticking of the grandfather clock by the fireplace. Her only warning of his approach was his soft footsteps on the carpet before he grabbed her ankles and swung her around to make room for him.

She let out an indignant squawk and raised her hand, which happened to be clutching a thick, hardback tome. She considered dropping it on his head for his impertinence in manhandling her.

Blissfully ignorant of any danger she might pose, he collapsed down next to her with an exaggerated sigh. His smile was so charming she knew he must employ it often to get him out of troublesome situations.

Against her better judgement, Leda softened. It was nice to have someone actually seek out her company.

"May I help you, Castor?" She shuffled away so that they were a more respectable distance from each other. His body radiated heat and that was frankly a bit much.

"What's this?" He scooped a letter off the coffee table, freshly sealed with wax and ready to be sent.

She snatched it from his grasp so roughly it nearly tore. "A letter to an old friend in Saint-Trevale," she said in a tone of forced calm, shoving it into the pocket of her dress.

Ordinarily she wouldn't have had such a panicked reaction, but the contents of that letter were more sensitive than her usual ones. In it, she'd asked Iris to leverage her contacts across Saint-Trevale and find out more about the kind of person Zephyr was. She wanted to know whether he'd got into any trouble in his home country that they should all be aware of.

And Castor couldn't know that she was studying the five families with suspicion, couldn't be tipped off that he needed to protect Pan's secrets.

Luckily he hadn't been watching her face as she'd taken the letter back and so, to him, nothing was amiss.

His focus was, for some bizarre reason, on her hair. He reached forward to touch a tendril that curled down past her collarbone. "You look radiant today, Leda. Full of life." He was awfully comfortable with touching people; she'd seen it in his interactions with the rest of the court. A clap on the shoulder here, a kiss to a lady's hand there.

It made Leda feel cold; she barely touched anyone, ever.

Perhaps she should get more comfortable with it.

"Thank you." She smiled. "Are you not busy? I thought you and your brothers would be preparing for the next trial?"

Castor waved a negligent hand and helped himself to a few grapes she'd brought to snack on.

"That's not for a while yet, plenty of time to get ready. I'm free as a bird today." Again with that grin. She could probably count his teeth.

She drummed her fingers on the cover of her book. "Are you close with Pan? Do you get on well?"

If he thought that a strange question he didn't show it. He shrugged. "Closer than you and any of your siblings, I suppose, but that's true of any family!" He sobered as she frowned. "If I'm honest he's not fun, Pan, too into his books and his botany. Growing up I wouldn't have wanted him at a party with me, but he was always there to help whenever I got into a scrape. Dull but reliable, I suppose. Much like our current king, eh?"

She firmly ignored that last question.

So Pan was responsible but not exactly inspiring. Maybe that was what the kingdoms needed in their next monarch. Someone stable and predictable. Then again, how much could the word of Pan's brother be trusted? She'd need to dig deeper elsewhere.

Castor was looking at her hair again. "Anyway, I was wondering whether you might like to—"

Before he could finish his sentence, several things happened in unison. The royal librarian dropped a stack of books on his foot and yelled out a curse that made Leda's jaw drop, Pyrrhus appeared in the doorway, and a piercing bark rent the air.

Leda was primarily concerned with one of those events and scanned the floor, looking up only to see Pyrrhus regarding Castor with barely concealed disdain as he approached.

She flung her book on to the coffee table and sprang to her feet.

"Which dog is that?" The bark had sounded close and she'd be damned if she didn't know Creoste's distinctive rasp by now. The old King's dog had tormented her for so much of her childhood that the sound was imprinted on her brain.

Pyrrhus was focused on her companion. "Are we not supposed to be meeting your brothers for lunch?"

Castor looked at the grandfather clock in bewilderment. "We are? I forgot. You must understand, Pyrrhus, when present company is so diverting."

Castor didn't bother to employ his smile on Pyrrhus; it seemed he was smart enough to know it would have the opposite of its intended effect.

Pyrrhus finally looked over at Leda. She shrugged at him before bending double and scanning the aisles between bookshelves to see if any canines had made it into the library.

"Indeed," he said, his tone inscrutable.

"She does love to hear tales of our childhood, Pyrrhus," Castor said, getting up and dusting off his trousers. "Don't worry, I haven't told her about all the philosophical debates you lost to me at school." He tried and failed to share a conspiratorial smile with Leda. "He was a solitary soul, was Pyrrhus, and overly bookish even amongst our kind. He quailed before an audience."

Leda barely managed to stop herself from glaring at Castor. She didn't know what battle of wills was going on between these two but she wanted no part in it. It was obvious Castor had an axe to grind with Pyrrhus, and she wouldn't be surprised if he'd decided that she was the best way to get under his skin.

That showed what he knew; Pyrrhus was as remote from her now as he'd been when he first came to the palace. She barely existed to him.

Pyrrhus didn't dignify Castor with a response in the common language, instead switching to their native River-nesse tongue. It was a rolling, smooth and ever-so-slightly guttural dialect and Leda could not for the life of her understand the words.

His fluency, though, that low tone of voice, it did something to her that made her shift uncomfortably. Thankfully, neither of them noticed.

Castor's mouth had set into a grim line at whatever Pyrrhus was saying.

Another bark, this time from alarmingly close proximity. Leda muttered the same curse the old librarian had just emitted and Pyrrhus made a stifled choking sound.

"That's Creoste," she said grimly, watching as the little ball of teeth and fury rounded the corner of the farthest bookshelf. He looked at her with the pleased determination of a hunter who had at last found his prey. "If you'll both excuse me."

She was sprinting through the library doors before either of her companions could respond, Creoste hot on her heels and barking up a storm. He was more unhinged than ever, chasing her with a determination she couldn't understand.

She managed to get to the stairs leading down into the entrance hall before he reached her, jumping up to try and catch her arm in his teeth.

"Creoste, no!" Pyrrhus had caught up to them, Castor nowhere to be seen. He pulled a long silver whistle out of his pocket and blew it, producing a sound that made the dog's ears go flat against his head. Creoste backed away from her immediately.

"Away!" Pyrrhus said, and Creoste raced down the stairs.

Leda couldn't believe it. How were they here *again*? Pyrrhus calling off Creoste as he made his attack, once more in this stupid entrance hall by her father's stupid painting of the Locarno family that Pyrrhus for some reason hadn't removed.

One thing was different, though. As a guard ran to scoop up Creoste and hurry him away Pyrrhus didn't remain in the shadows as he had the last time.

Her breath caught in her chest as he moved abruptly, striding down the steps towards her. Then his hand was on her lower back and he was guiding her forwards in a way that told her she didn't have much choice in the matter.

He was breathing harder than the stairs warranted and Leda looked up to see his tight, furious expression. She was incredulous as she realised that he was trying to stifle his anger with *her* and not that demon dog.

Well, she wasn't about to stand for that.

Leda stepped neatly out of his reach as they entered a deserted corridor on the second floor and rounded on him.

"Is there something you'd like to say to me?"

"Oh, there are a great many things I would like to say to you."

"That's rich coming from someone who's been avoiding me since I got here."

Pyrrhus scoffed. "You've hardly been seeking out my company yourself."

"I find myself not having much to say to you, nowadays."

He reared back slightly, as though she'd reached out a hand and shoved him. "I'll make sure not to bother you in future, then. You clearly don't need my help." He gestured towards the entrance hall where Creoste had accosted her.

"You're quite right. I can handle myself, thank you." The sarcasm dripped from the last two words.

"I suppose you'd have preferred if Castor followed you instead of me?"

She froze.

Pyrrhus's words were usually measured, calculated and thought through well before he spoke them. But not this time. Jealousy had pulsed in every syllable of his voice.

Leda hissed out a breath. "Do you hear yourself? If your subjects heard you talking like that they'd *overthrow* you, you child!"

Something had overtaken Pyrrhus; he didn't even seem offended by her attack on his leadership. It wasn't until her back nearly hit the wall that she realised he was crowding her against it.

"I didn't bring you back here to alternately ignore and insult me," he said curtly.

"If you want someone to drop to their knees every time you enter a room, go and ask anyone else in this bloody palace. You should know by now not to expect that from me."

Pyrrhus's breathing changed at her words, faster. His face, normally so expertly arranged into neutrality, clearly transmitted every thought that crossed his mind. That was how she knew, seconds before he did, that he would press her up against the wall.

Leda went without protest. The heat of him scorched her through her dress.

She would not make any kind of whimpering, breathless sound. She would *not*.

"I'd appreciate if you were more respectful."

He seemed unconcerned that he had her pinned against a wall in a highly trafficked corridor that could see anyone come upon them at any moment. His power and his confidence in it were sealed. She had half a mind to remind him that he wasn't supposed to be touching her, but her head was too filled with rage to properly articulate that thought.

"You want my respect?" Leda said instead, her heart beating so strongly she wondered if he could feel it from her chest through his. His lips were a hair's-breadth from hers despite their height difference. He smelled like the richest, darkest chocolate. "Abdicate."

No other word could have cut through the fog of anger drenched with desire more effectively than that. Pyrrhus reeled back as though she'd slapped him, pupils still dilated despite sanity beginning to return.

His face fell back into emotionlessness.

"Castor is a reprehensible person and always has been. You should stay away from him."

She gave him an obnoxiously exaggerated salute in the style of one of his guards as she pulled away from the wall. She missed the feel of his body against hers and loathed herself for it. "Yes, *sir*."

His face darkened at the word. "Careful, Leda."

She couldn't resist goading him, feeling wildly irritated and alive in a way she hadn't for a year. "Why? What are you going to do?"

His response was obliterated by a boom of thunder that shook the palace so hard the chandelier above their heads swung in a huge arc to crash against the wall.

CHAPTER 8

*L*eda and Pyrrhus sprang apart as though lightning had struck them through the walls of the palace itself.

Another boom, then the relentless gush of rain hitting the windows.

It hadn't even been drizzling a minute ago.

Leda went to the nearest window, watching the glass rattle in its pane and hearing the shriek of the wind as it found its way through the tiniest gaps in the walls. Pyrrhus let out the ghost of a groan as he came to stand beside her, before jolting in shock.

"Is that—" He pointed out of the window in sheer disbelief, and Leda followed his gaze until she saw something that made the bottom drop out of her stomach.

"No," she breathed. "It can't be ... we don't have tornados here. Only in Slofray."

It appeared her information was outdated judging by the dark funnel that stretched up into the purple sky by the river, ripping trees from their roots as it approached the palace at a pace that made Leda want to run screaming in the opposite direction.

"Should we go to the basement?" she whispered, as though afraid if her voice were louder it might attract the tornado's attention.

"Yes," Pyrrhus said steadily, voice low. "We all need to get to the basement. Now."

There was a second of tense, excruciating inaction before shouts began to echo from downstairs and they were both sprinting down the corridor. Leda fell behind almost immediately, her leg protesting. Pyrrhus looked like he was about to stop to lift her in his arms and halted when she snarled, "Don't you dare!"

He stepped back, though his annoyance was clear to see. As they descended the stairs hundreds of people joined them from all sides, servants and courtiers alike, guards directing them down into the basement with muffled yells. It struck Leda as something that must have been planned in advance, and she wondered what other calamities had befallen the palace over the past year to necessitate it.

People streamed into the basement as the wind roared around them. Leda looked frantically for any sign of her family, moving deeper into the labyrinth of corridors that stretched away from the kitchens. Eber was at the very end, huddled against the wall opposite the entrance to what had once been their mother's rooms.

"Eber!" She grasped his arm and he wheeled around to face her, terror in his eyes.

"What's going on?"

"The tornado is about to hit us," she said. "Where are the others?"

"They're all down here, I think; we were together in the gardens when we saw it. Elina fell when we were running, nearly got trampled, but she's alright. Ambrose is with her."

"And Azaria?"

"She was here before we arrived." He shook his head,

dazed. "She's more animal than human, I swear. She could probably sense it before any of us."

That should have surprised Leda, but it didn't. Nothing about Azaria could shock her anymore. Still, she should probably find her.

She tiptoed through the shaking and muttering crowd until she came across a sight that had her stopping in her tracks.

Pyrrhus was moving through the crush, comforting people, clasping their shoulders like a real statesman. It was so antithetical to the version of him that she'd once known that she gaped at the display. The court lapped it up, drawing him eagerly into their conversations.

Even Melia gave him her full attention when he stopped to talk to her. She seemed unconcerned that her precious gods were at that moment attempting to pull apart the building above her head. She did, however, look ill. It occurred to Leda that she must have caught the flu that was sweeping the palace and causing Ambrose to just about tear his hair out. His infirmary might as well have had a revolving door for all the people bustling in and out each day.

Pyrrhus seemed to notice Melia's state, offering her a hand as she sank into a chair. She took it gratefully.

Leda sat on an upturned bucket outside one of the cleaning cupboards, watching him continue to move through his subjects.

It wasn't something her father would have remotely conceived of. In his eyes people had been there to worship him, to serve him. He was not responsible for their comfort.

Pyrrhus had an entirely different view, it seemed.

Leda was quickly reminded of the flu she'd assumed Melia had when someone sneezed beside her, almost falling on to the bucket beside hers.

Leda reached out instinctively, grasping the girl's elbow and helping to lower her down. She nearly dropped her entirely when she saw her face and recognition flashed through her.

"Ismene?"

Ismene was a servant girl with the sweetest face anyone ever saw before she'd been blighted with a knife across her skin, leaving a long, thin scar. The punishment she'd been dealt by Leda's father when it was discovered that she'd befriended her. They'd only been young teens at the time.

And she'd barely spoken to Leda since. It was completely justifiable, but it hurt all the same.

Ismene seemed equally surprised to find Leda beside her. If Melia was slightly under the weather then Ismene was knocking at the doors of the netherworld. Her eyes were streaming and as red as her nose. The rattling sound she made as she drew in air indicated that she could barely breathe too.

Leda leaned backwards as subtly as she could. This was not something she wanted to catch. "How are you?" she asked softly.

Ismene's eyes darted to hers and then away. "I'm alright, looking forward to being able to taste or smell again at some point in the distant future," she said. Her voice was a few degrees lower than usual and she whipped a crumpled handkerchief out of her sleeve with a groan. "I thought you got out of the palace?"

"It was temporary." Even down here they could hear the screaming wind above them. Leda shuddered. "I'm not pleased to be back at this particular moment, I have to say."

Ismene looked up at the ceiling and nodded grimly. "The lake by my parents' house in the south flooded, went all the way up to their doorstep and straight through most other homes in the village. They're talking about the Slofray volcano possibly erupting too. I don't think you'd be safe anywhere at the moment."

"That's probably true. I'm glad your family is alright, though."

"Thank you."

It was an awkward conversation, stilted. There was so much to be said between them, but neither could bring themselves to address it.

Leda decided she was the one who needed to be brave. In fact, she owed it to Ismene.

"Would you like to have lunch this week? To talk?"

They looked at each other then, and Leda felt the usual guilt suffuse her entire body as her eyes fell on the scar across Ismene's face.

Ismene blanched and got to her feet. "Maybe, I'm very busy with my work. I'll probably be even busier cleaning up whatever horror we find upstairs when all this is over." She let out a hacking cough. "I'll see you later, Leda."

And she hurried away, leaving Leda feeling even worse than before.

She couldn't seem to get any of her social interactions right nowadays. Most of them ended with the other party either storming off or running away.

The one slim upside of this kind of disaster was that it was quick. After a few more minutes of the tooth-rattling sounds of screeching wind combined with the smashing of windows and the gods only knew what else upstairs, the noise softened.

The palace lay still above them, with only the occasional creaking.

A guard went ahead to check the upper floors and they

waited with bated breath for his return. It took a few minutes, and when he came back his face was grim as he announced it was safe to ascend.

They streamed up into the palace, hundreds of people taking tentative steps and keeping together as a pack, as though that would protect them from any lingering threat.

Leda slipped to the front and out into the entrance hall, letting out a shaky breath when she saw one of the great front doors had been blown clear off its hinges. It lay at the bottom of the steps outside in two enormous pieces.

She turned and made her way upstairs, starting when she felt a presence behind her. Pyrrhus.

He'd followed her. He had a million things to tend to, an army of twittering advisors and nervous guards to direct, a whole court to reassure. A palace that needed fixing before it tipped right over in the wind. And yet, he followed her as though it hadn't occurred to him for a second that he shouldn't.

Leda didn't know what prompted her to move towards the armoury on the fifth floor, but her feet took her there anyway. On the way she noted the damage caused by smashed windows, but it was what greeted her when she reached the armoury that stole her breath.

"Oh, excellent," Pyrrhus groaned, looking up with irritation at the enormous hole that had appeared when half the roof had been ripped off. Weapons littered the space around them. Leda looked down at the pile of bricks surrounding her feet, some scored by strange markings.

Her chimney had been the first to fall. She fought the ridiculous urge to laugh.

"My chimney ...," she said faintly.

Despite the devastation surrounding him, a hint of satisfaction crossed Pyrrhus's expression.

"Well that's something, at least," he muttered as he

picked up a bronze axe from a pile of debris and brushed the dust from it.

Leda's attention fixed on the weapon in his hand. Her mouth went dry, as though she'd swallowed a fistful of sand. It looked like the younger brother of the ceremonial axe used to end the lives of the Counterparts. That axe wasn't kept in the armoury; her father had deemed it too precious. It stood instead on its plinth in the palace temple, giving Leda yet another reason to avoid that room like the plague.

Pyrrhus tracked her gaze to the axe and seemed to understand the direction of her thoughts. "I tried to have the Counterpart axe destroyed but the priestesses wouldn't allow it. They said it would anger the gods." He looked around the destroyed room. "I doubt there's room for much more anger as it is."

Leda made a pathetic attempt at a smile. "Thank you for trying. I should ... I'm going to get some rest."

"Of course." He set the axe against the wall and dusted off his hands. "I'll go and take care of ... this." The expansive gesture of his arm seemed to indicate the entire palace, and the extent of the burden he'd placed on himself was painfully clear.

Still, she let him go. She knew that nothing she said would make a difference.

Her growling stomach brought her to a halt next to a smashed window two corridors down from her rooms. With a sigh she turned around and headed down to the banquet hall.

She was astonished to see that the huge glass doors taking up one wall of the hall had held steady in their frames, not so much as a crack to be seen. A hastily assembled table of cold food had been set up in the middle of the room by harried-looking servants. Courtiers covered in varying levels of dust and grime stood around the table, picking at the contents.

Leda reached for one of the few items left, a shiny red apple, and made an indignant sound as it was snatched out from under her.

Azaria's teeth made an obnoxious crunch as she bit into it. She regarded Leda with a curious expression.

"What's the matter with you?" Azaria asked.

"Nothing," Leda grumbled. "I'm just tired and covered in dirt and witnessed a tornado rip through a building. Nothing to complain about."

If Azaria were capable of such an indelicate action, Leda was sure she would have shrugged.

"Worse things have happened. Nobody died. At least something interesting is finally going on around here."

"I'd hate to think we're not keeping you entertained," Leda said dryly.

Elina approached them, looking thoroughly windswept and as annoyed as Azaria was neutral. She held a plate stacked high with fruit and surveyed the dregs on the table.

She seemed to reach deep within herself to find the will to take a tangerine off her plate and offer it to Leda.

"Thanks, that must have been difficult for you," Leda said with a smirk, taking the fruit.

Elina looked like she had a mind to snatch it back.

"Well, you need food to fuel your usual schedule, don't you? How else will you stand dully in the corners of rooms, sew ugly dresses no one asked for, or follow Pyrrhus around like a sappy little puppy?"

That was unnervingly specific. But then, Elina always was. "On that note, I believe I'll go to bed."

Azaria perked up. "Where?"

"My bedroom?"

"How?"

"Sorry, do you not complete full sentences anymore? What are you talking about?"

"Your room was destroyed; the tornado blew half the roof off," Azaria said, finishing off the apple she'd stolen from Leda so methodically that all that was left was seeds, which she tucked into her palm.

"Are you serious?"

A snort from Elina. "Have you ever seen her not be serious?"

Leda was getting to be very tired of anyone she shared blood with. Staring up at the ceiling, she took herself back to the days in her little cabin where she came and went as she pleased. Bliss, a lonely kind of bliss. If only she could go back there.

With a groan she turned and left the banquet hall, trudging up to the sixth floor to find that her room was, indeed, in pieces and drenched to boot.

That did it. She was hungry, dirty and on edge. She was going back to somewhere familiar.

The door to Pyrrhus's old study was unlocked, which surprised her.

Not one to look too closely at a gift, Leda slipped inside and sighed in relief as she saw that not a single thing had changed. Books still lined the walls, two stories high, interrupted only by the fireplace, which sat cold and empty. Her favourite armchair was still there, the blanket she'd knitted for Pyrrhus last year folded neatly over the arm.

So this was what it felt like to be home.

~

"Leda? What brings you here?"

Leda shut her book with a snap. Pyrrhus was framed in the doorway at the top of the staircase.

She looked down at the book and briefly mourned the fact that she'd lost her place. It was on the gifts and curses of the gods, barely worth the paper it was written on, but she'd found herself desperate.

So far it had done nothing but praise the power of the gods and tell her how many sheep she may wish to sacrifice to encourage them to send her a husband. There was nothing in there that even hinted at the reason for these dire weather events.

Pyrrhus was still waiting for her response.

She wondered how many sheep she'd have to offer to get the gods to send him to her.

There probably weren't enough in the entire kingdom.

Focus, Leda.

"You saw what happened to the armoury on the fifth floor and didn't wonder what shape my bedroom on the *sixth* floor might be in?" Leda said.

Pyrrhus ran a hand through his hair, looking like a man who hadn't slept in so long he could barely wrap his mind around the concept of a bedroom. He gripped the bannister in front of him like it was all that was holding him upright.

"Oh gods, yes of course. How bad is the damage?"

"It's not terrible, just smashed windows, a small hole in the roof and some ruined bedding. Nothing they won't have fixed in a few days." She wasn't too pleased about the compulsion she felt to reassure him, and glared at him to make up for it.

He bore it stoically.

"Right, well, I'll have some new rooms arranged for you." With that he spun around and walked away.

The fact that he'd left the door open behind him with uncharacteristic absent-mindedness had her gaping after him. Not for the first time, worry spread through her. She had the horrible feeling that she was slowly watching a man unravelling.

Perhaps he needed help just as much as her siblings did.

Still, something about being back here, in Pyrrhus's study, made her calmer than she'd felt at any point since she'd stepped back into the palace. Here, once the door was locked, it was safe. Nothing could touch her. It was with this thought in mind that she allowed her head to tip back against the armchair and sleep to overtake her.

She woke blearily a few hours later, stretched out on a narrow bed with a blanket over her. She blinked in the pale grey light from the window, seeing the familiar shapes of the furniture in Pyrrhus's old bedroom. He was the only person who could have moved her there.

She found she didn't mind that much as she turned over, buried her face in the pillow and fell back to sleep.

CHAPTER 9

*P*yrrhus, as always, was proving elusive. Leda left his rooms the following morning and readied herself for the day, then set out to track him down.

She checked the throne room first, finding it full of courtiers who viewed her with varying emotions, from sympathy all the way to outright hostility. She hastily ducked out, finding nothing in the banquet hall, his new office or the library. The guards outside his official rooms remained frustratingly silent when she asked where he was, not even making eye contact with her.

Even her favourite guard, Atticus, merely shrugged when she asked him.

It was over an hour later that she found her way outside, stepping into the rose garden and blinking in the sunlight. The wind, fresh and clear, whipped her hair away from her face. Her feet crunched on a carpet of ripped-up petals mixed with gravel as she made her way towards a familiar face.

Elina was wearing one of her simpler dresses and a sensible hat to shield her eyes from the sun, standing surrounded by her gardening tools. She paid no attention whatsoever to Leda as she approached, already enmeshed in a conversation with Pan Ariti.

It was not a pleasant one, judging by the hissed whispers Leda couldn't quite distinguish and the way Pan gesticulated as he spoke. Elina had one of her most mulish expressions on her face.

"Then you should be applying it after—" Pan broke off as Leda joined them, his expression transforming. He seemed almost relieved to see her, like she'd rescued him. "Ledazaria, how are you this fine day?"

"Very well, thank you," she said, looking between the two of them. "I hope I'm not interrupting."

"Not at all," Elina said, all frustration. "Pan was just venturing some rather outrageous opinions on how I should be managing the plants in *my own* greenhouse."

He failed to hide how offended he was by that. "I've been a professor of botany for almost two decades, you really should value—"

"I know what I'm doing!" Elina sounded about as mature and considered as a toddler mid-tantrum.

Pan sighed before executing a short bow to them both, and then he was striding back towards the palace.

Elina took one look at Leda, straightened her hat, and proceeded to thrust most of her upper body into a wounded-looking rose bush.

Leda cut to the chase. Elina never was one for pleasantries. "Do you know where Pyrrhus is?"

"You can't find him?" Elina said, buried almost upside down in the bush with her shears. "I assumed you could scent him like a bloodhound."

"Very funny." Leda was disconcerted by how quickly she was coming to not entirely dislike Elina, despite her prickly nature.

Elina didn't care whether anybody liked her, and paradoxically seemed more trustworthy as a result. She just appeared to be glad to be out from under their father's thumb, with their brother and her childhood tormentor Agon dead, living her life in the palace with her plants and her gods. No countries to invade, no wars to wage, no expectations.

"What are you doing?" Leda asked.

"Baking a cake. What does it look like I'm doing?"

"You're so sweet; it's a shame we don't spend more time together," Leda said snidely.

"Don't get on my nerves, Leda. I've got herbs in my collection that will turn your teeth purple for a month or make you giggle uncontrollably every time you cough, not to mention one that'll make hideous boils appear on your face. I've got a flower that'll knock you out for twelve hours if you so much as breathe in the pollen. That would stop you blathering on, wouldn't it?"

Leda rolled her eyes. "Terrifying. Back to the matter at hand; have you seen him?"

Elina's sigh was so dramatic it rattled the bush she was in. "Pyrrhus went over there about an hour ago." An arm appeared from the leaves and a pair of shears pointed in the direction of the treeline to the west.

Elina wasn't the only gardener trying to salvage the grounds that day. As Leda made her way through the wet grass towards the woods she saw a small army of workers shaking their heads defeatedly as they plucked plants from the ground. Their sad remains were somehow both brown with thirst and sodden with water, and they stacked high on wheelbarrows. Those were the strong ones, too, that hadn't been ripped up by the tornado.

Leda looked up at the palace to see it largely put to rights, albeit with a few missing windows and roof sections, before progressing into the woods along the dirt footpath.

A bird cooed dolefully nearby. It was cool and quiet between the trees, and Leda followed the fresh footprints ahead of her until she entered a small glade.

Bright sunlight lit the man in the very centre. He stood surrounded by large grey stones in front of which grew flourishing beds of wildflowers in every imaginable colour.

The light glinted off Pyrrhus's dark hair as he knelt at the foot of one of the stones, pulling away a vine that had snaked up around it.

A twig snapped under Leda's foot and he whipped around. He visibly relaxed when he recognised her, and then something wary entered his gaze.

Leda came to stand next to him, careful to avoid stepping on the flowers, and looked at the stone he'd been tending to. It reached up to her hips, grey and polished with a top like a scroll. There were words carved into it in elegant script.

She bent down to get a better look.

Sofie Locarno.

Leda's heart contracted in her chest as though someone had taken hold of it and squeezed.

"Who ..." She peered around at the other stones and let out a long breath. They were almost identical save for the shapes on top. They bore the names Elea, Sira, Erdil, Mat and May. The older Counterparts, all of whom had been killed years ago.

Their bodies couldn't be here; they'd all been cast into the Blainchill River as part of the ceremonies.

Regardless, Pyrrhus had brought them all together into one final resting place.

"You did this?" she asked in a trembling voice, crouching

to touch her fingertips to the stone that bore Sofie's name. It was rough and cold to the touch. The grief overwhelmed her, as potent as it had been the day she'd watched her die in the throne room.

She'd fought so hard to scrub her mind of the image of Sofie's broken body, the blood that had spread in a pool around her, seeping across the floor. While she was usually able to suppress it consciously, it was a starring feature in many of her nightmares.

"I did."

"Why?"

His hands were clasped behind his back, and for such an eloquent man he seemed to struggle to find the words. "I ... it was right," he said simply.

Pain welled up in Leda's chest and she fought the urge to cry, to sink to the ground and sob like a child. She bowed her head over Sofie's stone. It was beautiful, but grey and lifeless. A stark reminder that she was gone, and she was never coming back.

Did Elina know that this was here?

Her voice trembled. "I hadn't realised ... I didn't think that their deaths had affected you."

She wished she could take back the careless words as soon as they left her mouth. They were selfish, focused on her own pain and not on that of others who'd been forced to witness the ceremonies.

Pyrrhus straightened up and looked at her with such disappointment she recoiled.

"I only meant—"

"Excuse me." He nodded curtly, ignoring her plea for him to stay and exiting the glade.

Leda dropped her head into her hands. How could she be so unfeeling? She'd implied that he was heartless, that he'd watched children be slaughtered and felt nothing about it. She knew that wasn't true. Why did she have to constantly behave so reprehensibly around this man?

"What is going on with you?" Eber appeared from the trees so quickly he must have caught her exchange with Pyrrhus and hung back until the appropriate moment. She wouldn't be surprised if he'd followed her from the rose garden in the first place.

He stood next to her as she stared numbly at the ground. "Are you capable of opening your mouth without inserting your foot into it nowadays?"

"Apparently not," Leda said weakly, scrubbing her hands over her face. "I don't know what's wrong with me."

"You're contemplating a long life for the first time ever, and it scares you," said Eber with a wisdom he shouldn't possess. "You're not used to thinking about people other than yourself."

"Yes, alright," Leda said dully. "You've told me that already, multiple times. I'm aware."

Eber lowered himself to the grass and crossed his legs like a child, plucking a daisy from the nearby flower patch to twist between his fingers. Leda watched his hand tremble slightly, the way he swayed as if caught in a breeze, though the clearing shielded them from wind.

"You're *so* angry with me," Leda said. "Why? It can't just be because I left."

He stared into the middle distance. "You know Pyrrhus had that stupid paper sculpture of us removed from the temple? Now none of us will burn away into nothing. We're here now, proper people."

That did nothing to answer her question. There was a long pause as she tried to decipher his words.

"You found your purpose," Eber continued quietly, throwing the flower he had squashed in his fist back on the ground. "You know what you want from life, or you think you do at least. You made yourself a home. I have nothing. No one I'm close to, no calling. I look at the life ahead of me and I just see *nothing*. My god stopped caring about me years ago."

"Your ... you used to be close, with your god?"

The topic she'd danced around for years, the fact that she'd never heard from hers.

"I heard the whispers in my mind in the temple for years, felt them guiding my decisions, making sure I didn't get into danger," he said morosely. "Then it all just stopped. They don't want me either."

"Eber—"

"You always used to talk about how no one noticed you, but you'll find that everyone wants you here. I came to get you, Elina came to get you, Azaria demanded your return. Pyrrhus put himself in danger travelling away from the palace to bring you home. How many people do you think would do that for me?" He braced his arms on his knees and shook his head. "I don't fit anywhere."

Tentatively, Leda lifted her hand and let it rest on his shoulder. He flinched at the contact, but didn't shake her off. His head bowed further.

"I'm so sorry," she said, and she meant it. "I had no idea you were feeling this. You do fit here, of course you do. You're the life and soul of this insane little family we have. And you have so many talents, there are lots of callings you can choose from. Your god hasn't abandoned you, that's a blip, and there's so much you'll do in the future. We've got all the time in the world, I promise."

"We?"

"Yes, we," Leda said firmly.

She wasn't going to watch her siblings fall apart one by one in the wake of their father's death. She hadn't believed

Pyrrhus when he said she could bring the dregs of her family together, but that wouldn't stop her from trying. It was time to stop feeling sorry for herself and actually do something. "The first thing we're going to focus on is cutting down on your drinking."

Eber stopped sifting grass through his fingers and looked up at her in shock. "What are you talking about?"

"Don't try and fool me, Eber Locarno. You think I don't know what it's like to hide a dependency from the world?" Her hibcus use hung heavy and unsaid in the air between them; the headaches and the vomiting and the vacant stare she'd done such a mediocre job at hiding. "You're belligerent and lethargic and I can see it in your eyes. We're going to go to Ambrose together and he's going to wean you off. This stops now, Eber."

She'd grown up under the shadow of a drunken Dalev, a man who'd been most comfortable beating her when he was deep into his drink. She would not see Eber fall to the same vice.

"It's not a problem," he said stubbornly. "Half the court is drunk by noon."

"This court is comprised of vacuous, idiot nobles who have nothing going on in their lives," Leda said sharply. "That is not, and never will be, us."

She got to her feet and dusted her skirts down, before offering Eber a hand. He hesitated before taking it and allowing her to pull him up. He went to break away but she kept her fingers locked around his.

"Meet me in the infirmary at sunset and we'll speak to Ambrose. I mean it, Eber."

"Yes, madam," he said, a hint of a smile twitching at the corners of his mouth.

"Good." She released him. "Now I need to see Melia and finish off her dress before tomorrow's ball and then I'm helping Ami with her reading. You'll be alright until we meet?" Looking at him, she wasn't sure, but he nodded and waved her away.

She left him standing in the clearing with his hands in his pockets, eyes fixed on the graves of their siblings.

CHAPTER 10

Melia stood in the centre of her bedroom, arms crossed as she observed Leda. Her face was extremely beautiful, except for the fact that her lips tipped down slightly at the corners, giving her a permanent look somewhere between disapproval and sadness.

Her hair rippled gently in the warm breeze coming through the open window, her jewelled headdress glittering in the sunlight that flooded in.

Her presence made Leda sweat.

She didn't know what to do under such intense scrutiny from the most famous priestess the world had ever seen and so busied herself with fussing around the dress, which was propped up by the bed.

"Are you sure this is what you pictured?" Leda asked, spinning her fabric scissors nervously in one hand.

"Of course it is," Melia said, not sparing a glance for the dress.

"This fabric you provided is beautiful; I've never seen anything like it."

"We weave it in the Grand Temple in Slofray; it is only found there."

That was the sole reason Leda would consider that someone should visit that temple.

Leda couldn't keep the question from escaping her. "Why did you come to Saint-Trevale? Why commission this from me?" The story Melia had fed Pyrrhus about Leda's prodigious talent was one she'd love to believe. But she was a realist too, and though she might become great one day, it would take a lot more practice to get there.

Melia seemed to be suppressing a smile, or perhaps a sneer, but her response was polite. "I was in Saint-Trevale already, as I told you. And I'll admit I was curious about you, as were the gods. I wanted to see the woman who had instigated all of this."

She gave a grand sweeping gesture to represent the upheaval that had occurred at the palace since the old King's reign had come to an end. Leda didn't believe that she was the instigator of any of it at all. She was merely a pawn who'd been swept up in the current of events.

"If the gods want to know me, surely they can just look down."

Melia looked amused. "They work in mysterious ways."

"That, we agree on," Leda said, inspecting one of the dress seams to ensure it wasn't crooked. She looked up to find Melia still watching her. "And will you work in mysterious ways too, if you become queen? Or do you have plans for what you'll do?"

Perhaps it was an impertinent question, it certainly felt that way coming out of her mouth, but she needed to ask it. It had been impossible to find anyone who knew more about Melia than the fact that she was the Exalted Priestess and beloved by her priestesses. If Leda was to glean anything else about her character, it would have to be from the woman herself.

"What would I do with that kind of power?" Melia

asked, eyes sliding away from Leda as she considered it. "That is the ultimate question, I suppose. I would try to make life better for those who are suffering; that would be my guiding philosophy. It would be an extension of my current work for the gods, for what they ask of me. They require that I have a positive impact on others' lives while I am in service to them."

That positioned her ahead of Linus and Zephyr in terms of suitability for the throne, at least in Leda's opinion. Melia clearly had morals, considered them to be important, and had sympathy for those less fortunate than herself.

"I like the way you put it," Leda said with a smile.

Melia returned it. "I am glad that I went to see you in Saint-Trevale, Leda. It has been most enlightening getting to know you."

"I probably wasn't what you expected," Leda said ruefully. Melia had likely been looking for a woman who made things happen—someone impactful and confident. Someone people took notice of. Leda fell short of that.

"You are exactly what I expected," Melia said, surprising her. "You don't know who you are yet, child, but you will. The gods have plans for you; don't you worry about that." Finished with the conversation, Melia left the room.

Hours later Leda frowned in frustration, a fistful of pins in her mouth as she stared down this obnoxious puzzle of a dress. It just wasn't working. Was it the frilly sleeves? The ruffles so close to the waist? Something needed to go.

Decision made, she jerked to the side to grab her scissors as a whistling noise came from behind her.

The sound of metal tinkling on to stone as pins were spat from her mouth.

Leda stared down at where they'd fallen, vaguely aware she was bent almost double with her scissors dangling from one hand. The pins on the floor were red, glistening. Had she cut her mouth with one of them? She touched her lips and her fingers came away clear.

She tried to draw in a breath and wheezed with the effort, feeling warmth spreading down her arm to drench her fingertips. That wasn't good.

Steeling herself, Leda glanced up into the mirror, and screamed.

An arrowhead protruded from her left shoulder, blood soaking the silver of her dress in shocking scarlet. She was losing so much so rapidly she had no idea how she was still standing.

"Is someone here?" A small head poked around the door. Ami. "Leda!"

Her little sister ran into the room, her face white and panicked. She nearly crumpled beneath Leda's weight as she tried to hold her up, and they both went down to the ground in a heap.

"Get ...," Leda rasped, seizing Ami's wrist. "Get help ..."

Ami looked reluctant to leave her but cast another look at the arrow and let out a shrill sound. She scrambled to her feet and sprinted out of the room, leaving bloody footprints in her wake.

Leda emitted a low groan as she pressed her right hand against the wound in her shoulder, aware she was trying to dam a river with a pebble.

"Oh gods, Leda!"

It could have been seconds or minutes later, her grasp on the concept of time draining from her as steadily as her blood. She knew that voice anywhere, though, and it cut through the haze encompassing her mind with knifelike clarity.

Pyrrhus.

She looked over at him in a daze, straining to keep her head up so he didn't slide from her view. This man, who sprinted across the room to get to her, still had the presence of mind to ensure he didn't knock Ami aside as she stood in his way.

He was on his knees. "No, no." His face was bloodless, lips white in stark contrast to his hands, which were already stained red as he pressed them to her shoulder. "Leda, no."

She felt vaguely chastised, as though this had been something she'd chosen to do for sport and she was being told off for it.

"I'm fine." The wet gurgle that was her voice belied that somewhat. She shook her head, trying to get her thoughts in order.

He cupped her cheek in an attempt to keep her still and she leaned into it. His hand was warm. The rest of her was cold. She gave a violent shiver.

There was a ruckus as Ambrose skidded in, his speed so excessive he had to brace a hand on the doorframe to redirect and launch himself into the room. Two of his medical assistants barely avoided crashing into one another as they arrived on his heels, panting and red-faced.

Leda would have laughed if it hadn't been excruciatingly painful. She supposed she should be flattered by the panic on Ambrose's face as he dropped to his knees beside Pyrrhus. She thought if anyone would be pleased to see her skewered on an arrow, it would be him.

"Pyrrhus, keep her upright," he muttered, all business. "Don't touch the arrow and for the love of the gods don't attempt to take it out."

Leda heard a distressing tearing sound and looked down to see strips of Melia's new dress being wadded up and pressed against her wound by one of Ambrose's assistants.

The hissing sound she made was either from pain or the indignity of having her work ripped apart; she couldn't tell which.

"Melia's dress ...," she croaked out.

"I'm sure she'll understand," Ambrose said in a long-suffering voice, unable to conceal how annoying he found her even as he attempted to keep her from death. That was normal, at least. It couldn't be too serious then. "We need solution of honey wax," Ambrose snapped to an assistant, who went sprinting off again. "Pyrrhus, look at me."

It took Pyrrhus a second to process the words and move his focus from Leda to his friend.

Ambrose spoke slowly, as though to a child. "I'm going to cut off the arrowhead and staunch the flow of blood. Then we'll need to move her to the infirmary and I will remove the rest. We'll sedate her there. Do you understand me?"

"I—"

"Do you understand me? I need you to hold her still through this. Ami, come and take her other arm."

That got Leda's attention. She was sitting perfectly still already, thank you very much. She opened her mouth to tell Ambrose so and nothing came out except a thin scream as he brought some sort of sharp tool to her chest and snapped off the arrowhead, jostling the wood through her shoulder.

It burned like he'd set fire to every vein in her body.

That did it, and she sank gratefully into the welcoming arms of unconsciousness.

CHAPTER 11

On the one hand, Leda felt better than expected for someone who'd just had an arrow fired through her. On the other, she felt like she'd had her wrist tied to a galloping horse and spent the last few hours being dragged behind it on a field of broken glass.

She shifted and let out a pitiful moan into the soft duvet that had been tucked under her chin.

The lightest touch of a hand caressing her cheek, and then it was gone.

With the speed of a striking serpent, Leda's good arm shot out from under the duvet and she grasped the mystery person's arm before they could back away.

She recognised the surprised sound that followed.

Pyrrhus was sitting at her bedside.

One by one, she pried open her eyes and peered at him through the flickering candlelight.

His hair was a mess, as though he'd run his hand through it one too many times. His shirt was in an even worse state, rumpled and misshapen. There was something familiar about it, though. The stitching was slightly off. Leda recognised those hems, the ones she'd cursed over so many times.

He was wearing the shirt she'd made for him over a year ago. She'd felt so guilty that the karascus oil he'd used to heal her when she'd been whipped had ruined his old one that she'd been compelled to replace it.

Pyrrhus didn't want her to know that he still wore it judging by the speed with which he snatched his arm away, removing the crooked cuff from her view.

"How are you feeling?"

Leda looked up at the ceiling to see a full fresco depicting the gods at work in the heavens. The rest of the bedroom was opulent to the extreme. It bore signs of continued use: the neatly pressed clothes in the wardrobe that stood half open, the comb on the dressing table, the luxuriant black robe hanging on the back of the door.

Pyrrhus's new rooms. He'd brought her into his safe place.

"You have a habit of bringing me to your bedrooms," she said, her voice gritty and unfamiliar. "I like this one."

His expression told her that Pyrrhus had not expected that to be her first observation. He recovered quickly, though.

"How are you feeling?" he asked again.

"Like I've been ripped apart and poorly sewn back together."

"I'll be sure to tell Ambrose how grateful you are for his healing efforts."

"He already knows. We have a special bond, he and I." It was a bond comprised mainly of disapproval and annoyance, but special nonetheless.

Still, Leda would have to thank him eventually. How unpleasant that would be.

"I should have never brought you back to the palace,"

Pyrrhus said, hands fisted on top of her duvet.

"Yes you should; this has nothing to do with you. I chose to be here." She decided to change the subject, his guilt provoking something in her that she didn't want to examine too closely. "Do you know who shot at me?"

"There were no witnesses before, during or after. They were quick, extremely so." That sounded like someone they both knew. He asked the question she'd been dreading. "Do you think it was Azaria?"

"You can never rule her out," Leda said grimly. "But this isn't her style. When she decides she's done with me she'll probably try to stab me in the face; she'll want to watch the light leave my eyes." Pyrrhus was visibly unamused at the blasé way she presented that image. It didn't make it any less true. "And she'll do it in public; she loves a crowd of terrified admirers."

Leda shifted her position and put more weight on her bad shoulder than was wise. She flinched with a yelp of pain and Pyrrhus leaned forward.

"For the love of the gods," he muttered as he tucked the end of her bandage back into place. "Would it be too much to ask that you stop sustaining critical injuries?" His hand ran down the nightgown over her shoulder blade, tracing the pattern of thin scars there.

She smiled weakly at him. "It's not strictly under my control, but I'll try."

He nodded, and she took the opportunity to get a proper look at him.

Stress had broken the man.

His eyes were the dull red of someone who hadn't slept for at least two nights, and the facade he kept up at all times to shield his emotions from the world had been shattered. He looked like his heart had climbed out of his body, tried to make a dress and been shot through with an arrow.

But that wasn't possible. She was not his heart. They weren't together.

His eyes widened in surprise as she reached up to tug at his rumpled collar.

"You need to sleep," she said. "Right now."

He looked over at the small armchair he'd clearly been dozing in while he watched over her.

She shook her head, her attempt to pull him further on to the bed pathetic in light of her weakness. Still, he moved at her prompting. "No, here. Now, please."

"Leda—"

She made plenty of space for him to join her on the bed. There didn't need to be anything indecent about it. They were friends. Friends could sleep near each other. They could offer comfort. He needed support just as much as her brothers and sisters did, and she wouldn't leave this palace until she was sure he was as stable as she intended to leave her siblings.

Her own eyelids were drooping with fatigue as she gestured an 'off' motion at his shoes. "Don't say no," she whispered as she let her heavy head fall back on the pillow. "Just sleep."

She could sense his body a foot away from hers, his hand resting on the sheets mere inches from her own. She sighed, a small smile curling her lips as sleep pulled her down.

A sharp pain had Leda waking with a gasp. Bright yellow light streaked through the open window and she threw an arm over her eyes to shield them as she shifted her other shoulder.

More pain lanced through her and she fell back against

the pillows.

"Ow ..." She wasn't surprised to find the bed empty beside her, a faint depression in the mattress the only sign that Pyrrhus had been there. That, and the fact that his pillow had been fastidiously straightened and the duvet folded into neat lines.

With a yawn, Leda dragged herself out of bed. She donned the long robe that lay over the settee like a cape to avoid jostling her shoulder.

Her eyes caught on the elaborate dressing table beneath the mirror and she frowned to see her own hairbrush and pins set out on the marble surface. She brushed her hair with her good hand, but felt suspicion deepen as she walked into the bathing room and found her toothbrush and tooth powder next to Pyrrhus's.

It took her a few minutes to make herself look human, and therefore presentable to the masses once more. She didn't have to wash any blood off herself; it looked like that task had been taken care of.

She was immensely thankful for that.

She opened one of the double doors to Pyrrhus's rooms and took a hasty step back when she came up against a stone-faced guard. He was clad in full armour, copious chainmail, and carrying a spear to top it all off.

"Ah, hello," she said. "Do you mind if I?" She tried to sidle around him, and he angled himself to block her from leaving the room.

Oh, please gods no.

Leda's mouth thinned into a harsh line. "Let me pass."

"I'm afraid I can't. Our orders are to keep you within."

Leda peered around the guard to see no less than three others, all bearing an excessive number of weapons, standing outside the doors to Pyrrhus's rooms. It seemed they were there to protect her, with the side effect of not letting her leave.

The *presumption* of the man. He had no right to control where she went without discussing it with her. She was not a dog to be locked away on her owner's orders.

"Bring Pyrrhus here, now," she said from between gritted teeth. The guard raised a brow and she shook her head at him. "*Now*. Please." She shut the door crisply in his face, turned around, and let out a snarl of rage.

The sound of shifting armour along the corridor told her that her message was about to be relayed, and quickly. Good.

When Pyrrhus entered minutes later it was to find her sitting on the edge of his bed, her glare so powerful his movements were careful as he closed the door. He looked like he was preparing to do battle with an injured bear.

"Good morning."

Leda's eyebrows were raised so high she was sure they'd disappeared into her hair. "What do you think you're doing?"

Her legs had been so tightly crossed while she waited for him that she'd cut off her own circulation. They almost buckled when she surged to her feet.

Pyrrhus stayed by the door, posture stiff as he observed the flush on her cheeks and anger lighting up her eyes. "You seem to be feeling better."

He wasn't wrong. Her rage had given her something to focus on other than the pain in her shoulder, but she wasn't about to let him know that.

"How *dare* you try to lock me up?" she hissed.

"It may have escaped your notice, Leda, but someone is trying to kill you," Pyrrhus said patiently. "Forgive me if I attempt to prevent that using the resources at my disposal."

"Without consulting me?" Leda snapped, approaching and halting with only inches between them. Something ignited in his eyes, but his gaze fell to her shoulder and he stepped back.

"Very well, let's consult," he said sharply. "You're to stay in this room until the person who tried to kill you has been captured."

"Not in a million lifetimes," Leda bit out. "That could take weeks; I'll go mad if I'm here for even a day."

After she'd had a taste of freedom, she wouldn't give it up. She couldn't. Still, she wasn't completely out of her mind; she knew the danger that awaited her outside. "I'll consent not to leave the palace grounds, but I'm going where I want when I want to within it."

"Oh, *very* helpful." Pyrrhus crossed his arms. "Considering your assassin is already operating within the palace, how comforting to know that you won't be out touring the city."

He was almost vibrating with anger, but it was tightly controlled within him as always. Whatever emotions he'd expressed the previous night had been bottled up once more.

It made Leda want to shake him, but instead she took a deep breath and retreated to give them both some space.

"A guard can follow me through the public areas of the palace."

"No."

"Fine, they can follow me wherever I go in the palace."

"No."

She threw an arm in the air in exasperation. "You need to work with me on this."

He shrugged. This man had never, ever shrugged in her view before. She hadn't known he was capable of the gesture.

"Fine," she said darkly. "Two guards, just let me out."

Pyrrhus made a show of thinking it over. "Ten."

"Ten?" Leda choked. "I'm hardly the *Crown Jewels*. Why not put me in a full suit of armour while you're at it?"

Again with the frustrating silence from him.

"Four guards," she conceded. "But they need to give me space; they can't be walking in my shadow."

"Eight guards, and we can go to breakfast right now."

"Six, and I am not sitting with you at breakfast. I've seen quite enough of your smug face for one day."

That had his lips tipping up into the slightest smirk. "Very well. Six it is."

As he stood aside to let her leave she had the unsettling feeling that she hadn't come out on top of that negotiation. When she saw exactly six guards clustered in the corridor she threw him a furious glare. He responded with a blandly innocent look that boiled her blood.

She hated the Rivernesse school system for training him so well in debate.

"After you, Leda."

As she stepped out into the corridor she immediately lost her bravado. Despite the phalanx of guards trailing them, staring down every statue and candelabra they passed as though they meant to do her harm, she'd never felt more vulnerable. An arrow had come through an open window, completely unseen, and nearly killed her. How was she supposed to keep on constant alert for dangers like that and not lose her mind?

Perhaps the guards were a good idea after all.

She rolled her shoulder and let out an imperceptible grunt of pain, shrouded from Pyrrhus's hearing by the loud noise of shifting armour. At least she'd been able to take her medicine that morning, plus some more concoctions that Ambrose had whipped up. They seemed to be helping some. Her leg was throbbingly sore, but it held her weight. That was all she required; she could cope with the pain.

A shout echoed down the corridor. "Leda!"

They halted as Castor approached. Pyrrhus was looking at the guards as though they'd failed in the one thing he'd asked them to do, but said nothing.

"I heard about your injury."

That was putting it lightly, but Castor's face was consumed with concern.

"Are you alright?"

Leda tried to paste a gracious smile on to her face. "I'm on the mend, thank you."

"Who could have done such an awful thing?"

"That's what we're going to find out," said Pyrrhus.

Castor threw him a glance that was slightly theatrical, as though he hadn't realised he was there. "You're hardly one for properly leveraging your resources, Pyrrhus. Leda, I will launch another investigation with my own coin, to show the esteem the family Ariti holds you in."

Leda had no idea what the point of that would be, but it seemed a response was expected of her, so she nodded blankly.

"We'll find out who did this to you and take our revenge, I promise."

"I ... well, thank you."

Castor reached forward to take her hand for a kiss. A courtly, respectable gesture. Unfortunately, he'd forgotten which of her arms was injured.

Leda yanked herself back with a hiss of pain and in a blur of movement Pyrrhus was in front of her and Castor was staggering several steps backwards. There was a deep clang as he knocked his elbow into the breastplate of one of the guards.

He eyed Pyrrhus with undisguised dislike.

Leda blinked. She hadn't even seen Pyrrhus touch him. He was *fast*.

Castor appeared to know there was no salvaging this situation with Pyrrhus seeming close to breathing fire and Leda hunched over and cradling her shoulder. With a muttered apology and a hasty bow he marched off in the direction from which he'd come.

Pyrrhus turned immediately to Leda. "Did he hurt you?"

"No, no, he just jarred me," Leda said, flexing her shoulder and feeling the answering screech of pain. That would be fun to live with for the next few weeks. She sighed. "I've lost my appetite, though. I think I'll go and find Eber instead of breakfast."

Pyrrhus accepted that with more grace than she expected, and though they had a brief debate over how many guards each of them should take, they were soon going their separate ways.

"It looks like Pyrrhus has figured out that someone is hunting down Locarnos."

"You think?" Eber said from his spot on a bench near the throne room.

He sat mere inches in front of the three guards who had squeezed themselves into the alcove directly behind him. They hadn't left themselves enough space so a thick, armour-clad arm was squashed up against Eber's shoulder.

"Be lucky you've only got three," Leda said glumly, glaring behind her as her own cohort of four guards was joined by another two. "Give me a couple more hours and we'll have enough for a full country dance."

There was a kerfuffle at the back of Leda's guards.

"Touch me and you shall regret it."

Leda turned to see Azaria pointing at a particularly young and terrified guard.

"Azaria," Leda said blankly. "What are you doing here?" She waved away the guards who would have formed a barrier between them.

"Leda," Azaria nodded as she came to stand between her and Eber. "Golden retriever." She said snidely to Eber. He scoffed but said nothing, his fear of Azaria as palpable as that of the guards. Azaria turned to look critically at Leda's bandaged shoulder. "You're recovering?"

"Trying my best."

"Do you know who did this?"

"No. I don't suppose it was you?"

Anyone else would have been mortally offended and demanding Leda apologise for the accusation that very moment. Not Azaria.

"No," she said simply. Just like that. And Leda was inclined to believe her, of all things.

Eber looked hugely sceptical from his perch on the bench, but wisely said nothing.

There was another kerfuffle as Ami came through the corridor, joined by her own brace of guards. They were so tall compared to her that they shrouded her in shadow.

She looked up at Leda with wide, fearful eyes. "Are you okay?"

Something in Leda softened. "Of course I am, thanks to you." She looked around at the people crowding them all in and felt the immediate need to be somewhere, anywhere else. She held out a hand to Ami, who took it instantly in hers.

"Why don't we go to the library, hmm? You can read me some of your book."

Ami had been working hard on her reading and writing, spending so much time hunched over the desk in the library with her nose in a book Leda was sure she'd outstrip her own ability in a few years' time.

They walked through the corridor and had just begun to climb the grand staircase when Atticus joined them, slipping through the group of guards as though he'd been one of them all along.

"Really?" Leda said, her frustration potent. "You, too?"

The head guard held up his hands and pivoted so that he was beside her as they ascended the stairs. "I'm here on nobody's orders. My purpose is to protect my guards from your temper."

Leda huffed, turning to her sister. "Do you think that's fair?"

Ami giggled. "Yes."

"Traitor." Leda ruffled Ami's hair, now as long and out of control as her own, and Ami squawked and threw her hand off. "Fine, Atticus can join us."

She lowered her voice as they traversed an empty corridor. "Any more news on who shot at me?"

"No," he said softly. "But I've been tasked with leading the investigation and I'll keep you updated when I make progress." He lowered his voice until it was almost a whisper and she had to lean in even closer to hear. "I have my suspicions about Linus based on stories I've heard from his time in Doviet. Reports say he's vicious, cares nothing for killing children who threaten his position, and he hated your father. But it's all rumours, no evidence." He took in her stricken expression and patted her uninjured shoulder. "I want you to be wary of anyone who shows too much interest in you. Whoever killed Caspari and came after you is unlikely to stop until they've finished the job, and that puts all of you in danger."

That was very much what Leda was afraid of.

CHAPTER 12

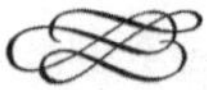

For the next three weeks Leda couldn't take a step without tripping over a well-meaning occupant of the palace. They watched her like hawks, displeased by how much she exerted herself after her injury. The master of horse almost had a heart attack when she asked for her horse to be saddled for a ride.

Pyrrhus always seemed to have an eye on her from the other side of a room, Azaria watched her from dark corners like an overgrown bat, and Eber was stuck to her side as surely as if he'd applied glue. Even Ambrose kept appearing from nowhere to check on her, though he looked as pleased about that as she was.

Leda responded to this by secreting herself away as much as possible, coincidentally keeping far away from Linus and his family. She spent most of each day in an empty corner of the library with Ami, making sure that she was protected too.

It had the added benefit of ensuring progress on another of her goals: helping Ami to become more trusting and less abrasive, and encouraging her to pursue her interests. Leda had Ami read aloud to her and they made up spelling games to play. When Ami was able to read out a full paragraph of a complex medical text, so chosen because she'd proclaimed she was going to be a physician like Ambrose, Leda was ecstatic. She rewarded Ami with an emerald hair tie she'd braided together from the leftover silk of her latest dress creation.

Ami's face had been unreadable when she accepted the gift, but Leda never saw her without it in her hair for the following days, even when the colour clashed horribly with her dress.

Eber and Elina started to join them in the library, making a show of doing other things while watching Leda with fanatical intensity. She looked back with equal fervour, trying to figure out how to help them to a position where they could live independently and accept her absence.

It was an overwhelming task.

One morning Leda sneaked into the rose garden before the sun had risen in search of some peace and quiet. A cracked twig sounded behind her and she turned to see Prince Fessler and Eber following her like silent ducklings. How they'd found her she had no idea.

"Alright, that's it!" she'd announced, turning on her heel and charging back into the palace. They'd followed her, of course.

It had taken an hour of negotiation with Pyrrhus to allow her to make one outing outside of the palace and into the city where she might actually interact with some normal people.

When she'd asked to go alone he'd let out a scoff so loud his advisors had looked up from their paperwork in clear concern for his well-being.

She'd braced her hands on his desk and given him a glare that had made his eyes narrow. "You've let everyone leave the palace as they please for weeks as long as they have chaperones. Why am I the only one trapped?"

He'd relented at that, though he required Leda to present a list of the places she wanted to go for his security team's approval. She also had to take ten guards and the royal carriage.

And so one rainy day Leda was able to visit a dress shop in Gemdark that Iris had once told her about, famous for stocking some of the most sumptuous fabrics in the kingdom.

She stayed in the shop far longer than she'd anticipated, engaged in conversation with the enthusiastic saleswoman. She was short, curvaceous and wonderfully well attired, not to mention extremely knowledgeable about her work.

The shop was small and cosy, with mahogany walls and thick white carpet. Candles burning in their brackets illuminated more fabrics than Leda had ever seen in one place before.

She traced a hand over the bolt of fabric she'd spent the last few minutes admiring. "And you'd recommend the damask?" she asked.

The woman nodded, lifting it from the shelf and bunching it at her waist to demonstrate the fall of it. "Oh yes, it'll give the dress a right nice bearing, especially the skirt. You can settle for the plain silk if you want, but it won't have half the impact."

It was a beautiful style, indeed. "No, I think you're right. I'll take seven yards, please. That should be enough."

As the saleswoman bustled off to get her scissors Leda was momentarily distracted by the clatter of horses' hooves in the courtyard outside. She went to the window to see what was causing such commotion on the road, but the glass had fogged up. Her gaze fell to a dress in the display and she cooed.

"This is an excellent pattern; I've never seen sleeves like these before."

The saleswoman looked pleased by the compliment as she rejoined Leda, the fabric she'd purchased folded under one arm. "One of my newest designs!" She surveyed Leda for a moment, and seemed to come to some sort of conclusion. "I can show you the pattern if you like. It's in the back."

"That would be fantastic."

"Just don't go selling it and putting me out of business."

Leda grinned, turning to follow her. "Oh, there's no danger of that."

The door to the shop opened and slammed so hard against the wall that the bell detached and fell to the floor with a *thud*. Leda didn't have time to turn before a hand grasped the collar of her dress and yanked her backwards. She staggered into her assailant with a gasp.

"What the—" She choked on the words.

"Time to go, Leda."

"Eber!" She allowed him to manhandle her out of the shop with minimal struggle, bewildered. She nearly fell at the speed he was moving them. "Wait, my fabric!"

"Someone will get it for you later, hurry!"

"Why?"

In place of an answer she was hauled like a sack of grain through the driving rain and unceremoniously stuffed into the royal carriage. She landed on the bench on all fours, dripping wet and gasping.

The door on the other side opened and Elina was similarly shoved inside. She looked as dumbfounded as Leda felt as Eber slammed the door behind him and Ambrose clambered in on the other side, jostling Elina to make room for him.

"What are you doing here?"

"I could ask the same question!" Elina spluttered, turning her accusing gaze on Ambrose.

Ambrose directed his answer to Leda. "Elina was with the Ariti brothers at the shrine; they're in the carriage behind us. We need to go, *now*."

He slammed his fist twice against the ceiling and the carriage jerked into motion, so quickly Leda lifted off her seat by a couple of inches. Elina grabbed her uninjured shoulder to stop them colliding as she fell back down.

Elina was still clutching her prayer garland with half the flowers torn off. Leda had seen the shrine before, a towering golden spire that sat in the very heart of the city. She didn't know much about it, but if Elina was spending so much time there it must be the place where only the most obnoxiously devoted prayed.

Leda levelled Eber with a furious look as he bent double to get his breath back. "What in the gods' names is going on?"

"Language!" Elina barked, raising her hand as though she'd like to throw her garland at Leda's disrespectful head.

"You weren't followed?" Ambrose muttered to Eber, who shook his head. "Nor were we, I think. Though there were too many people at that shrine, I couldn't be sure."

He cast an aggrieved look at Elina, as though the citizens' piety were her fault.

"I was safe," Elina said indignantly. "Pyrrhus said I could go out as long as I had someone with me and Pan, Castor and Arsen have been accompanying me. They wouldn't let anything happen to me."

"Not safe enough," Ambrose said, peering out the window. That seemed an overreaction given Arsen's reputation and military experience. Anyone who dared attack Elina would have been reduced to ribbons by the time he was done with them. And that was putting aside the fact that she was a formidable fighter herself. "Everyone needs guards, now, many of them. We should be going faster; what's the delay?"

There was a clatter of hooves as the palace guards circled their carriage in tight formation. One of the horses was so close Leda watched its snort fog up the glass of the window.

Elina brought herself up to her full, royal princess height and Leda could have sworn the light in the carriage dimmed. Elina was many things, but she was no wallflower. She could pull off being imposing as easily as breathing. "You will tell me what is going on and you will tell me *now*."

Ambrose ran a hand over his face. "Markus and Prince Elov are dead."

Time seemed to stop.

Markus was just thirteen years old. Leda had taught him to swim, alongside Ami. Upon finding out that he'd no longer be a Counterpart, he'd decided he wanted to be a pirate when he grew up.

She hugged her arms around her stomach as she saw Elina's head drop into her hands from the corner of her eye. Her gasp was ragged.

Leda turned to Eber. "How? What happened?"

"An assassin attacked them in their village yesterday. There was a struggle, and they were stabbed."

"It seems Prince Elov attempted to defend Markus," Ambrose said grimly. "He was found shielding his body; it seemed to ... it took him longer to die."

Elina let out a whimper.

Leda saw tears trailing down Eber's face and looked at her feet. The mural of the royal family from the entrance hall flashed in her mind, assaulting her with images of her siblings. Twenty-three of the King's children, over half of them dead. How he thought all of this was the gods' plan Leda could never understand.

This awful, desolate feeling of loss. It was her constant companion.

They were thrown unexpectedly from their grief-stricken silence by a ruckus outside the carriage. Leda couldn't see what was going on, the windows clouded by rain.

Their carriage slammed to a halt and fear touched Elina's eyes as she braced herself on her seat.

"Why are we stopping?" Elina demanded, her voice shaking. Whether from grief or fear, Leda couldn't tell. "We can't be at the palace yet."

Leda was of a mind to agree, and flinched when the door on her side burst open. A guard appeared through the pouring rain, the visor of his helmet lifted to reveal only his eyes, and held something out to Leda: a large squirming bundle of blankets.

A child.

"*What?*" Leda nearly overbalanced as they were thrust unceremoniously into her arms. Nearly deafened by the shrieks, she turned to gape at Ambrose and Eber. "What is this?"

"That would be your sister," Ambrose said.

"Mira?" Leda blinked at the child who was drenched, shivering and clearly unhappy to be there. Leda barely recognised her; she'd been three years old the last time she'd seen her, and the King hadn't had any patience with his younger children. They were generally ordered out of sight of court during the summer sojourns until they were at least eight.

Mira twisted violently in Leda's grip and kicked her square in the stomach. Elina decided that the situation wasn't weighty enough for her to prevent her instinctive snort of mirth, and Leda cast her an ugly look.

"Why don't you take her?" Leda asked. Elina looked away.

"Pyrrhus has ordered the remaining children of the previous King to be brought to the palace for protection," Ambrose said grimly. Eber, disturbed by the noise Mira was producing, had his hands over his ears and was missing the conversation. "Prince Fessler is already there, Princesses Annagret and Gabriell are on their way, and now you've taken delivery of Mira all the remaining Counterparts will be together."

Elina shifted in her seat, clearly discomfited by the idea of having all royal children and Counterparts in one place when she'd adjusted to life without their company forced on her. Her old prejudices ran deep, it seemed.

Sofie's name hung in the air, though, unspoken.

Eleven Counterparts born to the King and his mistresses. It was supposed to be twelve to match the number of royal children, but Mistress Aina had disappeared during the battles before she gave birth.

Elea, Sira, Erdil, Mat, May and Sofie, all dead at their royal siblings' hands. Markus killed by the gods only knew whom. Only four Counterparts left: Leda, Eber, Ami and Mira.

"What do we do now?" Leda said as Mira finally quieted and began to settle against her.

"We stay in the palace under guard, and we wait until the king's investigators uncover what happened. There will be no more trips into the city. Pyrrhus isn't about to see any more of you die." Ambrose's tone brooked no refusal. He looked meaningfully at Leda, as though expecting her to be the biggest problem he'd face.

Still blindsided by the news about Markus and Elov and

the appearance of her sister in her lap, Leda couldn't muster the energy to fight him. She simply nodded. Beside her, Elina appeared to have gone into shock. Eber's hand was shielding his face, but Leda could see the tears tracking over his cheeks and down his neck.

She'd never felt more determined than at that moment. She was not going home, was not leaving this place, until each one of her remaining siblings was safe, no matter how long it took.

"Alright," Leda said soothingly into Mira's hair. She looked up at Ambrose. "Alright. We'll stay at the palace, and we'll keep ourselves safe until we know what's happening."

Whatever it was, by the light of the gods, it was nothing good.

Atticus waited at the steps to the palace, arms folded, a group of guards behind him. He was opening the carriage door before it had come to a stop, and then he was helping Leda down to the ground, Mira still clutched in her arms.

"You two," Atticus said, lifting Mira gently from Leda and handing her to the guard on his right. He then pointed at Leda and Eber. "With me, right now. Elina, go with Belen."

"Leda! Are you alright?" Castor had alighted from the carriage behind them and was hurrying towards them.

Atticus was having none of it. He put an arm around Leda's shoulders and another around Eber's and herded them up the steps. "Not now, sir, I have to get them to safety."

Castor stopped in a spray of gravel, his face falling. "But—"

Atticus waited until everyone else was out of sight as they ascended the staircase in the entrance hall before releasing them from his grip.

"We still don't know who did this; almost everyone on

our list of suspects was away from the palace for some reason or another yesterday, which does *nothing* to help us." His face was haggard with strain and lack of sleep. "But I meant what I said to you both before. Stay away from Linus and his delegation. Leda, don't let Castor get too close."

She turned to him in surprise. "You think *he* could have something to do with this?"

"Honestly? I don't think so. He's no killer. But I sense something about his interest in you that's not genuine."

"Thanks for that," Leda said, highly offended. "Any evidence? Or is this another one of your hunches?"

"You'll be thankful for my hunches if any one of them keeps you alive," Atticus said, far too dramatically in her opinion. "He hates Pyrrhus and he knows there's history between you. Will you just be careful, please?"

"I'm always careful!"

Atticus and Eber threw her identically exasperated looks.

"I'll ... alright, I'll try. I promise," she said sheepishly.

Neither one looked like they believed her.

If Leda had thought she'd been under scrutiny before she'd been allowed on her ill-advised trip to Gemdark, it was nothing to what awaited her when she got back to the palace. Guards followed everywhere she went.

She went to meals and sat with her brothers and sisters, who could not be consoled about the loss of two more siblings. She attempted unsuccessfully to stop them from manifesting their anger in bickering and hurling food at one another.

It was particularly difficult given the fact that she needed to set an example; she had to be a steadying influence. But she wanted to scream and throw things like the rest of them.

She spent her afternoons with them all, trying to save books from being ripped and flowers from being stamped on. On one tense afternoon she had to wrench Fessler's bow and arrow out of his hands and tell him that if she ever saw him point them at Azaria again Leda would become the scariest person he'd ever known.

It was almost a relief to go and view the second trial, to be respectably out in the open and viewable by the guards, but also to get some breathing room from her siblings. She was sure none of them would be in the royal classroom on that day to watch the representatives of the five families be tested on their economic understanding.

Leda had an entire row to herself at the back of the room, and the seat she had was comfortable. The people bustling in barely paid her any attention. She couldn't have asked for more.

She glanced to her left. "Good gods!"

Azaria was sitting so close beside her they were almost nose to nose. Leda reared back violently, nearly toppling out of her chair.

"What are you doing here?" she hissed. Azaria moved with all the sound of a shadow and it never failed to disconcert her.

Azaria looked at Leda like she was the strange one. "I'm interested in the outcome of the trials, of course."

"Yes, I understand that, but it doesn't explain why you're sitting next to me," Leda said. "Come to think of it, it also doesn't explain why you were pretending to read by me in the library yesterday or why you followed me during my horse ride the day before. I swear if the dream I had about you standing over me as I slept was real I will—"

"Don't be dramatic, Leda. I hardly desire your company.

Now move over." Azaria snapped her fingers and Fessler, Ami, Eber and Elina appeared. They shuffled down the row of seats to reach them, each face a varied degree of unenthused. When they had settled themselves Azaria withdrew a wicked-looking dagger from the depths of her skirts and inspected the blade.

"Gods help us," Eber said weakly, clearly regretful that he'd drawn the short straw and was sitting next to Azaria. "Fessler, swap seats with me."

"Eat dirt," came the succinct response. Fessler had put his feet on the back of the chair in front of him, to the ire of the courtier sitting in it, and cried out when Ami brought her bony elbow down on his thigh. He returned his feet to the floor with a mutinous look.

Leda was strongly reminded of why she'd decided to live far away from these people.

"Are you sure you want to be here, Counterparts?" Elina asked, leaning across Eber. "This is likely to go over your heads."

"Shouldn't you be off licking statues in the temple or whatever it is you do all day?" Eber shoved her back into her seat.

"*Children.*" Leda whipped around, a headache already beginning to form at the base of her skull. "That's enough."

Elina ignored her. "Of course, Leda thinks she'll understand the trial. She's probably read a book about it."

"I have, actually. Now shut up."

"Make me, you insipid dullard."

Leda was close to climbing over Azaria's lap when a cleared throat sounded from the front of the room. It seemed their bickering had gathered an audience of its own, unbeknownst to them. The representatives of the five families stood gathered around Pyrrhus by the window, staring at them. The rest of the crowd had turned fully in their seats to observe them too.

"We'd like to begin, if that's alright with you?" Pyrrhus said pointedly.

Leda felt her face flame and looked across to see Elina straighten up quickly in her seat. She suddenly became very interested in her hands and nodded with a minuscule dip of her chin.

Why they'd chosen to open this particular trial to spectators, Leda would never know. It appeared to be a largely written test for the representatives of the five families, facilitated by economists from Pyrrhus's newly created Ministry of the Treasury; learned scholars from all over the kingdoms. Great charts had been pinned to the walls showing complex equations of currency information and measures of interest that Leda could barely wrap her head around. She wished she'd brought her economics book with her so she could look up some of the terms they were throwing around.

As the hours went by Leda was made very aware of how much her siblings regretted attending. She had to shush Ami and Fessler repeatedly as they attempted to play a game, and she threatened to do something very nasty to Elina if she kept sighing so frequently.

Azaria sat like an ice sculpture through it all, and Leda had no idea if she was focused on the trial or her mind was elsewhere. She didn't want to know where else Azaria's mind might go; that was too scary a place to contemplate.

The economists and Pyrrhus spent a further hour in deep consideration as they made their judgements. Leda confiscated a glass of wine that Eber attempted to take from a servant's tray and he gifted her with an extremely ugly look. She was glad of the reprieve when Pyrrhus finally stood up to announce the results to the crowd.

There went the trumpets again.

"Another excellent effort," he said smoothly. "And not an easy decision for any of us."

His economists nodded in solemn agreement behind him. They looked at him with the kind of devotion one usually found on Elina's face when she was praying in the temple. "I'm pleased to announce that the winner of this trial is Thalia." That made sense, she'd looked unruffled for the duration of it, not fazed by a single thing on his horribly complex charts. "Followed by Melia, Pan, Zephyr and finally Linus. Thank you for your contributions today, and I look forward to seeing you at the next trial."

Leda watched Linus carefully for his reaction.

He got up so quickly he overturned his seat. He didn't bother to right it and his wife did so instead as he stormed from the room with his hands curled into fists at his sides.

Pyrrhus watched him go with a grim expression on his face. Leda knew that these trials had taken months of careful diplomacy to agree, that they needed to be run fairly. Still she wondered, not for the first time, if she should ask Pyrrhus to ensure that Linus didn't win.

Someone that quick to anger should never be in charge of their broken kingdom, and perhaps that should take precedence over a fair and open competition.

CHAPTER 13

The morning after the second trial Pyrrhus decided to spend the hour following breakfast in the throne room. Of course, that meant the five families needed to join him to talk his ear off. Attracted by the concentration of so many powerful individuals in one room, the rest of the court came sniffing around shortly afterwards.

Hearing voices echoing off the walls, Leda paused in the doorway. She held a plate stacked with two enormous waffles she'd just drowned in honey in the banquet hall. She'd planned on taking them to her room and embarking on the doomed task of reading while she ate without getting the books sticky, but the scene in front of her looked more interesting.

Castor and Pan were in tense conversation with Linus, who was looking around the room as if he'd rather be anywhere else. Zephyr stood in the corner as usual, like a haunted version of his twin. Leda followed his gaze to find Azaria, who sure enough was in the shadows of the opposite corner.

Their shared theatrics would be laughable if they weren't so strangely threatening.

Azaria was looking at the five families with an inhospitable expression, and Leda thought she'd better see what that was about before arrows started flying.

Repositioning her plate more securely in her hand, she shouldered her way through the crowd and returned Azaria's curt nod.

"Good morning," Leda said.

Azaria had no time for pleasantries. "Behold the vultures, picking over the carcass of our father's throne."

Leda hadn't noticed how close to the throne the small group had gathered. Seeing it empty, she cast a look around to locate Pyrrhus. He was near the door, trying and failing to look inconspicuous as he hoisted a large wicker basket into one hand.

That was odd.

"You could try talking to them," Leda said, tearing a piece off the corner of her waffle. "Thalia and Melia are pleasant, at least, and have some promising ideas for the future of the kingdom. Pan is, well he's a bit dull, but ..."

Azaria scowled. "I will not speak to a single one of them. And if you don't stop talking with your mouth full I will launch you from the nearest window."

Leda took her time to swallow. "Well, I can't make you speak to them," she said. "Why don't you start thinking about what you might like to do with the rest of your life, Azaria? Eber and I have been making some interesting plans for him, perhaps you could join—"

"I can think of nothing worse," Azaria said. "I have plans for my future, but there will be many steps to bring them to fruition."

The words and tone were neutral and yet what lay unsaid beneath raised the hairs on Leda's neck.

"I hope they don't involve Zephyr," she said. "He's not a companion you want around you."

"Forgive me if I do not trust your ability to judge a person's character, Leda," Azaria snapped. "Perhaps you should stop prying. This conversation is going nowhere."

That was that then. With a muffled sigh Leda turned back to where she'd just seen Pyrrhus. The basket stood empty on the ground by his feet, and he'd produced a scroll from somewhere, which he was writing on.

A cry went up from the crowd, but not one of fear or alarm. Instead, it was a collective cooing at the tiny kittens that were suddenly spreading throughout the throne room.

The representatives of the five families broke apart as the cats entered their ranks.

Thalia exclaimed in surprise and ushered her daughter over to see a black kitten with huge yellow eyes. Melia merely observed them. Castor, Pan and Arsen got down on the floor in unison to let the kittens play all over them. Linus glowered and ignored them, steering his wife out of the room with a hand on the back of her neck.

Leda looked up to see Pyrrhus writing down observations. If this was one of his secret trials it was perhaps the worst execution she'd ever seen. She wasn't sure the reaction to fluffy intruders should be measured as stringently as economic or military prowess.

Still, she supposed their reactions said something about their characters; that was not nothing. She muffled a snigger behind her hand.

"I think these trials may have driven Pyrrhus a little mad," Leda said.

"He has completely taken leave of his senses," Azaria said damningly. "Yet you moon after him as intensely as you always have."

That wiped the smile off Leda's face. "I do not." She pointed her fork at Azaria. "We're friends."

Azaria made a noise that was pure scepticism. "I see nothing resembling friendship."

"Well you wouldn't know anything about that, would you? Name one friend you've had in your entire life."

"Stop attempting to argue with me," Azaria said. "It's exhausting."

She walked away towards Zephyr, who was shaking off a kitten that had dug its claws into his trouser leg.

Azaria's previous position was taken by Elina so quickly it was a wonder she didn't slam into the back of her.

"A whole town in Doviet was lost yesterday. An earthquake."

Elina always knew how to start a conversation that would make Leda feel a mix of nausea and guilt.

"I ... I'm so sorry to hear that."

"Are you?" Elina fixed her with an intense look that had Leda suppressing the urge to take a step back. "Are you really sorry to hear it?"

"Of course I am." Her sister's stare made Leda want to squirm. "Stop being weird, people are looking," she muttered.

"She can't help it, weirdness runs through Elina's veins." Eber joined them and took an obnoxiously large bite out of a nectarine as Elina glared at him. In his other hand he clutched the neck of an ornate violin, polished to a high sheen.

"What do you want?" Elina said. Like a striking snake she seized Leda's plate and fork and was halfway through a waffle before Leda could do more than squawk in outrage. She grimaced as she chewed. "Trust you to make the most bland beige food your favourite, it's so in keeping with your personality."

Leda went to slap her own hand, covered in honey as it was, on to Elina's gown, but Eber dropped his nectarine and caught her wrist in mid-air.

She strained against his hold. "Let's see how funny you find your little quips when you're choking on them!" she snarled.

Elina snorted, with derision or humour Leda couldn't tell, on account of the food stuffed into her mouth.

Eber squeezed Leda's wrist tightly before letting go.

"Play nice, sisters, the whole court is watching. I'm only here to invite you both to the stables this afternoon. The master of horse purchased some new steeds and Pyrrhus thought you might like to peruse." He rolled his eyes at their blank expressions and waved his violin in their faces. "Cheer up, it's not all disaster and death. I'll see you in the stables at five."

He strolled away, towards a guard standing in the corner. Kadir, clutching the bow that matched Eber's violin. His face lit up as their brother approached. Interesting.

"Eber is a halfwit," Elina said.

"Eber is closer to happiness than any of us nowadays," Leda said. "The rest of us could stand to be more like him sometimes. We're far too serious."

Elina scoffed. "We're in a grave situation, Leda, though as it doesn't directly affect you I suppose you wouldn't care. I, however, think about others more than myself. I'm joining a delegation of priestesses from the temple to travel to Doviet to dispense aid next week. Melia is leading it."

Leda ignored the insult. They came so often from Elina she was getting good at tuning them out. "Melia? But isn't the next trial imminent? Surely she's not missing it?"

"You didn't hear? She relinquished her place in the trials."

Leda stared at her, stolen waffles forgotten. She hadn't heard that at all. How curious.

As she mulled that over, she noticed Elina's face becoming more and more strained in the silence that stretched between them.

"What?"

"Can I ask you something?"

As far as Leda knew, Elina had never sought permission to ask a question in her life. And she'd never looked as tense in front of Leda as she did at that moment, as vulnerable.

"If you like."

But the question never came. Elina's mouth opened and then snapped shut as they were interrupted.

"Leda, Elina." The voice came from behind Leda, as though waiting to enter the conversation at the most inopportune moment.

Elina nearly jumped out of her skin.

Melia stood behind them, face serene and fiery hair falling down her shoulders in a pin-straight sheet so shiny it reflected the candlelight.

"Melia, hello. You resigned from the trials? Why?"

"Don't be rude, Leda," Elina hissed.

That was rich coming from her.

Leda ignored her, waiting for Melia's reply.

"I am fated to rule the Grand Temple, not the Five Kingdoms. I must admit I was curious to see my competition, and so I came here. I have been away from Slofray for too long, however. The gods urge me back. First, I must ask a word of you, Leda."

Elina's fingers twitched around Leda's plate like she would dearly love to strangle her for being singled out by her idol. She smiled instead. What a sweetheart she could pretend to be, when she wanted to.

Leda allowed herself to be drawn into the shadows of an alcove at the side of the room.

She looked enquiringly at Melia. Lines of anxiety marred her brow; that was new.

"I am fortunate to be a conduit for the instructions of the gods."

"I ... right, yes." Was Leda supposed to congratulate her on that? She wasn't sure of the etiquette.

"There is a curse upon the Five Kingdoms."

Leda swallowed and looked across the room at Pyrrhus, who was striding away looking somehow more exhausted than the last time she'd seen him. "The weather? The destruction?"

"Yes."

It was what they'd all feared, but none of the priestesses had been able to confirm it. Until now.

"Is it because he took the throne from my father?"

"In a way," Melia said cryptically.

"So he needs to abdicate?"

"He does."

"For once I find myself on the same page as the gods."

Melia's face twisted, and she struggled to get her next words out. "I should not be telling you this, but you were injured in my rooms where you should have been under my care. I owe you this information. There is more to the intentions of the gods than you know, Leda. Your family is in grave danger."

"My family?" Leda looked up in surprise. "The curse refers to more than just my father and his successor?"

There was a flicker of white as Melia cast her eyes up at the ceiling, real fear on her face. She winced. "I have said too much." She sank down into a perfect curtsey, much lower than Leda thought she merited. "I bid you goodbye. May the gods bless you."

The gods had never blessed Leda before; she couldn't think why they'd bother now.

When Melia had gone Leda looked up at the ceiling herself. "If only you'd leave us all alone."

Leda watched Elina dart after Melia and shook her head in disbelief. Her sister's passion for the gods was frightening in its intensity. She wondered why Elina didn't become a priestess herself, she had all of the required dedication. Perhaps that was why she shadowed Melia so obsessively, she was hoping she'd be recruited to the Grand Temple in Slofray.

Between Elina's rages, Azaria's strange bond with Zephyr and Eber's struggle to break his habit of drinking wine like it was water, Leda had a real problem on her hands.

She walked out of the throne room almost in a daze, so much so that it took a moment for the sound of shouting to reach her. She rounded the corner and froze.

Linus had his daughter's elbow in one hand, pulled so high it was a wonder he hadn't wrenched it right out of its socket. Her eyes were squeezed shut in pain; her other hand braced against the wall of the corridor.

"Roll your eyes at me one more time and I will remove them from your skull," he boomed, voice echoing off the stone. He didn't fear an audience, clearly didn't see a problem with what he was doing. "Insolent brat, how can I consider my life successful if I leave only *you* as my legacy? I won't tolerate this behaviour, do you understand?"

His daughter nodded tearfully.

He released her and she whimpered, cradling her arm. Then his huge hand was spanning the top of her head and he was using it to shove her forward. She scurried to comply and they disappeared into the entrance hall.

Leda stood rooted to the floor, one hand absently on her right thigh as it throbbed with pain. But this was not the time to give in to it, and she forced it to work as she followed Linus and his daughter. They were gone by the time she got to the entrance hall, but she didn't care.

She'd made a decision, and she had a different destination in mind.

Pyrrhus wasn't in the library, his official office or any of his other favourite haunts. She was almost surprised when she finally found him alone in his old study.

He made no comment as she descended the staircase towards him, looking up only when she came to stand before his desk.

"You need to make sure that Thalia or Pan win the trials."

He set his quill down. "Hello to you too, Leda. What exactly are you asking of me?"

"You created the trials; you can ensure that the right person wins. The right person is Thalia or Pan."

"And you reached this conclusion how, exactly?"

"I just saw Linus treat his daughter in a way that had me questioning whether he was possessed by the spirit of my father. He's brutal and ruthless and would drive the kingdom into the ground. You'd have accomplished nothing with your coup. And then there's Zephyr, sneaking around and whispering malevolence into Azaria's ear. I don't have much on him yet but I don't trust him. He isn't suitable for power either."

"I agree, as it happens. But what you ask isn't within my gift."

Frustration filled her. She should have known this would be his response. "What are you talking about? You have close to ultimate power; you can do whatever you want!"

"It's my responsibility to wield that power fairly and objectively," he said. He took in her mutinous expression and leaned back in his chair, his face infuriatingly full of judgement. "You're on board with that approach until it conflicts with something you want, it seems."

She threw up her hands in exasperation, ignoring the twinge in her shoulder. "I want what's best for the kingdom, for the people who live here."

"Then you should want the process for selection of their next monarch to be unbiased and honest. I designed these trials to achieve that, Leda. If someone isn't worthy of the throne, they won't win. Our preferences will not unduly influence the results." It was said with such certainty. She only wished she could feel the same, could quench the feeling of foreboding that sat like a stone in her stomach.

"You have that much confidence in a process that you've never run before?"

Oh, but now he was offended. He straightened in his seat, tugging irritably at his cravat. "I spent months on the design of the trials, consulted with the wisest minds across the kingdoms. I will not manipulate the process."

"Then you'd better hope that Linus and Zephyr show their true colours in those assessments, or we're all doomed."

On that rather dramatic statement she took a book from the stack upon his desk, swivelled and made herself comfortable in one of the armchairs.

The one he usually took for himself.

"I'm not going to let this go, you know," she said.

He was staring down at his work with a frown on his face, as though it were written in one of the few languages he didn't understand.

"Precedent has taught me to expect that," he said dryly, but there was a hint of amusement hidden somewhere in the words.

She frowned at him as he picked up his quill, unaffected

by her attempts to corrupt his process. But was it really corruption if it ensured that evil didn't take the throne once again? She hardly knew anymore.

"Have you always been this morally upstanding?" she asked. It was admirable and irritating all at once.

His laugh was low, unexpected. "Since the moment I could talk, according to my mother. It drove my brother Nestor and sister Ophelia insane. They couldn't put a toe out of line without me reporting it. My parents were thrilled, as you can imagine, it saved them a lot of trouble." He looked up to meet her gaze, something wry in his expression. "You'll not be surprised to learn that I was a timorous child, extremely risk-averse."

She couldn't imagine him any other way. She had a picture in her mind of a small, serious boy who took the weight of the world on to his shoulders even then. "You thought that following rules would keep you safe?"

He nodded, his attention dropping back down to his writing. "It took me a while to learn that the world was not as black and white as that. Of course, you knew that very young, didn't you?"

She blinked at him. She'd never thought of it that way, but he wasn't wrong. "I suppose I grew up in a system constructed against my interests, so I tried to break every rule I disagreed with if I could get away with it. Hence all my book thievery. Just because a powerful person decrees something doesn't mean it's right. Or that's what I always thought, at least."

Pyrrhus grimaced at that but made no response. It took a few seconds for the scratching of his quill against paper to resume.

Her eyes fell to the flex of his hands, the confident, curling script that he left on the page.

When he dipped the quill in the ink pot and idly stroked

his jaw as he surveyed what he'd written, her stomach clenched and she got to her feet with a loud scrape of the chair against the floor.

"Just ... think about what I said, alright?"

"I always do. And Leda?"

She paused with one hand on the door. "Yes?"

"I'll have Atticus look into protecting Linus's daughter. I won't tolerate violence against innocents here."

Her hand tightened on the doorknob, the wood biting into her skin. "Thank you."

CHAPTER 14

That afternoon found an odd assortment of people gathered in the royal stables as the master of horse showed them the new steeds he'd brought in from Doviet.

Leda, Eber and Ami, all still new to riding, hung back warily. Linus and his wife talked quietly in the corner.

"Perhaps this pony would be a good match for you, Ami," Pyrrhus said from his position beside Elina as they inspected the creature.

"We know there's nothing for Leda here, unless you happen to have any donkeys available? That's really the pace she prefers to ride at." Elina addressed the master of horse but her eyes were on Leda, who gave her a scornful look in return.

"I'm content with Willow, thank you very much," Leda announced as Eber barely contained his laughter. Willow was a sweet and docile horse who had never once tried to throw Leda off, despite her lack of skill. That had earned her loyalty. "Ami, you're stepping on my foot."

Leda lifted the tiny weight that was her sister and swivelled her away. Ami barely noticed, cautiously moving to inspect a handsome brown pony munching hay in the corner.

"This is the one!" she said, stroking a careful hand down his braided mane. "His name will be Midas."

Pyrrhus nodded at the master of horse. "Then Midas she shall have."

Eber lifted Ami so she was eye level with the horse and Elina handed her a carrot to feed him. Finally, they seemed to be learning to get along.

Leda was brought out of her reverie by a tap to the back of her hand. Atticus had emerged from the shadows behind her, all but silent. He held out a letter. "This just arrived for you."

She recognised the handwriting; it seemed Iris had managed to track down something worth knowing about Zephyr's history in Saint-Trevale.

She stepped back from the rest of the chattering group, tearing the letter open. She'd read only the first sentence of greeting when the creak of the door sounded. Azaria had arrived, dressed in a smart riding habit.

"I've tired of my—" Azaria's words cut off abruptly and Leda's head snapped up. Azaria was never one to leave a sentence unfinished.

Her sister had stopped dead in the doorway, one hand holding a dangling glove and the other, still gloved, up in the air as though whatever she was looking at had wiped all thought from her mind.

"Azaria?"

Azaria looked over at Leda as if surprised to see her there. Her gaze moved over Leda, Pyrrhus in front of her, Ami and Eber feeding carrots to the dappled grey and Elina sitting on a hay bale in the corner.

Linus turned at the sudden silence, his long ponytail whipping around his back. He took in Azaria for no more than a second before returning to the horse he was inspecting, clearly deeming her beneath his notice.

Azaria stared at Linus's back as she spoke. "I've a mind to have a new horse." Her voice was measured, but something, barely perceptible, was wrong with the cadence of it.

"You may want to take a look at Cyrus, then." Pyrrhus pointed to the chestnut in the corner who watched them all with deep suspicion. He tossed his head as they turned their attention to him, pretending not to preen under their view. He was Azaria given animal form.

"That is a fine horse indeed."

Leda jumped at the voice of the newcomer, who had snuck in behind Azaria in that disconcertingly subtle way of his. Zephyr's hair gleamed in the light that filtered through the gaps in the roof. His hands were clasped behind his back as he looked Cyrus up and down with an approving nod.

Leda slid Iris's letter into the pocket of her dress.

"He has spirit; he'd suit you," Zephyr said to Azaria, turning towards her as though they were alone in the room.

Zephyr didn't appear to be attracted to her, in Leda's opinion. At least not in a romantic way. He looked at her with the fanatical intensity of a man seeking a source of warmth in the iciest depths of winter, like she held the solution to all his problems. He looked most content when stood just inside her orbit, murmuring as close to her ear as she'd allow.

As though he sensed Leda's inspection, his gaze cut to her. He raised a pale eyebrow. Whatever he felt about her sister, he didn't share the same sentiment towards Leda. Her, he looked at like an annoyance, an obstacle in his way.

A great whinny sounded through the stables as the horse Linus was inspecting decided it had finished being poked and prodded. Leda gasped as the sound was followed by a resounding *smack*.

Linus had struck the animal for its disobedience.

Pyrrhus was across the room so quickly Leda was surprised he hadn't run. "No more of that. I believe we're finished here," he said to Linus. "It's time for dinner. Let's return to the palace."

Scandalised, Leda turned to leave, and nearly walked into Azaria, who was standing stock still. All the blood had gone from her face, and she was breathing as though she couldn't find air in the room.

"Are you alright, Azaria?"

"Yes," Azaria said sharply. "Zephyr, come with me."

He followed as she swept out of the stables. They outstripped the rest of the party in seconds.

"What's wrong with her?" Eber murmured as he fell into step beside Leda.

"I've been trying to figure it out for two decades," she responded. "Haven't succeeded yet."

As they crossed the rose garden and entered the cool shelter of the palace Leda could have sworn she heard the echo of voices raised in anger, but Eber shook his head when she asked if he'd heard anything. She shrugged it off, promising to meet him at dinner and returning to her rooms.

Leda still wasn't fond of the dining situation she found herself in each evening, crammed around a table with her siblings when they were giddy from music and wine and riling each other up. Elina clearly felt the same and so had invited Ambrose to join them that night. It benefitted everyone but Leda, who found him as insufferable as always.

Azaria was quiet, which wasn't uncharacteristic, but she

stared at her plate with a burning intensity that was alarming. Leda, who had the dubious honour of sitting next to her, turned to her as the starters were laid in front of them.

"Are you alright?"

"Obviously." Azaria sawed into the turkey on her plate as though it had personally wronged her.

Leda decided not to push it, turning instead to Ami and enquiring about the book she was reading. Ami dove into the conversation with an enthusiasm Leda wouldn't have thought her capable of a year before. It warmed her heart to see.

Leda was laughing in response to Ami's joke about the wily sea captain in her novel when a shadow fell across her plate.

"Good evening, Locarno family, brother." Zephyr nodded in that courtly way of his. Leda was surprised he hadn't doffed his hat and swept a bow to them all, he was so foppishly ridiculous.

The table looked up from their conversations to pay him vague greetings.

Ambrose merely glared at him.

"I'd like to speak to Azaria," Zephyr announced, undeterred. "Would you mind if I took your seat, Leda?"

Leda looked up in disbelief, her mouth full of turkey. His face was pleasant, as though what he was asking of her wasn't at all presumptuous.

She stared into the depths of those strikingly black eyes as she swallowed and arranged her face into her most stubborn expression.

"I'm not finished eating." She put a roast potato into her mouth to underscore her point, uncaring of how childish she was being. She did not know this man and she didn't like him and his weird fixation with her sister.

Zephyr laughed and dared to place a hand on the back

of her chair as though about to pull it, and her with it, away from the table. "I must insist. I'm sure Pyrrhus would love a visit from you, he's been staring at you all night."

Her mouth opened in outrage as she deliberated between telling him where he could stick his insistence and commenting on his hypocrisy given the hawklike intensity with which he studied her sister.

"Enough. Don't fight, you know how it bores me," Azaria cut in. She waved a dismissive hand. "Leda will move. Tell me what you have to say, Zephyr."

Leda had half a mind to protest loudly, but she locked eyes with Eber across the table. He shook his head in a clear indication he thought it not worth her time. Leda looked down at the knife and fork clutched in her sister's hands and her childhood sense of self-preservation kicked in.

She stood, glaring at Zephyr as he bestowed on her one of the most insincere smiles she'd ever seen.

Iris's letter burned in her pocket. She couldn't wait to read it, to find out what depravity was in his past, because she was certain there must be *something* there.

He was in her vacated seat so fast he trod on her skirts. As she looked down at the boot print he left on the fabric she was filled with the kind of instant, all-consuming rage that her sister was renowned for.

"Thank you, Leda."

Her reply was a guttural scoff. Luckily, unlike Azaria, Leda knew how to control her temper. With great effort she buried her anger and looked across the room at Pyrrhus, who was watching the action at her table with a raised brow, oblivious to Castor as he wittered on from the seat to his right.

She gave Pyrrhus an exasperated look and his lips tipped up into a smile as he looked away. Drawn to him by that ever-present invisible string that bound them, Leda approached his table.

"Leda!" Castor stood from his seat and offered a bow as she came to stand behind Pyrrhus's chair.

"Castor." She smiled. "Pyrrhus," she said quietly, taking the tankard of hot chocolate beside his plate and treating herself to most of the rest of it. The drink was warm and rich and she hummed with delight at the taste.

Pyrrhus rolled his eyes but didn't attempt to snatch it back. Castor, however, seemed less than pleased by her overly familiar display. Various high-ranking courtiers around the table were watching them with poorly disguised interest.

"Can I offer you my seat?" Castor said, recovering quickly. "Though I fear you'll find Pyrrhus a dull dinner companion this evening. He's barely got anything to say."

"How different our problems are, Castor. I often find he has too much to say." Leda braced her hands on the back of Pyrrhus's chair and leaned over his shoulder to peruse the paper he'd been writing on while eating. "Can you stop working for one moment?"

Pyrrhus tilted his head back towards her and sighed. His shoulders relaxed a fraction as the swirling sound of violins from the orchestra lifted the mood of the room, transitioning seamlessly into a new, languid song.

He opened his mouth to no doubt put her in her place when Leda felt a prickle at the back of her neck. Swivelling around, she looked back at her siblings.

Something was wrong.

Zephyr was speaking urgently into Azaria's ear, closer to her than she would normally allow anyone. The fact that he wasn't on the floor with a knife in his chest was impossible. Leda let out a choked sound that was immediately lost in the hubbub of courtiers' voices when she saw his hand caress Azaria's shoulder.

Her sister remained still. She was stone-faced, staring across the room at the table housing an assortment of the five families with her cutlery fisted in her hands.

She put down her fork.

She did not put down her knife.

If Leda hadn't been watching with her own eyes, she wouldn't have believed what was happening.

Graceful as a dancer, Azaria stood. She pulled her arm back.

And hurled the knife across the room.

The blade sank into the back of Linus Bolsh's head with a dull *thunk* that was immediately absorbed into the noise of the hall.

"AZARIA, NO!"

Leda wasn't the only one who'd been watching. Ambrose flung his chair aside and dove towards her sister, only to be blocked by Zephyr.

Most of the room hadn't realised what had happened, barely even picking up on the smash as Pyrrhus's tankard fell from Leda's hand and broke upon the floor, sloshing hot chocolate over her shoes. She watched the stream of blood pour down the back of Linus's neck, dripping obscenely from the tip of his long ponytail.

A scream rent the air. His wife, Hermiette.

The musicians stopped playing.

Linus's body crumpled sideways to the ground with a resounding *thud*.

CHAPTER 15

There were two, perhaps three, seconds of silence, and then the room turned itself over.

The court's voices grew into a cacophony of yells as they saw the fallen man. They scrambled for the doors, over-turning tables and chairs and each other in the process. Those who were feeling brave or morbidly curious tiptoed towards the hulking body on the floor.

Linus was gasping and trying to take hold of the knife in his neck. A sobbing Hermiette slumped on the floor beside him, trying to stop him instantly ending what little life he had left.

There was the clatter of footsteps as Pyrrhus and his advisors ran to them. Guards tried to intercept Pyrrhus, but he evaded them. Feeling completely outside of her own body, Leda took a floundering Eber by the arm and they approached the scene together.

In a flash, Azaria was standing over Linus's prone form. What remained of the crowd hesitated, with no idea what she might do next. The circle rippled and widened with trepidation, and Leda and Eber swayed as the people nearby moved back, using the two of them as a barrier to shield themselves.

Azaria crouched to take herself closer to Linus's eye level, her gown spreading around her in a perfect pool of midnight blue. "You shouldn't have hit that horse."

It was incomprehensible, Azaria cared nothing for living creatures.

"Azaria." Pyrrhus approached the centre of the circle, once again shaking off the guards who tried to pull him back. "What have you done?"

"The question is not what I've done," Azaria said, still balanced perfectly in her crouch, watching Linus's body weaken. "It's what he has done. Isn't it, Linus?"

Leda was astonished that Linus was still alive. He twisted himself painfully to look up at her sister and spat blood on to the floor.

"Should've killed you when I had the chance," he ground out, his voice difficult to distinguish over Hermiette's sobs. "Locarno *scum*. Curse you all."

His eyes rolled back into his head and he slumped forward, moving no more. Hermiette let out a gut-wrenching wail as she was prised from his body by Thalia.

What happened next was quick. A white-faced Pyrrhus made a gesture at his personal guards and seconds later they were surrounding Leda and Eber.

"Atticus," Leda said warningly as he approached her. As was custom for him, he smiled but gave no indication that he'd do what she asked. She nearly shrieked as he bent down, shoved his shoulder into her stomach and righted her so she dangled over him. Then, he ran.

While she tried to keep the vomit from surging, Leda saw glimpses of the scene they were leaving behind: Eber and Ami being removed by guards in a similarly undignified manner and a brace of new ones flooding the room.

Leda lasted until the second floor before saying, "Atticus,

if you don't let me down now I can't promise I won't be sick all down your back."

That did it. He lowered her with the level of care that she'd come to expect from him, but he beckoned the two other guards who'd followed them to maintain a punishingly fast pace to her rooms. Leda's vision swung violently before her eyes, partially due to shock and also the discomfiting nature of having been upside down for longer than anyone should be. Her leg trembled underneath her and she felt the sudden, overpowering urge to take hibcus, to dull everything she felt.

She stamped it down.

"What's happening?"

"It'll be alright, Leda. Stay in your rooms until one of us retrieves you," Atticus said as they finally reached her door.

They hurried inside and once he'd completed a thorough sweep of the room that included examining the lining of her curtains and sifting through the drawers in her wardrobe, he departed.

She heard a click of the lock in the door. One of the sounds she hated most in the world.

Leda sank on to the comforting softness of her mattress, trying to get her breath back in stuttering gasps. What in the gods' names had she just witnessed? What had Azaria been *thinking*?

She heard the click of a catch opening and looked instinctively towards the door, frowning when she saw it closed.

There was a creak, and she turned slowly to see a hand flat on the glass of the window behind the settee. She watched in mute horror as it opened, the frame hitting the opposite wall with a clatter, and the dark head of Azaria became visible.

She had scaled the palace wall, because of course she had.

Leda jumped up from the bed and located the closest weapon she could find, which happened to be a solid silver candlestick on her bedside table. She shook out the wax candle and it tumbled to the floor at her feet.

Azaria climbed through the window, sure-footed and agile as a cat.

"Why would they put you in a room next to a drain pipe?" Azaria wondered aloud, snapping the window shut behind her. "That's not secure at all."

She turned to see Leda's defensive pose and Leda could have sworn she saw something vaguely resembling humour cross her face.

"Our father took me to Doviet to put down uprisings and I killed over one hundred fighters in a single evening. But that's really frightening."

Leda wasn't aware Azaria knew how to convey sarcasm.

It was not a welcome discovery.

Leda brandished the candlestick like it was a more formidable weapon than it was. "Why are you not in the dungeon?"

"I declined to go."

That was definitely true judging by the number of scratches she bore across her hands and face. Leda would hazard a guess that whoever had attempted to get her into the dungeons had fared much worse.

She raised her meagre weapon even higher, for all the good it would do.

"Are ... are you here to kill me?"

Death at Azaria's hands, what she'd always feared more than anything else. Her blood glugged through her veins like it was made of honey, and her brain screamed at her to run. But where? She was locked in.

Well done to Atticus for exploring all options when devising his security protocols. He'd just accidentally signed her death warrant.

"Are you ... killing the royal children, too?" Leda said, her voice tremulous.

Azaria inspected the dirt covering her skirts with outright annoyance. "I have no interest in killing any of you. Why would I? It does not benefit me." She looked at Leda as though she were particularly dim-witted. "It was probably Linus, he hates us all. Well, *hated*."

Leda ignored that last part. "Then why are you here?"

"I wanted to tell you why I killed him," Azaria said simply, as casual as though she'd just popped in for tea.

Leda's arm sagged and she tossed the candlestick on to her bed. Her shoulder throbbed.

"I assume he looked at you wrong, or perhaps made a single joke at your expense," Leda snapped.

"No. I recognised him as the man who had me kidnapped when I was a child."

"*What?*"

"Yes, he took significant pleasure in my torture, when his men brought me to him. Of course I was too young to remember his face, but something about him was familiar when I saw him last year. When he hit the horse, I knew. It was him. He made the same sound of satisfaction when he struck me. I'll remember that until the day I die."

Oh gods.

Leda sank down on to her bed. "Why would he have kidnapped you?"

"Don't be naive, Leda. He hated father and always has. He sought to damage the King through his attacks on me."

"What did he do?"

A flicker of emotion in those perpetually dead eyes. "Some of the worst things a human can do to another. Only the gods could have dreamt up such torture, people don't have the imagination. It appears they ensured he led a blessed life. Until now." She looked up at the sky as though daring the gods to show her their wrath.

Leda could barely believe what she was about to say, but her heart was hurting too much not to. "I'm so sorry, Azaria."

"Why? It's not as though you did anything. I'm fine," Azaria said, whatever flash of emotion she'd let slip now back under ironclad control. "And I have my revenge now. Though perhaps it isn't enough. He has a child, doesn't he, the Bolsh heir?"

Leda nodded wordlessly. The child was small and weak for her age, spent all of her time at court staring at the floor. She had clearly suffered very much at the hands of her father.

Azaria looked towards the door. "Perhaps I should end that line as well. For completeness."

Leda felt renewed anger surge within her and was grimly satisfied as it replaced the aching sadness. This feeling, she knew what to do with. "This is not embroidery and you are not snipping off errant threads," she spat. "You'll leave the girl alone, she's innocent."

"Her father's abhorrent blood runs in her veins. What's to say I'm not preventing atrocities down the line?"

"Your father's abhorrent blood runs through your veins! Should I put *you* down?"

Azaria's lips pursed. "Not with that as your weapon." She gestured to the discarded candlestick. "My point still stands."

"I'm not arguing morality with you right now, Azaria." Leda got to her feet, aware that her raised voice was matched by those of a group of people approaching her rooms.

She looked over at her sister in panic as the door rattled on its hinges, but Azaria showed no intention of moving.

The door slammed against the opposite wall and at least ten people piled in, one after the other, a mix of guards and advisors and Pyrrhus himself. Ambrose had a hand out, trying to call him back, but dropped it when he registered Azaria's presence.

They all froze as they took in the scene before them: Leda and Azaria in the midst of a civilised conversation. They probably expected to find her sprawled in a pool of her own blood.

That's what Leda would have expected, anyway.

A racket of voices rang through the air as they all reacted. Pyrrhus was across the room in seconds, blocking Leda from Azaria with his body. As if that would have done anything more than slow her down for a moment. The remaining guards and Ambrose surrounded Azaria.

Atticus was flushed and startled-looking, but nevertheless stepped up until he was a foot away from Azaria. She regarded him with something approaching curiosity.

"By order of the king you are under arrest for the wilful murder of Linus Bolsh and under suspicion of the wilful murders of Prince Caspari, Prince Elov and Markus Locarno. In addition you are detained on suspicion of the attempted wilful murders of Eber Locarno, Leda Locarno and Princess Elina Locarno."

Azaria was frowning as she was ushered towards the door with a respect no one else would have been treated with.

"That list is excessive," Azaria said to Atticus, though she followed him. "I only killed one, and you all witnessed it half an hour ago. I did nothing to the others."

"Forgive us if we don't believe you," Pyrrhus snapped, his back to Leda as he tried to crowd her away from her sister. Leda had nothing in her to rebel with; she was only standing in the first place from sheer willpower. She stepped back silently, hands twisting uselessly behind her.

"You are a fool," Azaria said simply as the guards chivvied her towards the door, justifiably afraid to put their hands on her. "If I were the one carrying out these killings there would be no other living Locarnos." She pointed at Leda. "If I had been the one to loose the arrow, it would have gone straight through her heart."

Leda was close enough to Pyrrhus that she *felt* him flinch, and though he quickly recovered he appeared more furious than Leda had ever seen him. "Get her out of here, NOW!"

CHAPTER 16

The request came from the dungeons roughly thirty minutes after Azaria had been locked inside.

"She's asking to see you, madam," the guard said.

Pyrrhus made a disbelieving sound from behind his desk. Leda, who was staring out the window at the sumptuous view afforded by the luxurious office her father had once occupied, didn't turn to look at the messenger.

She was still shaking from the events of the evening, had refused to contemplate not following Pyrrhus when he'd been ushered away by his advisors.

"Azaria can sit in quiet contemplation," Leda said. "She's not getting a visit from me any time soon."

The guard hesitated.

"That's the final word on the matter," Pyrrhus said. "Leave us, please."

The guard did so.

"She never quite understood the point of prison," Leda sighed. Pyrrhus made a sound of agreement, and loudly shuffled the papers on his desk.

"She has no idea the havoc she's caused," he said.

Leda turned to face him. "He tortured her until something fundamental in her mind broke," she said quietly. "I don't believe she was thinking of anything beyond that."

Pyrrhus's expression softened. "If I'm honest I can't say I wouldn't have done the same in her shoes. Still, she's called the veracity of the trials into doubt. She deliberately sabotaged the selection of the next monarch. If the people of South Doviet don't rebel for this it'll be a miracle. The kingdoms are falling apart as it is."

An interesting thought. "Perhaps it's best to let it happen."

"Then there would be war," Pyrrhus said simply. "Horrific war. We're too intermingled to break apart now. Trade would suffer, tensions would rise and people would become desperate. We'd be fighting under the banners of unscrupulous fiefdoms once more."

"So you're saying my father was right to conquer them all?"

"Good gods, no. However, undoing his mistakes will cause more pain than trying to keep the kingdoms together as they are. I've assessed every factor in great detail; in fact I've written a book about it."

Leda stared at him. "You've written ... a *book* ... about the future of the kingdoms?"

Pyrrhus looked at her like that was a completely normal thing to have done. "It helped to get my thoughts in order."

"Right."

"And it will explain how I reached my conclusions to any citizens who care to know. I'm having it published and placed in libraries across the kingdoms."

"I see."

This man was adorable. And insane. An unbearably sweet maniac.

Pyrrhus seemed to have some awareness of the oddness

of it all, though, given the quirk to his lips as he looked up at her. "Do you not write books to sort through complex problems you encounter?"

"No, I think you're the only person in the world who does that."

Her eyes fell to the cuffs of his shirt, to the uneven stitching. He was wearing the one she'd made for him again. She'd been in a troubled state of mind when creating that, trying to process her feelings for him. It was no more strange a way to get all of that excess energy out than writing a book. They all had their idiosyncrasies, she supposed.

"Do you really think it's Azaria? That she's trying to kill our siblings?" she asked.

"Ambrose and Elina are certain it's her. I, however, find it difficult to believe. Azaria is violent and vengeful, but has she ever been secretive about it? As you said before, if she were behind this I suspect we'd all know. It's possible that it was Linus, given his feelings about the Locarnos and the depravity that he proved himself capable of through his assault of her. Atticus certainly believes it's him, and I trust his opinion."

Leda was inclined to agree. Besides, when Azaria had reminded them all that she didn't miss, that she would have hit Leda with that arrow, she hadn't been boasting.

She shifted away from the window and paper rustled in her pocket.

She withdrew Iris's letter. She'd completely forgotten about it in all the upheaval that had occurred that evening. Unfolding it, she began to read.

Leda,

Zephyr Bixel, there's a name I haven't heard in

a while. Our old junior prince has a reputation, though, I can tell you that. He was involved in scandals at the Saint-Trevale court, before and after your brother conquered, but nothing was ever pinned on him.

I have no proof, but a friend I trust who worked there tells me he gave his parents' whereabouts to the invading forces during the battles in exchange for clemency for himself. They were killed.

He had no friends at court, just political allies. His own brother reportedly can't stand him.

Be careful around him, Leda. He doesn't like the spotlight but if he wants to be king he'll resort to underhanded tactics to get it—that, my friends and I are sure about. If he senses you poking around in his past he might lash out, so ensure you're being safe.

I'll see what else I can find.

Love,
Iris

PS: Don't apologise for trying to fool me about your identity. I knew who you were from the moment I met you, silly girl, you think I didn't see sketches of you in the newspapers?

PPS: Keep writing to me, I want to make sure you're still well.

Leda looked up to find Pyrrhus watching her carefully. "I wrote to my friend Iris back in Saint-Trevale to see if there's anything in Zephyr's past we should know before the trials conclude."

Pyrrhus groaned and slumped back against his chair, as though he'd lost all the energy required to keep himself upright. "Yet another unnecessarily dangerous activity. I wish you'd stop investigating the candidates yourself."

"And I wish you'd abdicate your own dangerous position, but I suppose we're all going to be disappointed, aren't we?"

The look he gave her could only be described as sour. "What does the letter say?"

"Iris says he's sneaky, has no loyalty and will sink low to get what he wants. He might've turned his parents in to my brother during the invasion, to save himself."

She could see the effect that revelation had on Pyrrhus and knew he was thinking of his own parents who were killed when Rivernesse was invaded. He would have died before turning them in; she knew that without question.

But then something like satisfaction gleamed in Pyrrhus's eyes. "If that's the case, he'll be caught out in the trials."

"You're sure?"

She seemed to spend most of her time frustrating him these days, and this was no exception judging by the way he closed his eyes as if in pain. "Do you trust me?" he asked brusquely.

"Yes," she said instantly. It shocked her that she didn't need to think about it, she who trusted people so little, who anticipated constant betrayals. But in all the time they'd known each other he'd never given her real reason to doubt him, and it was time she realised it.

"Then trust my processes."

She nodded reluctantly. If he said his trials would ensure that Zephyr wouldn't win, then she shouldn't question it. Or she'd try, at least.

Pyrrhus rose from his chair and picked up his coat from the back of it. "You're sure you don't wish to see Azaria?"

She blew out a long breath, distracted. "I watched her skewer a man through the back of the neck tonight, albeit for justified reasons. I need some time to wipe that image from my mind before I see her again."

"Understandable."

Pyrrhus moved towards the door.

"Are you going somewhere?"

"The news of Linus's murder will reach Doviet tomorrow morning and they'll be in uproar. I need to meet with the advisors and privy counsellors. We have to find ways to reassure the people that the trials are continuing and the final selection will be a fair one. Insofar as I can actually assure them of that, if candidates keep being murdered by the former royal family."

He brushed past her at a respectable distance as he left, and part of her wanted to go back in time and slap herself for forcing them into this strange, unnatural friendship. If she was honest with herself, as she so rarely was, it was less than what she wanted them to be.

But he was still on the throne, still wielded unfathomable levels of power. She needed to stop forgetting that.

She could help him as she was trying to help her siblings, but no more.

The third trial was the very definition of a mess. Everything had been thrown into disarray by Linus's death, no one had been able to agree on a replacement for him, and the trial attracted such crowds from the Five Kingdoms as to make the candidates nervous. They therefore agreed to keep any spectators who were not senior members of the royal court or the Five Families' delegations out of the room.

Leda wasn't too upset by this, given Pyrrhus had told her the trial would be a gruelling assessment of the laws that her lunatic of a father had created. It would involve endless debate on which should be kept, forming the basis of the new Ministry of Law and Justice that had just been set up.

Leda sat at her siblings' customary table for lunch and busied herself with writing a list of books for Ami to read to continue building her vocabulary. She needed fuel for that task, and so was eating a cheesecake that was really meant to serve the whole table. But it was delicious and buttery and she was ravenously hungry.

She nearly dropped her fork when Elina entered the banquet hall with a bruised face, a muddy dress and a towering temper that Leda suspected was all interconnected.

"What happened to you?" she said as Elina snatched an apple from the bowl on the table.

"Her horse threw her," said Ambrose, who had entered the room so closely behind Elina that Leda hadn't noticed him. He seemed minded to fuss about her, and she was not receptive.

Castor came in at a jog and made his way over, concern on his face.

"Princess Elina, are you well? I saw you fall from my window." He turned to Leda. "It looked nasty; her saddle flew off almost before she did."

"It did?" Leda said, getting to her feet. "Did someone sabotage it?"

"No," Elina said grumpily. "Azaria's in the dungeons;

she's not in a position to hurt any of us. It was just a stupid accident."

None of this was an accident, Leda was certain. And still they didn't know *why* it was happening in the first place. She had a horrible feeling that it was bigger than mere revenge against the Locarnos, that she was missing something consequential. It more than likely had something to do with what Melia had refused to tell her about the curse, but she couldn't put the pieces together in her mind in a way that made sense.

"But if Azaria isn't the one who's carrying out these attacks—"

"Will you be quiet, Leda? Your voice is giving me a headache."

Ambrose reached for Elina's face and she nearly fell over herself in her haste to get away. "I'm fine!"

He held up his hands but kept moving forward, like he was approaching a wounded cat. "Just let me check, Lina."

She batted him away. "Stop that, I'm alright. Oh look, here's Eber."

They turned as one to watch Eber as he entered, looking vaguely out of sorts. He held two wooden flutes, one large and the other smaller and more delicate.

"Have any of you seen Ami?" he asked. He looked at Elina and blanched. "Gods above, what happened to you?"

"My horse threw me," she said stiffly. "It's just scratches. And no, I haven't seen her. Why? Ow!" She'd opened her mouth too far and grabbed at her bruised jaw, eyes brimming with tears of pain.

Ambrose knew better than to approach her again, but his expression darkened. Stopping him from healing was a lesser-known form of torture, apparently.

"I'd have thrown her off years ago if I were her horse,"

Eber muttered to Leda. "Imagine having something that obnoxious sitting on your back and snarking all day."

Leda snorted and Elina's head whipped up.

"What?" Elina demanded.

"What?" Eber said innocently, before waving the flutes in his hand. "Look, I need Ami. We were supposed to meet for practice over an hour ago and I can't find her anywhere."

"Where are her guards?"

"She snuck away from them this morning. She's getting skilled at it, and it's bloody irritating. She's very small, can hide herself away in tiny places. I suggested to Pyrrhus that we put a bell on her but he didn't go for it."

Leda suppressed a laugh. "Strange, that."

Her heart leapt as Pyrrhus appeared behind Eber. He looked tired but otherwise in good spirits. "If I'm putting a bell on her then I'm putting one on all of you. You're menaces—Elina, what happened to your face?"

Elina threw her hands in the air. "For the love of the gods, I'm fine!" she shouted.

"Case in point," Eber said dryly.

"What happened in the trial?" Elina asked, a flagrantly desperate attempt to steer the conversation away from her if Leda ever saw one.

"Zephyr won."

"Really?" The sceptical response of his twin brother was very telling.

That was good, because it diverted everyone's attention to Ambrose. As a result they didn't see Leda glaring at Pyrrhus, fairly sure she was about to start breathing fire. He held her gaze, mouthing the words 'trust me' just for her.

She would, of course. But if the trials failed and Zephyr won, then she'd take things into her own hands. She had absolutely no clue what that meant, but she'd do whatever was needed. This was bigger than her now, bigger than her desire to simply return home. She couldn't leave a mess behind her, another toxic monarch, if she could have any influence over it. And she was sure at least a few of her siblings would support her in that.

Pyrrhus turned back to the others. "I was surprised too, but he approached it with logic and balance. Thalia was second and Pan third. Pan had some opinions on the death penalty that were ... unanticipated. Suffice it to say he's an enthusiast, in every possible scenario."

There was silence as they all digested that.

Pyrrhus continued. "Did I hear you say you're looking for Ami, Eber? Atticus told me he saw her outside a couple of hours ago; he sent her guards looking after she slipped away this morning. Did they not find her?"

"Your guards vary in quality," Eber said, looking back at his own group of them in the corner. Only one, Kadir, was watching them, eyes alert and focused. The others were all surreptitiously engaged in a game of cards where they thought they couldn't be seen.

Eber heaved a great sigh. "I spend half my life running after that girl; she'll put me in an early grave I swear. Oi, you lot!" He gestured to his guards and jerked his head at the window. "Let's look for her outside."

They left, and those who remained went back to fussing over Elina, who was having none of it. When Ambrose pointed out that her hands were shaking and she needed to be checked for a concussion she announced that she was going to help Eber and stormed from the room.

They all followed.

"Elina," Leda said as she caught up with her in the rose garden. "Get back in there, they need to make sure you're alright. You look like you've lost a fight with an elephant."

"I do not, I—"

A shout sounded from near the river. They peered over

the stone balustrade at the edge of the rose garden and down the hill that led to the water. A cluster of guards stood at the riverbank, and Eber was sprinting from the woods faster than Leda had ever seen him run.

Something clawed at her stomach.

She moved towards the steps without her brain consciously directing her to do so.

There was something in the water. The guards dithered at the edge as if they didn't want to go in.

Leda drifted closer, as though in a trance. Then she was running, but she didn't remember deciding to do so.

The river was flowing slowly today, almost at a standstill.

Her vision cleared, the picture becoming more comprehensible the closer she got to the riverbank. And yet, it was so very incomprehensible at the same time.

A body, floating face down in the water.

Was it an animal? No.

Small, it was so small.

It looked like a girl. Young. Her hair was long and brown, tied with a length of emerald silk that fluttered and danced through the water.

Elina seized Leda's arm so hard she knew she'd bruise, but as her lips parted nothing came out.

"Leda, oh gods," Elina choked out, trying to tug her away as she stepped up to the river's edge, reeds tangling in her skirts. Leda shook her head. This wasn't possible. It couldn't be.

"Ami?" she said, her voice high and thin.

Her sister couldn't hear her.

Leda fell to her knees in the dirt, her hand touching the very surface of the water.

That silk hair tie swirled mockingly beneath, the only thing that moved.

CHAPTER 17

*L*eda couldn't breathe.

No, this wasn't possible; her eyes were fooling her.

She went to lower herself into the water, panic welling in her chest. Elina, now retching into the bushes nearby, was all but forgotten.

"AMI!" Leda shouted.

As her knees touched the water a pair of arms encircled her waist and she was lifted into the air. She didn't need to glance behind to know it was Pyrrhus. She thrashed in his grip.

"Leda, don't—" He grunted with the exertion of keeping her still and she wouldn't be surprised if the scream she let loose partially deafened him.

"NO! No, it can't be her, I taught her to swim—I taught her—AMI!"

Eber was past them in a flash, effortlessly evading Kadir, who made a vain grab for his arm. He sloshed his way into the river fully clothed, reaching Ami in seconds. There was an awful splash as he turned her over in the water, and the sound he made when he saw her face made Leda's heart crack in two.

Pyrrhus overpowered her then, lifting Leda completely from the ground and turning back towards the palace. The fight went out of her and she crumpled into his arms with a broken cry.

"No," she sobbed into his collar. "Please, no."

She could feel him shaking, knew it wasn't from the cold. "I'm so sorry, Leda."

As he stepped over the threshold into the banquet hall Leda looked over his shoulder and caught a flash of the scene they'd left behind. The sun sparkling incongruously on the water, Eber standing waist-deep with his head in his hands. A cluster of guards around Elina who had curled into a ball by the bushes. Ambrose stopping only to remove his coat before splashing into the water towards Ami.

Just like that, the image was gone, and the banquet hall doors closed behind them.

The next week proved a struggle for the occupants of the palace to get the Locarno children to do anything at all. The air was dark and full of grief, everyone from the courtiers to the servants donning black mourning clothes.

The sight of it made Leda incandescently angry, given those courtiers had never worn a hint of black after the other Counterparts had been slaughtered. They did so now only to appease Pyrrhus, who was hit as hard as anyone else by Ami's death, though he maintained his composure in front of them all.

Eber refused to eat, sitting at the dinner table with an untouched plate and blank expression. He declined to even pick up his cutlery, no matter how much anyone pleaded with him. But he drank. Oh, how he drank.

Elina stayed in bed for three days straight, not permitting anyone to open her bedroom door.

Leda was better at going through the motions. She ate her food; it tasted like sawdust. She dragged herself out of bed and went where she was directed. But she didn't speak. She had nothing to say.

Pyrrhus had started to gently tell her what the review of Ami's body had revealed and she left the room. She didn't want to know. She was afraid that more details would crack the rest of her to pieces. She couldn't add any more information to that picture of Ami's body that she would carry in her mind for the rest of her life.

No one knew how Azaria was taking the news. Leda thought she probably didn't care, and imagined her sat in the dungeon in much the same mood as ever. Perhaps she was even pleased, as Ami's death drew suspicion away from her. It was unlikely that she was the attacker given she was under lock and key and watched by guards when Ami was killed.

It took a full week before Leda was able to step foot outside of the palace.

She moved faster than she thought possible down to the pathway into the woods and didn't glance up from her shoes. She couldn't look at the river; even the sound of it gushing made her feel sick. She would never swim in it, never so much as touch the water, ever again.

Her guards stayed a respectable distance away, for which she was grateful.

An hour later night had fallen and Leda wondered idly why she wasn't shivering. She was sitting in the clearing that Pyrrhus had made into a graveyard for her siblings, the heavens pouring a lake's worth of water over her. Her hands rested on what was quickly becoming muddy soil. She moved her sopping hair out of her face and resumed staring at the newest grave, fresh marble that had barely been weathered, that of thirteen-year-old Markus. She supposed Prince Elov, whose Counterpart Markus had been, was buried at the royal family tomb in the Temple of Gemdark.

Here was better. Here was where she'd prefer to be, at least, when her time came. And she could feel that ending looming closer every day. Someone was very determined that she and her siblings die, and there were only so many of them left.

Twigs cracked behind her and she looked up to see that Eber had joined her, equally soaked to the skin.

"She should go there," Leda said hoarsely, pointing to a space between two waterlogged patches of daisies behind Sofie's headstone. Daisies had been Ami's favourite. She'd liked to link their stems into chains and wear them as crowns in the summertime.

Leda wasn't sure how much of the water trailing down her face was rain and how much was tears. The weight of Ami's death had her physically slumped over, like her spine had lost the ability to hold itself upright.

She hadn't felt agony like this with her other siblings. That had been the upside to her being so self-involved back then, so driven by her own survival. She hadn't been able to focus on much else.

Eber nodded at her suggestion but said nothing.

"We need to find out more about this curse, Eber. It's the missing link to all of this."

He sat down beside her. His movements were slow and pained, like he'd aged a hundred years in days.

"You like to think that, because maybe then there's

something you can do about it," he said. "Isn't it just as possible that an enemy of our father is trying to finish off his bloodline?"

Leda shook her head. "Melia knew more than she was saying. I feel it, Eber. This has something to do with the curse on the throne."

He still seemed sceptical, but humoured her with a squeeze to the shoulder. "If you want us to go and see Melia we will. But what makes you think she'll tell us more?"

"She'll have to, we'll give her anything. This has to stop."

"Alright."

"And soon," she sniffed. It was likely a wild goose chase and could lead to nothing. But she needed to do something. They had to be moving forward. Her inaction had already cost them so much.

Eber nodded. "Soon. Or, at least as soon as either of us is in a position to go anywhere."

He was right, of course. Leda had been crying so much her eyes were a swollen, painful red and she couldn't move five feet without a gripping pain in her chest. Eber looked like the energy it had taken him to leave the palace and walk into the woods had wiped out any reserves he had left. His lips were bloodless and eyes blank.

"I failed you all," Leda whispered, a fresh wave of tears mingling with the rain. "I came back to help you, to make sure you were all safe and well adjusted enough to live independent lives after what our father did to us. And all I've done is watch each one of you fall further. And now Ami is ... she's gone. I'm so sorry." She choked on the final words.

"None of this is your fault," Eber said. "We'll find out what's going on, together. We'll"—his breath hitched—" we'll stop it before we lose anyone else."

Tentatively, Leda reached out to him. With a sigh, Eber

wound his arm around her and she rested her head on his shoulder.

They sat like that, statues staring at the headstones of their family, for a long time.

CHAPTER 18

*A*mi's funeral was beautiful, but it was also one of the worst experiences of Leda's life.

She kept her tears at bay watching the priestess give the long service on the grassy slopes by the rose garden.

When she'd seen the coffin pulled on an ornate cart by Midas, the pony Ami had loved so much, she'd broken down. Eber had enfolded her in his arms and they'd cried together.

She'd almost choked on the smell of wine on his breath, but couldn't bear to say anything. She'd intervene just as soon as she could, enlisting Ambrose's help, but this day was for Ami.

Ten-year-old Fessler, who had grown up with Ami and knew her as his Counterpart, was stoic, but Leda noticed he was never more than three feet from Midas throughout the ceremony. When Elina had attempted to put a hand on his shoulder he'd shrugged it off with a shake of his head, expression tight.

After the funeral, time seemed to move in odd ways for all of them. Each day passed in a blur of routine; breakfast, lunch and dinner interspersed with activities. But they spent those days like ghosts, the hours dragging. Everything was dull and uninspiring, barely distracting them.

It felt rote, empty.

Of all those who grew concerned about them as the weeks passed, Pyrrhus was the most agitated, though he gave them space. He was also distracted by a myriad of demands on his time, not least the machinations of the remaining members of the five families as they jostled for the throne.

One morning Leda woke up and couldn't bear the thought of breakfast in the banquet hall under the watchful stares of the court. She got dressed in a blank daze and went instead to the place she found comforting above all others. Pyrrhus's old study on the third floor.

It was just as she'd left it, albeit more dusty due to Pyrrhus's flat refusal to allow anyone to enter aside from the two of them, even to clean.

Leda did her best to restore it to its rightful state with the duster she found in a cupboard. With that done, she sank into Pyrrhus's favoured armchair with a book in hand that she had no intention of reading.

She stared out the window at the tops of the trees stretching out beyond the river.

She watched the sun rise over the leaves and burn in the sky as it reached midday, only turning away when the light became too much for her eyes.

She nearly jumped out of her skin when she heard the door open above her.

There was no need to be concerned, there was only one person who would track her down here.

Her gaze was wary as it followed Pyrrhus descending the stairs. He was as polished and aristocratic as ever, but there was no disguising his fatigue. It showed in every step he took.

He paused at the bottom of the staircase, a hand clasped around the bannister. He took her in, wrapped against the morning chill in a thick blanket. She was little more than a ball of fabric on his armchair, red eyes and a mass of curly brown hair peeking out the top.

Words seemed to fail him. She wondered if he felt the same déjà vu she did, if seeing her took him back to the nights they'd spent here so long ago, reading and playing chess and too awkward to meet each other's eyes.

This was where it had all begun. How ludicrous that she felt that had been a simpler time for them both, as she'd plotted her escape and he'd covertly arranged for the death of her father.

Pyrrhus approached her slowly, as though she were a wounded animal. Her eyes narrowed at him over the blanket as he sat opposite, gesturing to the chess table between them.

"Would you like a game?"

Leda looked at the table and a deep kind of weariness spread through her bones. She shook her head.

Pyrrhus nodded, relaxing his pin-straight posture to sink against the back of the armchair she normally used. "That's probably for the best, you'd only lose anyway."

She knew what he was doing, but it did nothing to stop her from bristling with indignance. She let the blanket fall from her grip to reveal her mouth.

"You're feeling sorry for me," she said, her voice gravelly with disuse. "You'd let me win."

He looked at her as though that were the gravest insult anyone had ever made against him. "You impugn my honour, madam."

Leda's lips curled into the most reluctant of smiles. Having him here in such close proximity cut her as much it always did, deep in her chest. Yet somehow it also made her feel whole, like a persistent, gnawing gap in her soul had been temporarily filled. She'd never felt confusion like she did with him. He turned her inside out.

With a long-suffering sigh she pushed a white pawn out by two spaces. He leaned forward slowly from the chair opposite, already focused on the board. That was how he approached everything he did, with complete, unyielding concentration. He would think of nothing but the game until it was over, and then he would move on to whatever came next.

She took the opportunity to watch him as they made their moves. She wanted to curl up into him, to have him hold her and reassure her that everything was going to be alright.

But it wasn't, and she had no right to demand that from him anyway.

Her head tilted to the side as he moved his castle to take her knight. He'd opened himself up inexplicably, an amateur move. In a few quick plays of her castle and her queen, she would have him.

"Checkmate."

Leda looked up, half-expecting him to be wearing an indulgent smile, pleased that he'd made her feel better by sacrificing the game. What she found instead made her smile grow into something genuine. He was staring down at the chess pieces as though they'd moved of their own accord and committed the most heinous betrayal against him.

He breathed into the hand that had come up to cover his mouth. "How did—"

The rusty laugh that emitted from Leda snapped him out of his trance, and he looked up at her with barely repressed annoyance.

"I beat you," she said. "How embarrassed you must be, Your Majesty."

She could see him grit his teeth at her mocking tone.

"I'm very tired, it's been a long day."

"Don't bore me with your excuses."

Something lit up in his eyes as he looked at her. "This is bringing out an ugly colour in you."

"Said the loser, to the winner." She scrunched her nose at him. "Don't lash out, everyone has to be beaten sometime. It builds character."

She watched as he got to his feet, carefully moved the chess table to one side, and her throat went dry as he approached. Before she knew it he was crouched in front of her, hands twisted in the thick blanket that covered her. She nearly fell off the armchair on to him when he tugged at the fabric.

"Hey!"

"You are being smug, and you do not deserve my blanket."

"I made this for you!"

"Exactly, it is now my possession. Mine." The last word was a growl as, with an almighty tug, he whipped the blanket out of her grasp and settled it around his own shoulders.

It looked very out of place on the austere black lines of his tailcoat. Leda gaped down at him.

"You used to be so polite," she breathed. "What happened?"

"I spent too much time with a very aggravating woman."

A real smile shaped her lips, and she could see his pleasure at the sight of it. That, more than anything else, had her grabbing the blanket on either side of his shoulders and using it to pull him towards her until their foreheads touched.

"Thank you," she whispered, watching his eyes shut and the movement of his neck as he swallowed.

His eyes flew open again as she pressed her lips to his cheek, and she lingered there for longer than she'd intended, pinned in place by the intoxicating scent of him.

She let out a shaky breath, turning her head oh so slightly, and her lips brushed the corner of his mouth.

They stayed there, frozen, for what felt like minutes. Everything in her screamed at her to turn, to close the distance and take the comfort that he offered. The tension in every line of his body indicated that he was feeling a similar compulsion.

She felt him begin to shift, and then he stopped abruptly.

A tear trickling from her eye had touched his cheek.

She wrenched herself away with a ragged gasp. Shaking her head, she slipped out from under his grasp and headed for the door.

When she looked back he was still kneeling before her chair, hands fisted on the arms.

She couldn't. For so many reasons.

Feeling hollow, Leda drifted up towards the infirmary to collect her next doses of medicine. She was taking enough by now to justify starting her own herb garden, but it was better than the pitiful attempts she'd made to medicate herself before Ambrose had started prescribing for her.

She was quiet and sullen as she approached the infirmary, padding down the empty corridor outside. Guards trailed her as always, but at a distance. Instinct told her to peer around the infirmary door, which stood ajar, before entering. What she saw made her come to a halt.

Ambrose was pressed against his open medicine cabinet, holding two almost overflowing vials of blue liquid and looking scandalised. At that moment her sister Elina was pressing him against the shelves, hands on his collar, her face moving closer to his.

Ambrose looked for a moment, for the slightest flicker of time, like he might consider giving in. And then it was gone and his eyes were like stone flints. He nearly overturned the cabinet in his haste to get away, and ducked under Elina's arm. She collided with the shelves and grabbed the wood to steady the cabinet before turning to him with pure fire in her expression.

"Please don't pretend as though you don't feel it too," she said. Her eyes were red-rimmed, as though she'd spent weeks crying, which Leda knew was true. It wasn't often that she could empathise with Elina, but now she felt it with her whole heart.

Ambrose gaped at her sister, holding his vials up in front of him like they would shield him from her emotions. Leda hoped that the blue liquid he'd slopped all over his coat wasn't corrosive.

She knew she shouldn't be watching this, but the sight of Ambrose flabbergasted and flailing was so rare she couldn't move away if she tried.

"I ... that is not ... Lina, I'm in a position of power over you!"

Elina put her hands on her hips. "What are you talking about? I was a princess; if anything I'm in a position of power over *you*."

Ambrose didn't appear to share the same view judging by how violently he was shaking his head.

"I ... that's ... I don't understand where all this is coming from," he said. "You ... I've enjoyed having you here helping me over the past couple of years, and the gods know your knowledge of medicinal plants has contributed extensively, but this was only ever professional. I can't think what you'd even see in me."

Was Elina visibly wilting under his rejection? Surely not.

She held herself in such powerful check, Leda had rarely seen her vulnerable like this.

"So that's it? I don't mean anything to you?" There was an unfamiliar waver to Elina's voice that made Leda look away in shame.

She really shouldn't be watching. She turned away from the door, but their voices seeped out into the corridor.

"Of course you do. I care for you deeply, but not in that way," Ambrose said. "You'll be married to a noble somewhere, Elina. You'll live an illustrious life and have your own court to oversee, I'm sure. That isn't something I could provide."

"You're a junior prince of Saint-Trevale."

"I'm a physician and that's all. We're not suited, Elina, our priorities differ too much—"

"Enough, I've heard enough. If that's your decision I'll respect it." Elina's tone indicated she did not, in fact, respect it at all. She sounded like she wanted to throw a great many items across the room.

"Elina, wait—"

Quick footsteps and then the door swung open violently, smacking into Leda's back and sending her sprawling to the ground with a curse.

Elina looked down at her with murder in her eyes. "Eavesdropping, were we? Having a laugh at my expense?" Her leg shifted under her dress as though she were about to kick Leda's prone form, but she hesitated.

"Of course not!" Leda grabbed the nearby windowsill and used it to haul herself to her feet. Elina crowded her against the wall, similar to how she had with Ambrose, but this time the only thing coursing through her was rage.

Leda was not about to be her punching bag, no matter how bad she might feel for her. It was time for the Locarno royals to learn how to deal with their problems without violence.

"Don't take this out on me," Leda said, holding Elina away from her by both shoulders. She was alarmingly strong, damn all that training she'd been put through her whole life. "Seriously, Elina, control yourself. What are you doing?"

Her sister was close to rabid, but whatever madness flowed through her veins was instantly extinguished by the appearance of Zephyr. He'd snuck up on them without either of them hearing so much as a whisper.

Reluctantly, Elina backed away from Leda. Leda shoved herself away from the wall and gave her a dark look that promised retribution.

Zephyr was fixated on Elina, his expression quizzical. He didn't seem to feel the need to say hello, or bow, or adhere to any formalities at all. He spoke as if they were already in the middle of a conversation.

"I find it intriguing that you and Azaria share blood," he said idly. "You possess so few of her fine qualities. You have the temper of an alley cat. There is nothing regal in you whatsoever."

Elina visibly deflated at the insult, coming from the twin of Ambrose, of all people. That face, delivering such a message. It must have been a blow.

If there were a faster way to reignite Elina's temper, Leda didn't know of it. She seized Elina around the waist as she dove for Zephyr, hands outstretched like claws, and dragged her down the corridor. A cushioned settee sat under a stained-glass window around the corner and Leda shoved her down on to it.

"What's the matter with you? Have you lost your mind? You can't attack one of the five families after what Azaria did!"

"He deserves it!" Elina spat, straining to look over Leda's shoulder to see if Zephyr had followed them. "Sneaky, oily little creep." She blew a strand of glossy hair out of her face and dropped her head into her hands. "I feel like I'm losing my mind."

Leda was inclined to agree.

"We've lost so much recently," Leda said. "Of course it's affecting you."

Elina's breathing was quick and laboured. "That's all very well, but what do I do about it?"

"You find answers."

"What do you mean?"

"Before she left, Melia told me about a curse that the gods put on the throne. She didn't say much, but she implied that it had something to do with the person, or people, who are trying to kill the royal children and Counterparts. She said we were in danger. Eber and I are going to her temple in Slofray to find out the truth. You're welcome to join us."

Elina watched her with shining eyes. Leda had expected her to jump with joy at the prospect of seeing Melia again. Instead she was still and thoughtful.

"What makes you think she'll tell you anything more than she already has?"

Leda shrugged helplessly. "What other option do we have? We'll convince her, bargain with her, anything."

Elina let out a shuddering sigh. "Very well. Action, yes, we need that. Let's go." She stood up.

Leda recoiled. "Now?"

"Yes," Elina said firmly. "Right now. Mostly because Ambrose has been eavesdropping on our conversation and I suspect he'll try to prevent us from leaving the safety of the palace." She tossed her head as Leda flinched in surprise. "I can see your sleeve, Ambrose."

Leda turned and caught a flicker of white material reflecting the light as Ambrose drew his arm hastily back around the corner.

A few seconds later he emerged into view with an irascible expression.

"I don't make a habit of listening in on private conversations."

"Clearly," Elina said glacially. "That's why you're so bad at it."

Leda could have cut the tension in the air with a knife, and suddenly felt the need to be anywhere else.

"You can't leave the palace," Ambrose said.

"You have no authority over me, nor over her." Elina pointed at Leda. "Or Eber, for that matter."

"I can have the guards keep you here."

Elina bared her teeth. "Why don't you try that?"

Ambrose looked seconds away from stomping his foot, his expression aggravated. "You'll sneak away, won't you, if I try to stop you?"

Leda and Elina nodded in unison. Ambrose released a put-upon sigh.

"Very well, then I'll accompany you." He held up a hand as they both opened their mouths. "None of you have been to Slofray before; you have no concept of the journey, the time, methods or expense of it. I know how to get to the Grand Temple and have done so before. I will not be moved on this. You're only going if I am."

Annoyingly, he offered a compelling argument, and Leda could see reluctant acceptance spreading across Elina's face.

Leda turned to her. "We need to get there fast, before anyone knows we're going." She would leave Pyrrhus a note in his rooms to tell him not to worry, that they were safe, but she couldn't tell him face to face. He'd win any debate against her in a heartbeat and she couldn't allow herself to be talked out of this.

"Fine, but you won't tell anybody that we're leaving or where we're going," Elina said to Ambrose. She gestured to Leda. "Pyrrhus would sooner fight an army single-handed than let her out of his sight for more than a second."

Leda felt that was inaccurate, but to her annoyance Ambrose nodded in agreement.

"Very well. Let's commence."

CHAPTER 19

*A*mbrose, Elina and Leda went their separate ways to pack for the journey and reconvened later that afternoon in front of the palace, where Eber had ordered their horses saddled.

Ambrose's face was grim as he swung himself up on his horse and waved away the host of guards who moved to follow them. "We'll only be gone an hour; we shan't stray out of Gemdark. Atticus has given permission for us to leave unescorted."

He lied with such ease Leda found it disturbing. He'd already told them all the plan, to go to the village of Falcon-glass at the edge of Gemdark to the east in the direction of Slofray. There, they'd give their horses to the, doubtless very surprised, king's master of horse who lived there and ask him to hold on to them.

They would then hire a carriage to take them towards the border until the roads ended and were replaced with small earth paths the carriages could not easily traverse. They would walk from there, towards the small town of Goldcrest, where they'd stay the night before crossing their final hurdle, the Slofray forest.

All things considered, Ambrose predicted it should take them a day and a night to get to Slofray, and to the Grand Temple, which sat so fortuitously close to its border.

It all went smoothly at first, and they made the transition from horse to carriage to foot with relative ease. They didn't speak much, which was for the best given the crackling tension that flourished between Ambrose and Elina. Eber hadn't been informed of what had happened, Leda hadn't had a chance yet, and so was looking bemused. Wisely, he didn't comment.

As night began to fall and they continued their walk Leda hung back and fell into step beside Ambrose.

"I assume that before we left you used the few minutes you were away from us to let the palace know where we were going?" Leda asked. Of course he had, he was the least spontaneous person she'd ever met and a stickler for all rules that he encountered. It was probably why he and Pyrrhus got on so well.

Ambrose showed no remorse. "Pyrrhus would have been beside himself if the three of you disappeared with no warning, and you know it. His brains are already close to leaking out of his ears because of you. I declined to make it worse."

Leda regarded him with narrowed eyes. She'd left a note for Pyrrhus, of course, but it was interesting that Ambrose thought she'd be careless enough with him not to bother doing so. "What a charming image."

"I've warned Pyrrhus countless times over the past two years to keep away from you, that all you'll bring him is trouble. Has he listened even once? No."

"I'm shocked he didn't fall over himself to take your advice, given you're the authority on relationships, *man with one identifiable friend*."

His jaw worked furiously. "Are you going to walk next to

me for the whole journey? Let me know if so, so that I can prepare myself."

"By all means, why don't you go and speak with Elina instead? I'm sure that'll be a delightful conversation. You can treat her to your views on who shouldn't speak to whom and why, they're so fascinating."

He was staunchly silent at that. She fancied she could almost see steam pouring out of his ears.

Leda snorted. "What she sees in you only the gods know. I'd never have taken you for a heartbreaker, Ambrose, but miracles happen every day."

It was clearly a very sore subject, and unwise of her to have pressed it mere hours after his encounter with Elina.

Anger ignited his features. "How lucky we are that we got to keep *you* instead of Ami."

Time seemed to stop as the cruelty of his reckless words sank in.

The full meaning of the statement struck Leda like a kick to the stomach and she came to a stop on the path. She was almost out of breath from the savagery of it.

"What did you just say?"

Did Ambrose actually look regretful? It would appear so. He stopped and turned to her, shaking his head. "Leda, no, I'm sorry, of course I didn't—"

She didn't stick around to listen to whatever trite apology he had for her. With her mouth in a grim line, she strode ahead and joined Eber at the front of their party.

Ambrose was a stick in the mud, but he wasn't often cruel. Elina must have really shaken him. That was the only explanation Leda could think of for why he'd spoken so thoughtlessly.

Eber took one look at her and frowned. "What's wrong?"

"I don't want to talk about it," she snapped.

"Oh wonderful, now you're in a bad mood too. That makes three out of four." He sighed.

Leda's sour mood continued as Elina joined them, made a snide comment about Leda's scarf, and they spent the next thirty minutes hurling the worst insults they could think of at each other.

Around half an hour into their fight Eber was staring fervently at the sky as though attempting to call lightning to strike him down.

They reached the picturesque little town of Goldcrest an hour later, each of them in a towering temper. Leda was, for obvious reasons, refusing to speak to Ambrose. Elina was of the same mindset. The strap on Eber's sack of supplies kept coming loose and he was dealing with his sore shoulder with all of the dignity of a cat with a thorn stuck in its paw. Ambrose was grave and serious and directed them wordlessly towards a thatched inn.

"I need a break," Eber announced. He didn't have to say who he needed a break from, it was obviously all of them. "I'll find my own accommodations tonight; I'll meet you back here in the morning."

"Eber, that's not safe," Leda said. "We need to stay together."

He shrugged and walked off. She was about to chase him but realised it would do no good, he could outrun her in a heartbeat. She let out an aggravated sigh and followed Ambrose and Elina into the inn.

It was a small and cosy place, with roughly hewn chairs and tables clustered around a fireplace that crackled with flames. Thick wooden beams, warped with age, crisscrossed the ceiling. Only a few patrons remained at this time of night, paying the newcomers no heed as they murmured to each other over flagons of mead.

Leda turned back to the makeshift reception desk by the kitchen.

"Aye, I've got two rooms free that you're welcome to," the innkeeper was saying, sweeping Ambrose's coins off the counter into his hand.

Leda looked at Elina, who was looking at Ambrose, who was staring at the innkeeper with an expression Leda had most recently seen on Pyrrhus as he tried to solve a complex equation.

"I'm not sharing with her," Elina said, pointing at Leda.

"So you're sharing with Ambrose, then?" Leda said pointedly.

Ambrose's head jerked up. "I am most certainly not sharing a room with either of you."

"Fine, you can sleep in the stables. Leda and I will take the rooms," Elina said. She held out her hand for the keys.

"I am not sleeping on a bale of hay to appease you, Elina," Ambrose said. "You'll stay with your sister."

"I'd sooner strangle her than share a room with her."

Just a couple of steps and a strong shove and Leda could send her toppling out of the open window behind her. It was tempting.

The innkeeper had been watching their exchange with his mouth hanging open. As though anticipating bloodshed, he hastily intervened. "We've a servant's room in the basement that's not got anyone in tonight, if one of you wants that? Just a straw mattress on the floor, but it's something."

Ambrose seized on the offer with palpable relief. "Yes, thank you, very kind of you."

Elina transferred her annoyance to Leda, as she so often did. "Perhaps Leda can sleep there, she grew up in that kind of accommodation, she'll be used to it."

"Shut up."

"Make me!"

"You have all the manners of a screeching bat today and I wish you would *shut up*," Leda hissed. "Don't your gods preach piety and simple living for their most devoted? I'm sure they'd love you more if you slept on the floor for them once in a while."

Elina did not like having her devoutness twisted against her in arguments, and she pressed her mouth into a thin line.

Before she could respond Ambrose let out a sound of pure aggravation that he must have been stifling for a while.

"I've had it with you two and your sniping! No wonder Eber left. You'd think you were a couple of twelve-year-olds, not grown women. Go to your rooms upstairs and I'll take the servant's room. You are not to speak to one another until we convene at sunrise tomorrow morning. Do you understand me?"

They both regarded him with wide eyes, appropriately chastened.

"Yes," they chorused.

When Eber joined them outside the inn the following morning he was wobbly-legged and haggard. Ambrose and Elina, engaged in deep debate about who should carry which supplies in their sacks, barely noticed his arrival. Leda, however, watched like a hawk as he approached.

"Morning," he said, blinking blearily in the sunlight.

"Did you sleep?" she asked. She doubted it based on the bags under his eyes and the smell emanating from him. He was so young he should be able to recover easily from whatever a night of sleeplessness could throw at him. That he hadn't was an indicator that what he'd done was particularly extreme.

"Of course," he lied. She was sure of it. "Don't scowl at me like that, Leda, you're not our mother."

"Where were you last night?"

"Ambrose! Let me help you with that." Eber shot over to help Ambrose adjust one of the straps on his bag. Leda watched him go with her arms crossed so tightly her shoulders seized up.

It was a three-hour walk spent mostly in silence to cross the border into Slofray and find the Grand Temple at the base of the famous Red Mountains.

Leda didn't mind that they weren't speaking, as most of the journey took them through a forest so beautiful it looked as though it had been conjured from descriptions in a fairy tale. The trees were ancient and towering, jade leaves shimmering in the shafts of sunlight that filtered through the canopy. Carpets of wildflowers bloomed amidst the springy grass. Butterflies danced on the light breeze around them.

All they could hear was the sound of bees buzzing contentedly amongst the flowers and the gushing of a nearby stream that snaked around the path.

Leda was sad to leave when they reached the edge of the forest, but was immediately distracted by the sight she'd read so many descriptions of in books.

The mountains of Slofray made the hills behind Gemdark look puny, rising so high Leda had to crane her neck to see the top. They glittered in the sunlight, the minerals in the soil throwing off a deeply coloured hue all the way up until the snow capped them.

Only, they were not the colour she'd expected.

Leda stopped on the path so abruptly Elina nearly slammed into her back.

"Have I lost my mind," Leda said, "or are these mountains pink?"

Eber drew to a halt beside her. "They look gorgeous."

"But they're pink ..."

"What do you have against pink?"

"Why would everyone say they're red if they're not red?" She wasn't sure why she was so caught on this tiny inaccuracy.

"Maybe they thought red sounded more impressive?" Eber shrugged, showing a more reasonable amount of emotion in response to this discovery than she was.

"Perhaps the colours faded over time," Ambrose interjected dryly, showing barely more interest than Eber. "So what if they call them the Red Mountains? The Emerald Lake in Saint-Trevale is blue, not green."

He had a point, but still. "I suppose we shouldn't believe everything we hear about the gods and their lands, should we, Elina?" Leda said pointedly.

She expected something snarky in response, but Elina merely gave her a nasty look and walked away.

It wasn't difficult to find the building they sought in the mountain range. Leda swallowed heavily as they paused in the field that stretched out from the threshold of the forest and made their way towards the place that she prayed would hold the answers they needed.

The Grand Temple made the temple at the centre of Gemdark look like a poorly constructed children's toy, designed by an architect with no flair.

This was the true monument to the kingdoms' obsession with their gods.

The structure towered above them, built half into a mountain so that it jutted out oddly from the landscape. The marble that made up its walls was blood red, the roof jet black. Hundreds of latticed windows gleamed, and yet it was not a welcoming sight. It looked hard and cold.

Leda felt every bone in her body tell her to turn around and walk away from it.

Elina, on the other hand, was bouncing on the balls of her feet. Her eyes were wide and wondrous as she took in the towering spires.

Eber, trailing far behind Ambrose, seemed to be wondering whether he could get away with staying out on the winding entrance steps for the duration of the visit.

On their journey to Slofray they'd passed numerous villages and towns devastatingly scarred by the weather disasters. This temple, however, was pristine, as though it had just been finished yesterday. The gods clearly weren't ones to work against their own interests.

The great double doors opened without them needing to knock, and Elina gasped as Melia strode out. The wind whipped her pure white gown around her legs as she stared down at them. There wasn't a hint of surprise in her expression; she'd clearly been expecting them.

She wore a silver fur stole about her shoulders and head, which made her face, peeking out, look comically small.

Leda heard Eber snort and stepped on his foot. The sound cut off abruptly.

"Exalted Priestess," Ambrose said. "We beg an audience."

"I was told that you were coming." Melia's eyes flicked up towards the sky and Elina vibrated with excitement in a way that made Leda want to shake her.

Melia graciously invited them in and Leda dragged her feet at the back of the group as they entered a cavernous, freezing-cold entrance hall. In the centre of the room, climbing twenty feet into the air, stood a cluster of statues of the gods shaped from gold and studded with every kind of precious metal Leda knew the name of. She was faintly surprised her father hadn't plundered them for his palace upon Slofray's invasion. Then again, he'd never have done anything to anger the gods.

Melia seemed disinclined to allow them further into the building. It was enormous and yet seemed strangely empty. There were no whispers or footsteps to be heard. Where were the local worshippers? Where were the priestkeepers and the other priestesses?

Eber reached out to touch one of the statues and Elina slapped his hand away.

"We wish to know more of the curse," Ambrose said.

"How do we break it?" Leda asked flatly.

"I shouldn't—"

"Ami is dead," Leda said, her voice cracking. "Please, tell us what you know. We can't ...," she faltered. "We have to know."

Melia's sympathy seemed to get the better of her. "There is no way to break the curse," she said softly. "The King bargained with the gods and made a dastardly pact with a priestess for his own selfish ends. He sacrificed his Counterparts to ensure his prosperity, but a curse was also attached, by his own design. If he was murdered, no other bloodline could sit upon the throne of the Five Kingdoms."

"Which priestess did our father collude with?" Elina looked around as though expecting the culprit to spring out at them from behind a pillar.

"You know, child," Melia said, the first hint of annoyance touching her face. "Do not pretend otherwise."

Elina straightened up. "Queen Celandine."

Leda and Ambrose let out twin sighs of realisation.

"Of course it was her," Leda groaned.

"No one's seen her since she escaped after the battles for the throne, she's in hiding," Ambrose said.

"Perhaps her daughter knows her whereabouts."

Leda shook her head. "Azaria hates her mother more than she does anyone else in our family. And she cut off our brother Elias's arm, if that illustrates anything."

Ambrose chipped in, expression thoughtful. "But Azaria's always on alert. She'll know where her mother is, if only to keep out of her way."

He most likely wasn't wrong about that.

"Do we want to make Azaria aware of the fact that we're investigating the curse? We haven't ruled out her involvement in killing our siblings yet," Elina said, a healthy amount of fear in her voice.

"I told you, it's not her," Leda said bluntly, silencing them all. "If she wanted me dead I would be."

Eber piped up. "It's true, I once saw her shoot an arrow through a rat's head from a hundred feet away. She took less than a second to aim."

Leda turned back to Melia.

"So, a Locarno royal must sit on the throne or the gods will rip apart the Five Kingdoms one vicious storm at a time? Is that the long and short of it?"

"To my knowledge. I'm afraid your trials will solve none of your problems."

All of Pyrrhus's effort, gone to waste. The sacrifices he'd made, that they'd all made, worthless. Leda wished she could call her father back from the grave and beat him senseless.

"Why? Why would the gods want this?"

"We are but pawns, fated to play the pieces in their divine chess match," Melia said that like it was in any way a good thing.

They were the playthings of deities who wouldn't even lower themselves to show their faces to them. Leda stifled the urge to kick the nearest statue.

"And the remaining Counterparts? What happens

to us?"

Melia turned away. "You would do well to speak to Celandine. I only know pieces of the curse and the deal that she struck between your father and the gods. I am sorry I cannot be more helpful. What I can tell you is this, Locarno children. You must be careful, your lives are in great danger. I don't know why this assassin is targeting you all, but they show no sign of ceasing their attempts."

Leda shared a discomfited look with Elina.

Ambrose was also looking at Leda, his expression tense.

"Before we depart, I'd like a word with Melia. Would the three of you wait outside, please?" He addressed them with more authority than Leda felt he had the right to, and while Eber moved towards the door, both she and Elina instinctively refused to move.

"What about?" Leda asked.

"It's a private spiritual matter," Ambrose said. Elina turned away instantly, as though that were perfectly reasonable, and Leda jerked her hands at him like he'd lost his mind.

At his stony-faced silence, she sighed and went to join the others outside. But not before casting a suspicious look back over her shoulder at him and Melia as he drew her into conversation, their heads close together.

Something that sounded oddly like laughter drifted through the open doors. That couldn't be right.

Why Pyrrhus was Ambrose's friend, Leda would never understand. What an unpredictable and irritating man he was.

CHAPTER 20

The atmosphere was quiet and morose by the time Ambrose joined Leda, Elina and Eber on the steps of the temple. He remained tight-lipped about what he'd spoken about with Melia and Leda gave up on questioning him after a few minutes. Elina barely paid attention, so lost in her own thoughts that she wandered away and Eber kept having to steer her back on to the path.

Tense silence wrapped around them as they followed the dirt track back into the forest. No one suggested staying the night in the nearby town. Leda didn't know if the other three were as desperate to get home as she was, but if their pace as they strode through the forest was any indication, they shared her sense of urgency.

Eber was the first to speak. "So we need to put a royal child on the throne? Just get it over with and satisfy the curse?" His voice was hoarse, like that was a horrifying possibility to even speak of.

Leda sighed. "It's not that simple."

"While the royal Locarno bloodline lives one of its members must sit on the throne. That's pretty self-explanatory isn't it?"

"There must be more to it," Elina said miserably. "The gods don't work in such simple terms; there's always a sacrifice to be made."

"I don't see how we can find out the full extent of the curse unless we can locate Celandine. If she created it, she may know how to break it," Leda said.

"What do we do until then? Halt the trials and put one of the old royals on the throne? Azaria, Fessler, Annagret, Gabriell, Elina?" Eber's tone implied he didn't find any of those choices appealing.

Elina flinched at the sound of her own name.

Leda shook her head as they trudged into a clearing flooded with the hazy light of the setting sun. "It's not possible. If we called off the trials and put a Locarno on the throne the people would rebel, and leading that rebellion would be the heads of the five families. Some would rather rip the kingdom apart than have it under Locarno rule again, even if it costs them a few hurricanes and tsunamis."

An owl hooted from a nearby tree. Leda looked up to see if she could spot the creature just in time to hear the telltale whistling of an arrow through the air.

This time she registered the sound immediately, the benefit of hideous experience.

She had just enough time to grab the scruff of Eber's neck and force him down to the ground with her. The arrow thudded into a tree trunk, shuddering inches above where their heads had been.

The dark figure of Azaria emerged from the trees, her dress sweeping the leaf-strewn ground. With a steely expression, she walked past them and yanked her arrow out of the bark. She pointed it at Leda, who was scrambling to her feet alongside a profusely swearing Eber.

"See how easy it would have been to hit you?" Azaria said. "I could have killed you all in the time it would have taken for you to spot me amongst the trees. This is incomprehensible foolishness."

Coming from Azaria that was bizarrely close to an emotional display.

Elina still had her arms lifted around her head, as if that would have done anything to protect her. "You are deranged!"

Azaria merely adjusted the bag she was wearing on her back, nearly as big as her and clinking ominously with what must have been a small armoury's worth of weapons.

Leda sank down into a crouch with a hand clutched to her heart.

Ambrose seemed to want to defuse the situation before strong words, let alone knives, were thrown. He jerked his head at Elina and Eber. "Let's go and rest a few minutes."

Leda and Azaria watched them go, not blind to the furious glances Elina sent back over her shoulder every few seconds.

"What in the gods' names are you doing here, Azaria?" Leda was not proud of how far her voice had climbed in octave.

Azaria climbed over a tree stump that separated them with admirable grace. She gave Leda as thorough as inspection as was possible with just a look.

"You are well?" Azaria asked, as if they'd just happened upon one another in a palace corridor. Anyone else would have offered a hand to help Leda up, but she knew the possibility hadn't so much as crossed her sister's mind.

Leda stood with a groan and dusted herself off. "I was until you scared the life out of us all. What are you doing here?"

"Ambrose told Pyrrhus where you were going before you left. I wanted to check that you weren't yet dead. These are dangerous times." Azaria scanned the treeline as though a band of screaming marauders might burst through at any second.

She didn't seem to realise she was the greatest danger in this forest.

"Sensitive as always," Leda said, taking in the belt of sharp weapons strung across her waist. She looked ready to take on an army. "Are you going to be our guard detail?"

"If I must. It was foolish for you to leave the palace without one in the first place. There have been multiple attempts on your life in the past month alone," Azaria said coldly. "I won't berate you further because I am tired of talking about it. The gods know it's all I've heard from *him* over the past few hours."

Leda froze. "Him?"

As though called, Pyrrhus appeared from between the trees. He looked particularly bad-tempered; overheated and rumpled in rough travel clothes.

Leda's mouth fell open at the sight of him without the pristine lines of his tail suit. The increase in her heart rate couldn't be solely attributed to the fact that, judging by his expression, she was in a whole new world of trouble.

Azaria turned her annoyed stare back to Pyrrhus. "It was like travelling with a whining child who's allergic to the sun."

Pyrrhus clearly did not appreciate that comparison. He turned to Azaria with all the bad temper of a person who'd been forced to spend an extended period of time with her.

"Oh, look," Pyrrhus growled. "There are Ambrose and Elina and Eber; why don't you speak with them about how we're all going to get back to the palace in one piece?"

Surprisingly, Azaria did his bidding without complaint. She probably didn't want to stick around to see Pyrrhus tear Leda apart for leaving without permission or protection.

He watched her go with such an aggrieved expression that Leda couldn't contain her snort.

"What?" he snapped.

For the first time in a long while Leda laughed, loud and unabashed. She would have paid all the money in her possession to watch her sister and Pyrrhus travel together as a team—equally intelligent, identically stubborn, one utterly deranged and the other steadfastly logical. That would give her enough stories to entertain her for the rest of her life.

A scratch marred Pyrrhus's hand and he was looking sourly down at it. When he sensed Leda's enquiring gaze he grimaced. "I was standing too close behind her, apparently."

Leda snickered. "You're lucky you got away with only a scratch."

Pyrrhus gave her the flat look of a man who would gladly pitch her sister into the shark-infested waters of Saint-Trevale if not for the fear that she'd come out the victor.

His expression turned dark; she knew she wouldn't have been able to distract him for long. "You left with no word, and no guards. You're well aware that someone is trying to kill you, and yet you put yourself in danger. Was what Melia told you worth it?"

Leda grimaced. She wasn't entirely sure that it was. "Perhaps. I'm sorry, though, for worrying you. We didn't want to draw attention to ourselves. We have to limit the people who know about this godsforsaken curse."

Except it wasn't godsforsaken, was it? It was their own work, co-created with the old King. Their father's final masterpiece, the legacy he left to the world, aside from a broken kingdom and a succession of increasingly damaged children.

Leda turned to follow the others but stilled as she felt

Pyrrhus's hand close around her upper arm. He was suddenly much closer to her than she'd anticipated, and every muscle in her body tensed.

"You need to stay away from Azaria." He bent his head towards her, voice so quiet she was surprised she could distinguish it over the sounds of the forest.

"What?" She turned into him until she felt his breath stir the hair at her temple.

"She's dangerous."

She looked up into those dark, dark eyes. His expression was unfathomable, as it so often was. "She's always been dangerous," she murmured. Azaria had been more lethal as a toddler than most grown men.

He narrowed his eyes at that. "Leda—"

"You're being ridiculous, you just travelled all the way here with her and you're still in one piece. Speaking of, why *are* you here? Why didn't you just send guards to get us?"

This conversation did not need to be conducted from such close proximity, but neither of them retreated. Leda vividly remembered the last time they'd been this close, how it had overwhelmed her into running away, and her blood heated in response.

From the look on his face he was experiencing a similar recollection. "I was ... unsettled. I couldn't focus not knowing you were safe."

She was surprised by the honesty of his response, and she knew she must look visibly flustered. His words implied things she wasn't ready to hear.

"Well, I'm quite alright, thank you," she said, taking a step back. The action felt so instinctively wrong it almost pained her. "Physically, that is. Mentally I feel like my brain has been pulverised beyond recognition."

He said nothing as she led him to where the others had gathered.

Ambrose let out a groan of pure exasperation when he saw Pyrrhus.

"What are *you* doing here? I told you just to send guards!" He looked at the trees around them as Azaria had earlier, as though expecting bandits to crash through and seize Pyrrhus. "This is so dangerous; what were you thinking?" His eyes slid accusingly to Leda, who maintained an innocent expression. If anything she was on his side; she didn't want Pyrrhus to come to harm through his recklessness either.

"I had Azaria with me," Pyrrhus said, unconcerned in the face of Ambrose's ire. "She's more frightening than any combination of guards I've ever seen, so I was in good hands."

Ambrose cast a dismissive look over at Azaria. "She's as likely to kill you herself as save you from anyone else."

"How lucky I am, then, that she chose the latter today," Pyrrhus said, a finality to his tone that quieted Ambrose. "We should make camp and then the four of you can tell me why you thought it was a good idea to undertake a journey through dangerous lands to talk to a famously unsocial priestess."

Eber looked up at that, mouth slack. "Make camp? We're not finding an inn for the night?"

"We could have until this fool turned up." Ambrose gestured at Pyrrhus. "We can't risk anyone recognising him; we'll have to stay here this evening and hurry back to the palace tomorrow. Let's hope nobody sees their king without protection and decides to take out their frustration on him."

"Alright," Leda said hastily as Pyrrhus opened his mouth to respond. "We can do that, can't we? We brought equipment for this. Let's build a fire and then we can sort out sleeping arrangements. Eber, would you gather some firewood please?"

Eber gave her the blank look of someone who had never built a fire in his life. When Leda directed Azaria to accompany him he didn't seem appreciative. He gave her a wide berth as they disappeared into the trees, nearly tripping over a sapling for his efforts.

Leda turned back to the rest of their horribly tempered group. Elina had sat on a log and was staring up at the sky as though she could interpret the thoughts of the gods from the shape of the clouds. Ambrose, meanwhile, was bringing Pyrrhus up to speed on what they'd learned in the temple.

Pyrrhus's expression became progressively grimmer as the story went on. When Eber and Azaria returned bearing armfuls of firewood Eber took one look at Pyrrhus's face and hesitated on the threshold of the clearing. Azaria strode right to the middle, loudly deposited her sticks on the ground, and began to build the fire.

Pyrrhus barely seemed to notice as he sank down on to the log next to Elina.

"So if I hadn't deposed the King, none of this would have happened. Thousands of people would still be alive, and hundreds of thousands more wouldn't be living in poverty."

"You weren't the only one involved in that coup," Ambrose said. "It was a choice that we all made, hundreds of us."

"It was for the greater good," Eber said. "Father killed thousands per year; it would hardly have changed the number of deaths. Only the method."

Pyrrhus had the look of someone who wanted to check the maths on that claim before he could be comforted by it.

"Stop this, Pyrrhus," Ambrose said firmly. "I'm tired of watching you punish yourself for what we did. That man enslaved millions, profited from their labour and killed them on a whim. And that's nothing compared to what he did to his own children. You need to move on."

"Ambrose—"

"No, I'm serious. You've done a lot of good since taking the Crown, and you'll be passing it on to one of the five families in better condition than when you received it. The new form of government will help the people immeasurably; in fact it already has. We saw the new wells when we crossed through the villages. That was the doing of your Ministry for Health and Prosperity."

Pyrrhus still looked thoroughly put out, but nodded.

Elina was focused on Azaria, who was looking in satisfaction at the fire she'd produced with no help at all from Eber. He was still leaning against a nearby tree looking cautious.

"Aren't you supposed to be in a dungeon right now?" Elina said.

"They found the men who kidnapped me. They were interrogated and confessed. My revenge against Linus was ruled lawful."

"Father's laws haven't yet been updated, then?" Leda asked Pyrrhus.

His face took on a conflicted expression. "Not quickly enough, it seems." She was sure he'd be rectifying that oversight quickly. "Also it appears all of the men disappeared on their way to the Gemdark prison. They haven't been seen since."

They all looked at Azaria, who stared back without blinking.

"Why are you even here?" Elina asked.

"Leda is in danger."

"Why would you care if she is?" The question from Eber was rude, but Leda was keen to hear the answer too.

"I'd prefer if she didn't die now."

"*Now*? When works for you, then?" Leda sputtered.

Ambrose's hands were circling his eyes with such force

Leda wondered if he was trying to gouge them out. "Azaria, would you please take your bow and secure us some dinner?"

They spent the next hour talking about the curse and what that could mean about the assassin who stalked them. When that became too frustrating a conversation to continue and the chilliness of night fell they broke apart and spaced themselves evenly around the fire.

Close to midnight, Leda became aware that she was being watched and raised her head to survey her companions. Pyrrhus sat between Eber and Ambrose opposite her. They talked across him in animated discussion, but his attention was focused on her through the flames. He clutched a tin tankard in both hands, and she had no idea what crossed his mind as his eyes fell to the skirts of her travel dress.

A twig snapped as Azaria sat down beside Leda and Pyrrhus turned away. He took a long draft from his tankard and yanked irritably at his collar.

"Why do you look so gormless?"

Leda turned to glare at her sister. "Did you have something you wanted to talk about?"

"You care about people, don't you?"

Leda had a distinct feeling she was not going to enjoy this conversation. She hesitated before replying to the strange question. "I do."

"Then why do you not lobby Pyrrhus to put a Locarno royal on the throne?"

She cast Azaria a scathing look. "Who should I advocate for, sister? Elina, who flies into rages more frequently than you do? Ten-year-old Fessler, who would be ripped apart by ambitious advisors? Annagret and Gabriell are practically babies so hardly candidates. I doubt father would have allowed for advisors treating his children as puppet monarchs anyway. And don't get me started on you ..." She'd saved the most unhinged for last. "Not to criticise your leadership style, Azaria, but I think the people would take their chances with tornados and tsunamis before they'd have you."

Azaria didn't seem offended. "You underestimate my abilities."

"Perhaps, but I know your cruelty. You're not meant to wield power over others, Azaria."

Her sister was quiet at that, contemplative.

"Besides, this is all moot," Leda said. "The five families have been brought together to compete fairly for the throne, for the first time in history. Their supporters will riot if the Crown is taken from them and given back to our father's line."

That didn't seem to trouble Azaria too much judging by the way she waved her hand. "They can be put down with ease."

"Really? You think the Bixel family wouldn't have the support of Saint-Trevale, who want them restored to rule? You think the tribes of North Doviet won't stand behind the Bakirts? Now that the gods aren't in father's pocket you wouldn't have battles, Azaria; you'd have full-scale wars and you'd be attacked from every front. These weather disasters would pale in comparison to the bloodshed."

"Where did you gain such knowledge of politics?"

"Pyrrhus talks a lot."

Azaria cast Pyrrhus an appraising look through the fire. "Wiser than all of us in many ways, and yet so singularly foolish." She shook her head.

"Speaking of foolish," Leda said grimly. "Do you know where your mother is? She appears to be the key to much of this. She'll likely know more than anyone about why the assassin is after us."

"I have no interest in the location of that woman. She could be dead for all I care."

Leda had expected nothing more than that, but was still disappointed. Ambrose had been wrong, then. "I see. Will you look for her? For us?"

"Perhaps. I will sleep now."

With no further fanfare Azaria left to the bed of thick leaves she'd gathered as far away from the others as she could reasonably manage.

Ambrose insisted on staying up to keep watch as the rest of them yawned. He ensured that his position gave him a clearer view of Azaria than anything else, so it was evident what he considered to be the real threat.

Leda rolled her eyes as she headed to her own sleeping spot near Eber.

The night was mild and the soft rustling of leaves quickly lulled them to sleep.

CHAPTER 21

*L*eda felt like she'd been asleep for mere seconds when she was awakened by a high-pitched sound.

Shooting up to a sitting position with a frantic rustle of displaced leaves, she followed the source of the noise to see Azaria tossing and turning on the ground, emitting what could only be sobs.

Surely not, Leda hadn't seen her cry in over a decade, she didn't even think her capable.

But her ears didn't lie to her. Azaria was caught in the grip of a nightmare, her face screwed up in anguish. Leda got groggily to her feet, ready to wake her, when a hand came down on her shoulder.

"It's best not to wake people from nightmares," Ambrose said quietly. "Particularly those who sleep with so many knives."

He was not incorrect.

"Since you're awake, and no longer creepily twitching like you're being struck by lightning," Ambrose continued, stifling a yawn as her face flushed to the tips of her ears. "You can keep watch now."

She winced, but she couldn't very well say no. Instead

she moved to the position Ambrose had just held, preparing to spend the night in a bored stupor. Azaria's cries had mellowed into barely audible whispers, and she was once more sleeping as immovably as a corpse.

~

Leda was shaking herself to stay awake when she heard the rustling of another member of their party getting up. Her heart leapt into her throat as she saw who it was.

Pyrrhus reached her with steps that were far too quick and precise for someone who'd been asleep so recently.

"What are you doing?"

"I'm keeping watch." Leda gestured out at the pitch darkness as though she could distinguish anything from the trees. There could be a vicious, bloodthirsty creature standing ten feet away and she'd probably be the last of them to realise.

She dropped the stick she'd been using to draw patterns in the dirt.

Pyrrhus sat beside her, closer than he usually would. He must have misjudged the space in the dark. "I've seen you fall asleep two pages into a book before the sun has set. You need someone to keep you awake."

He wasn't wrong, anybody could have crept up on their camp and Leda would have been more insensible to it than Eber, whose snores presently telegraphed their location to half the forest.

There were scant inches between Pyrrhus's arm and Leda's as he settled himself more comfortably on the leaf pile she'd scraped together.

She felt the proximity of him like crackling flames against her skin and glanced back at the camp a short distance away. The fire had reduced to glowing embers.

Nobody moved. She wondered how many of them were currently locked in nightmares like Azaria.

Musing on these thoughts as she was, she was oblivious to the building irritation in the man beside her.

"You drive me insane; are you aware of that?" Pyrrhus said abruptly. "Charging off into danger without a word to anyone."

Ah, that. "I really am sorry," she said. "I never meant to cause you stress."

"*Stress*," he scoffed, and then he was turning to face her, locking her gaze with his. "No one has caused me more stress in my entire life than you have over the last few weeks. Care to tell me what exactly happened in my study, before you ran away?"

She battled to keep her breathing steady. "I don't know what you're talking about," she whispered, more cowardly than ever.

"No more prevaricating," he said sharply.

Something in her snapped. "Fine, you want me to say it? It was a moment of weakness. We *almost* kissed, very scandalous; we should alert the newspapers."

"They'd be thrilled if you did," he said, voice low as his gaze moved over her face. "They're fascinated with my love life."

An ugly, unjustified bolt of jealousy shot through her. She was going mad; she didn't even know who she was jealous of, if there was anyone for the newspapers to speculate about in the first place.

"That wasn't ... it has nothing to do with ..." Her voice trembled as she trailed off.

"Liar."

She swivelled to look forward into the trees, breaking the eye contact that threatened to show him a depth of feeling she wasn't prepared for.

As usual, his being so near filled her brain with thick, undulating fog. His arm brushed hers as he shifted even closer and she huffed with a stab of what she felt must be annoyance. "Sorry, I appear to be in your way; would you prefer to sit on my lap instead?"

He was so, impossibly close. The frustration was clear to see on his face, but it took a different shape from what it had been mere seconds ago.

His eyes flicked up to hers and they were a bottomless black. He'd not taken her outburst for the weak sparring joke it was.

They'd played this game with one another countless times, each daring the other to move forward.

This time, he didn't back away.

"I think you'd prefer it the other way around," he said.

She let out a startled whimper as his hands clasped her waist and she was lifted and twisted around until she fell into his lap, clutching his shoulders to steady herself. Muscle flexed beneath her fingertips.

How could she feel so drunk having not touched a drop of wine? Her breath was coming fast, as though she'd spent the last hour running instead of scraping sticks against the ground. His body was firm against hers, the heat of him burning through her clothes, and she briefly wondered whether he'd developed a fever. She resisted the urge to put her hand to his forehead to check.

"What are you doing?" she hissed, her lips so close to his he probably felt her words more than he heard them. Desire shot through her veins like lightning, her body a complete traitor. "This isn't ... we're ... *friends*, Pyrrhus."

His breathing had sped up to match hers, and his eyes clamped shut as though he were in pain when she shifted restlessly on his lap. "I'm not feeling particularly friendly at the moment."

It took him a few seconds to collect himself as she stared at him, both of them balancing on the knife edge between action and inaction, as they always did. Leda bit her lip, her mind screaming that she should by no means tackle him down to the leaves mere metres away from her family.

Pyrrhus shook his head, as though lifting himself from a trance, and let out a rueful breath. "Sorry, sorry, you're right. You don't want this." He pushed her gently off him and she let out a deeply unladylike grunt as she was deposited on to the ground.

Then he was up and moving into the treeline with all the swiftness of a man being chased by a rabid animal.

That was a sensible way for him to move, Leda thought grimly as she staggered to her feet. He *was* being chased. By her. Enough was enough.

Her world was death and destruction and constant, unrelenting panic. Her principles lay in tatters around her. And nothing felt right when he wasn't around, as close to her as possible.

Something in her mind had broken, her thoughts rough and primal. She was tired of denying herself, of denying them both.

She caught up to him thirty seconds away from the camp, struggling to distinguish him in the darkness as the canopy of leaves deflected most of the moonlight. Pyrrhus moved deftly through the trees, unaware of her pursuit, lost in his thoughts as he was.

He quickly became aware, however. She made sure of it.

Taking his arm, Leda ignored his sound of surprise and used their combined momentum to push him against an oak tree ahead of him. His grunt when his back collided with the bark was guttural.

"I'm walking away, that's what you wanted," he growled. "You told me time and time again that you only—"

She kissed him. Went up on her tiptoes and pressed her lips to his. He tasted like the hot chocolate he pretended he didn't drink every evening. He must have brought some with him on the trip and heated it on the campfire, the lunatic.

It was wrong of her to do this. They were friends, nothing more. They'd agreed. She'd *made* him agree.

They were keeping watch over the camp. It was cold, damp and misty. She was too short to reach up and consume him properly like she wanted to.

Yet she couldn't stop. It was like a dam had broken, and she drowned in him.

Pyrrhus resisted her for all of five seconds before she felt his control crack into pieces beneath her hands. He went abruptly from a block of ice to a man seized by ravenous hunger. With a low moan he reached forward to grasp her by the hips and pull her body flush against his.

He broke away, leaving her gasping, and rasped against her temple. "Leda—"

Her lips were already fixed on the frantically beating pulse at his throat, just beneath the rasp of his jaw, and she felt him shudder down the length of his body. A heady, powerful feeling spread through her as she sought out his lips again.

This. This was what she needed. This was what made her feel alive. She could deal with the consequences later. They were future Leda's problem.

She was unaware that he'd spun her until she felt the tree up against her own back, his leg pressing up between hers to pin her in place as he consumed her with the ferocity of a man who had waited for so very long.

Every moment she'd looked up from her book and caught him watching her, the stroke of his hand over her back when he'd healed her after she'd been injured, the way he took her in his arms as he slept before she ran away.

It had all led to this, years of tension and denial releasing in one terrifyingly intense rush.

Leda whimpered at the pressure of his leg against her, pressing down when instinct told her to and gasping as a blazingly hot feeling shot up through her body.

She broke away from the kiss, her head hitting the bark behind her as she took in desperate pulls of air. Pyrrhus's lips blazed a trail of fire down her neck as his hands slid down to the curve of her lower back to pull her more tightly against him. She shuddered. "Please don't stop."

Where had this side of him come from? This was Pyrrhus: buttoned up, reserved and *controlled*, never speaking before carefully considering his words, never moving before he planned his next steps. He was not this man who looked at her with pure lust, setting her body on fire by running his hands over her as though he couldn't decide where he wanted them to land.

His hand was sliding under the fabric of her dress to clench around her shoulder before twisting the material as though he was going to rip it off her. Gods help her, she wanted to let him. "I—"

"Leda!" Though the sound came from far away it snapped them both out of their daze in an instant. Someone might as well have tipped a bucket of ice water over their heads.

Pyrrhus let go of her dress like it was covered in poison and staggered backwards. It took him a moment to recover himself, and then he was striding away into the darkness.

"Wait!" she hissed.

He stopped to look back at her and her heart clattered in her chest. The Pyrrhus she knew was gone, the man standing in his place debauched; his hair a mess, eyes glinting with an intensity she'd never seen before. His clothes were rumpled beyond recognition. She blushed brilliantly as she realised he looked like he could feasibly have been mauled by a wild animal.

He was a man undone, and, seeing Azaria approaching through the trees, he turned and left.

What a moron she was.

She'd broken one of the few rules she'd put in place to protect herself, to protect them both. She was supposed to *help* him, to provide support, not get swept up with the man on the throne.

She was such an idiot.

Leda tipped her head back against the tree, for a much less satisfying reason than the last time she'd done so.

Azaria took in Leda's hair half out of its bun, her swollen lips and rumpled dress and didn't bother to contain her disgusted expression. "Ugh ... why?" She looked out to where Pyrrhus had disappeared to and seemed to decide she didn't want an answer to that question. "You can't be trusted to watch over the camp when you're behaving like love-addled dimwits. Go to sleep; I'll take over."

Leda trudged numbly away and settled back down on her pile of leaves. This time nothing could calm her enough to sleep, and she spent the rest of the night staring up at the stars, hardly believing what she'd just done.

She'd opened a door, and she didn't know how to close it, or if she even wanted to.

CHAPTER 22

When Leda woke, she couldn't look at him.

Not that Pyrrhus would have noticed, as she was fairly sure he planned to go about his day as if they'd never touched each other in their lives.

Leda groaned at the effects of a night on the forest floor, her body frozen into a solid, immovable block that she had to coax into motion one limb at a time.

After they'd packed up and stamped out the remains of the fire, their ragtag group was on its way.

To their surprise Azaria was taking her self-determined role as protector of the group seriously, scanning the tree-line with ferocity. Her arms must have been aching from keeping her bow constantly raised, but they didn't so much as tremor in the hours it took them to cross the forest.

Pyrrhus headed up the group and Leda brought up the rear, breaking her silence only to shout at Azaria when she aimed her bow too close to her head.

When they reached the town they decided to hire a small carriage that could handle the rougher roads and get them back to Gemdark in good time.

Seeing the size of the transportation Ambrose had

managed to secure for them, Eber immediately claimed the seat next to the driver on the outside. The rest of them were left to pile into the carriage.

They attempted to situate themselves in the tiny space in a way that would lead to the least bloodshed. Azaria got one of the two benches to herself as she point-blank refused to have any part of her touching any part of them. Ambrose squashed himself against the opposite window and directed Pyrrhus next to him so he wouldn't be pressed against Elina. Elina, mortally offended by this, sat on the opposite end of the bench, forcing Leda to squeeze in between her and Pyrrhus.

His whole body was stiff as she approached. Though he didn't look at her, she had the feeling he was acutely aware of her movements as she settled in next to him. She could feel every place they touched, their legs pressed against each other down the length of their thighs. The feeling was intoxicating, dizzying.

Pyrrhus turned his head, jerked as he saw Ambrose's exasperated face staring back from inches away, and looked forward with a sigh. Azaria made unnerving, unblinking eye contact with him and Leda smirked as he closed his eyes to avoid it. He was probably cursing every decision he'd ever made that had led him into this carriage.

"Leda, you're crushing me to death," Elina announced as the carriage rolled into motion.

In her haste to avoid getting too close to Pyrrhus, Leda had sat partially on Elina's lap and was shoved none too gently off. Her shoulder collided with Pyrrhus's and his hand came down automatically on her knee to steady her as she pitched forward. He pulled it away at her sharp intake of breath.

Azaria watched them all with the air of someone who could not believe that she associated with such people.

Blushing brilliantly, Leda stared up at the roof of the carriage. She wished she were riding up there instead; she'd be happy to cling on to the top for dear life for the rest of the journey. It would be less uncomfortable than it was in here. Curse Eber for taking the space outside with the driver; he had an enviable ability to anticipate and skirt awkward situations.

The tension sizzled between her and Pyrrhus, but they stayed silent.

A huge number of guards met them en route, and to Leda's delight they'd brought carriages aplenty with them. Pyrrhus, Ambrose and Eber disappeared into one, and Elina, Leda and Azaria wordlessly agreed that they would each take a carriage themselves. They'd had enough of each other to be going on with.

Leda lay down on the luxurious velvet bench of her quiet carriage, stretching muscles that ached from a few hours' compression.

She thought about the look on Pyrrhus's face as he'd pushed her against that tree, the feel of his hands on her, the mist that had enveloped her mind as she'd dragged him down into madness with her. Then she forced herself to go to sleep, as those thoughts had no business swirling around her mind.

The gentle rocking of her carriage carried her in peaceful slumber all the way into Gemdark and up the road to the palace. The clattering of hooves on the gravel drive woke her, and she blearily sat up in time for a guard to open her door.

Zephyr waited on the steps for them, head turned in the direction of Azaria's carriage as though he could sense it was the one that carried her. No one had as much talent as he did for being vaguely disconcerting.

Leda hung back to watch everyone as they made their

way into the palace. Pyrrhus took quick strides, already issuing orders to the council members who had spilled down the steps at his arrival, Ambrose and Eber on his heels. Elina had yanked her prayer garland from the pocket of her dress and was stalking up the stairs, clearly heading for the temple.

Azaria had stopped to talk to Zephyr, and whatever he was telling her was clearly not pleasing her. She waved him away with a dismissive hand, but he persisted, following her into the shadows of the entrance hall.

It was a sleepy morning, and the court seemed content to linger late in bed or stroll slowly through the halls after too much indulgence the night before.

The situation outside Leda's rooms, however, was a different story. A cluster of guards stood outside her door in deep conversation, and she recognised Atticus among them. He looked even more serious than usual.

Wordlessly, he held a red velvet pouch out to Leda. The other guards fell silent as she peered inside.

"My hibcus," she said blankly. "Why do you have this? Have you been in my rooms?"

"Someone was seen sneaking out of Elina's rooms yesterday evening by a servant. I ordered a full search of every royal child and Counterpart's residence. We had a sample of all of your medicines tested. Nothing wrong with any except yours, this pouch of hibcus has been poisoned."

Leda felt all the blood leave her face. "Poisoned," she repeated weakly.

Atticus nodded. "Arcanroot, ground into a fine powder and mixed in. We're going to conduct a full search of your rooms to ensure we haven't missed anything. You'll be allowed back this evening when we've concluded our assessment."

Leda nodded. "I ... of course. Thank you, that's ... well, thank you, Atticus."

She became aware that the pouch of hibcus was dangling from one hand and turned away. She needed to report this, and she knew just who she had to go to.

It took her a little while to find him.

Pyrrhus was in the royal library at his favourite desk by the far window, two stacks of books piled before him. A glance at the covers revealed they were dense texts on theology and the workings of the gods, as though any of those authors could provide anything other than pure guesswork.

Pyrrhus seemed to be of the same opinion. He was staring down at one book with a look of mixed frustration and derision on his face. He glanced up as she emerged from between the shelves, and his face transformed.

He looked guarded, as though he expected her to either yell at him or sweep the books from his desk and accost him the way she'd done the previous night. The image of that, the sheer possibility of it, flooded her vision, but she kept her expression carefully blank. No good would come of that.

Oh, but it would feel excellent at the time.

"Leda," Pyrrhus said in greeting, snapping his book shut.

She stopped two feet away, bending over the desk to get her face level with his. He registered the view she'd inadvertently given him down the front of her bodice and looked as though he'd like to give her a strongly worded lecture.

"Look at this." She waved the hibcus pouch under his nose.

Academic curiosity consumed him as it always did, and he switched his attention to the powder. "What is it?"

"Poison."

His reaction was pure instinct. No sooner had the word left her mouth than he'd smacked the pouch away from him, clear out of her hand. It landed on the floor and spilled everywhere.

"That'll be tricky to get out of the carpet."

"Did you just put *poison* by my face?"

"Relax, it's perfectly safe unless you ingest it."

That did not stop his indignant sputtering.

Pyrrhus stood and rounded his desk to remove the obstacle from between them. Leda straightened up. Her breathing had quickened but she showed no other sign she was affected by his proximity. Thankfully, he wasn't in a state to notice.

"Where did you even acquire that?"

"In my rooms, the guards did a search before we returned and they tested my medicines. Someone laced my hibcus with arcanroot while I was gone."

Pyrrhus passed an exhausted hand over his face. "Of course they did."

"I thought it might be of interest. Anyway, I'll leave you alone now."

She should apologise to him for what she'd started between them in the forest, should beg forgiveness for being such a hypocrite. For pulling him towards her and pushing him away in equal measure. But the words died in her throat.

He muttered something and she turned to give him an arch look.

"Yes?"

Pyrrhus settled himself back behind his desk with a frustrated sigh. "Nothing. I'll see you at dinner. I—what are you doing?"

Leda had taken a few books from his pile and was crouching down to create a wall around the spilled powder.

"I don't want anyone accidentally stepping in this until it's been cleaned up." She pilfered more books from his desk and used them to create an unstable roof on her structure. "There, I'll go and alert some servants." She got to her feet.

He wasn't where she'd left him. The seat behind the desk was empty, still rocking slightly, and she stifled her gasp as Pyrrhus's arm brushed hers. He wasn't looking at her though, instead staring down at his books.

"I need those."

"They're full of nonsense and you know it," Leda said. "Even if they weren't just the self-important ramblings of priestesses they'll hardly contain instructions on how to break curses. You have hundreds of scholars at your disposal; why not set them to the task? Or any of us, we'd be happy to help. You should go back to planning the next trial and stop trying to fix everything yourself."

"Is that what you think?"

"Yes. Finish the trials, pass on that damned crown and step down, Pyrrhus."

"So I should focus on the succession? Ignore the curse that blights the kingdom and will do so long after a new king or queen takes the throne? And the numerous threats on your life, too?"

"There have always been threats on my life, it's who I am. There's nothing you can do about that."

Pyrrhus shook his head, stubborn as always. "There are answers somewhere; it's a matter of finding them."

"Let someone else. You've done enough; let it go." She sat down opposite as he resumed his seat behind the desk. As much as neither of them wanted this conversation, they needed to have it.

"No."

She could scream with exasperation. "Do you enjoy doing this to yourself? Piling the weight of the world on your shoulders and torturing yourself with impossible tasks? Driving yourself insane trying to predict who might try to kill us next? Do you derive pleasure from your own suffering?"

His chair hit the window behind it with a clatter due to the force with which he rose from it. It was almost comical, he'd barely lasted five seconds sitting in it since she'd entered the room.

Once again he was circling the desk and then he was right in front of her.

"You think I want this?" he said, his normally steady voice anguished. "Do you think I want to spend every second of every day worrying that something will happen to you? That I've dragged you from your home into even more danger? All the while forcing myself to remember that you want nothing to do with me?" He let out a furious breath, stepping away but only for a second before rounding on her once more. "Do you think that's a productive use of my time?"

Instinct told her it would be wise not to answer that.

His jaw clenched as he looked down at her. "I am the king."

She made a face as though someone had placed rotting meat under her nose.

He held up a hand as her lips parted, going to his knees in front of her and caging her in with his hands on the arms of her chair. "Regardless of your opinion on the matter, it's true. I chose this, and I know it was a choice that betrayed you but I made it nevertheless. I am the king, responsible for millions of lives, lives that are under threat as we speak. I have to oversee the selection of a new monarch, determine how to break your father's curse and protect your siblings. I bear *enormous* responsibility. It should be all I can think about. But it's not."

The air whooshed out of her lungs as if she'd been physically struck.

"I'm sorry," she whispered. "I made it worse. I shouldn't have gone after you in the woods; it wasn't fair of me. I wasn't thinking clearly."

His face was inscrutable. "We both made mistakes, as I recall."

She shook her head. "No, it was me. I literally stalked you through the trees like a predator, as if I was going to return to camp with your carcass slung over my shoulder."

He blinked at the image she'd forced into his head and opened his mouth to respond.

"A royal on his knees before a Counterpart; wonders never cease."

Azaria stood in a nearby aisle of books, bathed entirely in darkness like some kind of malignant shadow.

Pyrrhus's knuckles went white on the arms of Leda's chair and his head fell forward in frustration. Due to their proximity that meant his forehead was nearly in her lap, and Leda had to force herself to breathe manually as her body had apparently forgotten how to do it.

"What do you want, Azaria?" Leda said from between gritted teeth. Pyrrhus was standing then, putting distance between them, and she wanted to grab the last remaining book on his desk and throw it at her sister's face.

"I want to speak with you."

"Unless you're here to tell me that you've found your mother, or a way to break the curse, I'm not interested in having a discussion right now."

"Azaria!"

Zephyr rounded the corner, visibly out of breath.

"I've been looking for you everywhere! What are you doing with these two?" He didn't bother to bow to Pyrrhus, and Leda reassessed who she'd actually like to strike with a book.

A flicker of annoyance passed across Azaria's face, almost imperceptible.

"Do not presume to tell me where to go or who to see."

Zephyr's manner changed instantly. "Of course, Princess, my apologies."

Pyrrhus reached into a pocket, withdrew a green pouch, and threw it on to the desk. Leda and Azaria looked at it with confusion, while the colour drained from Zephyr's face at the sight.

"Where did you get that?" he asked.

"From you," Pyrrhus said simply. "I must admit I had a low opinion of you, Zephyr, but even I didn't think you'd sink to underhanded tricks to win the throne."

Zephyr was speechless.

"You said I should be working on the fourth trial, Leda, but it has already concluded. I had agents of the guard approach each candidate and offer to sabotage their opponents in return for money. Zephyr asked them to kidnap Thalia's daughter Selene." He turned to Zephyr. "Presumably you knew of the strength of their connection, that Thalia would focus on nothing else until she was found. She would have likely withdrawn from the trials."

Zephyr stared at him with a mutinous expression, but Pyrrhus needed no response. He picked up the pouch and tossed it at Zephyr.

He caught it, but not before it hit his chest with the telltale clink of coins.

"You'll be unsurprised to know that Thalia refused to sabotage you, and that Pan also declined. Though I worry that's more because he's famously cheap. Regardless, they both ranked higher than you in this trial."

Zephyr slid a careful look to Azaria. She appeared, as she often did, like she couldn't care less about the conversation going on around her.

"I suppose you've made me the fool, Pyrrhus," Zephyr said. "Let's see how long that smug smile sits on your face. I doubt you'll be happy for long."

Leda had had enough. "Azaria, can you take him away please? He's exhausting."

To Zephyr's surprise, Azaria jerked her head at him and disappeared back into the bookshelves. Reluctantly, he followed.

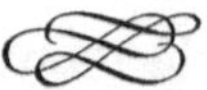

CHAPTER 23

As they approached their conclusion, the trials became uglier. Tensions boiled over between the five families, or three families as it was now given neither Slofray nor South Doviet had agreed on replacements for Melia and Linus.

Pan and Zephyr got themselves into such a fierce, wine-fuelled fight one evening that guards had to be called when Zephyr produced a sword that nobody had seen him enter with and swung it. He didn't do so with any accuracy, being quite tipsy, and so they'd had to help him extract it from where it was embedded in a wooden table.

Thalia also got into a screaming match with Arsen based on a salacious comment he made about her daughter. It ended with her husband dragging her away as she threatened to have him fed to her dogs.

The violence in the air made Pyrrhus more paranoid than ever. The palace was also bursting with dignitaries from all over the lands, the pressure of their scrutiny on the candidates causing them to lose their minds.

When Castor, tired of being followed everywhere by a stream of adoring fans from Rivernesse nobility, screamed a maid into tears upon finding her in his rooms when he wanted to be alone, Pyrrhus put his foot down.

He removed the candidates with him to Gemdark University. He asked Leda to join for good measure, given he apparently expected her assassination to occur the moment she stepped out of his eye line. She'd chosen not to examine her reasons for saying yes too closely.

He also brought around a hundred guards, but that was Pyrrhus's standard method of operation by that point, so it surprised nobody.

Though loathe to leave her siblings, Leda was happy with the idea of a brief change in scenery. She'd seen an illustration of the famous university in a book she'd stolen from the Leatherfell library when she was a teenager and was keen to see it in person.

It had been built to intimidate, atop a hill that swept up from the southernmost point of Gemdark. A cluster of white marble buildings in concentric circles around a central clock tower.

The best and the brightest from the kingdom studied and researched there. It had the added benefit of being well known to Pyrrhus, who had taught there and continued to give guest lectures in what little spare time he had.

The university was also, and she was sure this had no bearing on his decision, a fortress. It had once been the stronghold of a king, hundreds of years before the Locarnos had come sniffing around the throne.

The students were in a frenzy of excitement at their arrival and Leda found herself once again at the centre of attention. She spent most of her time in the secure rooms that had been allocated to her in the central tower, watching the hustle and bustle and raucous laughter of students from her balcony.

It was fascinating, how freely they talked and joked with

one another, how relaxed they seemed.

When she ventured out into the grounds herself she was watched with curiosity, but everyone who approached was fastidiously polite. They were likely intimidated by the guards that hung on her like a forbidding coat.

Even so, it was refreshing to be in a different environment, to see new faces, and to experience a library that made the one at the palace look like a single shoddily constructed bookshelf by comparison. It gave her time to think, to strategise about what she needed to do to keep her remaining siblings safe and well.

Even though the representatives of the five families were staying with them at the university, Leda saw little of them after they arrived.

Azaria was rarely at the university, so that explained where Zephyr was all day.

Thalia and her family could be seen around occasionally, but they kept to a tight group. They stayed far from the students with justified suspicion. They were high-profile targets and surrounded by strangers. Linus's barely cold body had shown them just how easily their lives could end, and Thalia was taking no chances where her daughter was concerned.

Pan, Arsen and Castor were in their element. Pan returned to the lecturing role he'd previously held for the university's botany department and swept around wearing stuffy old robes that most teachers had stopped wearing fifty years before.

Arsen and Castor weren't interested in the academic opportunities on offer, but Leda heard that they availed themselves of the free drinks available in the university inn whenever they spoke of their brother's possible ascension to the throne.

Castor couldn't have been imbibing too heavily, though,

given how he appeared at Leda's elbow numerous times each day in a perfectly charming state.

His excuses for approaching her wore thin after the third day. He'd insisted on giving her a tour of the campus. He'd brought her a basket of fresh oranges, supposedly filled with vitamins to brighten her complexion.

He also showed her a painting he'd made of the Grand Temple in the Red Mountains of Slofray, which was finely done. She'd resisted the urge to tell him that the priestesses were a gaggle of liars and their mountains were pink.

Leda had made all the appropriate noises at the painting and then looked at Castor as he'd stared at her expectantly. She had the constant feeling that they were speaking a different language, like he expected responses from her that she couldn't imagine.

The following afternoon Castor found Leda sitting on a bench in the courtyard with a book. He plonked himself down beside her with a grin. The bench was old and weathered and creaked miserably under his weight.

Leda closed her book with a tiny, suppressed sigh.

"Castor," she said with a smile. "How are you this morning?"

"All the better having seen your beautiful face."

She still wasn't used to the compliments, they made her fight the urge to squirm, but she tried to respond as gracefully as possible.

"That's good ... then. I mean, thank you." She wasn't doing well at the graceful part. Sometimes Castor's eyes flickered when she spoke and she was terrified that her awkward nature was so pervasive it was actually infecting the people around her. If she made this charismatic man lose his social skills when he was with her she might as well move to the North Doviet desert and abandon society altogether. "How—oh!"

He'd pivoted to face her, one knee up on the bench in between them, and had grabbed her hands. His skin was rough, unpleasantly so.

"I've tried to hold myself back, but I can do so no longer."

Leda gave an experimental tug on her hands and they didn't move in his grip. Wonderful.

"What are you holding yourself back from?" she asked warily.

"Declaring myself to you, of course."

"Declaring yourself?" Had her vocabulary shrunk to only the words he'd said to her? She feared so.

"You're a fascinating woman, Leda."

She couldn't fathom how he could find her interesting. That wasn't as self-deprecating as it sounded—she was plenty interesting to a small group of people, but she faded into the background whenever Castor entered a room. She was the audience to whom he performed; there was never much reciprocation expected from her, only laughter or an impressed smile. He would give a witty remark and look at her expectantly and she would wonder whether breaking into a round of applause would be too much.

He let go of her hands and she pulled them back with relief, occupying them with her book in case he got any ideas to repeat the action.

"Thank you, that's very kind of you to say."

"I mean it. You're beautiful and bright and demure. I couldn't have designed a more perfect woman if I tried."

Leda gave him a quizzical look, and an unwelcome realisation hit her like a cold slap. She knew exactly what she was to him; she was the blank canvas on to which he'd painted his ideal woman.

Oh, poor Castor. Poor her, come to think of it.

"Castor, why are you saying this?"

He gave a rakish smile. "I'm making such a hash of it, aren't I? I suppose you're not used to these kinds of declarations from men."

She was fairly sure she should be offended by that. "What kind of declarations?" If Eber was a golden retriever, then Leda was a parrot. She needed to get a grip on herself.

"My feelings for you, of course. I care for you deeply, Leda, and I'd like to court you."

She blinked. "Why?"

Castor pursed his lips as though thinking he'd praised her intelligence a little too soon in the conversation. A flash of what she could have sworn was irritation crossed his face. "All ... all the reasons I just gave?"

"Because I'm demure?" He didn't know her at all if he thought that was true.

Ambrose would choke in indignation if he heard someone thought that and then demand a written explanation from them as to why.

Castor's face was starting to fall. "I gather by how difficult you're making this that you're not interested in me courting you?"

And there it was. She wasn't going to give him what he wanted, and so the tantrum would be incoming shortly. She could see it in the pinching of his lips, the flush creeping up his cheeks. Goodness, growing up with Azaria had taught her a lot.

"I'm sorry if it disappoints you, but no. I think very highly of you, Castor; please don't mistake me on that. But we're not right for one another."

"Because of Pyrrhus."

She slumped against the back of the bench as something twisted in her chest. "No, not because of him."

Leda was sure she'd have the same perspective even if she'd never met Pyrrhus. Castor had an appealing face and charm but was so impressed with his own attributes there was no consideration in his mind for another person. His eventual wife would only ever be an admirer, a Castor devotee. She would never be a partner, his equal in all things. Leda couldn't live that life, she'd stood in Azaria's shadow for too long to swap it with someone else's.

She watched Castor's building rage and was vividly recalled to all the times she'd argued with Pyrrhus. There hadn't been a single moment where she'd seen danger in his eyes, no feeling in her stomach that told her she should be careful. He'd never done anything but respect her wishes, even when he disagreed, the most honourable man she'd ever known.

She never felt more safe than when she was with him.

"Don't lie to me," Castor said flatly. "Don't expect me not to notice how pathetically you pant after him. It's embarrassing and everyone in the palace can see it. They talk about it like it's all a great joke, the uneducated Counterpart lusting after the royal tutor. I was giving you a chance to move past that, to mature, but apparently you don't want to."

Her fingers dug into the spine of her book. She did not want this man, he was *wrong* for her.

And she knew with sudden, cutting clarity who was right for her, who had been all along, who would retain his vicelike hold on her no matter how long he sat on that wretched throne.

The unwelcome thought generated panic in her unlike anything she'd ever known, hitting her so hard she almost forgot what Castor was talking about.

She was such a fool, had been in denial for so long.

She took a moment to gather herself. "You're right." She swallowed, trying to calm herself down. "I don't want to move past that. I think this conversation is over—"

"I don't know why I bothered to consider you as an

option." Castor stood and towered over her, his face twisting to become something ugly in the harsh glare of the sunlight. "The most boring girl in the world obsessed with the dullest man I've ever met, it has a kind of poetry to it I suppose. Why should I want to get involved with your insane family anyway?"

"Now, wait a minute—"

"One psychopathic sister who's a second away from killing whoever she's standing next to, one preachy little gods obsessive, an attention-starved brother drinking himself to death and a gaggle of ill-bred, bad-mannered children."

It took great effort to refrain from throwing her book at him.

"Why did you proposition me, then?" she snapped. "If I'm so lacking in appeal and my family is repulsive, why approach me at all?"

"I don't know."

Oh, but they both knew. He saw an opportunity, petty magpie that he was, to take the mysterious shiny thing that had enraptured the boy he'd marked as his adversary at such a young age. If taking her hurt Pyrrhus, the courtship would be all the sweeter.

"You're not worth the effort, especially now," he spat.

"Leave, Castor, or I'll call over my guards."

She could see them peering around the side of a nearby building, their helmets gleaming in the light. They watched Castor with narrowed eyes.

Castor looked as though he were going to provoke her into calling them over, to test her mettle, but instead he bared his teeth and let out a disbelieving laugh. Shaking his head as though he couldn't fathom what was going on in hers, he stalked off towards the professors' hall.

Leda was glad to see the back of him.

CHAPTER 24

*L*eda tried to absorb herself in her book once more, but it was no good. She'd read the same paragraph four times by the time she gave up, too riled up to take anything in. She knew what she had to do next, to dispel the tight feeling in her chest, but it didn't mean she wanted to do it.

It would require her to make herself vulnerable in a way she'd never allowed before, to open up to something that thrilled and scared her in equal measure.

It took some searching, but she found Pyrrhus lecturing in the main building and waited in the shadows at the back of the theatre.

She remembered the moments she used to spend hidden away in a supply cupboard by his classroom in the palace, stealing the knowledge he was imparting to her royal siblings. The thought of how far she'd come since then made her smile.

He could engage a crowd of a hundred with as much ease as he engaged her back then. She wasn't surprised to see the absolute quiet, the lack of fidgeting, the riveted faces.

When Pyrrhus finished his lecture there was a great

scraping of chairs against the floor as students prepared to leave. Jovial chattering swirled through the room, echoing off the high arched ceiling.

As the final students filtered out around Leda there remained two people at the bottom of the tiered steps. Pyrrhus was smiling as he slid a stack of papers into his leather satchel and a student twittered on at him.

She was beautiful, with light red hair curled into a coil on top of her head, her dress conservative and tastefully tailored. She held a stack of books and fluttered her lashes in a way that made something ugly curl in Leda's chest.

The sight of Pyrrhus's smile normally made Leda's day. Today it made her feel rather ill.

Pyrrhus hadn't been smiling recently, certainly not at her. When he looked at her it was with worry and fear, as though afraid she'd disappear before his eyes.

"Thank you, that's very kind of you," she heard him say as she descended the stairs towards them.

He looked up at the sound of her approach and faltered with his satchel. "Leda?" There was that concern again, as though he had to block his first instinct to inspect her for injuries.

Every time he saw her he was palpably relieved that she wasn't dead. Sweet, but not really the effect she wanted to have on him.

The woman looked up at Leda with wide eyes, blind-sided by fading so quickly into the background of his attention.

Leda nodded at her. It wasn't her fault she was besotted with him, he was an intelligent and infuriatingly good-looking man who wore the crown well. Leda would be a hypocrite if she judged another for being attracted to the same qualities she was.

The woman's mouth curved into a polite reciprocal

smile as she took Leda in, eyes lingering on the slight falter whenever Leda rested her weight on her right leg as she descended.

She turned back to Pyrrhus and sank into a deep curtsey. "I'll leave you now. Thank you again for giving us your time, Your Majesty."

She nodded at Leda as she swept past and up the stairs to exit the theatre.

Pyrrhus's gaze hadn't moved from Leda's face since he'd first noticed her presence.

She ran a finger over the soft feather of a quill standing in a pot on the lectern. "Am I supposed to curtsey to you?" she asked idly.

His lips twitched. "You curtsey to no one."

"Quite right."

She watched him take a breath, as though he'd forgotten to draw in any air as she approached.

"That was a beautiful woman. And she was floored by you," Leda said. "Yet you showed no interest?"

He looked up at the door the woman had disappeared through with disbelief on his face, as though the mere thought was insane. Then he rolled his eyes. "No."

Leda swallowed, her attention on the thrumming pulse at his throat. "I never asked whether you'd ... whether you'd moved on. We ... I wouldn't have judged you if you had—" She broke off in frustration, couldn't get the words out in the order she wanted.

His jaw flexed, but he said nothing.

"You'd have been well within your rights to pursue someone else."

"Would I?" he asked dryly.

"Of course."

"Well, that solves all my problems, doesn't it? Now that

I've secured your approval." His mouth twisted around that final word.

There was a silence that had her fidgeting. "Do you *want* to move on?" Because she would let him if that was what he needed, even if it clawed something vital out of her to do it. Even if it meant she watched him abdicate and went home to Saint-Trevale alone and devastated.

He went to sit at the desk and evidently changed his mind, rounding on her instead. "How long were you gone from the palace?"

It was such an abrupt change in topic that she blinked. "I ... about a year?"

"Three hundred and forty-two days," he snapped. "And I thought of you on every single one of them."

Her lips parted and nothing came out.

Then he was stepping closer, filling up her vision. "Let me be clear with you, Leda, because I'm tired of equivocating on this. Any woman who showed interest in me ceased to exist the moment I looked out the window and saw you standing in that river," he said with a bluntness that astonished her. "When you walk into a room, everyone else disappears. It's a problem, has been for years, and everyone knows it. Everyone except you, apparently."

Now Leda was the one struggling to draw breath. "Oh," she said, an unjustifiably small response to the enormous piece of himself he'd just given her.

"I'm not asking anything of you," he said, his voice as stiff and formal as it had been at the beginning of their acquaintance. "I'm simply being honest. You want to know why I haven't moved on? There's your answer. But I respect that you want to be my friend, that you desire nothing more. You think I'm power-hungry and deplorable; I understand that."

She shook her head, so overwhelmed that she could

only focus on the least of her objections. "You are not power-hungry; you're a self-sacrificing martyr."

His lips quirked. "Semantics." He was admirably composed for someone who'd just revealed what he had. He seemed almost relieved, like he'd just lifted a great weight from his shoulders. "And you? Have you moved on? With Castor?" He said that name as though it were an abominable curse word.

She huffed, eyes fixed on the floor. "He did just ask if he could court me."

He moved away at that, putting space between them, and she hated it. "So that's why you're here. Given the tangent I just went on, if your intention is to announce your engagement that'll be appallingly embarrassing."

She shook her head, the very thought laughable.

"I said no," she said hurriedly. "He wants a meek wife, someone to laugh at his stories and watch for him constantly. He thinks I'm biddable and he can shape me into whatever he likes."

She was gratified to see Pyrrhus scoff like that was the most ridiculous thing he'd ever heard.

"You are many things, Leda, but biddable is not one of them."

"Indeed."

"You barely even listen to half the things I ask you to do."

She gave him a small smile. "You want obedience? Buy a puppet."

He shook his head and leaned back against the desk, surveying her with that penetrating gaze. "Were you disappointed? Was it the manner of his approach that you objected to, or the man?"

It was surprising that someone so intelligent, who could mesmerise crowds of restless students with his voice alone, could be so blind.

"Castor is a charming man of significant means." His arm jerked unnaturally as he gave the compliment.

"You'd support me, then, if I chose him?"

The word 'yes' seemed to take monumental effort for him to get out of his mouth, but he did it.

There was that martyr complex again. A surge of frustrated affection flooded Leda.

"He is nothing."

Pyrrhus's eyes widened at the bluntness of her statement.

"I'm not trying to be rude, or cruel," Leda said. "Castor just isn't *you*. And therefore he's not a prospect. I never considered him, even for a second. And when he was trying to convince me"—she finally met his gaze—"all I could think of was you."

His expression did not so much as flicker.

"That's *my* problem, you see? All I can ever think about is you," she said softly, as though the quieter her voice the less of an admission of huge vulnerability this was. "I had to come here straight away because I wanted to see you and talk to you and ask if you'd be open to"—her confidence faltered, but she ploughed on regardless—"to revisiting our previous agreement."

There was that unreadable expression on his face that always drove her to distraction. "Which one?"

He was being purposely obtuse and she deserved it. "About being together once you abdicate? The trials are ending soon and you'll finally be free and ... if we're both feeling the same way, it makes sense."

A less romantic proposition surely had never been made. It was so embarrassingly ham-fisted that she wanted to dig a hole in the ground outside and go live in it, never to be heard from again.

"How very logical," Pyrrhus said, but there was amusement in his voice. "And would the same rules apply as last time?"

She had only a second to feel relieved he was considering her proposition before realising that the air between them had started to thrum with tension. She'd banned him from touching her, the last time they'd struck this bargain. She'd known back then that the second he did her resolve would crumble into nothing.

That hadn't changed.

"I still hate the Crown."

"I don't want you to worry that you've been unclear about that," he said in that sardonic, teasing tone of voice she loved so much.

Agitation flooded her, igniting something hot and restless in her veins. She shifted from one foot to the other, not sure how to disperse the energy.

His eyes darkened. "You're moving about like you do when you're tipsy," he observed.

It *was* a kind of drunkenness, she supposed. Her entire nervous system was lit up and crackling with the force of what she felt for him, what she'd allowed herself to experience after such a long time spent repressing it. It consumed her.

Oh so slowly, realisation spread across his features. And then the calm, collected man before her disappeared between one breath and the next and he was stepping in to her and her chest was against his and the backs of her thighs were colliding with the desk.

He reached for her, and pulled away just as quickly as two people crashed into the room.

Bitter disappointment surged as they broke apart. Leda rounded on the intruders.

Two very similar-looking intruders, both with inky black hair and frosty eyes.

It seemed Azaria had brought her mother to pay them a visit.

Celandine was not doing this of her own free will judging by the scratches across her face and the fact that her arm was twisted viciously behind her back. Her stooped position didn't keep her from casting a superior sneer down towards Leda and Pyrrhus.

"Azaria, what are you doing?"

"You asked for my mother; here she is." Azaria punctuated this statement by throwing Celandine down the last few steps. She almost staggered into the blackboard but stopped just in time, turning to glower at her daughter.

"I had you trained too well, it seems."

Azaria ignored that. "I tracked her down, hiding like a coward in a temple in Doviet. She was trying and failing to blend in with the other priestesses."

Leda hadn't even known that Azaria had travelled out of Gemdark, let alone Viridiana. Come to think of it, she hadn't seen her skulking in shadowy corners for the last few days.

Pyrrhus recovered faster than Leda did. He lifted a nearby chair, placed it down next to Celandine and pointed at it. "Sit, please."

She gave him a look of utter contempt. "The only ruler of the Five Kingdoms I recognise is my husband. I do not obey *your* orders, upstart charlatan."

She spat at his feet.

But this was not a man who operated according to his ego, as she was accustomed to. The previous King would have lost his mind so quickly and violently that the spit on the floor would be joined in short order by the dead body of the person who'd dared insult him.

Pyrrhus, though, his expression did not change. He

didn't tremble with rage; redness did not reach his face. He merely stood there.

"It was not an order; it was a suggestion," he said glacially. "And need I remind you that your husband is dead?"

"I think of it always; I don't need reminding." Her point made, Celandine sank down on to the chair. She was shivering violently, as if she'd been thrown into a vat of icy water. Azaria had done some damage during her capture. "What do you want from me?"

"There is a curse on the kingdom," Leda said.

Celandine raised an eyebrow and kept her mouth shut, not deeming Leda worthy of a response.

She ploughed on regardless. "We went to see Melia at the Grand Temple." Celandine's mouth curled with derision at the mention of the other priestess. "She told us that a Locarno must sit on the throne for the gods to be content, and until then they will rip the lands apart."

Celandine was leaning forward, waiting for her to say more, and when Leda fell silent she tipped her head back and laughed. "Is that all she told you?"

A chasm opened up in Leda's stomach. If she was truthful with herself she could admit that she'd suspected as they'd walked out of the Grand Temple that they were leaving the truth behind, still largely concealed.

Celandine stifled her laughter. "Melia always was a hopeless, wet fool."

"Speak plainly, Mother," Azaria snapped. She hadn't descended the rest of the steps to join them, was still hovering above them.

"Melia cannot relay bad news, nor can she stand confrontation of any kind. She's famous for it. She cannot conceive of a difficult conversation and will avoid it at all costs. That's why she fled the trials and presumably why she fed you half-truths she thought you'd be able to bear." Celandine's eyes were lit up from within with malice. They'd placed an opportunity to torture them directly into her lap, and she revelled in it.

Leda was close to losing her patience. She didn't know how Azaria could stand so stoic and silent above them. "Why don't you enlighten us?"

She attempted to steel herself against what was coming. They would cope with it, whatever it was.

"What Melia told you is true," Celandine said. "But what's missing is critical. If you put a Locarno child on the throne now the gods would still rain destruction down upon the Five Kingdoms. For there is a second condition that must be met before the curse can be removed." She looked straight at Leda with those piercing eyes, so like Azaria's. "All of the Counterparts must die, as originally agreed with your father. Every single one. The method doesn't matter, only that it happens."

And there it was.

Some part of Leda, the darkest, most bitter place in her mind, hissed that she'd been naive to think the death sentence had been lifted from her. To think that she could be special, or worth anything. That she could actually do something with her life.

Leda shook her head jerkily. "No."

"Yes. The King was deposed against his will; he was murdered in a betrayal so heinous that it triggered the darkest times these kingdoms have ever known. A Locarno must sit upon the throne and the Counterparts must be dead. Otherwise the lands will suffer for eternity." Celandine slammed her fist on her knee. "*That* is the deal we made with the gods and we signed it in Counterpart blood. There is no way around it; I ensured it would be so with great sacrifice, the most powerful there is. Your life and those of your brothers and sisters were the requirement of the gods for it to be so and they will not be swayed. Ever."

Leda was barely aware that she was leaning on the desk, that it was the only thing holding her upright. Her thoughts were erratic, bouncing around her mind without direction. All she could feel was the panic suffusing her, paralysing her.

Azaria was finally moved to speak. "Knowing you, Mother, it is not so black and white. What else is missing?"

"Nothing," Celandine said, watching Leda's reaction with a smile so wide it looked almost manic. "It is my greatest achievement, my legacy, the one that I put in place for you and Elias to ensure that one of you would one day rule. Now, it all relies on you."

"What about the other secret Counterparts you always threatened us with?" Leda asked, her voice faint. "Father said they'd be sacrificed in our place if we ever escaped."

"They don't exist, as you well know by now," Celandine said icily. She seemed almost disappointed that Leda hadn't collapsed into tears yet. "The idea of them kept you all in line, though, didn't it?"

Azaria was looking down at the floor, her brow furrowed, clearly not following the conversation. "You wish for me to be queen."

"It's what I have trained you for since birth. I did every-thing necessary to prepare you for this life. I made you strong. Look at him." Celandine gestured at Pyrrhus with disgust. His back was to Leda; she could see nothing but the set line of his shoulders. "He is not a leader, he is weak; he won't make unpopular decisions for the good of the king-doms. He plays with his new ministries and privy counsel-lors like a child with toys. But you will succeed, my daughter. You'll continue in your father's footsteps and expand the kingdoms further. There are so many countries out there languishing in poverty and dust, you will bring them into the fold and elevate them."

The words she spoke were so wrong, so disgusting, that Leda felt the urge to retch on top of every other negative emotion that was attempting to pull her under. "Azaria, don't listen to her."

Azaria caught her eye and her expression shifted minutely. "I don't wish to rule."

"It doesn't matter what you wish," Celandine said. "It is your birthright and your duty. Kill your Counterpart and accept what you were always meant to be."

There was a horrible, tense silence.

Pyrrhus shifted into a position that put his body in front of Leda's.

Azaria turned to him. "I'll take her to the dungeons now."

Celandine looked annoyed, but not surprised. She allowed herself to be pulled to her feet.

Her gaze was fixed on Leda as she was shoved towards the door. "Don't be complacent, child," she called over her shoulder. "Azaria will change her mind, she cares nothing for you."

It was possible that she was right. Wasn't that always what Leda had thought? Wasn't that what she'd experienced growing up, even if Azaria did have flashes of mercy?

It hit her then, as Celandine looked at her with contempt and utter certainty that she would die. It was so similar to the looks Leda had received from her when she'd been a child, across banquet halls and ballrooms, that she felt her heart beat thick and fast and her breathing become harsh.

She was going to die. And so were the rest of the Counterparts. Pyrrhus's graveyard would be full the moment one of the royal children allowed the poison of ambition to get to them.

"Leda." Pyrrhus reached for her, his hand brushing hers.

She wrenched herself away. She staggered into the desk, a sharp pain flaring in her hip, which she ignored, and then she was running.

She sprinted up the stairs and away from the nightmare that had unfolded in front of her eyes.

CHAPTER 25

The world moved on as Leda sorted through her devastation at the fact that her father had doomed her to death from beyond the grave.

Part of her wanted to laugh hysterically.

He hadn't cared for her, had looked at her so little she was sceptical that he could have described her appearance. She was nothing to him, not a person but a possession. A means to an end. And so his evil ambition touched her still, even with his body cold in the ground.

She should have anticipated this, it was so in his character that part of her was disgusted with herself for being so naive.

He loved his royal children, they were his legacy, replicas of his own image. Or, maybe love was the wrong word, he was *obsessed* with them. They could have no impediments in their way, least of all the Counterparts.

Still, she'd allowed herself to hope and where had it got her?

Celandine had been sent to the palace dungeons and Pyrrhus had secured Azaria's word that she would tell no one the full curse. It presented too much danger to Leda,

Eber and Mira. There was no telling who else would join the effort to kill them if they knew it might help alleviate the gods' wrath.

Leda took the time to cry and rage and throw around the furniture in her room. She wrenched apart the sleeves and tore the bodice of one of her favourite dresses, scattering thousands of beads all over the floor.

They rained down on to the stone with a gentle tinkling sound, light and inconsequential and infuriating.

She screamed at the ceiling until her ears rang.

Then she got out her sewing supplies and began to piece the dress back together.

She could fall apart, could curl up in bed and not move until she wasted away to nothing, or until she lost what was left of her mind. Or she could acknowledge that there was a fixed end date to her life, as there always had been, and move forward. She'd done it before.

Pyrrhus had appeared at the threshold moments after she'd screamed, staring down at the carpet of glittering beads in shock. Then he strode in and shut the door on the guards who were trying to enter behind him.

Leda looped a length of silver thread through the eye of her needle. Her hand was trembling so much she nearly stabbed herself. "I'm alright, don't worry."

Her constant refrain, nearly always a lie.

Pyrrhus surveyed the carnage that was her bedroom with a sceptical eye. "If you say so."

Her voice was as flat and logical as she could make it. "I've contemplated death before. It's routine at this point. I was stupid to think I'd avoid it." No one was better than Leda at having ideas above her station, only to get smacked back down to the place she'd always occupied.

He sat beside her on the bed. "You're not going to die."

"You've said that to me a disturbing number of times,"

she said tiredly. "It shouldn't be necessary, but here we are." She rubbed at her bleary eyes with her free hand. "I should rescind the offer I made to you, about being together when this is all over. I won't be alive to fulfil it."

"No." He took the needle from her and laid it on the bedside table. "You're not going anywhere. The moment I give up the Crown you are *mine* and vice versa."

Her heart fluttered at the words, said with such certainty. She stared into the folds of the dress as though it might have answers tucked within the fabric. "You heard Celandine, I have to die to break the curse."

He shook his head. "There's always a loophole; we'll find it. Don't plan your funeral just yet."

She couldn't cry, and she scrunched up her face to make sure of it.

Maintain control, Leda. Keep some of your dignity for the love of the gods.

"Please, no matter what happens, I don't want a funeral. So many people pretending to grieve, I'd hate that."

If they even showed up at all.

"I'll take that into consideration. Or rather, I won't, because you won't be dying in the near future. Listen to me, we will find a way out of this. I'm not allowing any of you to be killed." His hand was wrapped around her wrist then, pulling it away from the dress. "Just give me time. Look at me."

She did so.

He didn't wear his emotions as plainly as she did. His eyes weren't red and swollen like hers, so puffy she could barely see. But he was tense, the lines of his face betraying the stress that followed him everywhere. She could practically see his mind whirring behind those dark eyes, sifting through and discarding every possible plan of action.

She hadn't given him time on the last occasion he'd

asked for it, not much anyway. But he was sitting here before her, refusing to give up on her. And so she would not give up on him.

"Alright," she said. "But we're not the only people who know about this. It must be why the assassin has been attacking us."

"Then we'll just have to find them too, won't we?"

So easy to say, nigh on impossible to do.

〜

Of all the places Leda wanted to be, oddly it wasn't the relative safety of the university or the sunny escape of her cabin in Saint-Trevale. It was the palace, where the people she cared about resided. She missed them. It was an odd, but not entirely unwelcome, feeling.

She'd asked Pyrrhus if they could return and he'd arranged it immediately. The number of students surrounding them had made him wary since the revelation about the curse, and his relative control over the inhabitants of the palace made it lower risk.

She breathed a sigh of relief when they crossed the threshold into the entrance hall. There was a clattering of sound as Pyrrhus's advisors descended on him like a pack of hungry wolves, chief advisor Ecgred at the front, red in the face from sprinting down the stairs.

Pyrrhus shared a grim look with her before allowing himself to be swept away, up towards his office.

She was almost glad he'd been distracted, giving her the time she needed for her next task. Resolved, she went to his old study and pulled down every single tome on religion she could find on the shelves.

She spread them out on the floor before her, a veritable

carpet of books, and hunched over them on her knees. She scanned the glossaries for a single word: *curse.*

There were fewer entries than she'd expected. The gods didn't seem to issue curses often, presumably because they'd become difficult to keep track of and Leda was of the opinion that they were lazy. Or ignorant. Whichever it was, it didn't paint them in a flattering light.

They liked to apply their curses to powerful people. The first example she could find a written record of had occurred decades ago: a plague of increasingly large rats in the lands of the noble who'd stolen golden sceptres from a temple in Rivernesse. They had stayed for five years, decimating every harvest, until the noble's death at the hands of his tenants had broken the curse.

Leda slammed that book shut, huffing out a breath. She didn't want to see examples of a curse working perfectly, she needed *loopholes.*

Unfortunately the next book did nothing to help. It told the story of the head of a tribe in South Doviet who bargained with the gods for the death of a powerful rival who sought to replace him. The gods struck his enemy down where he stood, and his eldest son for good measure, but also rendered the tribe leader infertile. He had clung to power for himself, but could never pass it on to his bloodline. He would not have the legacy he craved.

That was the theme of most of these stories, the gods seemed to like balance. They gave and took in more or less equal measure.

Leda frowned down at the pages, crinkled and yellowed with age. If only she could know what the gods got out of any of this, what the source of their interest was, it would be so much easier to understand. But their motives were opaque as ever.

She flipped through the rest of the books, coming upon story after story that turned her stomach. Diseased children and mass drownings and a plague of madness that caused the citizens of an entire town to murder one another. Hideous curses, all broken only when their subjects met whichever conditions the gods had set. Some accounts had even been torn from the books, the only evidence of their existence the ragged edges of their pages close to the spines. Those must have been so heinous that someone had felt compelled to rip them away.

As she sat back on her heels and let out a groan of frustration she realised that she was likely not the first person to have done this. Pyrrhus would have gone through all these books already. The fact that he hadn't told her about it must mean he was just as unsuccessful as she.

That feeling of doom that had followed her since she was old enough to know what a Counterpart was had returned with a vengeance, weighing on her like a set of hands pressing down her shoulders. The spark of hope she'd clung to had been extinguished.

There was no clear way around this curse.

And now she had to ask herself the horrific questions she'd been trying to avoid. What was her life worth in the grand scheme of things? How could she dedicate herself to ensuring the trials selected the right monarch for the good of the people, if she could in the same breath condemn them to die to save her?

Dusk fell outside the window while she remained lost in thought.

Leda drifted towards the banquet hall, trying to stifle her terrible mood. She could smell the delicious scent of a full roast dinner being served, and forced herself focus on that.

She didn't have answers but she *did* have limited time; she couldn't spend it in a stupor.

She found her siblings at their customary table in the corner with Ambrose, and they crowed in a cacophony of voices upon seeing her. Her breath caught at the sight of them, but she fought back the emotions that would drown her.

They could not know. She wouldn't torture them the way she tortured herself now.

Eber waved a chicken leg at her so enthusiastically he nearly flung it across the room. Elina made a show of being annoyed at seeing her, Ambrose seemed actually annoyed, and little Fessler copied his big brother in waving.

"You're finally back! How did you find the university?"

"Full of young people; it was a little alarming." The court had always been an older one, and Leda wasn't used to being surrounded by people her own age who she wasn't related to. It had been a pleasant change, even if all they'd done was gawp at her most of the time.

"Where's Pyrrhus?" Elina enquired.

"In negotiations with the five families."

Leda frowned as she saw the carafe of red wine and full glass beside Eber's dessert plate. Ambrose was glaring at it too, clearly holding himself back from commenting in front of everyone.

"I can't believe I missed this place," Leda said, bracing her hands on Eber's shoulders and squeezing just a little too hard.

"Really?" he said, wincing as he took a sip. "I thought you'd be too drunk on books to notice you weren't here."

She heard Elina snort from across the table and cast her a glare. Elina turned quickly away, striking up conversation with Ambrose. Was that amusement on his face? No, it couldn't be. His sense of humour was non-existent.

"Gods help me but I actually missed you all," Leda said. "Speaking of drunk." She picked up Eber's glass of wine and took a sip. "You're far too young to be taking alcohol at dinner, Eber, so I'm going to have this."

"What? That's not fair, I'm seventeen. I'm allowed." His performance was for the others but there was shame on his face. He refused to meet her gaze.

Oh, Eber. She should have been keeping a better eye on him.

"You also don't need two slices of pie." Leda pulled his second plate of dessert over to her along with his fork as she sat down. Steam poured out as she cut into the crust.

Eber's expression was long-suffering, but he didn't attempt to take his wine back. "I suppose I'll get juice instead." He scraped back his chair and sloped off to find a servant.

Leda smiled at Fessler, who interpreted this as an act of aggression and moved his own dessert far out of her reach. He gave her a contemplative look as he chewed.

"Did you catch any frogs while you were away?"

"No."

"Boring." He turned back to his plate.

That was her dismissed, then. Why must each of her brothers and sisters be constantly tap-dancing along the line between sanity and madness?

Leda began to eat. There was an explosion of taste on her tongue; sweet crystallised sugar on pastry and sharp apples, rich cream swirling through it all. She took her second bite before she'd even swallowed the first.

"This is delicious," she said.

Ambrose looked at her with barely disguised distaste. "It's not that good."

His taste buds were about as developed as his sense of humour, then. This was the most delicious pie she'd ever eaten; it was almost otherworldly, like it had been designed for her. Had food ever been this good before?

Leda waved her fork dismissively at Ambrose before diving back in.

Her plate was clear in less than a minute.

Elina seemed faintly repulsed as she put down her own cutlery. "It's like watching an animal. Did you just unhinge your jaw?"

Leda opened her mouth to retort. Bile rushed upwards with an unpleasant lurch. She clapped a hand over her lips and doubled over.

Elina rolled her eyes. "That's what happens when you inhale your food. Good to know you never grew out of the toddler stage of development."

Leda's stomach was roiling. She heaved into her hand, but wasn't sick.

Ambrose was watching her with a perturbed expression on his face. "What's wrong? Are you nauseous? Have you been taking your medicine?"

Leda nodded frantically, not trusting herself to open her mouth without vomiting all over the table. She tried to draw in a breath and it scraped through her lungs like they were full of broken glass. Her muscles felt as structured as jelly.

With a whimper she slid sideways off her seat and on to the ground.

They'd been roundly sceptical up until that point, but her descent to the floor got their full attention. With a succession of gasps and the scraping of chairs they all hurried to huddle around her.

A splitting headache sprang to life and Leda slammed her hands over her temples. It felt like her head was about to explode, the pressure unbearable. Her heart was beating so fast and hard she could hear it louder than any other sound in the room. The noise of her siblings and Ambrose and a few passing courtiers twittering around her faded into the background.

She was rolled firmly on to her back.

She was faintly aware that she was sweating profusely as Ambrose pressed a hand to her forehead and it nearly slid off. Rather than appearing disgusted, alarm spread across his face. Before she knew it, his arms were under her knees and behind her back and she was being hoisted up into the air as if she weighed no more than a feather.

"Infirmary, now. Elina, fetch Penelope and Orion and have them meet us there."

To Leda's astonishment, her sister took off at a run without raising a single objection.

Fessler watched them in shock, his napkin dangling from one hand. The sight of his tense little face, no doubt fearing yet another death, stayed with Leda all the way up to the infirmary.

She groaned as she was deposited on to a soft bed, not as gently as she'd have liked.

She glared up at Ambrose but didn't say anything because the moment she opened her mouth she would projectile vomit into his face and then he'd be very unlikely to help her.

And she needed his help more than anything at that moment, or she'd probably be dead by the time Pyrrhus came out of his meeting with the five families. One less Counterpart for anyone who wanted to eradicate the curse to deal with.

Ambrose was frantically grinding a mixture of herbs in a pestle and mortar, knocking over myriad jars on his desk before locating the liquid he needed with a triumphant sound. He mixed it into the disgusting-smelling concoction he'd crafted, turned around, prised her mouth open, and poured it down her throat.

Leda gagged. It was not only lumpy and cloying but it tasted like the stables smelled.

It did, however, alleviate the worst of her headache, and while she was slippery with sweat all over her body, that started to fade too. She was no longer in danger of sliding right off the bed.

She coughed and shuddered, but nodded at Ambrose's questioning expression.

He sank into the seat behind his desk with a long, slow breath. She could have sworn she saw his hands shaking before he clasped them together.

"Thanks," Leda croaked, managing to pull herself into a sitting position. She maintained it for all of two seconds before slipping back down. The muscles in her abdomen had gone dormant. "I take it that wasn't a reaction to a poorly cooked slice of pie?"

"I think you inadvertently intruded on an opportunity to poison your brother."

Relief and horror flooded Leda in equal measures. She pulled the thin duvet over herself to stave off the cold that followed.

The door slammed open and Penelope and Orion flooded in with Elina hot on their heels. The physician's assistants paused to peer into the pestle and mortar at the treatment Ambrose had created and bustled into the store cupboard, in deep discussion about the next dose required.

Elina approached Leda's bed and stared down at her. She looked like she couldn't believe that Leda was conscious, let alone sitting up.

"How is she alright? How is that possible?" Elina choked out, and then her hands were cupping Leda's face. Elina's cheeks were glistening with tears, and she visibly shook herself, also shaking Leda in the process.

Leda was reluctantly touched by this display. She didn't know Elina actually cared.

Elina then let her go so abruptly she nearly pitched forward and planted her face on the bed.

"They poisoned her!" Elina said to Ambrose, as though he might not be aware of that.

"Indeed."

"But she's alright?"

"I've been having rugosa added to all of your meals every morning to protect against poisoning," Ambrose said, holding the back of his hand to Leda's forehead and nodding in satisfaction at whatever temperature he could detect. "Take it easy, Leda, you'll be out of sorts for at least a day."

Elina whirled to face him.

"You've been adding substances into our food without our knowledge?" she hissed.

He appeared supremely unconcerned. Leda could admit that her judgement was impaired at that moment, but still, it seemed a foolish position for him to take. "Yes."

Elina was trembling with rage. "How could you do that? We haven't consented!"

"It was not harmful and was necessary to keep you safe. Stop trying to find any excuse to be cross with me," Ambrose said. "It's getting tiresome."

"Oh, well I'm sorry to have *wearied* you. That has nothing to do with you feeding us whatever you like and not telling us! I refuse to be treated like a science experiment."

"You're behaving like a silly little girl."

Leda cringed as Elina stopped dead, one fist frozen in the air. That had not been a smart thing to say. Leda pulled the duvet up over her eyes so she didn't have to watch this particular disaster unfold.

"You are the worst kind of man," Elina said, her voice

trembling. There was the tap of her heels indicating her stalking across the room and then the sound of her taking care to slam both of the double doors to the infirmary as she left.

"Smoothly done," Leda croaked, emerging from behind the duvet.

Ambrose glowered at her. "That's enough out of you, too!"

He strode off to his desk and grumbled something about the Locarno women being the bane of his life.

Luckily Leda didn't have to endure his mutterings for long as Penelope and Orion returned with armfuls of herbs and Eber hurried into the infirmary. He nearly tripped over his own feet in his haste to get to her, and then he was grasping her hands in his.

He smiled tremulously. "I just passed Elina and she nearly shoved me out an open window. I assume this is where she came from?"

Leda snorted and Ambrose roundly ignored them. Penelope and Orion were, as per usual, determined not to get caught up in any of their nonsense. They began chopping greenery on their workbench.

Eber sat gingerly on the edge of Leda's bed. "How are you feeling?"

"Like I've been turned inside out and had all the blood scraped from my veins."

Eber grimaced. "Vivid."

"You asked. Just be glad it wasn't you."

His expression twisted at that. "It should have been."

"I'm pleased it wasn't. I get injured all the time, Eber. It builds character. I get concerned if I've been healthy for more than a few weeks. You bruise like fresh fruit; it's best you avoid this kind of thing." She should tell him, right that second, should confess the full extent of the curse. But she couldn't. Instead she kept her mouth shut and rested a hand on her thigh, which was justifiably throbbing worse than usual.

Eber's laugh was reluctant. He must have known she was trying to cheer him up, that her words were a performance.

"I won't feel too guilty seeing as you seem to be in good spirits. Can't have been that serious if you're up and talking. What was wrong with Elina, aside from the usual?" He made the sign of prayer and rolled his eyes.

Ambrose slammed a hand down on his desk. "*Will* you two keep it down?"

Eber shared a significant look with Leda. "How do you feel about walking? Perhaps we should get some fresh air."

Leda threw the duvet off and swung her feet to the floor. "I'd love that." She staggered and Eber grabbed her elbow, but she otherwise felt better than she should have as she walked slowly out of the room with him.

"Stay out of trouble!" Ambrose barked after them. "Rest, Leda. I mean it. Go straight to bed."

"It's alright," Eber said. "I'll take her back to her rooms, she'll be safe there."

What Eber didn't know, however, was that by that point Leda had fallen into a somewhat altered mental state. Whatever it was, poison or antidote or some combination of the two, it was having an effect.

The journey back to her rooms was a blur of lights and colours. There was a distinct possibility that she'd stopped to laugh at a candelabra. By the time Eber steered her into her rooms she would have been hard-pressed to tell him what her own name was.

A nightgown was stuffed into her hand and she was shoved into the bathing room. Moments later Eber tucked her into bed, said something she didn't listen to, and left.

She let four or five seconds pass before flinging the

blanket that covered her halfway across the room and getting to her feet.

She was thirstier than she'd ever been in her life, but not for water.

Throwing a robe over her nightgown, Leda made her way down the stairs and through the back corridors of the palace. The stone was shockingly cold against her bare feet. Shadows slipped across the wall and she couldn't tell if they belonged to people or had appeared from nowhere. She had the vague feeling that she should be afraid of them.

Five minutes later she stood in the cavernous wine cellar beneath the banquet hall.

She'd shut the door in the faces of the nosey guards in their sparkly hats who'd followed her there, and was finally alone.

Water wouldn't do to quench this thirst. Leda wanted wine, but she didn't fancy anything someone might have poisoned, so it was best to go to the back of the collection for the older bottles. Her father would have had those meticulously tested.

Humming pleasantly to herself, Leda staggered down the aisle between the thousands and thousands of bottles in their racks and avoided those that looked like they were filled with blood. She blew the dust off a particularly nice-looking white.

She'd had quite enough red for one lifetime.

Gods, she was hilarious. She giggled at her own thoughts.

The cork was a mission to dispense with but she managed it with two hairpins and a great deal of swearing. Sliding down to the floor, her back against the soot-blackened wall, she took a swig. The swirling liquid soothed her itchy throat like a balm.

She'd nearly finished the entire bottle, her thirst an insatiable beast, when the door opened and Eber appeared from a nearby aisle.

He jumped so violently he nearly knocked over one of the long wine racks, but steadied it at the last second. "What in the gods' names are you doing here?" he cried, eyes fixed on the bottle dangling from her hand.

She was drunk, and only the gods he'd invoked knew what that would do in combination with the lingering effects of the poison and the treatment. Still, even in her stupor she knew how dangerous it was for Eber to be down here. She could control herself around all of this wine, at least she usually could, but the same couldn't be said for him.

Leda tried and failed to get to her feet. Why weren't her limbs listening to her?

"I was thirsty."

"I left a huge ewer of water next to your bed."

"It didn't suffice."

Eber looked at the empty bottle rolling across the floor towards him.

"You went for the ancient ones."

"Yes, I don't know why though." Leda wiped her mouth on her sleeve. "Tastes a bit like pickled cabbage. I prefer grapes. But I'll try a more recent vintage." She took the nearest bottle from a rack within her reach.

The label was so blurry she could barely read it.

He looked for a second like he might stop her, might confiscate it and march her right out of the room. But then his expression shifted, become despondent.

"I might as well join you then." Before Leda could move Eber had slid two bottles from the nearest shelf and was removing the corks with a deftness that was telling.

She watched in mute horror as he polished off the first

in less than a minute. He'd moved on to the second by the time she'd dragged herself to her feet.

"No!" She tried to swipe the bottle out of his hand but was made aware of the fact that he was standing several feet out of reach when he laughed at her. "Stop, I don't approve of this!"

"You were here drinking in the first place."

"But it's not a problem for me; if we were in a room full of hibcus it would be the same story for you!"

Eber took another drink. She knew she couldn't stop him, particularly because there appeared to be several versions of him in front of her at that moment. She had no idea which was real.

It took her a few seconds to realise she was pointing accusingly at a large oak barrel and not her brother. She blinked and pivoted towards him.

"What would Kadir think of you doing this?"

Eber lowered the bottle, eyebrows raised. "How do you know about Kadir?"

"I have two eyes and I've seen the way you look at him," Leda said. "You've teased me about how obvious I am with Pyrrhus, well you're twice as bad. You've never laughed at my jokes half as much as you laugh at Kadir's, and I'm really funny."

Eber smirked. "I should've known you'd be an obnoxious drunk. You're not funny whether you're intoxicated or sober, just so you know. Besides, I'm staying away from Kadir; I had him reassigned to Fessler's guard detail. He was furious about it of course, but I thought it made sense on account of the fact that someone's currently trying to end my life. Can't have him stepping into the line of fire, can I?"

He trailed off at that, staring down into the liquid swirling in the bottle. The thought of Kadir had made him pause, but the reminder of the danger to those he loved seemed to erase what little composure he'd clawed back.

He took another drink.

"This won't help you," she said softly, the wall at her back once more. "After a while it'll only layer on the hurt, in new and more painful ways."

"Will it?" he said lightly, as though he were merely indulging the nonsense she spouted.

She rested her head back against the wall, absorbed in the flickering light of the candles. "The pain never goes away, Eber. You can mask it, until the mask becomes more toxic for you than what you're covering with it."

"So I just bear it stoically, is that your suggestion?" His mouth twisted in derision.

She let out a dry, humourless laugh. "Hibcus dulled the agony of my leg, but it stole all my energy until I was a shell of a person. I'd just swapped one kind of suffering for another. And that's exactly what you're doing here."

"I get it, Leda, you're stronger than me. You cut down on the hibcus and barely feel your leg now, all through your marvellous strength of character. Congratulations, but not all of us have such a high horse we can climb up on."

The emotions took longer to rise through the haze in her mind, but the anger, when it hit her, was real.

"Just because you don't see it doesn't mean it's not there," she snarled, the truth spilling out of her like she'd never allowed it to before. "I'm fine until I'm not fine. I'm alright until there's a bolt of pain so crippling, so excruciating that all I can do is wait for it to be over. And I spend my whole life anticipating and dreading the moment it hits. It will never go away and so I accept it and I *manage* it."

"So I'm just supposed to accept that Ami's dead? And Markus? And Sofie?"

Their names still hurt to hear. "Yes. And it's awful and

unfair but if the alternative is drinking yourself to death, Eber, then it's not even a question."

A single tear tracked down his face, but he lifted the bottle to his lips once more. He wasn't listening and it killed something inside her to see it.

"Please, stop." He didn't. "That's it; I'm getting Ambrose."

Eber didn't seem as worried as Leda thought he should be as he watched her teeter towards the spiral staircase that would take her up into the banquet hall. When she opened the door the guards at the top looked at her with mixed relief and judgement as she emerged, blinking, into the light. Nevertheless, they followed her up to the infirmary in silence.

It took her a lot longer than it normally would, as she kept getting lost despite being in corridors she'd known all her life.

Eventually, Leda banged the double doors to the infirmary open with great ceremony and saw Ambrose jump up from his desk.

"Eber is drinking," she announced, and then realised she was still holding her own wine bottle.

Ambrose cast a nasty look at the guards that trailed in behind her.

"I don't suppose he's the only one," he said with a sigh. "Penelope, will you take Eber his medicine and see to it that he leaves the wine cellar, please? Then bring him here once he's well?"

A newly appeared guard stepped forward and spoke quietly to Ambrose. Ambrose scrubbed a hand over his face and looked at the ceiling as though praying for strength. "The rose garden, then, Penelope."

His assistant nodded and left with grace, but her face was grim as she passed Leda.

Leda barely noticed, however, as her legs had suddenly

become noodle-like and she'd sat down were she'd stood on the cold stone floor.

Unfortunately that meant she was still quite close to the door, so that when it swung violently open once more to admit Pyrrhus it missed the back of her head by an inch. She gasped at the whooshing sound and then laughed.

Ambrose looked like he'd dearly love to locate a barrel of the wine she'd just drunk and drown her in it.

Pyrrhus had just heard of her poisoning judging by the panic evident all over his face. He froze and looked down at her sprawled form. Slowly, as though approaching a wounded deer, he crouched down beside her.

He took Leda's chin in his hand as he studied her. She grinned at him.

"Oh gods, the poison has addled her mind."

"No, that would be the alcohol." Ambrose's sardonic voice filtered through the pleasant fog in Leda's brain. "She spent the past half hour in the wine cellar with Eber. The guards tell me he's sleeping it off in the bushes outside the rose garden."

Pyrrhus turned back to Leda with utter bemusement. "You're drunk?"

"No!" she said with what she thought was a disarmingly charming smile. "Why are you upside down?"

Pyrrhus admirably kept his composure when she cupped his jaw with both hands and shook his head from side to side.

He looked at her with poorly concealed affection as she ran her fingers through that thick, perfect hair that was the source of so much of her frustration.

"You're so ssserious," she slurred. "You should have some wine." She located the bottle beside her and the liquid sloshed as she brought it up to him.

He grabbed it before she could accidentally crack his head open with it.

"I think we've all had enough wine for tonight," Pyrrhus said steadily, ignoring Ambrose's snort from the corner. He glanced down at the label and his eyebrows rose. "Well, you certainly have an eye for the expensive vintage."

"The guard said the sommelier put the value of what these two idiots polished off at about fifty thousand sovereigns," Ambrose said, clearly not finding Leda as adorable as she found herself at that moment.

Now it was Pyrrhus's turn to snort. "Well, I can't say I don't respect that." He gently pulled Leda's hands off his head and looped her fingers through his. "I think it's time for bed, don't you?"

Come to think of it, she was rather sleepy, her vision hazy around the edges. And it would be nice to get away from Ambrose, who was somehow even less fun now than when she was sober.

"Can we go to your rooms?" she murmured into Pyrrhus's shoulder as he stood and lifted her easily into his arms. She clung to his neck as the world spun around her. "I don't want anyone else to try to kill me today."

Just like that, his good mood seemed to fizzle and dissolve in front of her eyes. He clutched her to him tighter than was necessary to carry her safely, and she felt the sigh in his chest against her side.

"No one is going to hurt you." He turned his head into the curly mass of her hair. "I promise."

"Don't forget to take a bucket!" Ambrose called after them.

It took longer than it should have to get Leda to Pyrrhus's rooms, mainly because she kept declaring they were going in the wrong direction and arguing the point with him until he looked ready to go outside and drop her into the fountain. Luckily by the time they were through the double doors into his room and he'd laid her gently on his bed she was half asleep.

She felt him lift her robe away to leave her in her night-gown, and let out a contented sound as he smoothed her hair away from her face. The mattress was soft, and when it dipped under Pyrrhus's weight she rolled across until she collided with his side. His arm immediately encircled her, and she buried her face into the warmth of his neck.

"Don't ever get poisoned again," he muttered, clearly under the impression she was asleep and lost to the world. "I mean it," he said, pulling the duvet up and over her shoulders. "I can't lose you, ever. I love you."

CHAPTER 26

*L*eda opened her eyes the following morning and came to two very quick realisations. First, it was possible that Pyrrhus had told her he loved her last night.

Second, someone was actively, and with ever-increasing desperation, trying to kill her and Eber and Mira. She'd been saved last night, and it could have been so much worse than it was, but it only added weight to the feeling of dread that had been threatening to crush her since Celandine had revealed her future.

They probably wouldn't be able to break the curse, and others would find out about it over time, just like this assassin likely had. The Counterpart lives were ticking towards their ends; there was no denying it.

Under the weight of those thoughts, it took her a moment more than it should to realise that her head felt like it had been cleaved in two. She groaned and rubbed her eyes, puffy and irritated by the light pouring in through the crack in the curtains.

She couldn't tell if it was the remnants of the alcohol or

the poison or the antidote. Either way, she'd been monumentally stupid the night before.

She was never, ever going down to the wine cellar again.

Pyrrhus lay next to her, a respectable distance away as always. He was fully clothed, as though exhaustion had pounced on him the moment he laid her down and had refused to let him do anything other than fall asleep himself.

Leda's mouth tasted like sand, and her teeth had a furry feel to them that made her want to gag. He absolutely could not see her like this.

She slid off the bed as quietly as possible, wobbled to her feet and took her shoes from where she'd apparently thrown them beside the dressing table.

Her leg twinged viciously, put out with her for what she'd done while her pain receptors had been dulled into oblivion. She clutched at it with a muffled curse. Ambrose would laugh her out of the building if she asked him for more hibcus now.

Still, she needed to speak to him. An idea, dark and depressing, had begun to form in her mind. And, her luck being what it was, he was the only person in this wretched palace who could help her with it.

The infirmary was quiet when she crept through the double doors, the orange and pink of sunrise casting the room in soft light.

She'd known Ambrose, legendary for being an early riser, would be there. Come to think of it, he was known for being late to bed too. When did he ever sleep?

He looked seconds from it at that point, to be sure. He was slumped in a chair next to the bed that contained a gently snoring Eber. His legs were spread out before him, eyes half closed.

"Ambrose?"

He jolted upright, instantly alert. "Leda, are you alright?"

She looked down at Eber, suddenly feeling cold. "Better than he is."

Ambrose was equally grim. "He's not improving right now, but it's a long road. Lifelong, in fact. There will be setbacks, but we'll get there."

She shook her head. "It won't be a long life, regardless of the alcohol."

That had Ambrose frowning. "What—"

The doors creaked open and they turned to see Thalia slipping into the infirmary. She wore a simple grey dress and her hair was wet and pinned messily on top of her head. She stopped short when she saw them, offering a polite smile.

"Ambrose, Leda, good morning." Her gaze flicked down to Eber and back, but she was kind enough not to comment. "Selene was practising sparring with some guards and came away with a cut to the shoulder for her efforts."

Ambrose nodded, getting to his feet. "Where is she? I'll come right down."

"No, no, it's alright," Thalia said softly. "It's a shallow wound; I can bandage it myself if you give me the supplies. You have duties to attend to here."

Ambrose disappeared into the storage room. Thalia could have waited for him in the corner as Leda had expected. Instead, she approached Leda and bent down to replace the rumpled blanket that Eber had kicked off in the night.

"My father struggled similarly," she said, her tone a kind of soothing that Leda had never heard from anyone before.

"Did anything help?" Leda asked dully.

"There's no quick solution to something like this," Thalia said. "But will you allow me to give you some advice?"

Leda nodded.

"We found it easier when he wasn't surrounded by the substances that tempted him. Perhaps you could have private family dinners with no wine instead of joining the big banquets. Seal away the wine cellar, don't drink in front of him and focus with him on the future he wants, that's very important. Support him."

Leda was painfully aware of her eyes filling with tears. She could barely corral the thoughts streaking through her mind. "I'm going to lose him."

A hand landed on her shoulder, squeezing gently. "No one knows the future, Leda. All you can do is be the best sister you can, and from where I'm standing you seem to be doing a good job at it."

Leda was reminded of the first trial, of Thalia praising Selene and gently guiding her in the right direction. This felt the same, and it was such a new experience that it made her want to cry harder.

"Thank you," she said, hating how her voice trembled.

"Of course," Thalia said, turning to take the bandages from Ambrose as he returned. "I'll leave you both now; I look forward to seeing you later."

Ambrose waited impatiently for the door to shut behind Thalia before he was rounding on Leda. "What did you mean when you said his life would be short?"

She was still staring at Eber's sleeping form, unable to get riled up by his tone as she normally would. "Is there a way to die that doesn't hurt?"

"*What?*"

"The Counterparts have to die to satisfy the curse. A Locarno must sit on the throne and we must be dead. Those are the full conditions," she said quietly. "Otherwise this weather continues and thousands more die."

Ambrose didn't look nearly as stunned as he should have.

"You guessed?"

He dipped his head in a nod. "Not for certain, but ... I knew your father well; I suspected he wouldn't leave the thread of the Counterparts loose if he was killed."

Leda drew in a deep breath. "So, a choice lies before us, doesn't it? We sacrifice ourselves and put a Locarno on the throne. Or we wait for this assassin to complete their task. Others will find out as time goes on, these kinds of things don't stay secret, and many of them will try to kill us too."

"What are you planning?"

She gave a short, humourless laugh. "Nothing, what power could I possibly have to plan? But if it does come to our deaths, if we see no other way, I want us to have a choice in how we go. I want it to be painless. Can you find something for us?" She gestured towards his cabinet of remedies.

He was gaping at her and she couldn't even take pleasure in having shocked him. "I don't kill, it goes against everything I stand for."

"You alleviate pain, Ambrose. You don't decide who lives or dies. All I'm asking for is an option."

He looked at her for a long, charged moment, and she could see his resentment for her plain on his face. If he disliked her before, it was nothing compared to how he felt after she'd put him in this position. "Pyrrhus would destroy me if he learned that I helped you with this."

She nodded. "I hope we won't need to use it, but he can never know. He wouldn't understand."

Ambrose sighed. "Sometimes I think you don't deserve his loyalty. He's in love with a woman who pushes him away every chance she gets."

The smile on her face was sad, defeated. "There's not much point in me pushing him away now, is there? My moralising around the throne doesn't mean anything anymore."

"Yes, but if you let him close you'll only ensnare him more deeply. It'll hurt worse when you do die. Then again, if you pull away now it'll probably drive him insane." He didn't indicate whether he considered either choice to be the better one. They both felt equally selfish.

"I know you don't like me and never have, but I'm asking for your help. Will you give it?"

"Leda—"

"What would you do in my position? What would you want for yourself? For Eber and Mira?"

Ambrose's mouth snapped shut at that, and she thought she could see the glimmer of something like understanding in his eyes. He looked over at his cabinet of medicines, his ensuing nod slow and reluctant. "I'll do some research."

"And you won't tell Pyrrhus?"

His gaze fell to Eber and his eyes closed, like he couldn't bear to look at him for more than a second. "I won't tell anyone; you have my word on that."

If Pyrrhus noticed Leda's distracted, absent state over the next few days he was in no position to address it with her.

The gods appeared to have felt that Viridiana had been left alone for long enough and unleashed upon them a heat-wave the likes of which they'd never experienced. It was hotter even than Saint-Trevale, a dry and crackly heat compared with the humidity Leda was used to, and the court roasted together.

By the time the river was starting to run dry, a foul mood

had befallen the palace, with every occupant sweaty and thirsty for water that was rapidly becoming unavailable.

Many turned to wine, which made them even more belligerent.

Leda, however, abstained, and she made sure that Eber did too. She took Thalia's advice and sequestered herself with him in the palace for days at a time, away from the court's influence.

Pyrrhus had considered that an excellent idea given it made them less of a target for anyone who might want to hurt them. Though it did have the drawback of keeping Leda away from him, a position she never wanted to be in again. But everything had become so complicated and they were both pulled in so many directions. It was difficult to remember the moment she'd admitted her feelings to him in that lecture theatre, it felt so long ago. And now her head was such a mess of dark emotions that she was almost glad he couldn't see the state she'd sunk into.

Ambrose's medicines got Eber through the worst of his withdrawal, but his mood matched hers most of the time. He was still sullen and in pain, barely speaking as the days passed.

The first time Leda saw more than a glimpse of Pyrrhus was a week into the heatwave. She and Eber were in the library working on his reading, stopping every few minutes to wipe sweat from their brows. She had a thick theological text open in front of her and was learning about yet more horrifying curses.

She'd frozen when Pyrrhus entered the room. He gave her a nod, Eber a concerned look, and kept his distance.

She watched as he took a stepladder from the royal librarian. He made quick work of rolling up his sleeves and climbed up to reach a book on one of the taller shelves nearby. Leda took in the corded strength of his forearms as he rifled through the tomes and then stared glumly down at her book.

She wanted to be near him, to spend every moment from the dwindling stockpile she had left in his presence. But her responsibilities to her siblings held her back.

The next day Eber was feeling well enough for a little more social interaction. He, Fessler, Elina and Leda picnicked on a blanket on the rapidly browning grass by the woods. Eber had pilfered some tin buckets from the stables and he and Fessler were running around collecting water from a nearby pond and flinging it over each other. Following a dire warning from Elina, they'd altered their play area to give the blanket she and Leda sat on a wide berth, for which Leda was grateful.

Of course, then Pyrrhus had chosen that moment to come out of the woods, deep in conversation with Ambrose, and neither saw Fessler leap out from behind a large boulder.

There was an almighty splash and Pyrrhus froze, as though he'd been shot. Ambrose let out a flurry of very colourful swear words that Leda was not pleased Fessler was hearing. He was probably already cataloguing them in his mind for use at the dinner table that evening.

Pyrrhus was silent, and even from a distance Leda could see his irritation. Eber fell about laughing in the background, no compunction whatsoever in pointing at the king as he did so.

With a flat smile that conveyed no mirth at all, Pyrrhus ripped the dripping cravat from his throat and squeezed a stream of water on to the ground. His shirt was entirely drenched, sticking to the lines of his body as though glued there.

The smirk all but fell off Leda's face.

She shifted forward on her knees to see better.

A splash of liquid to her own face.

"What the—"

"See how you like it when it happens to you, you deviant," Elina said, returning her glass to the blanket and picking up the book she'd been reading.

Leda spluttered. "That was wine!" She looked down at her pale blue dress and let out a half-choked sound of fury. "*Red* wine!"

Elina laughed.

The final secret trial was a fascinating one to observe from afar. One by one Pyrrhus and a panel of independent judges had brought the servants of Pan, Zephyr and Thalia into his office and interviewed them about the treatment they received at the hands of their superiors. Pyrrhus didn't reveal the results to Leda, but she was able to guess who came out of that well based on her observations of the second half of the trial.

It took place on an innocuous and unseasonably hot evening when the whole court had streamed on to the grounds and the musicians had followed. They danced and drank on the grass as the sky turned a star-spangled, inky black.

They were rowdier than usual, so drunk that Leda was happy Eber had chosen to spend the evening in his room. He didn't need to see courtiers vomiting in the corridors, starting fights with one another for imagined slights, and snoring huddled against walls, too intoxicated to find their rooms.

Pyrrhus had orchestrated the final part of his secret trial masterfully. He was five feet behind Thalia when a servant staggered and spilt a carafe of port down her pale green dress. Though visibly annoyed, she took the servant's apologies with grace and merely asked if he'd mind locating some napkins for her.

When another servant dropped a tray full of pastries that Zephyr was reaching for, Pyrrhus was right behind him to record the tirade that Zephyr let loose at the young man's incompetence. He used several expletives that had courtiers around him gasping behind their hands. Even Azaria looked at him like he'd lost his mind.

When a servant hurrying down the steps from the rose garden smacked into Pan so hard it sent them both tumbling to the ground, Pan merely got up with an irritable expression, brushed himself off, and walked away without a word. Pyrrhus was left to offer the servant a hand and pull him to his feet.

He glanced up as he did so, met Leda's eyes, and almost dropped the servant. His gaze had flickered, lightning fast, down to the thin white linen dress she'd donned for the hottest day of the year so far. The wind was whipping it around her legs in a frenzy.

His jaw flexed and he managed not to drop the servant to the floor, but only just. She could hear his profuse apologies from across the grass and failed to suppress her smile. Pyrrhus had no idea what was on her face, however, as he was striding back into the palace, a hand curled into a fist at his side.

The strain he was under was evident in every move he made, and the sight of it made her chest hurt.

CHAPTER 27

The next day, in defiance of what anyone expected, the heat wave abated. Unfortunately, it corrected itself to such an extreme that plants, brown and dead of dehydration, were covered in frost by the time everybody woke up. Though fires were quickly stocked and lit throughout the palace as they'd been during Leda's father's reign, the cold sank into the bones of every royal, servant and courtier.

Leda had woken violently shivering, buried under all the blankets she'd been able to find in her room at four in the morning. She'd feared that if she added any more the sheer weight of them would have crushed her to death.

The vague shadow of good news around the horrifying weather was that it at least seemed to be bringing people together. Quite literally, as they huddled for warmth. Even nobles who spent most of their time bickering and jockeying for position could be seen standing shoulder to shoulder that morning, albeit with long-suffering expressions.

The palace fires were so bright they hurt to look at as they roared in their hearths, but the air of the corridors was so frigid that courtiers and servants alike could be seen sprinting through the cold spots. Leda could have sworn that she saw the slight form of Ismene doing the same.

Ismene was still avoiding Leda, and she was still trying to accept it. She'd been so tempted to follow her former friend down to the servants' quarters, but luckily the frigid air emanating from the basement knocked her sense back into her.

If Ismene didn't want to speak to Leda any more that was fine, Leda had no right to push her.

As for the other occupants of the palace, Elina watched the rose garden die off almost instantaneously in the frost that morning and had a near breakdown. Though used to her sister's dramatic temperament, even Ambrose had seemed alarmed.

Leda saw him carefully approaching Elina with a fur wrap as she looked out the window on to the garden from the banquet hall and sobbed. He placed it on her shoulders and appeared to give some words of encouragement.

She continued to look devastated, but the tears at least stopped.

Leda herself was antsy, nervous. The final trial had concluded, Pyrrhus's abdication was finally on the horizon, and she'd never felt worse.

She needed to see him.

Having made sure her siblings were occupied, she stopped by the kitchens and asked the chefs for a platter of food. Pyrrhus favoured grapes, so she made sure they were on there, and she requested a tankard of his favourite hot chocolate. He most likely hadn't had any during the heatwave, so that might give him some comfort in the cold.

If there were any circumstances that warranted this little indulgence, they were now in place.

Pyrrhus was holed up, as he often was, in the old King's

office. His council stood around huffily in the antechamber wearing furs so excessive they looked like they were in peaceful embraces with a pack of brown bears. Their faces weren't peaceful, though; they were clearly annoyed to be denied an audience.

Ecgred, the chief advisor, appeared particularly sullen. He was a middle-aged man with large blue eyes, ruddy cheeks and a receding red hairline. The area around his eyes was crinkled with laugh lines, but Leda had never seen him perform the action. His gaze passed through her as though she were as immaterial as smoke.

To Leda's surprise, the guards let her into Pyrrhus's office immediately, as if they'd been waiting for her.

Pyrrhus was hunched over the grand desk, ink all over his sleeves, glaring down at the paper in front of him as though it had just gravely insulted him.

He looked up at her entrance and jerked as though he were about to stand up but thought better of it.

"Leda, I'm glad to see you've not frozen to death."

She placed the tankard and plate on to his desk and pointed at them. "You dehydrated nearly into delirium during the heatwave, don't think I didn't notice. I'm not going to watch you starve yourself now in the name of your people. They need you healthy."

He grimaced. "There won't be enough food to go around soon."

"And yet there's food before you right now."

Pyrrhus looked down at the platter as though she'd brought him a plateful of animal droppings. "I'm not hungry." The scratching of his quill resumed. His gaze touched on the hot chocolate, but he stubbornly didn't reach for it.

"Stop being a martyr." Leda took a fistful of grapes and held them between his face and the paper on which he wrote. He leaned back in his chair with a sigh of frustration and took them from her.

"There, satisfied?" he said as he chewed.

"For now," Leda said primly, going over to the fireplace and stoking the flames up as high as they would go. It did little to influence the freezing air in the room. The windows were layered in ice. With a sigh she gave up, drawing up a chair opposite Pyrrhus's desk and making herself comfortable.

She pulled her thick knitted shawl tighter around her, aware it made her look about triple her age. She could see in the reflection in the mirror on the wall behind Pyrrhus that the tip of her nose was red with cold too. Fantastic.

Pyrrhus placed his quill slowly and deliberately on the stack of papers piled before him.

"You're here to ask who the winner of the trials will be, I presume?"

No, she was there to drink in his presence like the helpless sap she was. To be soothed by the fact that he was near her. To torture herself with the knowledge that her relationship with him would be cruelly limited. But now was not the time to admit all that. "Am I really so predictable?"

He made a sound that gave no indication either way, a deep rumble in his chest. "I can't tell you, obviously, because that would be supremely unethical."

"But you can reassure me that it's not Zephyr?"

"No," he said staunchly, giving her a look that had her shifting in her seat. "Because, and I hate to repeat myself, that would not be *ethical*."

She stared up at the ceiling, turning her arguments over in her brain. "Will I be pleased by the result?"

He gave a sigh so pronounced it ruffled the papers in front of him. "I suppose you might."

Delight streaked through her, a brief flicker of positivity

in the mire of awful emotions that had clutched her since she'd seen Celandine.

Pan or Thalia, then.

"That's a relief, at least," she said.

Pyrrhus spun his quill absentmindedly in his hand. "At least?"

Leda fussed with her shawl, avoiding his eye. The coronation only solved one of their problems and they both knew it.

If this had happened months ago, before they knew what they knew, this conversation would have unfolded very differently. He would have confirmed his abdication and she would have leapt on him and demanded that he never be apart from her for the rest of their lives. They would have been together and they would have been happy.

"You're slumped over in a disconcerting way. What's going on?"

"There are other things we have to discuss." Things neither of them wanted to, but it was time.

"Such as?"

Sat before her was a man in a deep state of denial. She couldn't even blame him for it.

Leda looked out the window at the landscape, what little she could see of it through the ice. It was a frosted wonderland, too beautiful to be as destructive as it was.

Viridiana wasn't used to these extremes in weather. Eber told her that a supply cart hadn't been able to get up the hill to the palace that morning; they'd stopped halfway up and then slid back down. If the cold persisted for too long, they'd all be in trouble and Pyrrhus's tendency towards rationing food would be wise.

Her thoughts had been turning even more morbid over the past few days, as newspapers had arrived at the palace bearing news of ever-increasing death and destruction. She shifted erratically from terror that she and the other Counterparts would be murdered to wondering if them dying was the right thing for everyone. She considered again how much a life out there in the kingdoms was worth, compared to hers. Roughly the same, she thought. But five? Ten? A thousand?

Her life should pale into insignificance next to those numbers.

And yet here she was, stubbornly and selfishly living while she watched devastation unfold around her.

"A new monarch mitigates the risk of rebellion in the kingdoms for now, that's it. It won't fix the weather."

He jerked up at that. "Leda—"

But she'd started and she couldn't stop, the words spilling out of her, ripped painfully from her chest. "The longer we're alive, Mira and Eber and I, the more people are dying. Tens of thousands already have, and hundreds of thousands more have lost their livelihoods."

"I—"

Her voice broke. "The citizens are dying, innocent people ..."

"Leda, please—"

"In horrifying ways. They're drowning, and starving and being ripped apart by tornados. People in the city I can see from the window behind you are freezing to death in their homes as we speak. Parents have lost their *children*. Part of me doesn't blame whoever this assassin is for trying to kill us." It was her darkest thought, the one she was most ashamed of, but it was in her head constantly now, soaked in guilt.

Pyrrhus threw down his quill in frustration. "I don't know where you're going with this, but I doubt I'm going to like it."

Leda tried to blink the tears out of her eyes. "There are

three Counterparts left, just three lives. How can we hold those above tens of thousands? How can we possibly justify that to ourselves?"

There was a horrible pause as Pyrrhus stared at her.

"You make an excellent point," he said finally, voice dripping with sarcasm. "Why don't I just get a dagger and kill the woman I love right now?" Her heart seemed to stop beating in her chest. He said that word so casually, as though it were a given, as though it were so easy to voice he didn't even need to think about it. "Don't forget to send the seventeen-year-old and the *four-year-old* in here afterwards so I can finish them off too. Problem solved." He gestured at the stack of papers he'd been writing on. "Why didn't I think of that before? This is all redundant now!"

Leda had never seen him so undone, and the sight of it broke her. "You think I want this?" she cried. "Of course I don't, but you said yourself that I was selfish! That I need to think of others first, and that's the kind of person I want to be!"

Pyrrhus rose from his chair and stalked around his desk until he was looming over her.

"That's sound logic until you start sacrificing others on your behalf. You're happy sending Mira, your sister who just started speaking full sentences, to slaughter? Am I hearing that correctly?"

Reality hit Leda like she'd been plunged head first into ice water. Her hands clenched into fists in her lap, nails biting painfully into her palms. "I ... It's an impossible choice, I don't know what—"

"Exactly!" Then his hands were around her shoulders and he was pulling her to her feet until she was crushed against him. Her trembling hands came to rest on his back as his arms wound around her waist. He held her so tightly she could barely breathe. "It *is* an impossible choice. I will not kill you, or any of them. I can't."

She sagged in his arms, but he kept her upright. "You should."

"I won't. Ever."

Because he wouldn't sacrifice one life for another, would never be the one to make the choice to send someone he cared about to their death regardless of who it might help. It wasn't the person he was; it ran counter to every moral he had.

Did that make him a good person? Yes. Did it make him a good king? That, she couldn't answer so easily.

But what did she know about what it took to be a ruler, to hold the lives and deaths of millions in one's hands? She was so tiny, so inconsequential by comparison.

"I'm sorry, I'm so sorry, I don't know what to do," she whispered.

His lips were against her forehead, then her cheeks, then her jaw, and she let out a muffled sob.

"This is what makes me singularly unsuited to be king. I'm paralysed too. I won't do anything that will hurt you, even if *everyone* else I'm supposed to protect dies. That, Leda, is true selfishness. I should never have accused you of it—"

He couldn't continue what he was saying, because he'd been shoved rather unceremoniously backwards and her lips were on his.

There was no delay this time, no shock. He responded instantly, as though picking up where they'd left off in those woods was second nature, something he'd been waiting for every second that had ticked by since it happened.

His hands fisted in the silk skirts at her hips and he used the leverage to fuse her body against his.

She'd accepted that she was probably going to die, but

she couldn't go without being with him, even just once, if that was what he wanted as well.

And so she brought him back to her and kissed him harder, and he met her fervour with his own, spinning her around and lifting her on to the edge of his desk.

He let out a guttural groan when she wrapped her legs around his waist. It felt as natural as breathing, was without her conscious direction. She needed to get closer to him, was almost crazed with it. His eyes opened, dazed and drunk, and he looked around the room with something resembling dissatisfaction.

Her confidence faltered, but she could see the tightness of his fist around the silk of her skirts, hear the shuddering of his breath. What he was frowning about seemed to be the room itself.

He lifted her up in one smooth motion and pressed her against the bookshelves that covered the entire right wall.

When he took one arm away from her back and began to shift, she gasped. The shelf at her back rattled with the force he was applying to it. Hopefully he was doing something to make it more comfortable because the lines of the books digging into her back were threatening to lift her from the pleasurable feelings she would prefer to be drowning in.

"Wh ... what are you doing?" She pulled away with difficulty to watch the books spilling to the floor around her with loud thuds.

"Just ... just *there*," he said the last word in triumph, letting out a breath of relief mixed with something else as a metallic clink sounded behind Leda's head and the book-case swung outward. She would have lost her balance and toppled backwards if he hadn't held her locked up against him.

Pyrrhus let her down on to her feet, spun her until her

back was against his chest and she looked breathlessly at the narrow spiral staircase that seemed to go down forever. It must go right into the basement of the palace.

A secret passageway.

"How ... what is this?" Leda's words ended on a whimper as his lips descended to the most sensitive part of her neck and his hands tightened around her waist.

He didn't answer, instead urging her down the steps. They rocked up against the stone walls and Leda had to brace herself there as his hands traversed her body.

She barely knew where she was when she heard the creak of a door opening, the rustle of a tapestry being moved and found herself blinking in the light of a familiar corridor.

"Oh—"

Then her hand was in his and he was pulling her towards the door of his old study. She was gratified to see him curse at how many attempts it took to get the key in the lock, his distraction clear.

Finally, it was open and he had swept her down the stairs. He made it all the more dangerous by kissing her as they staggered down each step. She made it all the more dangerous by responding enthusiastically. They would both sustain some serious injuries if they fell, and yet neither of them could summon the will to care.

His hands were tangled in her hair.

The sounds of objects clattering to the ground, flung by the sweep of a strong arm.

Leda felt cool mahogany against her back. Clarity hit her and her eyes flew open.

"I'm sorry, did you just relocate me to your *preferred desk*?"

"I was going for the bedroom, but—"

He'd missed.

His pupils were blown wide. She must have smashed his IQ apart until it was less than half what it usually was. Pride licked through her at the thought.

She got her revenge by tracing her hands down the planes of his stomach through his shirt and he seemed to temporarily lose the ability to speak altogether.

He swept the final pot of quills off the desk with a groan. "Here will do."

Leda couldn't protest because they were both self-sacrificing idiots who should have done this a year ago and she was not waiting one second longer. If she couldn't be with him now then she never would, and the very thought was unthinkable.

She had no idea what she was doing, of course, had barely touched anyone else in her life. But he was the only person she'd ever wanted. It was this realisation that had her pushing things forward.

She wanted him. All of him.

She untied his cravat and wrenched his shirt over his head.

He caged her in with his body, his lips pressed against her chest above the bodice of her dress, just over the violent thudding of her heart.

"What do you want?" he said, his voice hoarse. "We can do anything you want. We can stop right here if that's what you desire."

A surge of frustration ripped through her at his gentlemanly questions and she thudded her head back against the desk in annoyance. His laugh was a huff against her skin.

"I'll take that as a no, then. What do you want, Leda?"

"I don't know enough to articulate it," she gasped. "I'd need to do some research."

He looked up and across the shelves near his desk. "I have some books on the subject—"

She let out a sound of mixed exasperation and laughter and pulled him back down to her. "I intend to learn through experience."

"Well I usually advise a literature review first, but I'll make an exception—" He cut himself off. Thankfully, he seemed to be bringing some experience of his own to the table that Leda was able to follow.

His hands were a brand across her skin, sliding under her skirts and over her thighs, eliciting a sound she'd never made before in her life. She felt like she was drowning in sensation.

He watched her face with the intensity of a man trying to memorise everything about her. She urged him towards her with her hands on his back.

She needed him to be hers, now. She was tired of waiting.

"Please," she whispered into his neck.

He didn't need to be told twice.

CHAPTER 28

The results of the trials were not announced immediately; in fact they took days, and the Five Kingdoms waited with bated breath for news. The inns of Gemdark overflowed with dignitaries from Saint-Trevale, Doviet, Slofray, Rivernesse and the lands beyond who had come to hear the results.

A huge platform stood in the palatial town square facing the Gemdark Temple, draped in gold cloth.

Leda watched the fountains flow with wine as she and her family approached in a small delegation of carriages. Pyrrhus had allowed them to take seats on the platform that would hold him, the three remaining families and government representatives for the announcement. He'd stipulated that their seats be behind a panel of frosted glass for their own safety, but they'd be involved at least.

There was a sense of festivity and excitement in the air, despite the fact that it was still bitterly cold and icy.

Leda watched Thalia, Pan and Zephyr, all splendidly dressed, line up on the platform next to Pyrrhus amid raucous cheers. Well, she watched their blurry shapes move from behind the frosted glass, but she was still happy to even be seeing part of this historic event.

A muted sort of excitement flared through her. Pyrrhus's abdication was on the horizon, and he looked happier about it than any of the misguided fools who competed for the throne. She was so pleased for him. He'd accomplished incredible things, had given so much of himself to keep the people safe. He deserved this reprieve.

And if she didn't get to spend the life he'd got back with him, that was awful, but at least he had it. Her father would take her life from beyond the grave, but he wouldn't get Pyrrhus's.

As though sensing her morbid thoughts, Eber reached over from beside her and squeezed her hand. She wrapped his in both of hers and refused to let go.

"Thank you," he murmured to her, too low for anyone else to hear. "For everything you've done for me since you came back. I'm feeling more like myself again. I wasted so much time in a stupor, I thought I wouldn't even have—ow!"

She'd almost crushed his hand between hers, fighting back tears. "I'm so sorry." She released him.

He let out a mild chuckle, not quite back to full force, but getting there. "Excitement of the day getting to you?"

"Something like that." She turned away so he wouldn't see her traitorously red eyes. She couldn't tell him what was coming, it would rip him apart. It would send him straight back to his vice. She knew that better than anyone because all she wanted nowadays was to obliterate her consciousness with hibcus.

She had to spare him, even if it meant keeping him in the dark. He might one day hate her for it, but she could accept that.

A flare of trumpets quieted the crowd, and Pyrrhus stepped forward to make his speech. The people listened rapturously to his summary of each of the trials and the winners and losers, and his careful explanation of how the scores had been tallied. He even went into detail on the nature and purpose of the secret trials he'd conducted, which Leda hadn't expected.

"I am honoured to be able to announce our next monarch. A leader who is strong and decisive, intelligent and fair. May I present the future Queen Thalia of the Five Kingdoms!"

A roar of triumph went up from the Doviet delegations. The rest of the crowd clapped politely, not knowing much of Thalia, but they seemed pleased to be part of the ceremony of it all. Leda saw the blurred form of Thalia embracing her husband through the pane of glass.

It was the right decision. Thalia wasn't particularly impressive on first impression, but she was wise and balanced. Her family adored her, which was more important than anything else in Leda's view as it reinforced the true goodness of her character. Unlike Linus, whose child had flinched whenever he entered the room, or Zephyr, who had sacrificed his parents to save his own skin.

Pan and Zephyr stood frozen as the rest of the officials on the platform converged around Thalia.

A few minutes later Atticus ushered Leda, Elina, Eber and Fessler down the steps at the back of the platform and into the red brick alleyway leading to the waiting carriages.

Elina let out a garbled sound of outrage, having been shoved out the way by Pan as he stomped down the steps from the platform, Arsen hot on his heels. He gave her a look that quelled anything she might have said and forced his way through the gathered guards towards the carriages.

He was taking it well, then.

Thankfully Castor managed to get down from the platform without causing bodily harm to anyone, though the look on his face was as dark as that of his brothers. His eyes passed over Leda, and he stopped as though some invisible force had taken hold of his limbs. Within seconds he was moving again, but this time it was towards her.

The aggression on his face had her backing up a few steps.

Castor completed the journey for her, placing a hand squarely where the arrow had gone through her shoulder and using it to shove her against the wall of the alley. All the breath left her as her back made contact with the bricks.

What in the gods' names did he think he was doing? She could throttle him. Metaphorically, of course. Physically there was no way she had the strength.

He really was very tall. It struck her that he could squash her like a bug if he desired, and that it would take him little effort.

There was an uproar behind Castor, nearly drowned out by the still-cheering crowd. Leda looked around his shoulder to see guards approaching and Pyrrhus nowhere to be seen on the platform he'd occupied moments before.

Castor seized Leda's jaw in his hand, squeezing until the bones hurt, directing her attention to him. He really had a handsome face; it was a shame it masked such a hideous personality.

"How dare you stand there and look smug at my brother's failure, stupid little whore!" he spat in her face. "You'll get what's coming to you, you upstart piece of vermin."

There was a blur of movement. A hand took Leda around the waist from the side and yanked her away from Castor as he was promptly removed from her front. She came up against a hard chest and recognised Pyrrhus immediately. His other arm wrapped around her so he fully encircled her as he stared over her head with an expression of absolute rage.

Castor, in the meantime, had been lifted clear off his feet by two enormous guards and was dangling between them, all dignity gone.

"We all see what's happened here!" Castor yelled, breathless in his struggle to be released. "You rushed the trials so you could be with your whore, because you know no one would ever accept an insipid mouse like her as queen. I'll bet everything I own that you rigged the competition against us! You couldn't bear to have someone more intelligent than you on the throne to uncover all the mistakes you've made—you've always been pathetic, Pyrrhus Selhurst!"

One of the many impressive things about Pyrrhus was that, even while enraged, he had control over his temper. Instead of surging towards the open target that Castor presented, as Leda could tell he wanted to by the tension in his body, he held himself in check.

Slowly, Pyrrhus removed a handkerchief from his pocket and handed it to Leda. She used it to wipe Castor's spit off her face and had to consciously stop herself from punching Castor in the stomach. She wasn't sure she had Pyrrhus's ironclad restraint.

"You are embarrassing yourself," Pyrrhus said, his voice glacial. "Guards, take him away."

Castor did not respond well to being dismissed like he was beneath the king's notice. He chose to express this by yelling every obscenity he could think of as he was removed from the alley.

The remaining guards stared after him with mouths agape, and swivelled back to Pyrrhus. He let Leda go and she had to fight the ridiculous urge to burrow her way back in.

"Are you alright?"

"Yes, of course, no harm done."

"Good." His face did not reflect that sentiment at all. "Atticus, take them back to the palace, now. When you get there, see to it that the Ariti brothers are escorted from the grounds. Do not let them anywhere near Leda, am I understood?"

"Of course, Your Majesty." Atticus put a firm hand on Leda's shoulder and steered her past an uncharacteristically silent Eber and Elina, towards the carriages. Leda allowed herself to be moved, missing the time in her life when she wasn't at the centre of so many spectacles. She was certain her face was tomato red with embarrassment.

The carriage was silent as they climbed in, and Leda watched through the window as Atticus strode over to the carriage into which two guards were trying to stuff Castor. Atticus wrenched him upright by his shoulders, and she could hear muffled shouting through the glass.

Her carriage rocked as the horses broke into motion, the last image in her mind the expression of mixed incredulity and disgust on Atticus's face at whatever Castor had just said to him.

What a way to end a day of celebration.

CHAPTER 29

Leda was in the grand king's office by the time Pyrrhus returned from Gemdark. She'd never felt nerves clawing at her like this before, could barely keep still. She paced back and forth behind his desk.

Castor's outburst had rattled her.

She paused with her hand on the back of the ornate king's chair, telling herself to sit, to calm down. But she baulked at the idea of sitting *there*. Instead, she settled on the leather reading chair in the corner.

Pyrrhus arrived as soon as she sat down.

He stopped short the moment he laid eyes on her, clearly not expecting to find her, palpably panicked, in his office.

She hadn't even opened her mouth to speak before Ecgred was banging his way through the door behind him.

"You need to calm down!"

That recalled Pyrrhus immediately to the conversation, or perhaps shouting match, that Leda had just interrupted.

He turned on his heel to face his advisor, who tried and failed to hide his annoyance when he registered Leda's presence.

"Do not tell me to calm down. He *spat* at her, Ecgred."

"And he's been ejected from the palace with his brothers; what more do you want?"

"I want him banished."

Ecgred tutted. "Hard to justify. It makes you look impulsive, ruled by emotion."

"Funnily enough, I do not care," Pyrrhus said from between gritted teeth. "Besides, I'm about to renounce the throne; you no longer have to concern yourself with my image."

Ecgred pursed his lips. "We need something concrete—"

"As far as I'm concerned someone who would assault her in front of that many people would have no compunction in shooting or poisoning her in private."

"You ...," Ecgred faltered, eyes widening. "You think he's the assassin?"

"Perhaps, or Arsen is more likely. Castor was terrible at combat at school; I doubt he's made a concerted effort to improve since."

"But ... why? Why would he do that?"

Pyrrhus exchanged a look with Leda and she shook her head minutely. Ecgred was a pragmatist, he served the throne over and above those who sat on it. If he learned of the curse he'd probably hurl the letter opener on Pyrrhus's desk at her without a second thought. Then he'd bustle off to dispose of Eber and Mira, whistling all the while.

"There are reasons."

Ecgred looked seconds away from childishly stamping his foot. "How can you expect me to advise you when I don't have the full picture?"

"I don't," Pyrrhus said coldly.

Ecgred started pacing in a style so similar to the one that Leda had just employed that she recoiled. He noticed her movement out of the corner of his eye and then his full attention was on her. "Perhaps we should conduct this conversation without Ledazaria present." He then displayed the terrible judgment necessary to open the door and point at it while looking meaningfully at her.

Cold filled her veins. She didn't move an inch.

"You don't direct me. Anywhere," Leda said, her tone matching Pyrrhus's. She couldn't believe this man had the nerve.

"These are matters of ruling, Ledazaria. They are too complex for you to fully comprehend, and misunderstandings sit at the core of poor advice."

"You would know all about that," she snapped.

Pyrrhus turned, ostensibly to look out the window, but she caught the shadow of the instinctive smile on his face. By the time he turned back to face them, his expression was grave once more.

Ecgred was stunned into silence before he sputtered. "Your Majesty, I must insist—"

"None of us are in a state to carry out this conversation now. Thank you for your input, but I must ask you to leave, Ecgred."

Now it was Pyrrhus pointing at the door, and Ecgred couldn't move to it fast enough. There was a magnificent slam as he yanked it shut behind him.

Then silence, for long minutes.

By the time Leda had managed to pull herself out of her thoughts Pyrrhus wasn't standing where he'd last been.

He was in front of the window, hands clasped behind his back. The line of his spine was so straight it was as though someone had drawn it with a ruler.

Leda directed her sullen stare to the bookshelves. "I missed it."

He jerked a little, as though he'd forgotten he wasn't alone. "What?"

"I was trying to ensure the right person won the trials, to protect the people from a reign like my father's. But I was blinded by Linus's aggression and Zephyr's scheming. I barely paid attention to Pan, I thought he was too *boring*." She shook her head, hardly able to believe her mistake, the conclusions she'd leapt to. "I should have investigated more, not taken Castor at his word."

"It's easy to castigate ourselves in hindsight," Pyrrhus said, still absorbed in the view outside. "What I can't deduce is why or how they'd have done this. They were accompanied at the shrine when Markus and Elov were killed."

"Hired assassins? Or one of them slipped away without detection? Who knows, but the *why* of it is easier to guess at. They found out about the curse and decided to kill the entire Locarno line to end it; it's why they got Caspari and Markus, not just the Counterparts."

Pyrrhus turned to face her as he continued her thought. "So that when Pan won the trials and took the throne there would be no curse hanging over it at all." He said grimly, as though he'd usually love to solve this kind of puzzle but all the pleasure had been stripped out of it for him. "Not a terrible plan, but poorly executed."

She couldn't agree more. "They assumed he'd win the trials."

Pyrrhus sighed. "He nearly did. But how could they have found out?"

"I'd guess Melia and Celandine aren't the only ones who know about the curse. The Aritis were in the temple or at the shrine practically every day; it's not infeasible that another priestess could have told them."

"Of course we can prove none of this."

She gave a humourless smile. "Of course."

"I'll have Atticus ensure they stay away while we investigate, by any means necessary."

She nodded. "Let's hope that's enough."

He planted his hands on his desk and leaned over it, surveying her with the kind of focus that had her feeling totally exposed, as though all her secrets were laid bare for him to see. It was for that reason that she refused to meet his eye.

"It's all rather bleak, isn't it?" she murmured.

"That had better not be you giving up. We have time."

But what good would time do against insurmountable odds? The Aritis would be the first in a long line of those who would want to end the Locarnos. Thalia's ascension to the throne meant nothing.

She wondered if Ambrose had found the painless method of death she'd asked for yet, resolving to find him and check. And then she'd have to figure out with Eber what the bloody hell they were going to do with it.

There was so much dissonance in her mind she wanted to curl up and scream.

But she couldn't, not in front of Pyrrhus.

And so she redirected the conversation. "Atticus may be able to keep the Aritis away for a while, but they're still a threat. You could have them all imprisoned."

Pyrrhus was already shaking his head, standing up to his full height once more. "No, Ecgred was right. No punishments without trial."

His reaction was instant, without thought, and it was at that moment she knew with certainty that, even after all he'd been through, the crown hadn't corrupted him. It had made him more self-sacrificing, masochistic enough to work himself to death trying to fix everything, but it hadn't poisoned his mind.

He was extraordinary.

"Pyrrhus," she said, emotion surging within her. "I—"

The door slamming open announced Ecgred's return.

He poked his head and none of the rest of his body into the room, clearly reluctant to be back so soon after being dismissed.

"Thalia requests an audience, immediately," he said with an expression that told them he wasn't pleased to be the messenger.

Pyrrhus nodded, reaching for the tailcoat he'd discarded on the back of his chair. As he pulled it on, his movements as assured and efficient as ever, he approached Leda. He didn't seem to care one bit that Ecgred's beady eyes were still fixed on him.

He looked down at her for a moment, expression contemplative. "Ten guards."

Her lips twitched, the fog of stress lifting, if only for a second. "Seven."

"Deal." He reached down, offering his hand to shake like he might at any of his official meetings. She grasped it and found herself instead pulled to her feet. Her lips parted as she came up against his chest, but he was folding her into his arms and kissing her before she could get any words out.

The sound of the door snapping shut as Ecgred hastily extracted his head from the room had her shaking with laughter.

When Leda finally found Ambrose he was transiting the corridors at a truly reckless speed, nearly knocking over a statue as he rounded the corner.

He had his medical kit tucked under one arm and seemed to be making a concerted attempt to inhale the sandwich in his other hand as he strode towards the infirmary. He raised a brow at her as she joined him.

"What's got you in such a hurry?"

"A squadron of guards got into a ridiculous fight about nothing and now half of them have bloody noses," Ambrose said, his voice one long groan. "And Eber forgot to take his medicine this morning. I need to ensure he gets it before the withdrawal symptoms kick in, leaving me with approximately half a second to eat this sandwich." He promptly shoved the rest of it into his mouth.

She'd never seen someone chew so resentfully before, but at least it momentarily shut him up.

"I think others know about the curse, Ambrose," she hissed. "We're in more danger than ever. Did you find"—she cast her eyes around the deserted corridor—"a way?"

His pace eased, allowing her to walk in step with him without her leg screeching in pain.

"It shouldn't be necessary, Leda, plans can be put in place to keep you safe."

"You know as well as I do that plans mean nothing. I'd prefer options other than dying surprised and in agony," she said. "Unless you've thought of a spectacular way out of all of this that you've failed to share with me? Because you're so much cleverer than the rest of us?"

She was concerned for a second that, now he'd finished his sandwich, he was able to reach out with his free hand and throttle her. Instead he slammed his eyes shut and came to an abrupt halt.

His expression was strained and she realised then that he'd looked that way for a long time.

"Gods give me patience," he growled. "You're even more irritating now than when you were rip-roaringly drunk; you make me want to—" His eyes flew open as he cut himself off. He had a vaguely stupefied look on his face, as though he'd just been struck by a blunt object.

"What is it?"

Something lit up his eyes. "*Finally!*" He was speaking to

himself more than her, must have been, given she had no clue what he was talking about. "Listen, I ... I have the serum you'll need, but ... give me a few days more, alright?"

She supposed she could allow him that. Not that she had any choice. He didn't wait for a response, a new energy in his step as he tore off towards the infirmary at a speed she couldn't match if she tried.

CHAPTER 30

Though the weather was caused by the freakish machinations of gods, it did create a merry air for Thalia's coronation. The grounds of the palace were blanketed in pure, dazzling white, and local tradesmen crafted beautiful statues of ice to decorate the hibernating rose garden.

The throne room had been filled with hundreds of candles and glittered with light on the evening before the coronation. The palace was full and bustling as dignitaries from the conquered kingdoms and beyond arrived to bear witness to the event. Leda couldn't walk through a corridor without passing excitable groups of people there to celebrate and laugh and finally move on from the horrors of her father's reign.

It was faintly painful to watch the servants putting up bunting in the banquet hall, the atmosphere more jovial than she'd ever seen it.

The knowledge that this coronation wouldn't fix all these people's problems ate at her. The Counterparts weren't dead and a Locarno didn't sit on the throne, and so the weather would continue to rain down the gods' wrath.

The future was so uncertain.

Princess Gabriell was three years old, so the kingdom would need to suffer through ninety or so more years until the entire Locarno bloodline, Counterpart and royal alike, was gone. And that was if all of them agreed not to have children of their own. That would be its own struggle. But then the people would prosper again. It was abhorrent, but there was no other path she could think of. Perhaps, when Mira had reached her majority, Leda and Eber could speak to her about it, and they could all decide what to do with themselves.

If Leda happened to be the last of the three to die naturally and the people were open to a Locarno royal taking the crown again, perhaps she would take herself out of the equation using whatever painless serum Ambrose had managed to find for her.

She decided not to workshop that particular idea with Pyrrhus.

As if her thoughts had called him, Pyrrhus appeared at her side, watching with a wry smile as a servant dropped a length of bunting and loudly cursed. He wore no crown, and looked ten times better for it. He'd seemed keen not to wear it since Thalia had been announced as the new ruler, and no one had worked harder than he to arrange for her coronation to happen as quickly as possible.

"Are you well?" Pyrrhus asked her.

The back of her hand skimmed across his. "Quite well, thank you. You seem to be in good spirits today."

Eber came up behind him before he could respond, clapping him soundly on the shoulders. "Of course he is!" her brother said. "He just abdicated this morning."

Music to Leda's ears.

She turned to Pyrrhus with a smile. "And how do you plan to celebrate?"

"I can think of a few ways."

Eber dropped his hands from Pyrrhus's shoulders, scrunching up his whole face in disgust. "I'm standing *right here*." His shudder was so pronounced it wracked his whole body. "I would vomit if it weren't such a happy day."

"You seem to be feeling better," Pyrrhus observed, finally taking his eyes off Leda.

Eber shrugged. "I'm ... alright," he said. "Leda and I decided to take some time over the next few months to help right some of the wrongs caused by the gods' curse, given it's all stemming from our family. We'll go to some of the worst affected towns and help with the relief efforts."

He'd lit up when she'd made the suggestion, delighted with the prospect of bringing some purpose to his life. It would also provide them with the opportunity to speak to others about the gods' curses, to try and find a way to break theirs given books and priestesses were leading them nowhere.

Pyrrhus turned to Leda. "Will you require assistance?"

It was the most *Pyrrhus* way imaginable of asking to come along. So polite, like he was offering to help her down some steep steps. She'd foolishly made the assumption that he'd accompany them, and flushed as she realised quite how presumptuous that was.

"We can probably squeeze one more into the carriage. If you're available, of course." She attempted to be cool and collected and failed miserably judging by the look he gave her.

"Given there's still an assassin out there the fact that you think you and Eber could go gallivanting around the kingdom without protection is laughable. Of course I'm coming."

Eber snorted at that. "If your concern is about protection we could bring Azaria."

Azaria would strike paralysing fear into the hearts of anyone who gave them so much as a second look. Of course there was also the fact that the probability of her maiming Leda or Eber on the trip was higher than nil. It would be best to avoid that.

Pyrrhus frowned, clearly thinking along the same lines. "No."

Leda sighed. "Very well then, I suppose it had better be you."

"And six guards?" he asked hopefully.

Eber made a noise of disgust and walked off.

Leda gave Pyrrhus a dour look. "I am not having this conversation with you again."

"The point is moot, I suppose. I don't have any guards left to command after today."

She couldn't believe how pleased he looked about that. At one point he'd have been only too happy to see hundreds of guards buzzing around her like she was a human beehive.

Elina stalked into the room, her hair piled carelessly on top of her head, the bags beneath her eyes so pronounced they were almost purple.

"Where's Thalia? The priestesses need to paint her with the blessings before tomorrow's ceremony."

"She was in the rose garden, last I saw," Pyrrhus said.

"I was just there and she isn't." Elina let out a huff of annoyance. "She treats me like a bloody servant; I'm not at her beck and call. I shouldn't be running around after her all day."

Leda and Pyrrhus exchanged a look and stayed silent.

"Sir!" Elina pointed to Thalia's husband, whose name no one knew even now. He'd just entered the hall and seemed to be contemplating walking straight back out again. "Where is your wife?"

There was quiet as they all remembered that he did not

speak to them, and Elina gave another growl of frustration. "Just point!"

He cast around as though expecting Thalia to emerge from one of the walls and settled for a shrug instead. Concern flickered across his expression.

Elina cut an exhausted glance at Leda. "I can't wait until this is all over."

"I couldn't agree more."

Elina's expression faltered. "Oh, I almost forgot." She extracted a crumpled envelope from her pocket. "Atticus asked me to give this to you, because apparently I am the messenger for every occupant of this wretched palace." She stuffed it into Leda's hand and walked off in a huff.

Leda broke the seal and unfolded it.

I need to tell you something
Mistresses' rooms, as soon as you can
Come alone, tell no one, trust no one

Before Leda could slip away to meet Atticus, Thalia's daughter went into a full panic. Selene didn't know where her mother was and was building herself into a towering rage in her anxiety. When she began to hyperventilate, Pyrrhus stepped in.

He brought in Ambrose to calm her and assured the rest of them that there was nothing to worry about. He did, however, ask that they assist the guards in locating Thalia.

Perhaps she'd got cold feet and had ensconced herself somewhere to build up the nerve required to sit on a throne like this. Why anyone would want it, Leda couldn't fathom. As far as she was concerned Thalia was chaining herself to a life of misery. She'd never look over her shoulder without fear again. She'd likely fall into corruption and greed and arrogance just like Leda's father.

Still, hiding didn't fit with what Leda knew of Thalia. They'd only spoken on brief occasions but she seemed to have a solid, dependable head on her shoulders.

Nevertheless, they all agreed to search the palace to lift the uneasy air that had befallen them.

Leda suggested that she and Eber search the mistresses' rooms in the basement, giving her the perfect cover to meet Atticus. He'd told her to bring no one, to trust no one, but Eber didn't count. She trusted him completely, couldn't switch it off if she tried.

He was unenthusiastic as she dragged him down towards the cold and draughty corridors.

They descended the stairs with little grace. They had to take a candle of their own into the pitch-black halls, and when Leda stumbled and trod on the back of his foot Eber howled like she'd stabbed him.

"I hate this place," Leda muttered as Eber lit the sconces on the wall. He kicked what turned out to be a large, loose cloud of dust and they spent the next few moments coughing.

"Is anyone here?" she asked, but Atticus did not step out of the shadows. They were alone.

Perhaps he was running late. An uncomfortable feeling lodged somewhere around her diaphragm told her that she might be wrong, that the reason could be much less innocent.

But they were nothing if not dutiful, and they were there to search for Thalia. They spent the next thirty minutes in the abandoned mistresses' rooms, exploring ever more dusty and disused living spaces. They saved their mother's rooms for last, dreading the reminder of her and of Ami, but couldn't put it off forever.

The door creaked gratingly as they pushed it open, and they stood on the threshold for a long moment, taking in the sitting room. A chair lay overturned in one corner, a nearby wall hanging ripped in two. A stack of rotting logs stood by a fireplace that hadn't been used in over a year.

"They always said she was our father's favourite mistress; the room sizes seem to bear that out," Leda mused, moving aside so Eber could enter.

"This is so boring," he announced, dramatically pulling back the curtains that framed a painting as though Thalia might be crouched behind them. "What would you do, if it were your coronation tomorrow?"

Leda was looking at the fireplace, and attached chimney, with more suspicion than anyone else might. "My coronation? What in the gods' names are you talking about?"

"You know, if you were queen? How would you run things?"

Leda snorted as she checked behind the settee. All that greeted her was dust and grime. "Who knows? I'd probably do a bloody awful job and run the kingdom into the ground. What do I know about anything? Who would even listen to me?"

Eber sighed dramatically. "Shame on me for starting an interesting topic of conversation. Of course you'd use it as an opportunity to talk yourself down. You're hardly a fluff-brained slug, Leda."

She laughed. "High praise, that. What would you do if you were king?"

Eber opened a decorative china teapot and peered inside. "I'd probably go travelling around, I don't know what any of these countries look like. I'd get a feel for the land-scape, you know? And while I'm at it I'd actually pay the guards and servants properly and make music lessons mandatory for all children across the Five Kingdoms."

Such an *Eber* set of policy priorities there. "You've clearly thought it through."

"I can't believe you haven't. All these years we've been stuck here staring at that godsforsaken throne, and you never once thought of what you might do with all that power?"

"I didn't imagine it because the thought is ludicrous, Eber. First of all, you know I think power is awful. If you managed to finagle your way on to that throne it would turn you into a bratty little despot to rival even Azaria. Besides, I'm not the kind of person who could lead anybody. Elina once called me the depressing ghost that haunts the corridors. I'm not exactly awe-inspiring, am I?" She stuck her head into the bathing room.

Eber stretched out his arms to the side and moved them as though he were treading water. "So much self-pity in the room all of a sudden, I'm afraid I might drown in it."

He dodged the sofa cushion she hurled at his head.

Having found nothing, they proceeded into their mother's bedroom. Here there were also signs of a hasty escape: wardrobe doors open, dresses all over the floor in a riot of silks and satins.

Leda could feel both of their moods dim at the sight.

'She really cleared out her jewellery collection when she left, didn't she?' Eber said grimly, looking from the empty box on the dressing table to the clumsily embroidered cushion that Ami had made for their mother. It was small and maroon with gold stitching, and hideously ugly. It lay abandoned on the seat, clearly not a treasure worth taking to Olora. That surprised neither of them.

Eber picked up the cushion, dusted it off, and tucked it under his arm. Leda had half a mind to ask for it herself and was stamping down on the selfish urge when a shadow appeared under the door.

"Thalia?" Leda called out. No response. "Atticus?"

Exchanging a bewildered look with Eber, Leda opened the door.

A masked figure clad entirely in black lunged at her. She shrieked, trying to slam the heavy door closed. They heard the sickening thud of a knife slamming into the opposite side and Leda cried out as a great force had it swinging open again, crashing against her previously injured shoulder. She dropped to the ground as Eber dashed over to her.

But their assailant had made it into the room, knife recovered from the wood and glinting wickedly in the faint light. The masked figure stepped clear over Leda and ran at Eber with the weapon held aloft.

The way out was clear, safety within her reach, but Leda didn't consider it for a moment.

Panic, pure and focused, streaked through her veins. She sprang forward to seize the intruder's ankle before they could reach Eber. They went down but caught themselves with their hands with all of the grace of an acrobat. Grasping the knife once more, they lunged at a terrified Eber.

Unwieldy slashing and stabbing motions missed his body by inches.

Not on Leda's watch. This was *not* going to happen again.

With a strangled "no!" Leda launched herself to her feet and hurled herself forward to tackle the attacker to the ground from behind. She hurt a faintly surprised sound amidst the grunt as they hit the stone floor, hard.

Her leg protested viciously but she couldn't care about that, boxing the pain away in her mind as she'd trained herself to do. She took the attacker's shoulder and roughly rolled them to face her.

They were staring through their mask at Leda. Something was familiar about their eyes, but it was too dark to tell.

Her heart beat so fast it felt ready to tear itself out of her chest, and the feeling persisted as Eber joined them and pinned the attacker's hands to the ground. Leda wrenched the knife out of their grip and flung it away, earning a stinging cut to her arm in the struggle.

The knowledge that this must be the person who'd killed Ami, who was murdering Counterparts and royal children alike in cold blood, was all she could think of as she straddled the squirming figure. She took the base of the black mask and battled the sudden paralysing fear that she was about to reveal a headful of black hair.

But it couldn't be, if this were Azaria she wouldn't have been subdued this quickly.

If this were Azaria, Leda and Eber would have been dead within seconds of her entering the room.

Oddly reassured by the thought, Leda ripped the silk mask away from their assailant's head.

A beautiful face with an angular jaw that had once sent the court painter into paroxysms of compliments. Rich, dark hair. Eyes burning with familiar rage.

Elina.

CHAPTER 31

*L*eda sagged on top of her sister, the shock hitting her with all of the impact of a slap across the face.

"No," she breathed.

"Elina ...," Eber said, voice wavering, though he continued to hold her wrists firm against the ground.

There was no way ... this couldn't be. But the truth was staring them both defiantly in the face.

Leda got to her feet with slow, methodical movements and crossed the room to retrieve Elina's knife. The knife that she'd intended to kill Eber with.

She returned and sat back on top of Elina's stomach, so carelessly she took vicious pleasure in hearing her lose all of the air in her lungs at the impact. A white hot, quiet kind of rage flowed through her, but she felt calmer than she had in months. She levelled the knife at Elina's throat and watched her eyes widen in fear.

"Eber," Leda said. "Go and get help." He hesitated, and she cast him a speaking glance. "Now, do it now."

"But she'll hurt you."

He didn't have faith in Leda's skills, and she wasn't offended. She'd had precisely none of the training that Elina had. She was sitting on top of a woman who had been instructed in murder since she was old enough to hold a sword.

But Leda could see the tears leaking from the corners of Elina's eyes, could feel the trembling in her limbs.

"She's almost as highly trained as Azaria; if she had the guts to kill either one of us we'd both be dead already. Go. Now."

His reluctance was clear, but he nevertheless scrambled to his feet, nearly staggering. The shock had got to him; he appeared completely unmoored from reality. He made his way out of the room at a run.

There was silence.

Leda was the one to break it. Her blood felt like it was boiling in her veins. "So, you're the one."

All of the fight seemed to go out of Elina and she slumped her head back on to the floor. Even the trembling stopped. "Yes."

"All along?"

"Yes."

"Caspari? Elov and Markus?"

Elina wouldn't meet her eye. Tears slid down her temples and on to the floor. She dipped her chin in the smallest of nods and Leda could have screamed.

She pressed the blade into Elina's throat and a bead of blood bloomed at the wickedly pointed end. Leda never wanted to do great violence before, had thought herself more of a pacifist, but at that moment something funda- mental had shifted in her. She knew without a shadow of a doubt that she could plunge this knife into Elina's chest and, for one bright flash of a second, it would bring her satis- faction.

"Ami?"

Elina closed her eyes as though the word pained her

more than the cut, but did not nod. She didn't need to, the guilt was written all over her traitorous, murderous face. Leda let out a shuddering breath.

"You killed her? A ten-year-old. Your sister."

Elina's eyes were still closed, her expression agonised as she shook her head. "She *had* to die."

Oh, Elina. What had she done? And what would she lead Leda to do in revenge?

Now it was Leda's hands that were trembling.

"You shot me with an arrow, and poisoned me, and the gods only know what else."

Elina's eyes flew open. "I didn't want to; you have to believe me! It's the gods' decree, it's for the greater good. You all have to die. I'm so sorry, Leda, but it's true. It's the curse, the part that Melia left out." Her whole body was wracked with a sob that had Leda shifting with her.

"So you took it upon yourself to take the Counterparts out, then?"

"It was my calling from the gods; I had to set things right. Don't look away, Leda, you need to listen to me! This is why they put me through so much growing up, to make me strong enough to do this." She continued despite Leda's violently shaking head, her voice frantic. "People are dying all over the Five Kingdoms, Leda, just because the Counterparts live. What were five lives compared with tens of thousands?"

Elina's hair was glimmering wet with her tears, her voice beseeching. She really was trying to make Leda understand.

The unwelcome memory of Leda repeating almost the exact same reasoning to Pyrrhus made her feel physically sick. But though the guilt had eaten at her, she was never committed, could never have brought herself to do something like this.

These acts were evil, reprehensible. They were unfor-givable.

"And what was your plan for Mira, Elina? How were you going to kill the four-year-old?"

"I ... I don't know."

"It seems ending our father's life gave you a taste for murder."

"No, no!" Elina struggled underneath her, though was clearly not putting her full strength into it. "I didn't enjoy it, I was doing it for the good of the people. I was saving thousands of lives."

"Don't you dare speak as though that absolves you. You *killed your family*," Leda spat.

Leda had been dragged back to the palace kicking and screaming, desperate to avoid that family. She'd spent months coming to terms with the fact that they were some of the most important pieces of her life, no matter how much they might annoy or exasperate her. They were *hers*, and she was theirs. The people who cared for her were sacrosanct.

Elina had apparently spent the same period learning the exact opposite lesson. It was sickening.

Elina bit her lip to try and stifle her sobbing. Leda had rarely seen her cry before. But it didn't matter. She was an easily led, morally repugnant weakling. "I started all this, Leda. I killed our father and brought the curse down on us all; I had no idea it would happen. It was my responsibility to fix it. I did it for the good of the people."

"You did it for your own selfish purposes, so that you could take power for yourself."

"No! No, I never wanted to rule, but I have to. Can't you see? I'm the only one who can do it. It can't be Azaria, and Fessler, Annagret and Gabriell are too young. I have to take the throne for the good of everyone. I'll give it up, I promise, if any of the other Locarno royals want it when they come of age. But I have to protect the kingdom in the meantime!"

She sounded alarmingly like Pyrrhus.

"*Liar.*"

Elina let out a frustrated sound from beneath her. "We wouldn't be having this conversation if you'd just behaved the way you were supposed to! Why did you try to save him?"

"What? Who?"

"Eber! I thought you'd run away while I ... while I killed him." Her voice cracked on the penultimate word, as though she had a right to the misery that was all over her face.

Her logic hung in the air between them. Elina thought Leda was a coward and always had done. She'd screeched in Leda's cabin that she was selfish and only cared about herself, and not her family.

Therefore when she'd taken the opportunity to attack them she'd expected Leda to see danger and flee for her own life. She thought Leda would never sacrifice herself for someone else after she'd spent her whole life trying to survive.

How wrong she'd been.

"Your understanding of me is outdated," Leda said coldly. "Your activities over the last few months have unhinged you and you have no comprehension of anyone in your world anymore."

It was an odd sort of betrayal, her sister's lack of faith in her, paling into insignificance against the bigger ones. Still, it hurt.

"Where's Atticus? What have you done to him?"

"Nothing, he's fine. He realised what was going on and tried to get a message to you but we intercepted it. He'll be released when everything calms down."

Leda's blood ran cold. "*We?*"

The clattering of multiple pairs of feet announced the arrival of Eber with reinforcements. Elina relaxed under Leda as Castor, Pan and Arsen hurtled in and skidded to a halt.

It took only a second for Leda's relief to transform into panic.

She cried out as she was lifted bodily from Elina by Castor. She watched in mute horror as Pan offered a hand to her sister, guiding her gently to her feet, and Arsen restrained a violently struggling Eber.

The knife was ripped from her hand.

"What are you doing?" Leda elbowed Castor in the stomach and was rewarded with a pained snarl.

But she knew what they were doing, and it snapped something in her mind to see it. How could she have been so stupid, so blinkered? Elina hadn't been their alibi for the murders; they had been *hers*.

Castor seemed to enjoy having his arms locked around Leda far too much, and she considered smashing her head back against his face. Unfortunately he was too tall, but she might get his windpipe if she aimed properly.

Eber had gone for help and inadvertently brought back the worst possible people. A bunch of cowardly, snivelling traitors.

"I see the coup you're orchestrating is more sophisticated than you let on, Elina."

Elina tore the rest of her mask from her face. "The Ariti family shares my cause. They want the safety and prosperity of the citizens of the Five Kingdoms over and above their own selfish goals."

There was that word again, selfish. Leda didn't know when Elina had learned that was the weapon she could use to strike closest to her heart, but she didn't seem afraid to wield it.

How could Elina, so intelligent and caustic and witty, be so unutterably *stupid* at the same time?

"The Ariti family wants the safety and prosperity of the Ariti family, Elina. I suppose they scurried over to you like rats when it became clear Pan wasn't winning the trials?"

The brothers shook their heads. She refused to make a sound as Castor squeezed her hard enough for her ribs to bend.

Pan raised his eyebrows at Castor. "Why you ever attempted to court this feral thing I have no idea."

"Nor I," Castor said into her ear, though the excitement with which he held her belied his words. He was so much stronger than her, and he revelled in the display of it. "Though there's something intoxicating about seducing a woman who's doomed but doesn't know it. With the added benefit of driving Pyrrhus insane with jealousy, of course."

Leda felt the urge to vomit rise within her, but ruthlessly suppressed it. Best not to waste it unless she could be sure to target him with it.

"You knew about the curse," she breathed.

"Elina told us long ago," Pan said, his voice infuriatingly flat and logical. "This way, everyone wins. I'll marry her, so both a Locarno and an Ariti will sit on the throne, satisfying the curse and restoring our family to our rightful place."

Arsen smirked. He was hot-headed, couldn't resist grinding salt into the wound. "You should be on your knees and grateful, Ledazaria. Pan wanted Pyrrhus killed and Castor ordered you signed over into his possession until your death as their original conditions, but Princess Pious here negotiated them out of it."

So there was a glimmer of humanity left in Elina. That did nothing to stop Leda glaring at her with a hatred so powerful it nearly buckled her knees. She didn't know how all of these emotions could coexist within her at the same time, but they made her want to scream at the top of her lungs.

"I'd be grateful if we could stop talking about me as if I weren't here," Elina said tersely. "Loosen your hold on Leda, Castor, she's still a Locarno and you'll treat her with a modicum of respect."

He did as instructed, and Leda took a deep breath from newly unrestricted lungs.

"Arsen, take Eber and hide him somewhere he can't be heard. I don't care where, as long as nobody finds him until we need him."

"And Leda?" Castor panted, starting to feel the exertion required to prevent her from throwing him off her.

"She can be locked in here while I speak with Pyrrhus. We'll use her to get him to comply. He doesn't need to know that she'll die regardless of the choice he makes. The curse will be broken by tomorrow night."

Icy cold spread through Leda's veins at the dispassionate words. All of Elina's shuddering and crying had been ruthlessly cut off. She was calm now, her purpose overtaking her.

"We could offer Pyrrhus the chance to say goodbye before we kill her," said Pan.

"Perhaps," Elina said, her voice wavering ever so slightly. "He'd do anything for her, though. He's obsessed." She wouldn't meet Leda's eye. "If he knows she'll be killed he'll do nothing but try to stop us until his dying breath."

That was what Leda was most afraid of.

Pan cast Leda a mistrustful look, as though she were capable of letting Pyrrhus know their dastardly plans telepathically. "Shall we strategise upstairs?" He waited for Elina's nod.

Leda snorted loudly as Castor reluctantly let her go.

"You're bending the knee to a spoilt little girl with no

experience of the world, very laudable. I'm sure the people of Rivernesse will be thrilled with you for prostrating yourself before a Locarno." She spat the last word, driving the knife home. "*Again.*"

Pan visibly flinched, but her words didn't stop him from leaving, followed shortly by Arsen who had a violently squirming Eber over one shoulder.

Elina directed Castor out of the room ahead of her and gave Leda a long, inscrutable look before leaving herself. Leda heard them all filing out of the sitting room and the door to her mother's rooms locking behind them.

She'd been able to feel her death looming for so long, but she couldn't quite believe it now that it stared her in the face.

How could she have spent so much time suspecting the wrong people, not looking around her at who had most to gain from the Counterparts' deaths?

She'd seen Elina as high and mighty and moralising. Annoying? Of course, but no threat to any of them. Leda had even cautiously begun to like her, to enjoy their verbal sparring.

She was an abominably bad judge of character. Once again, she'd been swept up in others' schemes and blindsided. And she would pay the ultimate price for her mistakes.

As night fell she dragged herself over to lie on her mother's bed, staring at the ceiling and straining with all of her might to hear what was happening in the palace.

Silence greeted her, the stone between floors too thick to transmit anything, but she could imagine what was going on. And those thoughts horrified her. She could picture Pyrrhus being told of Elina's great plan and what might happen to him if he refused to let her take the throne.

She lay frozen with terror at the prospect.

CHAPTER 32

*L*eda started awake at the sound of the door to her mother's rooms opening. Still half-conscious, she scrambled back to the end of the settee she'd relocated herself to in the middle of the night, squinting in the darkness.

She expected Elina or one of the traitorous brothers from Rivernesse, but instead she saw a golden blonde head duck through the doorway. And a face that would usually be handsome were it not for the furious scowl that now occupied it.

She staggered to her feet. "Ambrose?"

Was he friend or foe? She had no idea anymore.

He opened his mouth to reply and the cry of a child sounded from behind him. He turned to usher in Eber, who was unsuccessfully trying to soothe a bawling Mira as she strained to get out of his arms. Ambrose shut the door behind them all and bolted it.

Leda took in the sight of Eber and Mira, two terrified children who'd been marked for death their whole lives. The only other Counterparts left.

There had once been so many of them.

The thought was devastating.

"What's going on?" she asked, her voice cracked and dry.

Was that sympathy on Ambrose's face?

"Elina made a move on the throne. She secured the support of Rivernesse through the Aritis and has convened the royal council to vote on killing the rest of the Counterparts and restoring a Locarno to rule."

She hissed out a breath. "Pyrrhus would never let—"

"It's become too big for Pyrrhus. Everyone knows the full detail of the curse now. He's lost control; the remaining royal families and the nobles have stopped listening. They'll take the decision."

Leda clutched at her throat, trying to slow her frantic breathing. "The five families hate the Locarnos; they won't give up their claims to the throne."

Ambrose shook his head. "Think, Leda! Who's left who won't bow to the pressure? Linus is dead, Thalia and Melia are the gods only know where, Pan has thrown his support behind Elina and Zephyr is only arguing the point that Azaria be queen instead. They don't care for three Counterpart lives that were always doomed."

That was Ambrose, forever seeing the bright side.

"Always doomed." Eber's voice, higher and thinner than it should be. He sounded like a child again. "You knew about the curse and didn't tell me."

"We needed time to find a way out of it, I was going to tell you but I couldn't ..." Put that look on his face. Hopelessness and regret and a rage so deep it broke her apart. She'd wanted him happy for as long as she could manage it. She wanted him to have what she couldn't.

But they had bigger problems than Leda's omitted truths at that moment. Swiping a hand over her wet cheeks, she swivelled back to face Ambrose.

"Did you bring it? Can you kill us painlessly?"

"*What?*" The word was choked. Eber looked at her like he'd never seen her before. "You planned our deaths with him?"

"I didn't want you to suffer if it came to this," Leda said softly. She'd thought she'd run out of tears. She'd been wrong.

The look on Ambrose's face was conflicted and she wasn't in any way reassured by it. "I found a way, but a while ago you gave me another idea, Leda, and I want to try it. It's extremely high risk and may not work. I think we should attempt it anyway. Can you trust me?"

That was an intriguing question. Something in Leda rebelled against the idea. Ambrose was the first to sigh when she entered a room, as though having to hear her speak was torture. He'd never taken much trouble to hide how little he wanted her around. But he'd also never faltered in helping her when she was injured.

Besides, what choice did she have? The alternative was certain death for them all.

Eber was staring sullenly at the ground, his eyes red and swollen.

Against her better judgement, Leda found herself nodding shakily. Ambrose had never intentionally hurt her. She could trust him to do right by her and her siblings.

He blinked, as though expecting more of a fight, but recovered quickly. He produced three vials from within his coat.

"I've been sent here to sedate you and have you brought up to the throne room. They've been debating all night and will reach their decision in an hour. Elina wanted you all unconscious because ... well ... it was thought to be kinder that you not know your fate."

"How sweet of her," Leda said stonily.

Ambrose held up the vials and turned to Eber. "I need

the three of you to drink this. It will sedate you, but not completely. You'll be drowsy, Mira the most given her age and size. When you're brought up to the throne room you must not draw attention to yourselves. They'll pass down the verdict and if you're to be killed they will ask me to administer the fast-acting poison." He took a deep breath, and Leda wondered when he'd last slept. The shadows under his eyes were purple. "I will not do so. Instead I'll give you a serum I created that will interact with what I'm about to give you to mimic death. While Elina is crowned, Pyrrhus and I will get you out and away from the palace before they realise the curse remains unbroken."

They locked eyes at that, aware that the gods would continue to rain down their wrath if they were successful. Leda looked at Eber and Mira and the conflict inside her eased. They needed time to find a way around the curse, and this was the only way to procure it.

"Elina is a skilled botanist; won't she know what you're doing?"

Ambrose gave her a grim look. "She trusts me not to betray her. She thinks I value the well-being of the kingdom over the three of your lives. She also believes that I dislike you and your effect on Pyrrhus and that it would prevent any crisis of conscience."

"She's right about that last part, isn't she?"

"Yes. But this isn't about that. I'm a healer; I don't want to kill, ever," he said. "Elina has a habit of believing everything she sees on the surface. Whatever I tell her, she takes at face value; she doesn't dig into hidden context. I told her I'd administer the poison if asked, and though she dislikes me at the moment she still trusts me. She's not suspicious."

Leda opened her mouth to respond, but Eber cut in. "Why debate? We have no choice." He placed Mira down on the settee. "Here, give me the vial."

He snatched one up and swallowed the murky green liquid in a single gulp. It made quick work of him given how few seconds ticked by before he was staggering. His eyes fluttered shut as he descended on to the cushions.

Leda turned to Ambrose. She needed one last question answered before she took the vial he offered. "Where is Pyrrhus?"

"He abdicated in preparation for Thalia's ceremony, so he's no threat to Elina's position. She did, however, have him put in the dungeons."

"To stop him protecting us."

"Yes."

And if Leda struggled now, or attempted to run away before Ambrose could execute his plan, Pyrrhus might suffer the consequences. That tipped her over the line into her decision.

She threw her hands in the air. "I can't believe it's come to this. Let me help you with Mira."

Mira accepted her vial with good grace, though she complained at the bitter taste, and Leda carefully laid her down next to Eber. Her hair was fine and soft as silk, and Leda gently moved it away from her face.

She raised her own vial to Ambrose in a mock toast.

"Let's hope this works." She threw it back, grimacing at the taste, and settled down next to Mira as a curious heaviness enveloped her limbs one by one. It spread through her until her eyelids shut as though someone had pressed their fingers against them.

It was an odd sensation. She could feel her body, but not move it, and was aware of what was going on around her. Her state of mind was dreamy, even relaxed. She heard the guards entering the room, felt them lift and carry her through the hallways.

They were gentle with her. That was nice.

Leda sensed the moment they entered the throne room as the chattering of hundreds quieted to a shocked ripple of gasps. She supposed she and her siblings must have presented a disquieting sight, draped as they were over the arms of guards, appearing unaware of the danger they were in.

The surface Leda was laid on was hard and cold, and she didn't make a sound as someone smoothed her skirts to ensure they shielded her legs from the frigid air. A series of fierce whispers reached her, and she recognised the sound of Azaria and Elina bickering. She'd heard it so many times over the past few months, though never over anything as serious as this.

The very idea of either of these two immature twits taking the throne was horrendous.

Speaking of the throne, she prayed that Pyrrhus wasn't anywhere near it. She silently asked the gods to ensure that he stayed in the dungeons, safe until whatever escape plan Ambrose had set up could be put into action.

Leda strained to hear but couldn't pick up his voice in the flurry of sound around her. She was light-headed with relief at the thought that Elina hadn't allowed him in the room. He held too much of the court's love and respect, and he would fight for Leda's life. He couldn't be allowed to do so in front of all of these witnesses.

Elina and Azaria's conversation was slowly becoming louder and more heated. Leda could make out their voices clearly now.

"Leave me alone!" Elina hissed. "*I* did this, not you. I sacrificed everything to kill the Counterparts, I ripped myself apart to do it, and I will sit on the throne. You won't step in at the last second and take it from me."

"I am fated to be ruler," Azaria said. A supportive mutter came from near the source of her voice and Leda surmised

Zephyr must be next to her, always there to prop up her insane beliefs. "You will step aside."

"No."

"I am the oldest living royal."

"You're unhinged and not mentally fit to take the throne."

"That is a matter of opinion."

"You have *no* idea what I've done to get here. This is mine."

Azaria seemed to be running out of patience. "I know every desperate, pathetic step you have taken to get to this position. I knew from the moment Markus and Elov were killed. I trained with you, remember? I know your style with a sword. Or rather, your lack of ability. You aimed for the Counterpart and killed Elov by accident. You hacked them both to death like a talentless butcher, leaving your calling card for all those who cared to look closely."

What sounded like a rasping gasp from Elina.

"Your attempt to poison Eber was another mark of your desperation. I know the kinds of plants you used to slip into Prince Agon's tea to put him off visiting your rooms to beat you. I know the dose you could use to ensure death. I made it my business, early on in life, to understand how my siblings might kill."

Elina's voice was dull and lifeless. "If you knew it was me, why didn't you say anything?"

A pause. "It saved me effort. I did consider having you killed, of course, for what you had done. That's why I had Zephyr sabotage your horse, but I changed my mind in the end. An effective ruler delegates, you see. Pyrrhus said that during the trials, and he has always been wise beyond his years. You took care of multiple deaths for me." The words were harrowingly clinical.

"You're a monster," Elina choked out.

"I think our siblings would bestow that honorific on you, not me. There is one thing I'm curious about, though," Azaria said, and Leda heard the rustle of her gown as she moved closer to her prone form. Leda could feel the weight of her sister's gaze on her. "How did you find out the true nature of the curse? That the Counterparts must die or the disasters will continue in perpetuity?"

"Caspari figured it out. He told me a few seconds before he tried to kill me. He planned to take out his competition early." Elina's voice shook with the memory.

"A wise strategy," Azaria said without a hint of surprise. "Though foolish to begin with you."

Their conversation was interrupted by the sound of trumpets, and Leda strained to hear as a member of what must have been the royal council got to his feet.

Once the crowd had quieted, the man's reedy voice passed over them. It took him a long time to say it, so many redundant, pretentious words used to explain the verdict they had reached in conjunction with representatives from the five families.

The curse needed to be satisfied. The Counterparts were to die, and Elina was to be placed upon the throne.

Someone next to Leda drew in a sharp breath. She couldn't tell whether it was Elina or Azaria. Footsteps approached, and then she felt what must have been Ambrose next to her. She prayed with all she had that his plan would work.

A hand stroked her hair, too small to be his. It was warm, and shaking.

It disappeared for a moment, hesitating.

Then the hand prised her jaw open and three drops of a foul, corrosive substance fell into her mouth. It burned like acid on her tongue.

If Leda had thought the experience of sedation was odd,

it was nothing compared to this. She could hear the beating of her heart in her head, could feel every second of it slowing as the pumping of blood through her veins became sluggish.

The beats in her mind sounded further apart. Then, they stopped altogether.

Her heart had stopped. Ambrose had given them a concoction to kill her. That dour prat. That traitor. He'd gone against his promise, as she'd been terrified that he would. As she'd been terrified that he *should*.

Wait ... if he'd killed her, how could she be aware that he'd done so?

Another, struggling heartbeat, so many seconds from the last she couldn't believe that anything in her body was still functioning. Her breathing had slowed to an imperceptibly shallow dip and rise of her chest.

Then blackness. Nothing at all.

CHAPTER 33

It could have been minutes or hours or days later, Leda didn't know, but she felt herself being yanked painfully back to the surface of reality.

Rhythmic, pounding blows to her chest. Air breathed from someone else's mouth into hers, burning like smoke in her lungs.

She let out a groan, and the assault stopped. The hands on her body flew off her.

Leda blinked her eyes open and she fought not to roll to her side and vomit the residue of that foul liquid on to the floor. Out of the corner of her eye she could see Eber on an identical stone slab to hers. He was half on, half off, covered in sweat, with an alarming pallor she might have expected of a creature dragged up from the netherworld. His eyes were maroon, like every blood vessel in them had burst simultaneously.

He closed his eyes, feigning death once more.

Elina and Azaria paid the Counterparts no attention, and nor did the crowd, who had their backs facing their presumed dead bodies. The two contenders for the throne had moved to the dais that held it and were bickering so loudly the entire room was riveted on them with a mixture of fascination and dread.

Leda turned her head slightly to see an empty slab that Mira must have been spirited away from in the kerfuffle. Ambrose stood by Leda's side, blocking her from her sisters' view. One of his assistants, Orion, held the same protective position over Eber.

"Funny thing," Leda hissed through a mouth as closed as she could manage. "But I could have sworn I just *actually died* for a moment there. That wouldn't be the case, would it?"

"You all died," Ambrose said tersely, just as quiet. "Technically. We just revived you. That part of the curse should be broken now. I negotiated it with Melia and the gods allowed it. A thank you will suffice, whenever you're ready."

If it hadn't been imperative that she pretend to be a corpse she was sure she'd have let out a loud noise of disbelief mixed with that emotion she hated so very much, hope. There was no way Ambrose could have done this, could have saved them despite impossible odds.

But he'd stayed behind when they'd visited the Grand Temple in Slofray, had emerged from his conversation with Melia looking grim but focused. He'd figured out the truth, had planned something like this all along, and had only been lacking the means to do it.

"Why didn't you tell me?"

"Honestly?" His voice was a low rumble. He'd turned to her, would look to anybody observing from the crowd like he was simply checking her body. "I was worried it wouldn't work. I searched for months but couldn't find anything that would kill you in a way that would allow you to be brought back. Then the solution came to me when we spoke in that corridor—alcohol. It counteracted the worst effects of the clyve serum, allowing you to be resuscitated. I hadn't considered it before, and it *worked*." He looked as stunned about that as she did.

So that was why he hadn't told her his plan, had fed her and Eber yet another half-truth to avoid bringing their hopes up. Acute gratitude warred with anger inside her. She was seconds from leaping up and wringing his neck or giving him a hug, she couldn't decide which, but before she could a more pressing matter grabbed her attention.

Azaria had a handful of Elina's glossy dark hair in one fist and was using it to drag her off the dais. Elina went with an incoherent screech, nearly tripping over the throne, feet sliding on the floor as she tried in vain to throw Azaria off. Leda knew from painful experience that Azaria had the upper body strength of a bear, and it seemed Elina was relearning that lesson the hard way.

"You hesitated, sister," Azaria said, barely out of breath while Elina panted in her grip. "You didn't want to kill them? You're as weak as ever."

Elina looked up to the ceiling as though expecting the chandeliers to detach and fling themselves at Azaria of their own accord.

She was appealing to her gods, but they didn't seem to be listening.

Under Azaria's arm, Leda caught the merest flicker of doubt crossing Elina's face. Would her precious gods abandon her in favour of Azaria? Surely not. She was their chosen one.

Judging by the lack of divine intervention as Azaria flung Elina to the hard floor and delivered a vicious kick to her stomach, the gods had turned their backs on her, or at the very least lost interest.

Elina was only momentarily thrown off her game. She spun with feline grace to sweep out Azaria's legs from under her. It made her stagger, but only momentarily.

Strength of a bear, balance of a ballet dancer and aim of an expert huntress, it had never seemed fair.

Another figure entered the fray. Pan. But he was not a skilled fighter, was ungainly and clumsy. He was protecting his chance at the throne more than he was Elina and so they didn't form an effective team. He got in the way more than he helped and was quickly slammed to the ground by Azaria with a moan of pain.

She didn't look at his sprawled form, her attention fixed on Arsen and Castor, who had edged out of the crowd. They both seemed to be deliberating entering the fight, Arsen with relish and Castor with a frown that indicated he wanted to be nowhere near any of this.

Azaria was ready for them, a predatory gleam in her eye. She'd always been more animated, more viciously human, when she was fighting than in any other situation. Her fingers twitched at her sides as though desperate to tear into flesh, to dole out as much pain as they could.

Castor, coward that he was, melted back into the crowd. He was wise to do so.

Arsen was not. He strode into the space in front of Azaria, obscuring a doubled over Elina from her view. His hand jerked as he went for the dagger sheathed at his side and then he appeared to think better of it. He brought his arms into a boxing fighting stance, an arrogant smile curling his mouth.

He was a legendary martial mind in Rivernesse; he thought he didn't need the weapon.

Then he was even more stupid than Leda had first thought. An untested brute. For all that he'd studied combat and military strategy all his life, most of it existed inside his head. Aside from sparring with guards, she doubted he had much experience executing it in real life.

And Azaria wasn't even real life. She was no average fighter.

She lulled him into a false sense of security. She stood still as a sculpture carved from ice, hands on her hips. Her entire body was presented to him, every vulnerable part, without the slightest apprehension. He seemed to read that as weakness.

He made the first move, barrelling towards her, having allowed her the time she needed to study him. His arms came around her torso, as though attempting an embrace, and they went down to the ground with an incongruously quiet thud.

The crowd surged closer, bloodthirsty as ever.

Azaria was light and small, but had trained her whole life to wield her opponent's strength as though it were her own. Within seconds Agon had been rolled beneath her, his legs tangled in hers, and she was extracting his dagger from its sheath.

He shoved her off with a strangled yell and staggered to his feet.

She was up almost before he was, a blur of movement. And then she struck, quick and precise as a snake.

A ribbon of red stretched across his collarbone. Dark, viscous blood streamed down his skin to soak into the white linen of his shirt.

"Retreat or the next wound will be three inches higher." Azaria's eyes lingered meaningfully on his throat. She wasn't even breathing heavily.

He ignored her, his face puce with fury and embarrassment. He went for her with a scream that got progressively higher pitched, and then he was on the ground once more, only this time without her.

He lay on his front, face pressed against stone, a brilliant line of red open across his side. She'd sidestepped and slashed him, enough to spill a dizzying amount of blood but not to kill him. A kick to his lower back had sent him sprawling.

And then she was crouching over him, almost but not quite sitting on him. She dangled her knife over the back of his neck, a curious expression on her face. It dropped down an inch, nicking the skin, and the crowd gasped.

"Stop!" Elina collided with Azaria with a bone-shakingly loud thump, sending both of them tumbling to the ground and away from Arsen's limp body.

Azaria snarled and returned the full force of her attention to Elina, who was failing to extract herself from the tangle of heavy skirts that weighed her down.

Elina looked again towards the heavens, her face a mask of disbelief. She really believed they would save her, that her path was righteous and she'd sacrificed her siblings for the moral cause that would lead her to the throne.

It was clear the moment she realised that no help was coming, and it was gut-wrenching to see realisation dawn that she'd committed the most heinous acts a person could for the benefit of her cruellest sister. Elina had unwittingly swept the path clear to allow Azaria to gain power and bring misery to the people she'd wanted to protect in the first place.

Leda watched through half-closed eyes with a detached kind of horror as the blows from Azaria's fists rained down on Elina until she fell into unconsciousness. In seconds, her body lay limp at Azaria's feet.

Blood dripped grotesquely from Azaria's fingertips as she rose to her full height.

She looked up at the crowd, now flushed and panting but otherwise impassive, as though a sack of flour lay at her feet and not a sister. "Would anyone else like to contest the crown?"

Horrified silence answered her. Even the royal council members seemed to have nothing to say.

"I thought so. Guards, dispose of her."

Azaria turned and looked straight at Ambrose, who did an admirable job of not cowering.

Her eyes dropped to Leda, who by that point was sitting up warily on the slab, her limbs curled in tightly to her sides.

A rare expression of shock crossed Azaria's face. She didn't bother to look for the other Counterparts.

"How is she alive?"

Ambrose's hands had become fists at his side. "I killed them all, but temporarily. I revived them, and the curse relating to the Counterparts is broken. A priestess confirmed it to me. A new bargain was struck with the gods for it to be so."

All of a sudden, sound broke out, but only inside Leda's head. It was a kind of ringing laughter, dark and musical, and it absolutely did not belong there. She clapped her hands over her ears and whimpered.

The laughter cut off as abruptly as it had started.

She was breathless as she looked around, searching for the source, sure it couldn't have originated inside her own mind. The rest of the room was stone-faced, no mirth to be found anywhere.

Whatever concoction Ambrose had given her must have rendered her insane. She could only pray it was temporary.

Or ... she looked up at the ceiling, towards the heavens. Could it be?

Azaria's eyes narrowed. "Prove it."

Ambrose looked out of the window at the pouring rain, buffeted by wind so powerful it was coming down almost horizontal against the ground. He was as steady as a man who dealt with unhinged and murderous people every day.

"Place the crown on your head, become queen, and watch the rain stop."

Azaria regarded him with great scepticism.

He held up his hands in front of him. "If it doesn't, then you can kill them properly."

Leda glared at his back. He'd better be right.

Azaria cast an unreadable look at Leda.

Zephyr stepped up to her sister, and Leda could have cursed. His face was alight with malice.

"You need to kill Ledazaria regardless of the curse," he said to Azaria. "She's the remnant of your past, the one who holds you back and ties you to the weak person you were before you killed Linus." Something flickered in Azaria's expression. "To be a strong ruler like your father you need to sacrifice your Counterpart. It has always been your destiny, and hers."

Leda's heart caught in her throat. The logic he poured into her sister's ears was deeply flawed, but it had been believed by the court and the kingdom for years. It was written into the foundations of the palace in which they stood, carved into its bones.

Azaria looked away from Zephyr as though he hadn't spoken.

"Take the Counterparts to the dungeons."

As the guards hurried to carry out her instructions Azaria strode to the throne and sat upon it. She was a magnificent sight against the gold, with her blood-red gown and the regal turn of her head. She knew everyone in the room was focused on her and could imagine no other feasible scenario.

"Crown me." She barked at the council, who stood uncertainly against the wall. They parted to reveal Melia, who it seemed had returned to the palace with a small delegation of priestesses.

They'd watched all of this unfold and did nothing. Even now, all Melia did was pin Azaria with an assessing gaze.

"Do it."

Leda allowed the guards to pull her to her feet and followed Eber out into the corridor. Her legs barely held her up; she was dizzy with a potent mix of relief and lingering fear.

She stared out of each window they passed on the way to the dungeons, absorbed in the driving rain that battered the manicured gardens.

It stopped.

Leda stopped, too, and the guard behind ran straight into her back and bounced off with a curse. She barely noticed, letting out a choked sound as the rain disappeared from one window to the next, leaving a pristine and star-spangled sky in its wake. Even the clouds were gone.

The foul weather had stopped, as abruptly as though a command had been issued to it.

Ambrose had been right, the Counterparts had all died and a Locarno sat on the throne, the curse was satisfied.

She no longer needed to die. If Azaria freed her, she'd get her life back.

But at what cost?

CHAPTER 34

*L*eda had complained too much about the restrictions she'd been under when Pyrrhus was trying to protect her. Compared with sitting in a dungeon for two weeks, she'd had unimaginable amounts of freedom before.

She spent most of her days lying on the pallet in her cell imagining the crystal clear waters of Saint-Trevale. There had been a brilliant array of fish there, painted in colours she'd never seen before, darting back and forth between coral reefs. Such peace and tranquility in the most beautiful place in the world.

She counted her lucky stars that Pyrrhus was in the cell next to hers, though the fact that he was there indicated that Ambrose's plan to get them all out had failed miserably. She'd been frantic when she caught sight of him as she was led into the dungeons, and seeing him unharmed had made her sag with relief.

His expression had transformed into something completely unrecognisable when he'd noticed her. There was a man who thought, for the briefest amount of time, that he was seeing a ghost.

A wall of solid stone divided them, but if they sat near the bars they could hear each other. He attempted to divert her with conversation for hours each day, but she became more morose and unresponsive as the time passed. Being so close and unable to touch him was torturous. He seemed to struggle with the same, though he bore it with more dignity than she did.

One evening she sat with her back to the wall they shared, her hand curled around a bar.

"I wish I could see you," she whispered.

"Me too. You have no idea how much."

She drummed her fingers against the cold metal. "How did this happen?" she said brokenly. "What did we do to deserve this?"

"The gods don't care about what we deserve," Pyrrhus said. "Their whims change at random; we're ants to them. Nothing we said or did triggered this."

It made sense, and yet at the same time it didn't.

"I hate them," she whispered, as though they might not be able to hear her. But she knew they could if they wanted to, could crack open her head and peer at all the thoughts in her mind if the impulse struck them.

Still, who cared if they did and got offended? What more could they possibly do to her?

She thought of the man beside her and her stomach dropped. There was more that they could do to her, so much more. Her heart resided in her body, here in this cell, but a significant part of it was tied inexorably to him. It lay exposed, raw and vulnerable, outside of her, ready for anyone to strike at if they wanted to hurt her.

She closed her eyes against the thought, summoning another instead.

"I don't want to die," she said quietly. "This back and

forth, fear and then relief and then devastation again. I can't take it." She was afraid it was driving her mad.

She heard him shift in his cell, closer to the wall.

"You won't die. There's no need for it, the curse is broken. She'll allow you to live, Leda." His voice was low and soothing. "You may be exiled from Viridiana though, if you can bear it."

Her mouth curled into the smallest of smiles. Perhaps foolishly, she allowed hope to bloom within her, just for a second. "My home in Saint-Trevale is still waiting for me. I hope one of those books of yours has instructions on how to fix water damage. Gods, there's probably all kinds of mould in there by now."

A pause. "You want me to come with you?"

As if she was going anywhere without him ever again. The very thought was ludicrous.

"I can't imagine it any other way. We'll get you a book-case and some maps and you'll be quite content."

She couldn't see him, but she knew he was smiling. "I do like that image."

"You may have to give up your hot chocolate habit, though. Not only is it ludicrously expensive, it's just too hot out there."

"That's a compromise I'm not willing to make."

She choked out a laugh.

A day later, the queen blessed Leda with a visit.

Azaria was richly dressed in a purple gown that cut away to reveal a skirt of deepest black, her shoulders draped in matching ermine. The crown was perched on top of her hair, almost too big.

It looked like a strong breeze might topple it off her head.

Leda fixed her gaze on the straw on the floor, swirling patterns in it with her feet. "When you were imprisoned the lodgings Pyrrhus gave you were considerably nicer than these."

From the corner of her eye she saw Azaria looking around in bemusement, as though she hadn't spent a moment considering her sister's comfort.

"You appear to be surviving," Azaria said, supremely unconcerned. She swept her skirts aside and sat beside Leda on the hard pallet that served as something close to a bed. She kept her distance as usual, at least two feet between them, but the position allowed her to stare out at the bars of the cell and not subject herself to extended eye contact.

"What do you want?" Leda fisted her hands in her lap.

"It's all over. The fires, the earthquakes, the storms. The rightful ruler is on the throne and the kingdoms are rejoicing. Bonfires burn in my honour every night; wine pours from the fountains. Feasting will be held across the lands."

"Rightful ruler," Leda scoffed. "There is *no one* less suited to ruling the Five Kingdoms."

"You are incorrect."

"Am I? You vacillate wildly between being emotionless and violently angry. No one can predict what you're going to do on any given day. You *cut off* one of your brother's arms," Leda ground out. "It's well known across the kingdom that you're incapable of caring about anyone but yourself."

Azaria's blank face indicated that she wasn't offended by that assessment. "I seem to recall saving your life many times, for someone who only cares about themselves," she said levelly.

"You didn't try to save me on the night you took the

throne, though, did you? You didn't knock the poison out of their hands. You watched me die. Only *you* know why you ever kept me alive before that; I can barely understand why you bothered when all of the scars on my body are from you."

Not a flicker of remorse in those bright blue eyes. They were more remote than ever.

Leda could see that being queen had changed Azaria already, was making her an infinitely worse version of herself. Just as she'd expected, just as she'd feared would happen to Pyrrhus. She imagined the crown dripping with corruption, iridescent golden tendrils of it snaking over Azaria's hair and skin until it was absorbed into her very pores. The object pulsed on her head like something alive, something implicitly evil.

Leda couldn't understand why she was the only one who could see behind its facade.

"What does Zephyr want you to do with me? Kill me, I suppose? He was keen on it when you took the crown."

"I don't know what his most recent position is." Azaria looked off into the distance. "He's down here for the moment."

"He is? Why?"

"He tried to kiss me."

That, Leda did not expect. "Oh."

"I threw him across the room when he tried, of course. But then he attempted to argue his case, so I thought a week down here would restore his mind to the right place."

Leda couldn't believe they were having this conversation. "Yes, well, that should do it."

"Ambrose patched him up. His pride is more injured than his body."

That was a useful piece of information to have, and Leda was glad to know it would reassure Pyrrhus. Ambrose being pardoned and restored to his position was a glimmer of good news in this mire of doom.

"Anyway, we're not here to talk about Zephyr. This is about you." Azaria still had that faraway look in her eyes, and that never meant anything good. "I have these thoughts in my head now. New thoughts. I think, in some small way, part of me always knew that it was meant to be me."

It was gibberish delivered in Azaria's usual calm, confident tones. It took Leda a moment to process the words, yet still she was lost. "What are you talking about?"

"The one who kills you. It was always meant to be me. You are my Counterpart, after all."

Leda took a deep, steadying breath. It did nothing to quell the panic rising in her. "Not anymore."

"No, you are, in every way that matters. You are mine to do with as I wish; you always have been. My possession."

It was the most chilling thing anyone had ever said to her. It was too much, even for Azaria.

"So you're going to kill me even though the curse no longer dictates it?"

"Most likely," Azaria said. "I need to look to the future, and sever the ties that connect me to the past, and to those that challenge me. That requires all your deaths eventually. Not just you, but the other royal children as well. If a Locarno must sit on the throne, then I have to be the only one eligible. I will not be usurped. I'll give you a week here, though"—Azaria's eyes flicked over to the wall that was shared with Pyrrhus's cell—"to tie up any loose ends."

Leda stared at the space her sister had occupied long after she left.

"Leda," came the low sound of his voice, all of his concern infused into that one word.

"She's all talk," Leda said. "She won't go through with it."

His silence told her he didn't believe her.

She didn't either.

~

Azaria was true to her word, and exactly one week later the guards arrived to escort Leda out of her cell. She was bedraggled and dirty from so long spent in one room, but held her head high as she followed them beyond the bars. She cast a look into Pyrrhus's cell as she passed, catching his eye as he leaned against the wall.

He was all she'd wanted to see, for so long, but the image of him caged there burned her eyes.

They shared a look that communicated so little of what she wanted to say that she could have cried before the guards chivvied her onwards.

If that was the last time she saw him, she wouldn't be able to bear it.

It wasn't enough.

It had never been enough.

"Where are you taking me?"

The guard to her right shot her an uneasy look. She recognised him from only a few weeks ago, when he'd been part of the detail protecting her. He seemed to feel the whiplash of the change as much as she did.

She wondered where Atticus was, hoping he was alright. It might have been reassuring to have him with her, as she approached the end. He'd always had a soothing presence about him.

"We're going to the throne room, madam."

"To my sister?"

"That's right."

Leda nodded, but stopped short as they came to the top of the stairs that deposited them into the entrance hall of the palace.

There was a new monstrosity to behold. A statue of Azaria, cast in solid gold, standing by the back wall of the staircase. It obscured most of the Locarno family portrait from view. It was gaudy and audacious and not at all Azaria's style.

Yet another sign of her sister deteriorating into the altered state she'd entered as soon as that crown had touched her head.

Leda suspected Zephyr's influence too. He'd whispered poison in Azaria's ear, made her think she was favoured by the gods and the only one who could rule this kingdom full of people she didn't care about.

Leda looked up at the expressionless face of the statue, perfection itself, and felt a wave of disgust build. She turned away and allowed herself to be led to the throne room.

She took a deep breath, ready to approach whatever faced her with dignity. Above anything else, she was tired. Tired of the flares of excitement that she might survive, in between crushing assurances that her life would end. This death, it was what she'd trained for, all her life. She'd had over a year of wonderful freedom, a different life in Saint-Trevale, and now she had been pulled firmly back into her reality.

There were no more chances. This was the plan her silent god had for her, all along.

As she stepped over the threshold and into the throne room, her gaze locked on the ceremonial axe resting on its grand plinth in the centre of the room. Its handle had been polished to a high sheen, jewels winking innocently in the light of the chandeliers.

The Counterpart axe.

Leda promptly lost her mind.

With a guttural sound she hadn't even known herself capable of producing, she turned and tried to run in the opposite direction. All her resolve, her mature acceptance of her situation, evaporated. Guards, those traitorous guards who had spent months keeping her safe, seized her by the arms and lifted her off her feet.

They dropped Leda on the ground in front of her sister. The stone was bitingly cold under her hands. She stared up into Azaria's eyes as she felt Eber being forced to his knees at her side. The chirpy sounds of a young child sounded from her other side and she looked down in horror to see Mira.

"No," she breathed. "Azaria, no. You can't kill a child this way. Please, don't."

Azaria was unmoved. "It is expedient." She turned to the royal council, lined up against the wall, and received their grim nods, indicating they'd do nothing to stop her. The court stood silent around them, their attention fixed with dread on Mira.

Almost against her will, Leda's eyes were drawn to the dark figure by the columns at the side of the room.

Pyrrhus stood in almost the exact same position he'd occupied for Sofie's ceremony so long ago, before all this madness had really begun. Back then he'd stood proud, emotionless and unaffected, though now she knew what he'd really felt.

Anyone could see the truth of his feelings as clear as day now. He was restrained this time, two guards gripping him by the shoulders with great difficulty. His expression was one of mute horror as he struggled, and he looked at Leda so intensely that she felt the tears she'd fought off finally begin to fall.

No, he couldn't be here. He couldn't see this.

She shook her head at him and searched for the courage to mouth those words, the words she'd felt for so long and suppressed. The words that made her vulnerable, that showed she wasn't as detached and independent as she'd always hoped.

This man had occupied a huge part of her heart and soul for such an extended period she could barely remember a time when he wasn't there. Even when she'd been away from him, she felt his presence everywhere she went. He was so strong and moral and awe-inspiring, utterly unique, and she was so lucky to have been able to spend the time with him that she had.

It wasn't enough time.

But she couldn't tell him she loved him like this, not as he was about to watch her die. It would make her final act one of cruelty.

Leda turned back to Azaria amidst the sounds of Pyrrhus's renewed struggles against the guards. She kept her head high as she watched her sister lift the axe from its plinth. She wondered absently if it still had their father's blood on it. She hoped not, she wouldn't want it to sully her and her siblings more than it already had.

A hand grasped hers. Eber.

She squeezed it so tightly she was likely cutting off his blood supply, but she couldn't bear to look at him.

The crowd was restless, unsure. They muttered amongst themselves, and didn't seem to be feeling their usual blood-lust. All of their goblets of wine rested full in their hands.

No one was drinking, and no one was celebrating. Pyrrhus's struggling had spooked them.

Azaria pointed to the silver block, which had been positioned for Leda to place her head on to. "If you wouldn't mind."

Leda forced her chin up and met her gaze. "Don't think for a second I'll make this easy for you."

Azaria let out a terse breath, and something indefinable flickered through those bright eyes. She made an odd jerking motion with her hand, and looked down at it quizzically, as though it had moved without her permission.

"Very well."

Was that hesitation Leda saw in the way Azaria raised her axe? It certainly took her a few more seconds to lift than it should have.

Leda stared into her eyes, refusing to blink. She would make Azaria feel every second of what she was about to do.

Her whole body was shuddering, nearly out of control. She shoved Eber away from her, out of Azaria's path.

If Leda thought she saw a flicker of doubt on Azaria's face, it must be her own adrenaline-soaked mind fooling her with what she so desperately wanted to see.

"Goodbye, Leda. I am sorry."

It was the first time her sister had ever apologised to her.

CHAPTER 35

*L*eda's courage failed and her eyes snapped shut as she waited for the telltale whistle of the axe through the air. The sound she'd anticipated since she'd been old enough to understand her fate.

Instead, there was an almighty clang of guards falling to the ground behind her and then everything happened at once.

A flash of dark hair as Pyrrhus appeared in front of her, his hand on her chest pushing her backwards so powerfully she slid a clear foot across the floor.

All the breath was knocked out of her.

Azaria had been mid-swing, already committed.

Leda screamed as the axe embedded itself in Pyrrhus's back. She screamed so loud and so long that it tore at her throat.

There was a moment of chilled, horrifying quiet, and then the crowd descended into anarchy.

The courtiers screeched and howled like dying animals, and they converged on them with such speed that Azaria hastily retreated, her hands dangling by her sides. Her face was sickly white, her mouth open. She was finally speechless.

Leda caught Pyrrhus as he fell forwards on to her. She cried out as a well-meaning courtier reached forward to extract the blade of the axe, and they pulled their hand back with a hurried apology.

"AMBROSE! Someone find Ambrose!" Pyrrhus was heavy and warm in her arms, though her sense of touch was dulled by the blood that covered her hands as surely as if she'd dipped them into a vat of it.

His blood, she had *his* blood on her hands. No. No. She could barely comprehend the idea of it. The realisation had her shaking so powerfully she nearly dropped him.

She sobbed with relief when she saw the distinctive form of Ambrose shoulder his way through the crowd and fall to his knees beside Pyrrhus. His mouth opened and no words came out.

Pyrrhus's skin was the white of fresh paper, a horrible contrast to the scarlet of his blood.

"Help him!" Leda screeched through the noise of the crowd as the guards tried in vain to calm them down. But the mob was baying, unwilling to be silenced. Out of the corner of her eye Leda saw Eber scoop up a crying Mira and disappear into the mass of people.

Ambrose swallowed and his hand hovered shakily over the axe. His eyes were darting back and forth as though he couldn't settle on a thought. Leda couldn't understand why he wasn't doing anything. He always leapt into action the moment he spotted an injury. He'd healed worse, and he'd do it again now.

But Ambrose was in shock.

Pyrrhus's breathing was shallow, rattling, and Leda placed a hand on his chest as though she could manually force his lungs to work.

Azaria's voice boomed over the fray. "ENOUGH."

The swarm of people around them froze and the guards were finally able to force their way through.

Leda screwed her eyes shut, taking Pyrrhus's hand in hers and pressing her face into his neck. Her next words were just for him.

"You will not do this," she said desperately. "You will not martyr yourself for me, do you understand? I cannot live in a world without you in it. Please, *please* don't do this."

He let out another shuddering breath, but no words, and that scared her more than anything. If there was one thing Pyrrhus didn't have trouble with, it was words.

Firm hands on her shoulders, dragging her away from him. She kicked and wailed so loud it blistered her throat.

"NO! No, no, no, Pyrrhus, no, please—"

Her vision was hazy with panic. The crowd swallowed Pyrrhus up as she was pulled through it. Her breath came out in desperate pants as she was lifted to her feet by the guards and saw Azaria crossing the room towards her, mouth set in a grim line.

"Guards, find Eber and Mira and put them back in the dungeons with Leda. Leave them all there until I've dealt with this." She gestured at the chaos around them.

Leda could have sworn she saw the most minute tremor in her sister's hand.

The guard hesitated. "Are you sure—"

Azaria's next words were not for him, nor for any of them, it seemed. She was looking up at the ceiling, towards the gods. "Something is wrong," she muttered, wringing her hands in a way Leda had never seen her do before. She turned her glassy stare to the guard, who seemed to immediately regret having questioned her. "I need them out of the way, now."

Leda struggled so hard that pain screamed through the

shoulder the arrow had gone through. "Let me see him!" she begged.

"There would be no point. He will be dead in minutes."

That hit Leda like every single one of her organs had been ripped from her body. Misery clutched at her so tightly she could barely draw air from her surroundings. It was like breathing in mud. "Then let me be with—"

"No. Enough. You don't need to watch him die." Azaria looked at the guards, and Leda realised that, in her own twisted way, she was trying to be sensitive. It absolutely enraged her. "I told you to take her away, I need time!"

Something very cold settled over Leda, and though the tears continued to stream down her face, the uncontrolled sobbing paused.

"I will kill you," Leda said, cursing as her sister turned her head away dismissively. "No, look at me, Azaria." Azaria tilted her chin up to met her gaze. "I. Will. Kill. You."

Azaria finally saw something in Leda's expression that wiped the condescending look from her face, and her lips thinned into a tight line. "You don't have it in you."

Leda threw her head back and let out a sound that was half laugh, half screech. "Oh, trust me, I do. I swear upon the gods that I will *end you*."

Speaking of those gods, where were they? They had to save Pyrrhus, they must, as recompense for all they'd done, the fun they'd had with their curse. They owed him his life.

Azaria rounded on the guards. "MOVE!"

Leda went, kicking and shouting as they dragged her off. She could see glimpses between bodies in the crowd, Ambrose and his assistants finally descending on Pyrrhus, and a spark of hope flared within her.

Ambrose would save him, because he had to. Because there was no world in which he couldn't.

He *had* to.

As Leda was stuffed into a cell and felt the shock of the cold metal bars under her hands she finally fell silent.

She would not go quietly to her own death whenever Azaria plucked up the nerve to try again. She'd get out of here, she'd find Pyrrhus, find the remainder of her family, and she would save these lands from the rule of her sister.

That would be the purpose of the Counterpart.

She knew Azaria better than anyone, knew the horrors she'd inflict on the people she ruled, even if it was without malice. But the reverse wasn't true. Azaria didn't know Leda at all, viewing her as a bemusing object who did inexplicable things and felt love for people Azaria did not think deserved it.

Leda's sister never failed to underestimate her. And that would be her fatal flaw.

She would tear her reign apart with her bare hands.

No Locarno would sit on this throne, ever again.

www.ingramcontent.com/pod-product-compliance
Lightning Source LLC
Chambersburg PA
CBHW021730110726
47902CB00005B/1410